HU...
WATCH

Oz let the helicopter continue to climb until they were at a safe distance above the sea.

The pilot let out his breath as he spied the *Montana*'s navigation lights through the gloom. He clicked on his transmitter. "BB-58, this is Sea Wolf One. I have a visual and am proceeding to your helideck. Over."

Static answered his message and then the radio became intelligible. "We repeat," the radioman on the Montana said. "Proceed to helideck. Our crew's standing by. Over."

"We're advancing to the helideck," Oz said.

With the tail wind shoving the chopper forward, the MH-60K refused to come to a stop when the pilot pulled on the control column, tearing ahead instead like a runaway sled on a steep hill.

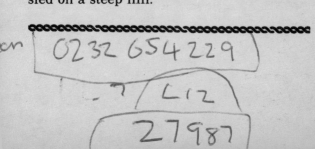

**HarperPaperbacks by
Duncan Long**

NIGHT STALKERS
GRIM REAPER
TWILIGHT JUSTICE
DESERT WIND

Night STALKERS

SEA WOLF

DUNCAN LONG

HarperPaperbacks
A Division of HarperCollins*Publishers*

This is a work of fiction. The characters, incidents, and dialogues are products of the author's imagination and are not to be construed as real. Any resemblance to actual events or persons, living or dead, is entirely coincidental.

HarperPaperbacks   *A Division of* HarperCollins*Publishers*
10 East 53rd Street, New York, N.Y. 10022

Cover art by Edwin Herder

First printing: March 1991

Printed in the United States of America

HarperPaperbacks and colophon are trademarks of HarperCollins*Publishers*

10 9 8 7 6 5 4 3 2 1

SEA WOLF

P R O L O G U E

Lieutenant Erin Croll pulled his heavy coat around himself, half crouching against the wind that pelted him with frigid drops of rain. As he grasped the brass knob of the starboard hatch and unbolted it, lightning revealed his sharp features.

He stepped onto the dimly lit bridge, carefully securing the hatchway behind him. He turned his ice-blue eyes toward the captain standing at the wheel beside the helmsman.

"The decks are secured, Captain," Croll reported. "I'm here to relieve you."

The captain glanced at his watch, nodded, and barely stifled a yawn. He grasped the blue-gray equipment console as the frigate mounted a towering wave and plummeted back down the watery slope.

"Thank you, Mr. Croll," the captain said in a voice that revealed his patrician heritage. "We're heading into quite a squall," he added. "Don't hesitate to call me if you run into trouble."

"Aye, aye, Captain."

The skipper left the bridge through the hatchway at the back of the large steel room. Croll crossed to one of the square windows at the front of the bridge and looked out. The ship lurched in the North Atlantic storm as another flash illuminated the ocean.

"How are we doing, Mr. Hogg?" Croll asked, turning away from the fogging porthole.

"As well as can be expected, sir," the grizzly-looking helmsman replied.

"Keep a close watch on the radar," Croll instructed the young crewman seated behind the Type 910 radar equipment console. "You're all that's between us and a crack-up."

"Very good, sir," the technician replied. He studied the scope more intently, aware of the lieutenant's watchful gaze.

Croll clutched the radar console as the ship reeled upward on another swell. "Do we have SCOT?" he asked the radio technician.

"No, sir," the sailor answered. "The cloud cover is too dense for us to contact satcom. But we took an inertial reading a half hour before the storm hit."

"Good," Croll replied, turning back to the view ports stretching across the forward wall of the bridge.

The storm was perfect, he realized. His stomach muscles tightened and he felt like he needed to vomit but he beat back the nausea and reminded himself that if he passed up this chance, the likelihood of another such opportunity was remote.

Lieutenant Croll turned from the windows and

checked their speed. "Mr. Hogg, reduce speed to one-third," he ordered.

"Ahead one-third?" the helmsman asked doubtfully.

Croll stared at the sailor.

"Yes, sir," Hogg responded nervously. "Ahead one-third."

As the ship slowed, Croll produced an envelope from his jacket and handed it to an ensign standing next to Hogg.

"Take this to Petty Officer Stuart Grapper at once," Croll ordered.

Within minutes Petty Officer Grapper and two of Croll's other men had overpowered the guard of the armory and distributed the few pistols and rifles among the sailors Grapper had roused from their sleep. Ten minutes later a flurry of shooting erupted in the crew compartments.

The thunderous storm that roared outside buried the screams and much of the gunfire. Only when a frantic message from the engine room reached the bridge was Croll forced to act.

"Captain!" the chief engineer screamed from the intercom. "They're killing us!"

The unmistakable sound of gunfire was transmitted to the bridge, along with the frantic screams of men dying below in the engineering section.

"Lieutenant?" Hogg queried, turning toward Croll.

"Ignore it," Croll ordered, unbuttoning his jacket.

"But it's gunfire, sir!" Hogg protested.

Croll extracted the Walther PPK from his waistband. He pumped the double-action trigger before anyone on the bridge could react. Hogg was the first to fall, a ruby hole in his neck spurting blood. Croll fired the pistol until it was empty, leaving the bodies of four crewmen in bloody pools on the heaving floor of the bridge.

The only survivor of Croll's attack was the radar technician who managed to escape through the port hatch. The door was left ajar, instantly chilling the bridge as the icy wind sliced through the open exit.

The technician didn't get far; he was cut down in a salvo of automatic fire that ricocheted off the steel deck.

Croll looked out the open hatch to see Petty Officer Grapper, illuminated by the lightning, standing over the body for a moment; the officer fired a single bullet from his L85A1 bullpup rifle into the still-breathing technician. He kicked the body through the open railing, knocking it onto the deck below; then he picked his way across the swaying ship toward the bridge.

Grapper stepped in and swung the hatch closed. "All's secured, *Captain* Croll," he said, saluting.

"Good job, Grapper," Croll commended. "Send in our radioman and radar technician at once. Then have your men get the bodies cleared away. Dump them overboard as quickly as possible so we can get under way under cover of the storm."

"Aye, aye, Captain," Grapper responded, leaving the same way he had come.

Croll smiled to himself as he recalled that no one had committed a successful mutiny on a British naval ship for over a hundred years.

What had started as an angry daydream after he'd been passed up for promotion was now reality. His actions wouldn't have had any chance of succeeding even ten years earlier, but with the computerization of the British naval records, it had been surprisingly simple for Croll to befriend a mousey young data-processing technician in the personnel office of the British Royal Navy.

With Croll's combination of attention and bullying, the young woman had altered and modified records and orders, gradually assigning Croll's key friends and contacts to the HMS *Fox*.

The day before the ship left for sea—the day Croll had promised to marry the girl—he had strangled her and hastily buried her body in the unkempt garden behind her tiny flat.

C H A P T E R

1

From the first, Captain Jefferson Davis "Oz" Carson had felt uncomfortable about the joint exercises with the new Omega Force, the elite company created by the Greek government to deal with terrorist threats at its airports.

The American helicopter pilot was part of a select US Army Night Stalkers team that ferried CIA agents and antiterrorist forces to trouble spots around the world. Today, he found himself trying to offer advice to the Greek airmen about how to execute such operations. The Greeks were proud and cocky—a dangerous combination in Oz's view.

The American pilot flew a Sikorsky MH-60K helicopter specially designed for antiterrorist missions. Today, the chopper flew unarmed, leaving the pilot with much the same feeling he would have had if he had been naked.

Holding the control column steady, the American glanced at the rocky, sunlit slope of Cape Sounion where the chopper's shadow scampered. The steep drop led to a tiny beach where—according to the Greeks—Ulysses and other ancient Aegean sailors had set sail thousands of years ago. Atop the crest of the slope were the ancient columns of a temple built in the days of Pericles for the sea god Poseidon. The ruins glowed in the mellow morning brightness.

Oz turned his attention to the three Greek choppers flying ahead of him, skimming above the waves twinkling in the intense sunlight. The pilots of the aircraft fought the breezes blowing off the ocean to keep their machines on a steady course. They rounded their reference point and headed back inland.

The Greek convoy consisted of two Bell AH-1S "Cobras" and a single Italian-built CH-47C "Chinook." The single-engine Cobra gunships sported three-barreled 20mm cannons under their chins and bore missile pods on their stubby wings.

The gunships were to supply cover for the unarmed transport chopper following them; within the tandem-rotor Chinook was the newly formed Greek antiterrorist team. Twenty-five men rode inside the tan-colored chopper emblazoned with the Greek military's insignia of a blue dot inside a circle.

The American pilot noted with alarm that the Chinook was getting dangerously close to its gunship escort. "Omega Three," Oz called on the radio, "I'd give Omega Two a little more space if I were you. Over."

"It's okay," the accented voice of the Chinook's pilot answered. "We'll spread out when we reach the target area. Over."

Oz glanced toward his copilot, Lieutenant Chad "Death Song" Norton, and shook his head in disbelief.

The Native American sitting to Oz's right flashed one of his rare smiles. He glanced through the window and then checked the cathode ray tube display in front of him. "We're nearing their DP now," he said.

"Good," Oz said. "I'm going to be glad to get this over with."

The wind buffeted the four helicopters as the Greek pilots rounded the walled ruins that served as a landmark and continued inland, flying above a rocky outcropping. All of the choppers flew low, hugging the ground as they would during an actual operation to avoid enemy radar.

"They're on their final approach," Death Song remarked, consulting the electronic map displayed on one of the cathode ray tubes in front of him.

Behind Oz in the crew compartment, Warrant Officer Harvey "O.T." Litwin spoke into the intercom. "We've got an aircraft coming up behind us. Looks like a small passenger plane."

Death Song swore and checked his radar, wondering how he could have failed to detect an approaching aircraft. "Yeah, real low and fast," he remarked as the plane appeared on the scope. "Must have been hiding in the ground clutter. It's accelerating toward us now."

Oz toggled on his radio, "Omega Three, we've got company. They're approaching at six o'clock."

"What's that?" the puzzled Greek pilot asked.

"A plane's coming up behind us," Oz explained.

An unfamiliar voice erupted from the radio.

"Hey, warmonger Yanks, get out of Greece. We don't want you here, you stupid imperialist pigs."

"What the hell?" Oz muttered. "Is this some kind of joke?"

"They're still coming," O.T. warned. "To our left."

Oz glanced over his shoulder and spotted the crimson and white Cessna Model 337 "Skymaster" as it advanced and drew even with the nose of the American chopper. A black-haired female passenger in the "push-pull" twin-engine aircraft gestured obscenely through her window.

"They even know our sign language," Death Song commented dryly as the radio exploded in another diatribe. "Want me to take out their radio?"

Oz lowered the volume. "No, we'd better not." He knew the Greek authorities wouldn't take kindly to disrupting radio communications with civil aircraft.

"Let's ignore them and hope they go away," the American pilot directed. "O.T., can you get the plane's ID number so we can report them to the authorities?"

"I've got it," Luger announced over the intercom. SP4 Mike Luger sat alongside O.T. in the gunners cabin behind Oz and Death Song.

The civilian aircraft passed and then darted dangerously in front of the American chopper in a tight turn.

"You stupid jackass!" Oz yelled, jerking back on the column and throwing everyone forward in their harnesses.

The MH-60K slowed abruptly, narrowly avoiding ramming into the Skymaster. The helicopter's landing gear was nipped by the whirling rear blades of the airplane.

As the American pilot hung back and watched, the civilian aircraft continued to drop below them, turning and accelerating toward the rear of the Chinook.

Oz triggered his radio on to warn the pilot of the Chinook. But communication was hopeless; the civilians persisted in shouting their anti-American propaganda on the military frequency.

It was impossible for Oz to tell if the pilot of the plane was trying to ram the transport helicopter or had simply lost control of his aircraft. But the result was the same: The nose of the Skymaster dropped into the horizontal path of the Chinook's thirty-foot-long rear blades.

The whirling metal rotors of the Chinook sliced through the cabin of the airplane, instantly decapitating both the pilot and his passenger and putting an abrupt end to the torrent of obscenity from the radio.

The bloody wreckage of the Skymaster plunged onward, careening into the rear of the Chinook whose rear blades slashed even deeper into the plane, ripping it apart. The Chinook shuddered in the collision as the plane sheered its right engine, weighing it down and buckling the chopper's frame.

One of the damaged rear rotors ripped free of its hub and the Chinook plummeted tail first to the rocky plain thirty meters below. Flipped on its side as it crashed, the helicopter raised a storm of dust.

The long blades of the front rotor whirled into the rock, pounding themselves apart.

Oz was stunned for a moment by the enormity of what he'd seen. He rapidly switched his radio to the international emergency frequency of 121.5 megacycles and activated the transmitter. "Mayday, Mayday. This is aircraft MH-60K NS-1. We have an air collision four kilometers north of Cape Sounion." He repeated the distress call as he slowed the MH-60K, kicking its control pedals so the chopper circled the wreckage below.

When the radio signal had been acknowledged, Oz switched to the military frequency of the Greek helicopter pilots.

"At least we don't have a fire," one of the Cobra pilots was saying as he set his chopper down a safe distance from the Chinook.

Oz remained in the air as the pilots and gunners from the Cobras raced on foot across the rocks to the downed aircraft.

"Looks like we may need the hoist, O.T.," the American pilot said, studying the buckled right side of the Chinook that faced up into the air.

Death Song agreed. "Their rear cargo door and the front of the chopper are both damaged."

"I wish we'd brought along the cargo hook," Oz said, thinking of the winch's meager lift ability compared to the seventy-five hundred carrying capacity of the hook.

One of the Greek pilots had returned to his helicopter and was on the radio. "At least some of them are alive—we can hear them inside," he explained to the Americans. "But the front doors are jammed and the rear hatch is totally caved in from the wreck. We don't have cutting tools and with the fuel leaking all over the place . . ."

"We're going to lower our hoist," Oz interrupted. "See if you can fasten it to the side door or some other point where a little leverage might create an opening. The hoist has a five-hundred-pound limit," he cautioned. "Much more than that and the cable will snap and we'll be out of luck. Over."

"Let's get into position then," the Greek airman advised. "We'll help guide you to the exact point where we need it."

The Greek pilot jumped out of his Cobra and sprinted to the downed helicopter. He told the other airmen what the Americans proposed to do and the four searched for the best point from which to lift. After what appeared to be a heated conversation from Oz's vantage point, they settled on the spot most likely to be opened: the right side door behind the nose of the chopper.

Oz centered his helicopter above the Greeks and then lowered the collective pitch lever in his left hand. The MH-60K responded smoothly and inched downward until they were forty feet above the wreckage.

"A little to the left," O.T. called.

Oz nudged the control column so the MH-60K angled a bit and then hung in exact position for the hoist.

"They're ready for the hoist," O.T. said.

"You take it, O.T.," Oz ordered. "You've got a better vantage point."

"Roger," the warrant officer answered, stepping to the backup hoist controls in the crew compartment. "I'm lowering the hoist now," he said. He leaned from the side door of the chopper and watched the end of the cable spool out from the winch mounted over the right door frame.

One of the crewmen on the ground grabbed the hook on the end of the steel cable. He hastily fastened it to the bent door wedged in its frame.

The other pilot gave the cable a hard tug and then signaled to O.T.

"They've got it secure," the warrant officer said. "I'm activating the winch."

The machine rapidly reeled in the slack of the thin cable that glistened like gold in the sunlight. Then the steel became taut, ringing in a low pitch as the cable tightened.

The door on the wreck refused to budge and the winch began making a clacking sound, automatically disengaging itself as its limit was exceeded.

"We're not having any luck," O.T. yelled.

"Tie the cable into place," Oz said.

O.T. loosened the winch and wound several loops of the cable around the mechanism so it was locked in place. "Cable secured," he called.

"Signal the Greeks to stay back," Oz told his warrant officer. "Then you get away from the door. If the cable goes, it's going to come zinging back at us."

Oz wondered what the chances were of having the cable get tangled in the MH-60's blades should it snap. If that happened, the Greeks might have another wrecked chopper to contend with. He pushed the thought out of his mind and concentrated on the task at hand.

"We're clear," O.T. informed Oz seconds later.

The pilot eased the collective pitch lever upward, inching the chopper higher into the air.

The hoist cable became so tight that its twanging pitch reverberated through the metal frame of the helicopter as the door of the wrecked Chinook gave way. The hook and the door came storming upward toward the American chopper. Before they had traveled far, however, gravity overcame their upward momentum and the cable and door dropped away, bouncing on the end of the steel cord.

"Door's free," O.T. called. "Everyone managed to stay clear and it looks like they're getting the injured out of the Chinook. I'm reeling in the cable."

Oz circled around the wreck and prepared to land fifty feet from it.

"Cable's secured," O.T. yelled as he tossed the bent Chinook door from the helicopter.

"Let's go offer them a hand," Oz said to the navigator and warrant officer as the chopper touched down. "Luger, you stay on board and get the passenger seats folded so we can transfer stretcher cases if we need to."

"Yes, sir," the gunner's voice answered.

The three Americans jumped from the MH-60K whose blades still cycled slowly. The men ducked their heads and sprinted toward the downed helicopter.

The Greek medic inside the Chinook had sustained a deep cut on his forearm but was otherwise uninjured. He worked inside the topsy-turvy interior of the helicopter, indicating to the Cobra crews which soldiers were in need of immediate medical attention. With the help of other survivors in the chopper, the wounded men were rapidly lifted from the open door of the Chinook.

One of the Greek pilots placed a moaning soldier onto the scraggly grass as Oz and his crewmen approached the wreckage.

"These men need to be transported to a hospital," the Greek said. "Probably it would be best to take them to Lavrion, twenty kilometers north of here."

The chopper medic concurred as he helped lift another injured soldier from the open door of the helicopter. "Lavrion's hospital would be the closest and they can treat most of the injuries," he told Oz.

"Let's start conveying the injured to our chopper then," Oz said as he removed a large combat bandage from his vest and handed it to the medic.

"Thanks," the Greek said. "We'll transport those who need immediate attention out of here first. What's your copter's maximum capacity?"

"How many stretcher cases?" Oz asked.

The medic thought for a moment. "Five stretcher cases and four can sit. The rest are either dead or not that seriously injured."

"We can get them in one trip then," the American pilot responded as he helped lower an unconscious soldier to the ground.

The medic nodded and then ducked out of the doorway. An injured soldier climbed through the narrow opening and was assisted to the ground by two Cobra gunners.

The medic's head reappeared in the doorway. "That's the last one that needs immediate attention," he notified the Americans.

Oz and Death Song carefully lifted one of the unconscious Omega soldiers onto a stretcher they'd improvised from a camouflage poncho and carried him to their chopper. O.T. transported one of the wounded men by himself, the muscles straining in the warrant officer's burly arms. The Cobra crews pitched in, and after two trips, the seriously injured were secured in the MH-60K.

"We're ready for takeoff," O.T.'s voice crackled over the intercom.

Oz lifted the chopper into the air and watched the map Death Song had retrieved from the data cartridge of the on-board 1750A/J73 dual mission computer; the information was now displayed on the pilot's left CRT. After aligning the chopper onto the proper course, Oz shoved the control column forward and sped above the craggy rocks toward the hospital at Lavrion.

2

The first few hours after the mutiny aboard the HMS *Fox,* the remaining crew members had barely been able to keep the ship afloat in the storm. Captain Croll manned the ship's wheel himself to keep them running with the wind and to prevent the huge ocean waves from swamping the vessel.

"Captain, this is engineering," Brian Ewing called over the intercom at the height of the gale.

"What is it?" Croll snapped as the ship lurched with the gut-wrenching impact of a wave.

"Our starboard gas turbine's developing troubles with its bearings, sir. If we don't shut down soon—"

"We need full power in this storm," Croll bawled at the engineer. "We can't afford to stop one of the engines now. Keep it running, do you understand?"

"Well, yes, sir, but there may be hell to pay later when—"

"Just give me full power," Croll demanded, cutting him off. "Do what you can to minimize the damage."

"Aye, Captain."

By the time daylight finally broke, the storm had almost exhausted itself. The mountains of water had changed to hills and by midmorning the men were swabbing the last of the bloody stains from the ship.

Three hours later Croll was examining the spare transmitter that the radio technician Winston Bammes had rigged into a rubber dingy. "This better work," Croll told the sailor as the rubber boat was being lowered over the side of the quarterdeck.

"Don't worry, Captain," Bammes said, running a greasy hand through his hair and jacking up his glasses. "I double-checked everything. The two-stage timer is set to contact the satcom in four hours. Then the explosive goes off thirty minutes after that. I've even got it so it'll automatically recycle if it fails to connect to the communications sat."

Croll scrutinized the cobbled collection of wires and electrical equipment sitting in the dingy and hoped the technician was as skillful as his records indicated.

"Doesn't it need a bigger antenna?" Grapper asked.

"No, sir," Bammes answered. "The satellite is overhead so the signal goes straight up. No need for a high antenna if you have enough power to hit the satellite."

"Lower away," Croll directed Grapper, who had been promoted to second in command.

"Lower away," Grapper ordered. The four sailors standing next to the dingy on the quarterdeck lifted the rubber boat and carefully lowered it over the stern. When the boat hit the water, it cruised along with the ship as the sailors holding its ropes verified that it was properly balanced.

The chief in charge of the detail turned to the officers. "Looks good, Lieutenant Grapper," he reported.

Croll nodded to his lieutenant.

"Release her," Grapper instructed the sailors. Croll watched the dingy float free, rapidly falling behind the HMS *Fox*. When the rubber boat was clear of the ship's wake, Croll crossed to the intercom on the metal wall beside him and toggled its button. "Captain to bridge."

"This is the bridge, Captain."

"Full speed ahead."

The deck below the captain's feet throbbed, the twin engines revving to their full speed and the propellers churning a boiling storm of bubbles that rose to the surface in the *Fox*'s wake. Croll wondered momentarily if Ewing's team had performed the proper repairs on the faulty bearing.

He recognized ruefully that so much depended now on how the members of the crew performed their jobs.

When Croll returned to the bridge, he ordered the ship's active radar arrays disengaged and instructed that the sailors on the bridge keep careful track of all radio and sonar activity around the frigate. One chance encounter, Croll realized, and all of his careful planning would be for nothing.

The engines continued to function properly, and within four hours the HMS *Fox*, traveling at thirty knots, had put 120 nautical miles between itself and the rubber dingy adrift in the North Atlantic. The timer in the rubber boat activated the SCOT satcom terminal, sending a distress signal and the transmitter's coordinates. By the time the British Royal Navy initiated its search, the dingy's secondary timer had activated its explosive charge, destroying both the transmitter and the small craft.

Since the rescue effort was centered on the location of the transmitter, by the time the first search chopper had arrived, the HMS *Fox* was 150 nautical miles away, steaming for the Caribbean. Croll intended to make good on a deal that had been offered him there.

The biggest problem Croll would face once he reached his destination was securing fuel for the gluttonous two-shaft COCOG Rolls-Royce Olympus TM3B engines that powered the ship. He had been promised a huge advance and safe harbor for repairs and refueling in return for helping smuggle drugs across the Caribbean to small boats just off the coast of southern Florida.

Since the HMS *Fox* could travel through the Caribbean unchallenged by the American authorities who policed the seas, the scheme had merit. Croll had planned to quickly amass a fortune for himself and his crew and then they'd scuttle the ship and go their separate ways with their shares of cash.

But the leader of the Colombian organization supplying the drugs, Carlos Rodriguez, had insisted Croll work for nothing on the first few runs. That was bad enough—but then Croll discovered that the drug lord had bribed some of the men on the *Fox* to take over the ship. Grapper had discovered the plot and, acting on Croll's orders, had loaded the four sailors into a rubber dingy in front of the assembled crew.

"I don't want any of you believing that another successful mutiny can occur on this ship," Croll harangued the crew as he paced the deck in front of them. "England hasn't imposed the death penalty for some years. But we're not in England anymore nor is this ship a British vessel." He strode to the mooring line that connected the tiny dingy to the side of the HMS *Fox.* "Release them," he ordered.

The sailor standing next to the line hauled the heavy rope off its chock and cast it overboard. The tiny dingy quickly fell behind the *Fox,* which continued to charge ahead at ten knots. Croll waited until the small craft was well behind the ship and then nodded to a crewman.

The man trained an Enfield L86A1 machine gun on the dingy and opened fire, raining scores of bullets onto the condemned sailors in the rubber raft. Before any of them could jump to safety, they were all dead. The air hissed out of the small craft and sank, leaving little sign that the men or boat had ever existed.

"Dismiss the crew," Croll ordered Grapper, leaving the deck and retiring to his quarters.

Only when Croll discovered how easy it was to approach unsuspecting yachts and private ships in the Caribbean did he latch upon the idea of actually pirating the vessels. The costly boats fetched good prices, although the cash was barely enough to keep the massive frigate going.

And then one day Croll's luck changed for the better.

Grapper had come to the captain's quarters late one afternoon in April during a stopover in Santa Marta. The *Fox* had been refueled and was preparing to leave its berthing position on the dock. "Mr. Grapper," Croll nodded, admitting the crewman to his cabin.

"Captain, I think I've got some good news," Grapper said excitedly. "It may be a trick, sir, but I don't think so."

"What have you got?" Croll said, returning to the desk where he'd been writing.

"I ran into one of Rodriguez's men on shore," Grapper related. "I told him you were pretty unhappy about the double-cross and that you weren't planning on doing business with his boss anymore unless he paid up front. I expected the guy to leave immediately and report back. Instead, he tells me Rodriguez can't be trusted. He offers to sell us information about Rodriguez's shipments in exchange for a cut of the take."

"Just what information does he have?" Croll queried.

"The routes and times of Rodriguez's drug shipments," Grapper grinned devilishly. "*And* the return shipments of cash paying for the contraband."

The captain sat back in his chair, lacing his hands behind his head. Revenge *and* a way to make money, he smiled to himself. It sounded too good to be true.

"What do you think, sir?" Grapper asked.

Croll did not answer immediately but tried to figure all the angles. "It may be a trick," he finally said, "but we have enough firepower on board to get us out of any trap they could spring. Plus I don't see any way they could take advantage of feeding us false information." He continued to deliberate for quite some time. "Let's give it a try," he said at last.

Grapper returned to shore carrying a compact military transmitter.

The captain of the HMS *Fox* soon discovered he had not been tricked. The intelligence came in regularly, and Croll began collecting huge stores of drugs that were hardly diminished by the few contacts with small-time dealers on shore. Eventually he planned to approach one of Rodriguez's Colombian rivals to secure a quick outlet for the drugs he had commandeered.

Things had gone very well, Croll mused, standing on the bridge of the frigate enjoying the Caribbean sunset. Even better than planned.

Selling the drug-running boats hadn't proven to be much of a problem. A crewman whose military records indicated a conviction for counterfeiting soon demonstrated he was more than capable of producing new titles for the stolen vessels.

Certainly no one thought to contact the British Royal Navy, since the idea that the ship might be operating on its own was too preposterous for the authorities to even imagine.

Even if someone should double-check, he had taken the precaution of changing the frigate's ID number to that of a ship still in service with the British Navy. It was only if someone compared the ship's ID with its assigned location that they might catch on. By that time, Croll smiled to himself, the *Fox* would be scuttled and at the bottom of the sea and he intended to be living happily ever after in some backwater refuge, fat and rich.

3

"Hurry," Billy hollered at his younger brother. "We need to hurry if we're going to find any empty brass before they start shooting here again."

Five-year-old Mike followed his brother under the hole in the chain-link fence, ignoring the warning signs plastered all over it. Mike's shirt snagged on one of the sharp twists of wire and ripped loudly.

"Mom'll tan your hide now for sure," ten-year-old Billy predicted, pulling his baseball cap around to what he thought was a rakish angle. "Hurry up, now. Quit poking along."

When Mike finally made it out from under the fence, the two boys raced toward the cardboard targets, snatching the empty brass cartridges that hadn't yet been policed from the field and jamming them into the pockets of their jeans. Neither was aware of the faint whopping of helicopter blades growing progressively louder.

The grassy North Carolina meadow raced toward the chopper, the shadow of the aircraft melting into and reappearing in the foliage below.

"There's the firing range," Death Song announced, double-checking his mission-control computer on the cathode ray tube. The range had been set aside for attack helicopters and was one of eighty ranges located on the 148,000 acres of Fort Bragg.

Oz triggered the radio on from his control column. "Range Master, this is NS-1 asking permission to commence test firing on range thirty-seven."

"NS-1, permission is granted for test firing on range thirty-seven," Range Master answered.

"Roger, over and out." Oz switched over to the intercom, "Arm the board, Death Song."

The navigator hit the appropriate switches. "Machine-gun pod and rockets are now armed," he announced.

"O.T. and Luger, we're going in," Oz warned. "Prepare to fire. Let's shake out the cobwebs."

Oz scrutinized the terrain ahead of him, aware that one pilot error could spell a fatal crash for everyone aboard. Nevertheless, he kept the chopper low, almost hugging the earth, just as he would when trying to evade enemy radar. He lifted the collective pitch lever and heaved the MH-60K skyward momentarily to leap the hill bolting toward them.

The four men in the machine were shoved into their seats as the earth rushed under them; a split second later they plummeted toward the valley. Oz drew upward on the collective pitch lever to level their path, and the G-load pushed the crew into their bucket seats.

"There're our targets," Death Song announced.

Oz caught sight of the first one. "Got them. Fire

at will," he instructed the others. As he spoke, he hit the firing button on the control column with his thumb. To the starboard, the dual guns clattered, brass raining from the pod as the 7.62mm bullets spewed out. A cloud of dust swept across the cardboard dummies as the chopper strafed them repeatedly.

O.T.'s Minigun roared thunderously in ten-round bursts, sending bullets zinging toward the targets, while empty brass cartridges gushed from the firearm. Joining in the cacophony, Luger's identical six-barreled weapon spurted flames and slugs from the other side of the chopper. Jets of dirt leaped into the air as the cardboard soldiers on either side of the aircraft were chewed apart as fast as they were spotted in the scrub.

Oz banked sharply for another run at the targets, almost scraping the top of a tree as the aircraft wheeled. The chopper darted across the ground, flame streaming from its artillery.

"Cease fire!" Luger shouted over the intercom. "Cease fire!"

Oz wondered what was going on. The order wasn't Luger's to give, but he wouldn't have done it without a good reason. "What's wrong?" the pilot asked.

"I think I saw someone on the range," Luger replied. "By the targets we just passed."

"Are you sure?" Oz asked incredulously. No one in his right mind would go over the fence with all the warning signs surrounding the range.

"Pretty sure," Luger answered.

"Let's take a look," Oz said, kicking his left

pedal so the chopper nosed around and racing back
to the targets.

"I see 'em," O.T. yelled. "Two kids. Can you
take us down?"

Oz's blood ran cold. "Yeah. Where are they?"
he answered.

"In the pits behind the targets."

The pilot landed the aircraft on the range and
within seconds O.T. and Luger were jogging toward
the two prone figures.

One of the boys peeked up out of the pit, and
then scrambled for cover when he saw the uniforms
and helmets of the approaching men.

"Come on out of there," O.T. ordered, greatly
relieved to see that both of the youngsters were uninjured. When he'd first spotted them from the helicopter, he'd feared the worst. "We're not going to
hurt you," he reassured them.

"Our mom says not to talk to strangers," the
older one said.

"Your mom's right," O.T. replied. "But this is
an exception. Did you know that you're trespassing
on government property?"

The boy didn't look convinced.

O.T. decided to try another tack before having
to drag the youngsters kicking and screaming back
to the chopper.

"Did your mom ever tell you not to talk to US
government personnel?"

"No."

"All right then. That's us. We're kind of like po-
licemen. Your mom'd think it was okay to talk to po-
licemen, wouldn't she?"

Within minutes the two boys were on board the MH-60K, enjoying their ride back to the Army base.

After filling out forms in triplicate and submitting signed statements to the fort's security personnel, the Night Stalkers crew returned to Simmons Army Airfield at the southeastern quarter of the military reservation.

Oz landed the helicopter. "Good job," he said, praising his crew as the twin T700-GE-701C engines wound down.

"I'm sure glad we didn't ace the kids," O.T. declared.

Oz said nothing but suspected the two youngsters would haunt his nightmares for some time to come. He shivered at the thought of what the outcome could have been. As he glanced through the window of his side door, the pilot was startled to see Captain Louis Warner, Division Commander of Task Force 160, approaching the chopper. The officer was trotting toward them, holding on to his hat to keep the rotor's wash from blowing it away.

A veteran of Vietnam, Warner was a skilled pilot and justly deserving of the respect shown him by the Night Stalkers and others under his command. He was rake-thin with an acne-scarred face, a smallish lower jaw, and a pug nose. Oz knew something important was afoot if Captain Warner was meeting them in person at the airstrip.

The pilot unlatched his side door and jumped out of the chopper, striding the ten yards to meet his superior.

"We've got another job for you, Oz," Warner

said in a pronounced Brooklyn accent as he returned the pilot's salute. He turned to Death Song, O.T., and Luger as they encircled him. "Gentlemen, you need to prepare to board a transport in three hours. You'll need warm-weather gear and your sidearms. That's all I'm at liberty to tell you at this point.

"Oz, I sent word to Lieutenant Tomlin; he and his platoon will be traveling with you."

Oz thought for a moment. Tomlin. The name sounded familiar but he couldn't place it. He turned his full attention to Warner as the officer continued.

"Get to my office at sixteen hundred hours for the briefing," he ordered the pilot. "In the meantime, I'll have the ground crew prepare your chopper for transport ASAP."

"Very good, sir," Oz answered.

"I'll see you then." Warner turned and swiftly made his way back across the airfield.

Oz and his men glanced at one another and then sprinted for their cars, parked at the edge of the field.

4

Captain Rogello Fernandez stood at the railing aft the bridge, his brown eyes watching the sweating workers bring the last of the boxes onto the *Leona*. The Cuban ship the wiry captain commanded was a Russian-built attack craft. It floated low in the filthy water, near its maximum displacement of 580 tons with the addition of the cargo he was taking on.

The ship had been a military gift from the USSR during the 1980s in exchange for "dirty work" Cuban troops did for their Soviet sponsors. Designated a *maly protivolodochny korabl*-class antisubmarine ship, the *Leona*'s hull-mounted sonar and antisubmarine warfare weapons consisted of four sixteen-inch acoustic homing torpedoes, two RBU-1200 250 mm mortars, and two racks of depth charges mounted at the stern.

For added combat flexibility, the vessel sported an ADMG-630 30mm six-barrel Gatling on the after superstructure, a surface-to-air missile launcher at the quarterdeck, and a three-inch dual-purpose gun mounted in a turret on the foredeck. On the large starboard side-deck, the Cubans had added two ancient .50-caliber Browning machine guns to deal with small-scale problems—such as boats.

The captain perused the dense Colombian forest that sweltered beyond the beach in the harsh noonday sun and realized how relieved he'd be to leave the port. As the last of the crates were loaded into the hold, Fernandez turned away from the railing, wondering who was behind his orders to transport the cargo—which he was certain was drugs. As an officer in the Cuban Navy, however, he knew better than to inquire. It was always possible that the nation's leader himself had issued the order, highly publicized national antidrug policy or not. Officers who checked into such things had a way of vanishing, and Fernandez was determined not to suffer the same fate.

"That's the last of it, *Capitán*," Lieutenant Garcia called in Caribbean-accented Spanish from the main deck below.

"Secure the boarding ladder and let's be on our way," Fernandez ordered.

Within the hour, the 187-foot attack craft sliced through the Caribbean waters, heading northwest. The captain's orders were to take his cargo through the Windward Passage between Cuba and Haiti to Tortuga to transfer the packages aboard the *Leona* to an awaiting American yacht, relieving Fernandez finally of his disgusting cargo.

"Captain, we're getting interference with our radio," Lieutenant Castillo declared, glancing up from the console.

Fernandez paced across the diminutive bridge and picked up a headset to listen. The high-pitched squeals he heard were obviously caused by electronic jamming.

Maldecir Yanguis! he swore to himself. The American Navy was always playing games at sea, behaving like bullies to make life miserable for the Cubans. "Go to condition yellow," the captain ordered Lieutenant Garcia, knowing it was unnecessary but deciding to be prudent, given the cargo they carried.

"Do you have anything on radar?" Fernandez asked.

"We had a blip up ahead a minute ago," answered the technician at the console. "Probably a helicopter. But it dropped below the horizon."

"What about sonar?"

"Nothing on sonar, *Capitán,*" responded the sailor checking the readings.

"Let me know if either of you get anything else," the commander directed.

It was inconceivable that the Americans would have the audacity to stop a Cuban naval vessel. But the inconceivable had a way of happening in the strange years that followed the Cold War, and Fernandez wasn't going to take any chance of being caught by surprise.

"The Lynx crew reports a visual confirmation, Captain," Lieutenant Grapper announced. "We've got a Pauk-class ship at starboard, just over the horizon."

Croll nodded. "Looks like our informant has scored again. Has the ship taken any countermeasures?"

"Negative, Captain," answered the ensign at the radar monitor. "Their fire-control radar's off."

Croll debated for a moment whether to get ahead of the Cuban ship to fire a missile at its bow, which was unprotected by the vessel's CIWS, or continue forward and attack from the port side. If the Cubans didn't have their fire-control radar on, a port attack might work and would certainly be quicker.

"Bring us around to three hundred fifty degrees, Mr. Grapper," Croll instructed at last.

"New course heading three hundred fifty degrees," Grapper echoed, passing the captain's orders along the chain of command. The helmsman altered course.

"Full ahead," Croll directed. "We'll need to close with them as quickly as possible after they realize they're under attack."

"Full ahead, sir."

The deck vibrated below their feet as the twin screws of the *Fox* throttled to their full power.

"Battle stations."

"Battle stations," Grapper called into the intercom.

There was a clanging of bells as the men on board sprinted to their assigned combat positions, and one by one the section heads reported over the intercom that they were prepared for the coming engagement.

"All stations are manned and ready, Captain," Grapper reported.

"Arm all weapons systems," Croll ordered, "but do *not* activate the fire-control radar," he added, attempting to avoid the possibility of giving the Cubans any early warning that something was amiss.

Grapper passed the order along and, within ten seconds, the missiles and guns of the British frigate were armed.

"What's the status of their radar?" Croll asked the technician at the scope.

"They're sweeping our area, sir," the sailor answered, studying the screens. "They must suspect that someone's shadowing them. But their fire-control radar's still off."

"Excellent. Launch Exocet One," Croll ordered.

Grapper issued the order and the MM.38 Exocet antiship missile jetted from the rectangular container ahead of the breakwater, showering the ship with flame as it shot away.

Captain Fernandez gazed from the starboard porthole of the bridge, watching in bored silence as a crew of sweat-soaked sailors on the deck below scraped at the railing to rid it of its ever-present scabs of rust. Although the *Leona* was well designed, the Soviets hadn't seemed to be capable of creating paint that could protect a vessel from the ravages of salt water.

A shadow over the sea attracted the commander's attention. Staring toward it, he squinted into the bright sunlight.

"Mother of God," he swore, whirling toward Lieutenant Garcia who stood next to the helmsman. "Activate the fire-control radar and the Gatling! Immediately!"

The startled lieutenant gave the order; Fernandez swung back toward the porthole, scanning the water.

There it was again, a shadow skimming over the ocean, approaching the vessel with lightning speed. "Battle stations," Fernandez ordered, convinced that what he saw was real. He watched the rocket hurtling toward them, threatening to destroy the ship. Why wasn't the Gatling engaging it?

The vessel burst into activity as the forty sailors aboard rushed to prepare for action, wondering why the captain would hold a drill during the hottest part of the day, but too fearful of his wrath not to perform at their best.

Above the bridge, the Bass Tilt fire-control radar on the superstructure flailed about, sweeping the sea with invisible beams. Abruptly, its radar locked into the incoming Exocet and within a fraction of a second an alarm sounded in the bridge. At the same instant, the computer for the ADMG-360 Gatling automatically plotted the ballistic coordinates for an incoming projectile.

The Gatling swiveled on its servo motors, precisely aligning with the incoming target, and commenced firing a stream of 30mm bullets from its six spinning barrels.

The large shells tore past the Exocet and plunged into the sea, raising gushers of water far behind the rocket.

Fernandez realized with horror that the defensive weapon wasn't hitting its intended target. Although he'd been told the weapon worked flawlessly, the missile continued to advance toward them and—in an instant—closed the space between it and the ship.

The frigate staggered with an explosion that splattered the outside of the bridge with shrapnel, the port next to the captain abruptly shattering.

Fernandez was surprised to see no fire or smoke on the decks below. "Damage report!" he bawled, yanking open the aft hatch at the rear of the bridge. Dashing outside, he caught a whiff of the acrid smell in the air, and raced along the rail of the deck to survey the destruction that he knew must have resulted.

He swept the decks, taking a mental inventory of the damage. A rack holding a 406mm ASW torpedo tube was empty, apparently having dropped its torpedo into the sea. A crewman lay next to the empty tube, a growing pool of blood surrounding him.

"Help him," the captain shouted at the sailor who stood frozen in shock next to the wounded man.

Except for the pocking of the steel surface on the side of the cabins, there seemed to be no other damage. Fernandez turned and strode back into the bridge. Since the missile had been coming right at the ship, he reasoned, it must have been struck at the last moment by one of the shells from the ADMG-630 Gatling. The explosive warhead of the Exocet had been too far away to pierce their armor plate.

"Minimal damage to the main deck, Captain," Lieutenant Garcia reported. "Four casualties—all on the main deck, sir. Weapons systems are now operational."

Fernandez turned toward the radio technician. "Send a priority message to Naval Command that we're under attack. Whoever fired the missile at us is probably still jamming our transmitter, but we might get lucky and get something through."

He noticed his men were all watching him, waiting for orders. Well, he'd be damned if he was going to run; his men were trained and they had the armament. "Lieutenant Garcia, bring us abeam and let's see who launched that rocket."

"The Exocet exploded, sir," the weapon's control officer reported to Croll over the intercom.

"But sonar reports that the ship is functioning perfectly," Croll objected. "What have you got on the radar?"

"They activated their fire-control radar just seconds before the missile reached them," the technician answered.

Croll nodded. "They must have stopped it then. Somehow they managed to get the CIWS up and hit our rocket just before it got to them."

"Shall we proceed toward them, Captain?" Grapper asked.

"Of course," Croll replied. "We'll have to close and finish the job now. We can't allow them to escape and tell tales. What's the maximum speed for a Pauk-class ship?"

"Thirty-two knots, sir," Grapper answered. "Same as us, if I remember correctly. Maybe a little less if they're in need of maintenance."

Croll swore under his breath.

"They're turning, Captain," the radar technician said.

"Their screw count's increasing, sir," sonar reported.

"They're making a run for it!" Croll seethed.

"Sounds like they're coming toward us, Captain," the sonar technician declared. Everyone waited quietly as the sailor listened. "Yes, sir, they're coming this way," he confirmed.

Croll was silent for a moment and then snickered. "They've got more stones than I would have given them credit for," he said. "Bunch of macho men more afraid of looking like cowards than of fighting us. Let's show these third-world losers what a real naval vessel can do, Mr. Grapper."

The two ships approached each other at full speed, probing in the electronic spectrum with their radars, their sonars snatching information from the ocean through which they surged.

At the sight of the large British frigate, Captain Fernandez realized his mistake in not retreating. His ship was designed for antisubmarine warfare, with only limited antiair and antiship capabilities. The *Leona* wasn't equipped to wage a major battle against a vessel nearly ten times as large.

Fernandez tried to persuade himself that the missile launch had been a mistake, but he knew better.

The continued jamming of their radio and the echoes on the screens from the British fire-control radar could mean only one thing: The English were attacking.

Fernandez considered whether they could still outrun the bastards. Better to run and fight another day than to be slaughtered like a dog. No one would think him a coward for fleeing such an overwhelming foe. "Reduce our speed to one-third, fire torpedo two, and bring us about," he ordered.

As the ship slowed, one of the three remaining sixteen-inch, electric-powered torpedoes scooted from its launch tube on the port side of the main deck. The acoustic homing device in its nose searched for the sound of the enemy ship as it churned through a wide turn, listening for the screws of the British frigate.

The torpedo traveled below the surface, leaving a white trail of bubbles that marked its passage. As it raced away, the *Leona* came around, its deck sloping steeply. Without warning, the ADMG-630 Gatling burst to life, its computers directing the weapon onto a new target.

"Where?" Fernandez shouted.

"High, at five o'clock," the radar technician responded.

The captain rushed to the rear of the bridge and looked past the railing aft. The Cuban ship twisted to complete its turn, the superstructure blocking Fernandez's view of the Gatling, but its high rate of fire was creating a cloud of arid smoke that marked its position. Far beyond the rear of the *Leona,* the captain spied the tiny dot of the approaching missile.

"This is L-63. We're in range," Ensign Albert Habiger reported over the radio. The pilot of the Lynx helicopter from the *Fox* continued his nap-of-the-earth flight, keeping his chopper precariously low as it raced over the water toward the Cuban attack craft.

"Hang on, L-63," Grapper's voice came back in the pilot's headphones. "They just downed our second rocket and we've stopped to let their torpe get past us. We'll launch a third missile in just a minute to tie up their fire-control system. Over."

"L-63 standing by," Habiger said, pulling back on his control column. The chopper halted, hanging just yards above the ocean, a mist surrounding the helicopter as its rotors kicked against the salt water.

A minute later the order came over the helicopter's radio. "Initiate your attack."

"Fire your fish," the pilot ordered his weapons officer.

The officer jabbed the red-glowing button on the panel in front of him. One of the four rockets on the helicopter's pylons dropped a few feet and then sputtered to life just yards above the ocean. "Missile away," the weapons officer announced.

Knowing the rocket could give away their position, the pilot jerked the control column to the left as he kicked the left pedal, sending the chopper through a banking turn that brought it dangerously close to the heaving water below.

"We've got a third missile coming in high at five o'clock, *Capitán!*" warned Lieutenant Garcia.

Fernandez scanned the horizon and caught sight of the rocket as the Gatling commenced firing, wondering all the time how long it would be before the six-barreled gun exhausted its ammunition or malfunctioned.

"Another incoming," the radar technician warned. "From three o'clock."

"What!" Fernandez exploded, striding across the bridge to glare through the starboard window.

There was a concussion aft as the Gatling destroyed its target; the ADMG-630, its barrels smoking, then spun around to face the newest threat. Quickly acquiring the starboard target, it immediately commenced firing, but after only a brief series of shots, sputtered to an abrupt halt.

"What's wrong with the Gatling?" Fernandez roared, his eyes riveted on the Sea Skua missile rushing toward them.

But before his question could be answered, the missile reached them, its warhead smashing into the superstructure below the bridge. The nearly instantaneous explosion ripped through the armored hull and engulfed the hold with flames. The spare depth-charge stacks stored in the chamber were bathed in fire and molten metal, exploding a split second later, their blasts ripping apart the bulkhead and buckling the deck.

Water flooded through the split in the hull as dazed crewmen in neighboring compartments struggled with watertight hatches in an effort to contain the cascade.

"What's the damage down there?" the captain shouted over the intercom to engineering, ignoring the yells of the radar technician.

"We're flooding, Captain," the chief engineer's voice answered. "We've got—"

"*Capitán!*" the radar technician screamed as another missile struck the ship.

The warhead smashed through the armor at the aft of the ship, sending deadly daggers of steel flying through the engineering section. Moments later, water spilling into the engine brought the *Leona* to a dead halt.

"The last two missiles came from an aircraft off our starboard," the radar technician hollered over the clanging of alarms in the bridge. "Looks like a helicopter."

"Fire SA-N-5 One," the captain ordered.

Within seconds, the surface-to-air launcher behind the sonar housing at the aft of the main deck swiveled about and coughed out one of its deadly SA-N-5 missiles. The rocket's main engines burst into life as the missile cleared the ship, the projectile hissing outward on a tail of fire and smoke.

Captain Fernandez watched the outgoing rocket for only a moment, enraged that he couldn't do more to satisfy his hunger for revenge. Then he gave his final order in a near whisper, "Abandon ship."

"What, *Capitán?*" Garcia shouted over the clanging alarm.

The captain adjusted his hat and stood up very straight. Then he spoke again, this time more loudly. "Give the order to abandon ship."

Ensign Albert Habiger had never had to evade a real missile. But he'd spent so much time in simulators that his reflexes took over when the weapons officer, Will Arnold, warned that a rocket was headed their way.

Instinctively, the pilot pulled the collective pitch lever of his Lynx helicopter, taking the machine upward for maneuverability. The thumping rotors overhead lifted him so fast it left a giddy feeling in the base of his stomach as he was shoved downward by the added G-force.

"Coming in at seven o'clock," Arnold warned.

Habiger jerked the collective pitch lever to the right, thrusting the chopper away from the missile as the weapons officer tapped buttons to release a flare and a cloud of chaff from the countermeasures compartment in the rear of the helicopter.

Habiger shoved the helicopter into a dive, turning in his seat in an effort to see the rocket chasing after them.

The Cubans' SA-N-5 missile flexed its wings, altering its course to home onto the helicopter that continued to jockey around in an effort to elude it. The radar-controlled guidance system of the advancing rocket ignored the flare that hung on its tiny parachute. But when the rocket neared the chaff, the metal foil scattered the reflections of the radar emanating from the SA-N-5's guidance system, causing it to turn abruptly and chase an electronic shadow.

As the cloud of chaff dropped toward the ocean, the missile lost its target, inducing its internal logic circuits to explode.

Ensign Albert Habiger heaved a sigh of relief as the wreckage of the missile dropped into the sea behind them. Turning the chopper around, he headed back to the landing deck of the HMS *Fox*.

"The boarding party is ready, Captain," Grapper announced. "What should we do about the lifeboats and the Cubans in the water, sir?"

"Let's take care of the survivors before the boarding party leaves," Croll answered.

"Sorry, sir, I'm not sure I understand," Grapper said, puzzled.

Croll looked the officer in the eye. "We don't want any storytellers to get away, do we?"

"No, sir, we don't. I'll have Mills take care of the problem."

The captain watched with detachment as Mills and his gunners slaughtered the Cubans floating in the water around the crippled *Leona*.

5

Oz strode down the hallway leading to Commander Warner's office, hastily replacing his ID card in his wallet.

When he looked up, a black muscled giant was blocking the corridor in front of him.

"Well, if it ain't the copter jock," the giant growled.

Oz's eyes narrowed. "Sudden?"

"Who you think, white boy?" the lieutenant laughed. "Sir," he added, saluting sharply.

Oz returned the salute, then shook hands with the man enthusiasticaly. "I *knew* that name sounded familiar," the pilot grinned. "But I'm so used to thinking of you as 'Sudden' that 'Tomlin' just didn't sink in. The last time I saw you, you were a buck private lugging an M60 in Nam."

"Yeah, those were the days," Sudden laughed. "It'll be a pleasure to serve under you, sir," Sudden said finally. "But if you'd try to keep things a little calmer this time . . ."

"I'll certainly try," Oz smiled, pushing his way

49

through the door leading to Warner's conference room.

"Right on time," Warner remarked, scrutinizing Oz and Tomlin as they took their chairs beside the three chopper pilots already seated around the oak briefing table.

"Gentlemen," Warner said, "I think this mission will very likely prove to be a wild goose chase." He tapped the keyboard in front of him and a map appeared on the monitors situated in front of each man at the table. "The good news is that you'll have a chance to bask in the Caribbean sun for a couple of weeks."

"I've been feeling a little pale," Sudden cracked.

"The bad news," Warner resumed, stubbing out his cigarette, "is that you'll be confined to an old World War II-vintage battleship most of the time you're there."

The pilot next to Oz groaned softly.

Warner tapped another key. "The dots you see spread across the map here mark areas where ships have been reported missing. The map's a little skewed, I'm told, since the missing boats are reported at the nearest port. The vessels have actually been lost somewhere on the open sea. But it gives you an approximate idea of where they're vanishing."

"There's a large concentration of dots along the chain of islands southeast of Puerto Rico," Oz noted, studying the screen. "It stretches to the northern shores of Venezuela."

"That's where the problem centers," Warner

said. "Even given the large number of private boats transversing the area, the pattern shouldn't be there."

"The Puerto Rican Triangle," someone cracked. The others at the table snickered.

"Don't laugh," Warner said. "If the press hears about this, I'm sure some Ted Baxter type will coin just such a phrase. One thing's certain, though; ships *are* disappearing in American waters, and the authorities suspect some type of modern-day pirate operation, maybe to procure boats for smuggling drugs into the US."

The commander lit a fresh cigarette and inhaled deeply before going on. "Because of the large number of tiny islands in the area, and the need for high-tech equipment capable of searching for and confronting pirates, the State Department has asked that a contingent of Night Stalkers be called in to deal with the problem."

Warner tapped several buttons on the keyboard in front of him and a picture of a battleship appeared on the monitors. "You'll be transported to the Air Force airstrip at St. Croix and from there, you'll fly to this old lady, the *Montana.*" He tapped his monitor. "It's a BB-61-class battleship, originally built in 1941 but refurbished during the late eighties. The ship's air pad accommodates four helicopters and she's been outfitted with modern equipment to aid in your search. Should it be necessary," he added, "she'll be capable of supplying additional fire-power."

"Where do the Delta Forces figure in all this?" Sudden asked.

"It's hard to tell from the maps," Warner answered, calling the Caribbean islands back up onto the monitors, "but there's a wealth of tiny islands scattered throughout the area. If necessary, your men may be needed to check some of the islands on foot to search for hideouts."

"Search and destroy?" Sudden asked.

Warner grimaced even though he knew the lieutenant was only joking. "Not exactly. You'll need to ask questions first and shoot later."

The commander studied the men sitting around the table for a moment. "That's about it," he said. "The operation's code name is Sea Hawk. But this isn't like a standard operation; you'll have to play it by ear and mesh with the Navy and Coast Guard crews as best you can. Your helicopters are being loaded onto a C-5A Galaxy now. You're scheduled for takeoff in two hours and fifteen minutes. Any questions?"

No one spoke while Warner crushed out his cigarette. "That's it then," he said, rising to his feet. "Good luck, gentlemen."

6

The lime and white gaff sail ballooned out in front of the yawl, sledding them across the rolling ocean. The large boat traveled only slightly slower than the warm summer breeze that propelled it.

Dr. Richard Adams stood behind the wheel, squinting into the noontime sky. The sun and light reflecting off the ocean seemed destined to burn more of his pink and peeling skin. He shuddered involuntarily at the thought of how much greater his chances of contracting skin cancer must be after four weeks in the Caribbean.

"Let me drive," Venessa begged, running her hand across his burnt shoulder, making him wince. He glanced down at her, her mop of glossy black hair trimmed short and the wet T-shirt she wore doing little to hide the melonlike breasts bouncing behind a likeness of Bart Simpson. Short and almost plump, her perky smile shined up at him.

The doctor scanned the sea and silently cursed a God that had created such a beautiful ocean and then compelled humans like him to subsist in delicate pale white skin.

"Come on, let me steer," Venessa whined, rubbing her torso against his side. "Pretty please."

"If it's the only way to get you to quit hounding me," Adams replied irritably. It seemed like Venessa spent every waking moment at sea begging to steer the boat.

When they went ashore, it wasn't much better; she wore him out dragging him from one tourist trap to the next trying to spend every last dime of his money. Adams was beginning to think he'd have to lose her at the next port or be forced to resume private practice to support her spendthrift habits.

He wondered what had ever possessed him to take her along on this voyage. He'd been divorced for four whole days when he'd picked her up in a bar in Key West. Out of the frying pan and into the fire, he thought, glancing again toward the sky.

But one look at her smooth, tanned legs as she took the helm reminded him of his reasons for bringing her along.

Oh, well, what the hell, the doctor calmed himself as he eyed the map lying on the bench aft of the wheel. This was what he'd always dreamed of, wasn't it? A willing woman, a boat of his own, and a splendid breeze to drive it across the sea. Why persist in bellyaching?

He walked back to the bench and sat down, picking up the divider and stepping off the miles on the map. As near as he could tell, they were about fifty miles west of Basse-Terre.

Give or take four hundred miles, he smiled to himself, leaning back into the cushioned bench and folding the map. His navigational abilities had gotten them lost more than once, but it didn't make any difference; as long as they reached port often enough to buy food and other supplies, what did it matter?

Adams cracked open the seal of a bottle of Jack Daniels and admired Venessa's backside. Then he shut his eyes, inhaling deeply to savor the heavy salt air.

Within minutes, he was asleep in the hot sunlight.

"Honey, wake up," Venessa was whispering, shaking his shoulder after what seemed only seconds. "There's a ship headed our way."

"What?" Adams mumbled.

The doctor sat up slowly, his head aching and his shoulder throbbing where Venessa had touched him. He immediately noticed his now beet-red sunburn and swore loudly.

The sun was low on the horizon. He'd been asleep for several hours lying in the sunlight.

"Why'd you let me sleep so long?" he demanded.

Venessa grinned wickedly. "I wanted you to *stay up* late tonight," she giggled.

"Damn," the doctor swore, rising sluggishly from the bench.

It felt as if his skin was crinkling when he moved. He glanced at the sails that hung flaccidly in the deathly still air. They'd be in great shape if he had to be hospitalized, he realized. Adams recalled several cases where . . .

"There's a ship headed toward us," Venessa repeated, pointing to the starboard. "I thought you might be interested in seeing it since it was so close."

She lets me boil like a lobster and then wakes me up to see a passing ship, Adams sneered to himself. He swore under his breath as he turned and stared toward the east. A gray ship was silently plowing through the water, coming directly toward them. The doctor turned and retrieved his binoculars from the compartment under the bench. He cursed as the bottle of Jack Daniels fell over onto the cushion and map, but he ignored the mess and lifted the binoculars to his eyes.

The ship was definitely a military craft. Bristling with radar and radio masts, its pointed bow sliced through the ocean as it continued to steam toward the yawl. The doctor eyed the square metal containers on the front deck that he knew contained missiles. He saw no markings on the ship and it didn't seem to be flying a flag. Though he prided himself on being able to identify the ships of the Western Hemisphere, he didn't recognize this one.

But it looked vaguely familiar. He tried to think.

"What is it?" Venessa asked, breaking into his musings. "Do you know what it is?"

"A ship, of course," Adams snapped.

"I mean what kind of ship, silly." She poked him in the ribs and made his burnt skin smart.

"I don't know what kind," the doctor answered. "But it's definitely not the US Coast Guard, so they won't be stopping us."

"They're headed straight at us," Venessa said.

"Shouldn't we get out of their way? What if they don't see us?"

"They see us. They'll be veering away soon since we're a sailboat and have the right of way."

But the frigate didn't veer away. It proceeded toward them until it was towering over them.

"I don't know what the hell they're doing," Adams finally admitted, unable to believe how close the frigate was getting. He tried to raise the ship's crew on the radio but got no response.

Adams was suddenly aware of how provocative Venessa appeared in her bikini bottom and T-shirt, which was soaking wet again. Had it been soaked for his benefit or the sailors'? he wondered idly. "Get below and put something on," he ordered.

"Sometimes you're no fun at all," she pouted, turning to go with a sway of her hips.

"Ahoy," a metallic voice called from the deck of the frigate that now towered over the yawl.

"What the hell's going on?" Adams demanded.

"Prepare to be boarded," the disembodied voice replied.

"By what authority?" Adams yelled back, knowing there was absolutely nothing he could do to prevent them from coming aboard. "I'm an American citizen," he continued, aware of how stupid such a remark must have sounded.

Standing at the railing that towered above the doctor, Croll turned toward the gunman standing next to him. "Show him by what authority."

The unshaven rifleman pointed his Enfield L86A1 machine gun over the railing and centered the doctor in its scope.

"Holy shit!" Adams whispered to himself.

Croll smiled at the expression, then his face became a mask. "I'll show you by what right," Croll's voice boomed over the loudspeaker.

He turned toward his ensign. "Fire."

The machine gun peppered the man below, killing the doctor on the spot.

Croll looked away, his face expressionless. "Prepare the boarding party," he ordered. "We now have another boat to add to our collection."

Fifty kilometers northeast of the *Fox,* a US Coast Guard HH-60J MRR helicopter was heading toward the WHEC-378-class cutter on which it was based.

In the cabin of the aircraft, Jeff Musil turned toward the pilot. "Lieutenant, you might want to hear this," he said. "It's really weird."

"Pipe it to me," Lieutenant Naldoza ordered, checking his course heading and glancing out at the sea. The helicopter's shadow seemed to be racing them from under the ocean's murky depths.

"—identify yourself, please," Dr. Adams's voice said in Naldoza's earphones. "Do you read me?"

There was no answer.

"You're on a collision course with our craft," the doctor radioed, "and we're unable to move out of your way. We're a sailboat with no auxiliary. Please respond. Over."

There was static and then the broadcast went dead.

"That *is* odd," Naldoza said, checking his fuel

gauge. "How far away would you say that was?" he asked his navigator.

"Hard to say, sir," Musil replied. "With the ship, it could have come from halfway around the world. You know how the radio's been lately. But it sure was a strong signal."

"Did you get a bearing?"

"Yes, sir."

The recent disappearance of ships in the area had put a lot of pressure on the Coast Guard to solve the mystery. Lieutenant Naldoza came to a quick decision. "It's probably nothing, but let's follow the bearing and see if everything looks all right."

"Should we report it?" the navigator asked.

"No, let's check first and see if it's anything serious." The pilot turned his chopper in the air and got onto the course Musil had plotted for the radio source.

Minutes later, the US Coast Guard HH-60J MRR helicopter approached the HMS *Fox* with the sun at the chopper's back.

"What in the world are the British doing around here with a civilian ship in tow?" Naldoza asked as they sighted the Royal Navy ship. "And what's wrong with the yawl? Let's try to raise them on the radio," he ordered his navigator. "What frequency do we need for the British Navy?"

"I'll get it." Musil threw several switches on the transmitter and then turned to the pilot, "All right, sir," he said.

"Ship number F92, this is US Coast Guard HH76 calling," the pilot radioed. "Do you read me? Over."

There was no response. The pilot tried several more times as he neared the British ship. "Are you sure this is the right frequency?" he asked Musil.

"Yes, sir."

"Something's wrong here." Naldoza dropped his speed and altitude, cutting his approach to the ship. "Switch to our Coast Guard frequency, and report what we've found. Send in their number, too."

"Yes, sir."

Naldoza studied the yawl bobbing in front of the ship and the fifty-foot yacht floating behind it. Why would those boats be with a naval ship? he wondered. And was that a body lying on the deck of the yawl? There was a sudden flurry of activity as sailors on the deck of the Royal Navy ship ran to the other side of the platform.

What's going on? Naldoza wondered again.

"Sir, our radio seems to be out of commission," the navigator reported. "If I didn't know better, I'd say it's being jammed."

Naldoza stared at the radio module and wondered what type of malfunction could possibly have knocked out the whole system. He looked back toward the ship in time to see the boxlike bundle of six GWS 25 surface-to-air missiles on the stern deck rotate into position and rise, as if locking onto a target.

Only when one of the tubes had popped open and the missile was jetting toward them did Naldoza realize his chopper was under attack.

The pilot breathed a prayer and dropped his helicopter toward the surface of the water, hoping his heat signature might be lost in the warm ocean below. He pushed the control lever forward to attain maximum speed.

"Try the radio one more time," Naldoza ordered the navigator as the missile continued to gain on them. "Send a mayday." Musil looked puzzled, but Naldoza knew he didn't have time to explain.

He thought fleetingly of his wife and three kids, and then all thought ceased as the chopper exploded. The wreckage dropped the few yards to the ocean's surface, raising plumes of water as it fell.

7

Oz and the Night Stalker crews had flown their four helicopters from Simmons Army Airfield just west of Smith Lake to Pope Air Force Base four and a half miles northwest of Fort Bragg. There the ground crews partially disassembled the choppers and prepared them for transport in a C-5A Galaxy.

The helicopters, stored on the lower deck of the transport, were strapped in place to prevent them from shifting during the flight to St. Croix. The Night Stalkers personnel, Delta Force troops, and an Air Force security team that would secure the runway at their destination all boarded the pressurized upper deck of the C-5A transport at eighteen hundred hours for the long flight.

O.T. reached an outstretched hand across the aisle. "So you're Sudden," he said, shaking the lieutenant's hand as they settled aboard the web seats in the C-5A cargo plane.

"Yep," the muscular man responded loudly so his voice would carry over the jet's engines as the transport prepared to take off. "But not hardly anybody calls me Sudden anymore. Things have changed since Nam."

O.T. nodded. "There aren't many of us old-timers left in this man's army."

"I know 'Sudden' is short for 'Sudden Death,' " Luger interjected. "But how'd you get the nick-name?"

"I'll let your captain tell you that story," Sudden grinned. "How 'bout it, Captain Carson?"

As the transport's engines droned on monoto-nously and they ascended into the nighttime sky, Oz settled back into his web seat with a sigh. "It's a long story," he warned, "and I'm not even sure if I can remember all of the details. You may have to help me out, Sudden.

"I was a green helicopter pilot who'd just had his chopper shot out from under him in Nam," he began. "One of the old Hueys. I spent most of three days hiding in elephant grass and stumbling around during the nights, navigating by the stars."

"That was when we found you," Sudden inter-jected, a distant look in his eyes.

"Boy was I glad to see you guys!" Oz said. "Sudden's patrol radioed in and were reassigned to escort me to the nearest LZ. They thought they had it made since they'd only been out a couple of hours. Boy were they wrong!

"We'd passed through a village," the pilot con-tinued. "We didn't stop to search it because there wasn't a hint of danger. Just a bunch of old men, women, and kids, with a few water buffalo milling around; everything appeared normal.

"There were two trails that led out of the village," Oz recalled. "The leader of our squad, Lieutenant Thompson, elected not to take the most direct route—it was too exposed and everyone was certain it would lead to an ambush or booby traps."

"So we took the jungle trail overshadowing the village. It looked dangerous, too, but we didn't have much choice; the vegetation was too dense to allow us to travel another path without making a huge detour.

"We plodded along sweating like pigs in the heat," Oz continued. "Halfway down the slope, the point man dropped and signaled a halt. The order was passed along the line with the same hand signal.

"Maybe forty yards ahead of us was a group of black-pajamaed Vietcong acting like they owned the place. They were laughing and smoking, sitting on a log alongside the path, their AK-47s leaning against a palm.

"As we watched, they were joined by four more Cong. The lieutenant ordered us off the trail. That was when I first started to wonder about snakes," Oz grinned.

"The cling vines were bad enough," Sudden added.

"Lieutenant Thompson told his men not to shoot until the M60 gunner did—Mr. Tomlin here," Oz said, indicating Sudden. "And he wasn't to shoot until Thompson gave the go-ahead. In the meantime the Vietcong on the trail were still making enough racket to be heard for miles. Pretty soon, the six of them rounded the turn of the path. They clomped into the kill zone of the ambush, completely oblivious to the danger, carrying their AKs slung over their shoulders and holding them by the barrels.''

"The lieutenant let the first six pass through our trap," Sudden explained, " 'cause we could hear more coming down the trail.''

"Four men and two women rounded the angle of the path," Oz resumed. "The lieutenant's patience paid off because one of the men coming up the trail was wearing an NVA uniform.

"Thompson gave the order and our guys let them have it. The Cong didn't know what hit them. After it was over, we stuck to the hill while the sergeant and the lieutenant searched the NVA soldier for documents.''

"That was when the rest of the platoon of Vietcong came streaming down the trail," Sudden grinned.

"That was when Sudden saved our asses!" Oz exclaimed.

"Oh, you're full of it, man," the black soldier growled, visibly embarrassed.

"We were hugging the earth while the Vietcong tore up the jungle," Oz went on. "We'd almost stopped returning their fire because there was so much lead coming at us. Sudden here leaps up and starts blasting away with his M60, oblivious to the incoming bullets.''

"I was too dumb to know any better," Sudden said, smiling and shaking his head. "And as I remember it, I had this green chopper pilot standing right beside me firing an M16 as fast as he could pull the trigger.''

"We blasted our way down the slope with the

rest of the squad following," Oz chuckled. "They were as crazy as we were!"

"We'd faked out the Cong," Sudden explained. "They thought from all the racket that we had 'em outnumbered and hightailed it out of there as fast as their little sandaled feet could carry them."

"We plastered the last of their column," Oz added. "Then headed the opposite way and finally reached our LZ. The Hueys picked us up an hour later and we were out of there."

"I was never so glad to see an Army base in my whole life," Sudden cackled.

The pilot of the C-5A landed in a giddy "slam dunk" at St. Croix, touching down at the aircraft's maximum safe descent speed. The transport's wheels screeched onto the runway, and the pilot taxied toward the immense hangar that was to serve as the assembly point for the helicopters traveling in the plane's cargo hold.

The squad of Air Force security guards from the transport fanned into the darkness to ensure that the area was secure, while their sergeant, using night-vision goggles, observed the region from the rear cargo hatch of the C-5A. The security guards were clothed in full combat gear, and all but two carried Colt M16A2 rifles. The others were armed with an FN Minimi and an M203 grenade launcher.

When the all-clear was given, Oz and the Night Stalkers crews disembarked from the cargo plane. The personnel of the C-5A, along with the helicopter ground crews, remained in the transport to aid in unloading the four Army helicopters.

While the choppers were being assembled, O.T. found a cool, sandy spot outside the hangar and stretched his camouflaged poncho over it. "A good soldier always conserves his energy," he explained to Luger as he climbed onto the improvised cot, positioning his helmet and ACR alongside himself.

Oz was too nervous to nap.

He paced the runway, mentally reviewing Commander Warner's briefing. The pilot unconsciously patted his hip holster, still slightly uncomfortable with the new rig he wore. Inside the holster was a stainless steel Ruger P-85 with a B-Square BSL-1 laser sight that rode below the barrel of the gun. The sight offered the advantage of much faster target acquisition at night—but its extra four ounces still would take some getting used to.

The ground crews labored on, unfolding, reassembling, and readying the three MH-60K SOGs and the AH-64 "Apache" attack helicopter that comprised Operation Sea Wolf's contingent. The cool nighttime breeze made the work go quickly, although the floodlights they'd set on the tarmac created a blizzard of bugs before their tasks were completed.

An hour and a half later Luger walked swiftly across the tarmac and spoke to the pilot.

"They're ready, sir," he said.

Oz turned, surprised at the gunner's quiet approach. "I'll be there in a second," he said. He crossed back to the tin hangar and retrieved his helmet; then he headed for the waiting helicopter. Grabbing the handrail next to the pilot's door, he stepped onto the bar that extended in front of the landing-gear support and swung himself into the MH-60K. He checked to be sure the stockless PK-15 submachine gun was stowed behind his armored bucket seat and then fastened his shoulder harness.

The Night Stalkers and Delta Forces left St. Croix immediately, heading directly for the battleship *Montana,* which cruised 150 kilometers southeast of the island.

Fifty kilometers northwest of the ship, Death Song spoke for the first time. "What do you suppose that is at three o'clock?" he said, pointing.

Oz looked past the copilot toward the horizon. The flames on the skyline showed as a bright spot of flickering white in his night-vision goggles. "O.T., do you see that?" the pilot called over the intercom.

"Yeah," the warrant officer replied from his narrow compartment behind the cockpit. "Looks like a boat's in trouble."

"Let's find out what it is," Oz said, passing the order for the convoy to alter its course to allow them to get a closer look at the conflagration.

Venessa Jenson had nearly gone into shock after being dragged up to the deck of the yacht to almost stumble over the bloody corpse of Dr. Adams. She operated on automatic, following the orders of the burly crewmen who boarded the gory yawl and lugged her into a boat that whisked her off to the quarterdeck of the HMS *Fox*. The dazed woman was impervious to the rough hands gripping her arm, forcing her into the steel bowels of the frigate.

"Take good care of her, girls," Grapper snickered as he shoved Venessa into the cabin that reeked with perfume.

"Whatever you say, dearie," hooted one of the three prostitutes occupying the plushly furnished room.

"Don't get smart with me, you stupid slut," Grapper sneered, hulking in the doorway as if daring the woman to say something else.

The rake-thin woman waited until the sailor had closed the door and then snorted like a grunting pig, gesturing obscenely. "Pig!" she called after him. "I swear, why can't he be like the rest of them and show us a little respect!'' she protested. "He's sure quick enough to drag one of us off when he feels the need.''

"Sit there,'' a tall, red-haired woman instructed Venessa, pointing to a leather couch in the corner. Venessa obeyed without protest, dropping onto the sofa and staring at the carpeting for a moment. Then she hid her face in her hands and wept silently.

Captain Croll watched from the bridge as a seaman finished repainting the bulwarks of the foredeck. The sailor worked in bored silence, oblivious to the sunset that seemed to stretch endlessly along the horizon. The whole crew is getting bored, Croll reflected. He'd tried to reduce the monotony with videos and shore leave; he'd even brought prostitutes aboard during the last month. But the only time the men seemed to be wholly engaged was during the raids on unsuspecting ships. Even Croll found he'd developed a taste for the violence when he was stopping Carlos Rodriguez's ship.

"Captain, what do you want us to do with the girl we found on the yawl,'' Grapper asked, breaking into the captain's reverie.

"What?'' Croll said.

"The girl we took off the yawl, sir. She's pretty well stacked. Several of the men were wondering if—you know.''

"Have her remain in the prostitutes' quarters for the time being,'' Croll answered. "We'll see what happens after she gets used to being on board. Alert the men on watch that she's not to go anywhere on the ship alone.''

Croll watched as Grapper went below and the bored sailor finished painting the rail. Our boredom and complacency may be coming to an end, the captain thought. Downing the US Coast Guard chopper had been risky. The Americans' reaction to losing a chopper would be controlled and measured—unless they discovered there'd been foul play.

Then there would be hell to pay if they traced the deed back to the *Fox*.

Croll had had no choice but to order the Coast Guard helicopter shot down. The chopper crew had seen the two boats that the *Fox* had commandeered, and it would have been impossible to explain why a Royal Navy ship would have done such a thing.

In the last few hours, Croll had put nearly sixty nautical miles between them and the wreckage. With any luck, they were now beyond detection.

Croll left the bridge and strolled along the port bulwarks to study the sea behind them. Somewhere out there was the wreckage of that damned chopper, Croll told himself as the ocean turned inky under the starlight. Most of it would have sunk by morning, but some of it might remain afloat.

Would anyone be able to trace it to them? was the question troubling his mind.

"BB-68, this is Sea Wolf One, come in please," Oz radioed the USS *Montana*.

"This is BB-68, reading you loud and clear," the radioman aboard the US battleship answered. "What's up, Sea Wolf One? Over."

"We've spotted a fire at the coordinates triple

A, 623," Oz answered. "Have any distress messages been sent from that area? Over."

"Hang on, Sea Wolf One, and I'll check."

Oz continued to scrutinize the flames through his windscreen, perceiving his own reflection in the glass as well. His face was rendered an eerie green by the instruments glowing in the cabin, and his features, hidden by night-vision goggles, made him look more like a sci-fi cyborg than a man.

The sea below rolled and heaved as the chopper hurtled overhead, flying low to avoid detection. The Apache gunship that traveled ahead of Oz's aircraft was only discernible as a black shape hugging the ocean, even with the pilot's night-vision goggles.

The other two MH-60Ks trailing behind Oz each transported a squad of Delta Force troops that sat in the shadows of the passenger compartments, blind but for the starlight coming through the open side doors. Although cool air whipped through the openings, refreshing the men on board, none of the soldiers spoke since the overbearing noise of the MH-60K's twin engines made communication impossible without shouting.

"Sea Wolf One, this is BB-68," called the radioman from the *Montana*. "We have no record of an SOS or anything about a fire in your area. Over."

"We're going to check it out then," Oz replied. "Over."

"If we don't hear from you in a couple of hours, Sea Wolf One, we'll send in the marines."

"Very comforting, BB-68. Over and out."

*   *   *

By the time the Night Stalkers convoy reached the site, the flames had been extinguished, and a cloud of steam was rising from the blackened fore-deck of the ketch. The mast still smoked and was devoid of its sails and rigging, which now floated in the ocean in charred tatters.

"Sea Wolves Two, Three, and Four," Oz radioed the other choppers, "hold your positions while we go in."

Oz stayed low until he had reached the yacht; then he lifted the chopper higher to prevent the wash from its blades from fanning the embers on the craft. The three people on deck, one woman and two men, were busy extinguishing the last of the smoldering bits of rigging that glowed in the star-studded night. As Oz completed his circuit of the boat, the copilot consulted his instruments.

"We're getting a call from them," Death Song informed the pilot, selecting the proper frequency on the radio module that sat on the console between their seats.

"Where in the world did you come from?" a male voice on the radio broke in.

"This is Sea Wolf One circling you. Are you in need of help? Over."

"That's a negative, Sea Wolf One. We have the fire pretty well doused. We were able to get a hose working to pump seawater onto the sail. But we've got enough repair work to keep us busy here for a while."

"Do you need assistance?" Oz inquired. "Shall we contact the Coast Guard and have them check on you?"

"That's a negative, Sea Wolf One. In fact, it'd be a big favor if you did *not* contact them. We were playing with fireworks and . . . Well, our insurance will probably be canceled if a report's filed. We'd just as soon handle this ourselves," the voice said. "We have an auxiliary so we can get to port on our own power without the sails. Over."

"Okay then," Oz grinned. "We'll let you get back to work. Sea Wolf One, over and out."

"I'm Crystal," the painfully thin prostitute whispered to Venessa, putting her arm around the weeping woman. "Look, kid," she advised, "you're gonna hafta pull yourself together or you're gonna wind up being shark bait. It won't be easy, I know," she consoled, "but if you put out around here, they treat you like royalty!"

"Yeah, we got it better than we ever had on shore," Tiffany chimed in through a cloud of cigarette smoke. "No pimps to beat on us," the red-haired woman marveled, "good food, and free medical care. *And* the British Navy screened all these guys for AIDS before they were brought on board."

"Plus the captain gives us a bonus almost every time they take a ship," bleached blond Mandy enthused. "I've got more money and jewelry squirreled away in that wall safe over there"—she pointed—"than I ever expected to own in my whole life."

"But they killed my boyfriend," Venessa protested.

"Right now, you'd better worry about saving your *own* skin, honey," Crystal advised.

"You got the bod for the job, kid," Tiffany reassured her. "It won't be that different. I'm sure your boyfriend didn't have you along just because you were such a great conversationalist!"

"It wasn't like that," Venessa objected.

"You two know each other long before you started your trip?" Tiffany inquired casually.

Venessa didn't answer; it had been only a few days since Adams had picked her up in Key West.

"I think maybe you're already one of us," Tiffany needled. "A whore is a whore whether she's working for money or a tour of the islands," she asserted. "I bet you're gonna fit in just fine around here, honey."

"This is Sea Wolf One," Oz radioed as they approached the *Montana*. "Come in, BB-68."

Even from a distance, the vessel was impressive, with its lofty superstructure bristling with antennae and radar.

Two large sixteen-inch gun turrets were nestled in front of the enclosed bridge, and a third complement of sixteen-inch guns perched on the aft deck. Ten turrets with 20mm Vulcan on five-inch guns were scattered on either side amidship, and what little space was left was filled with missile launchers for Tomahawk and Harpoon rockets. The old ship was 887 feet long and sported a heavy armor plate.

Any way you figure it, she's one tough lady, Oz thought to himself as the radioman answered. "Sea Wolf One, we're reading you loud and clear," he said. "Over."

"Sea Wolf One requests permission to land four

choppers on your helo pad," Oz responded. "Over."

"Sea Wolf One, permission to land is granted. Approach the landing deck from the north. The wind is from the southeast at four miles per hour and the seas are calm. Over."

"Thanks, BB-68. Over and out."

As they neared the enormous battleship, emblazoned with a white pennant number "68" near the anchor hawsepipe on her bow, Oz became aware of her mammoth proportions. The ladders and the hatches on the deck were dwarfed by the ship's guns and superstructure, making their dimensions appear as if the vessel had been designed for children rather than men.

Although the *Montana* seemed to have been conceived with helicopters in mind, her designers had never envisioned such an eventuality. The aft deck had, in fact, been created free of obstructions to ensure its swiveling gun turrets a clear field of fire.

Consequently, when the ship was taken out of mothballs and refurbished, it was a simple matter to create a landing pad on the aft deck. The renovated ship was updated with modern electronic equipment and missiles, making her one of the most durable fighting ships on the ocean—with a relatively low price tag for the American taxpayer.

The four Army helicopters homed in on the *Montana*'s bright navigation lights, with the chopper's own lights strobing like electronic fireflies in the night.

Oz switched his radio to the ultra-high air battle net frequency utilized when the Night Stalkers needed to communicate between helicopters traveling in a convoy.

"Sea Wolves Two, Three, and Four, this is One," the pilot said. "We'll stay in our trail formation and approach from the aft end of the battleship. Look sharp. Let's show the Navy what Army pilots can do."

The convoy approached the USS *Montana* from the stern and gradually matched speed with the battleship, enabling the Apache and the three MH-60Ks to hover behind it. The Apache then inched forward and centered over the white circle painted at the midpoint of the helideck.

The pilot of the chopper watched the yellow-clad deck crewman closely, reading the sailor's final cues and bringing the aircraft in safely. Once the Apache was on the shifting deck, the sailor motioned to cut the power to the helicopter's engines.

The ship's ground crew rushed to the aircraft, swiftly pushing it into position at the port side of the gun turret on the aft deck.

One by one, following the same procedure, the three MH-60Ks landed in the white circle, and within fifteen minutes all four aircraft had been wheeled into their parking spots on the helideck.

"Captain Carson?" a sailor inquired, saluting the pilot as he climbed out of his chopper and jumped to the swaying deck.

The Army captain returned the salute. "I'm Captain Carson," Oz replied.

"Captain Palmer would like to see you immediately, sir. We have somewhat of an emergency and the captain is hoping you might be able to help us out."

"Lead the way," Oz directed.

9

As second in command of the HMS *Fox,* Lieutenant Stuart Grapper had certainly never expected to be ordered to sail a pirated yawl. However, unlike most of the other craft they'd commandeered, the yawl didn't have a motor, and Grapper was one of the few sailors aboard the frigate who could operate a true sailing vessel.

"Pick out some crewmen to assist you," Croll had directed.

"I can get by with just one man, sir," Grapper answered. "Maybe Hawkins."

"Right. Take him. And get away from here ASAP. We can't chance having to down another chopper. We were lucky to have jammed the radio of the last one."

"What about the ID papers, sir?"

"They'll have new documents for you in a few minutes. The gunner managed to put a bullet hole in the original," Croll said matter-of-factly.

Grapper nodded, once again aware of the lack of emotion the captain seemed to display when it came to killing. The lieutenant figured Croll could order his own grandmother killed without a second thought if it would get him ahead. Grapper had decided long ago that the captain was a very dangerous man, and that no one in their right mind would dare to cross him.

"We'll meet you at Rouseau in a couple of days," Croll said. "Five percent of the sale is yours," he added, aware that the man selling the stolen boat bargained more shrewdly when he stood to profit from the deal.

Croll stifled a yawn and decided to call it a day. "Mr. Bammes, you've got the bridge," he announced to the sailor standing at the helm.

"Aye, aye, Captain."

"I'll be in my cabin, but don't disturb me unless it's an emergency."

"Aye, sir," the sailor answered, suppressing a smirk. When the captain demanded not to be disturbed, it meant one of the "hired hands"—as the crew called the prostitutes—was keeping the officer company.

"I know you and your men are worn out," Captain Palmer was saying apologetically to Oz, "but the Coast Guard's lost a chopper, and they were hoping the Night Stalkers might be able to search the area." The two men were gazing through the laminated glass port of the bridge on the USS *Montana* where a half moon was rising, glowing a honey color that reflected off the rolling ocean.

"Sure," Oz replied wearily. "Most of my air crews have had their bacon salvaged at one time or another after going down. We'll be glad to help out if we can."

Within half an hour the four Night Stalkers teams, along with the medics from each of the Delta Squads, had been briefed, their helicopters refueled, and were airborne.

Oz studied the surface of the troubled sea below him. The wind had recently come up and the waves were soaring several yards into the air. The pilot was thankful that the Caribbean was a warm body of water and that the Coast Guard aircrews wore life preservers as a standard feature of their uniforms. If the chopper crew had survived the impact of a crash, chances were good, Oz knew, that some of them would be able to stay alive for hours if not days in the ocean.

Raindrops splattered against the windscreen and then vanished as quickly as they'd come. Oz switched on the wipers, whisking the beads of water from the Plexiglas.

"It's odd that no one's detected emergency signals," Death Song said, tapping a button on his HSD. "This is the end of our section," he stated. "We need to double back around."

The pilot kicked his left rudder pedal, traveling two kilometers to bring them onto a new course, and then headed toward the USS *Montana.* He suppressed a yawn, wishing they'd brought a thermos of coffee along with them. Oz checked his HSD screen and shoved the pedal again to bring the MH-60K onto its new heading. "I know we're all tired," he announced to his crew over the intercom. "But let's try to stay sharp."

The pilot scrutinized the quaking sea below. With light from the rising moon and the NVGs he wore, the swirling water was brightly lit in varying shades of green and white. He tensed the stiff muscles in his long legs and scratched at the stubble on his normally clean-shaven chin.

"I'm getting a signal on the emergency frequency!" Death Song exclaimed.

"A beacon?" Oz asked.

"Yeah. One beeper. Just a second and I'll have the heading."

Oz toggled on his radio. "BB-68, this is Sea Wolf One. Come in please."

"This is BB-68, go ahead."

"We have an emergency beacon signal at"—he glanced at the coordinates Death Song had punched onto the VSD—"sixty-four degrees due south coordinates triple A, 687. We're headed that way now. It must be close since the signal's strong."

"Good work, Sea Wolf One. We'll relay your message to the Coast Guard so they can send in some more choppers. Over."

"We'll let you know when we reach the site. Over and out."

Oz brought the control column to its center position, slowing the MH-60K as he kicked it onto its new course. Then he shoved the column forward to attain the helicopter's maximum speed.

The waves rolled under the aircraft as it skimmed toward the emergency beacon, the pilot checking the VSD screen to be sure the helicopter was properly aligned.

"We must be right on top of it," Death Song

said, tapping a button to the side of his VSD and punching two more on the keyboard.

Oz slowed the chopper as the signal grew stronger.

"I see something," Luger called from the gunner's window.

"I've got it," Oz said, gazing through his side window. In the sea below was the scattered wreckage of a helicopter, the distinctive white pattern of the debris leaving no doubt that it was a Coast Guard chopper.

Oz studied the FLIR, hoping the infrared viewer might give him a better picture. "There's somebody down there!" he declared. "O.T., get the winch ready."

Captain Croll stood in the prostitutes' quarters, amazed at how the women had managed to transform the two large rooms from spartan gray officers' cabins into a plush bedroom suite. He recognized some of the furniture, filched from several of the larger yachts, but the carpeting and some of the other furnishings seemed to have materialized out of thin air. He made a mental note to himself: A sailor would do almost anything with sufficient motivation—and certainly sex was one of the major motivators for his men.

"How can we help you, Captain," Tiffany whispered provocatively, swaying toward Croll and slipping her arm around his waist.

Croll studied Venessa for a moment and wondered if he would ever be able to trust the woman.

She turned her face away from him.

"How about a little quiet talk?" Croll suggested to Tiffany.

"Why, Captain, whatever do you mean?" she replied, batting her eyelashes up at him. "See you tomorrow, girls," she called as she and Croll walked toward the door of the cabin. "Don't do anything I wouldn't do."

Venessa glared at the closed door. One way or another, she resolved, she was going to get off the HMS *Fox.* But before she did, she vowed to herself, she would see Croll dead.

Grapper and Hawkins sailed toward Rouseau, driven by the brisk western breeze that carried the yawl in the direction of Dominica. Three and a half hours into their journey, Hawkins spotted the navigation lights of an approaching ship.

"What is it?" Hawkins asked as Grapper studied the ship's lights through the binoculars they'd found on board earlier.

"Looks like a military boat," Grapper said. "Probably Coast Guard."

Hawkins swore loudly. "How in the world are we going to get out of this?" he demanded.

"Take it easy," Grapper advised. "We don't have any lights. They probably don't even know we're here. Besides, they won't stop us on the open sea; they have no jurisdiction here. And even if they stopped us, we have all the proper papers."

"Proper papers nothing, they're forgeries. Look, they're turning toward us!"

Grapper said nothing as the ship altered its course for a path that would intersect theirs. His confidence ebbing, he watched in disbelief as the ship, definitely a US Coast Guard vessel, matched their speed and pulled alongside them. He fingered the P7 pistol hidden under his shirt, painfully aware of the machine guns prominently displayed on the foredeck of the approaching cutter.

C H A P T E R

10

The crude laboratory sat north of Santa Marta, Colombia, surrounded by jungle on three sides and ocean on the fourth. White-masked lab technicians, carefully protecting themselves from the intoxicating dust that floated inside the primitive structure, cautiously loaded plastic sacks into boxes as they advanced along roller-topped conveyers to the outdoors. Sweating laborers then shouldered the heavy containers through the narrow gate of the complex, past the watchful guard armed with an Ithaca Model 37 pump shotgun.

The men moved like ants in a line that snaked through the jungle, following the narrow dirt path rendered invisible in the darkness. For three hundred yards they strained until the vegetation ended abruptly and the earth became sandy. Then they plodded the remaining distance to the twenty-meter *yate,* moored at the dock.

Guards from the ship lined the wooden pier, armed with Star Z-70 submachine guns. Ignoring the sentries as best they could, the workers cautiously climbed the swaying gangplank that rose and fell with the rhythm of the waves.

Juan Santos watched as the boxes were stowed in the ship's hold. Satisfied that the job was progressing properly, he turned to the captain of the vessel. "You must take care to stick to this course," he warned deferentially, referring to the paper in his hand. "It's been carefully plotted to avoid every US Coast Guard patrol. If you keep to it, you'll be safe."

The swarthy sea captain snatched the paper from the other man without a word and jammed it into his grimy jacket pocket, puffing voraciously at a hand-rolled cigarette that smelled of mint and marijuana.

In the silence that followed, Santos was aware of the waves lapping against the dock as he tried to determine whether he'd been dismissed. The captain had a reputation for losing his temper unexpectedly, and Santos didn't want to slight him.

"We'll stick to the route," growled the captain at last, inhaling on the butt one last time before flicking it into the ocean.

Santos muttered a reply, thankful for the chance to escape, and hurried off the ship as the final carton was being hauled up the gangplank.

The Colombian strode nearly a hundred yards into the jungle on the dirt path, then veered down a side trail and walked briskly through the darkness, stopping twice to make certain he wasn't being followed.

Soon he reached a dilapidated shack with a thatched roof. He listened intently to the chirping crickets for a few seconds to verify that no one was nearby and then knocked softly at the wooden door.

When there was no answer, he rapped a little harder.

"Un momento," a woman's sleepy voice called from inside.

Santos smashed a mosquito feasting on his forehead, vaguely aware of the patter of bare feet inside the hut.

"Juan?" queried a female voice close to the door.

"Yes," he muttered.

As the heavy crossbar slid away and dropped noisily onto the wooden floor, the door swung open. Santos stepped inside the hut, past his olive-skinned common-law wife. He closed the door behind him, plunging them into darkness, and felt along the floor with his foot. Locating the heavy bar, he grasped it and slid it into the iron clasps on either side of the entrance.

He struck a match, lit the candle sitting on the table, and crossed to the bed in the corner of the one-room shack, shoving it aside. Its legs grated along the rough floor.

The Colombian knelt, placing the candle on the floor next to him, and jerked at the loose floorboard. Laying the board down, he lifted the candle to check the hole for spiders; then he reached into the opening and retrieved the diminutive battery-operated transmitter hidden inside.

"Are you calling the British again?" the woman inquired anxiously.

"Shhh," Santos cautioned. "It'll be our necks if Rodriguez finds out."

"It's so dangerous!" she objected.

"Not if we're careful."

"How I wish you would stop taking these risks!" she implored almost tearfully.

"Soon we'll have enough money to leave this dump," he replied, switching the radio to the proper channel and turning it on. He looked up at the woman. "Have you forgotten the child we buried?" he asked passionately. "We can *never* raise a family in this malaria-infested jungle. We will never be truly safe here," he hissed, clicking the radio to the correct frequency. "These messages are our ticket out of here."

The woman fell silent for several moments as he telescoped the antenna of the transmitter.

She reflected bitterly on their lives in the Colombian jungle. They were virtual prisoners except for the infrequent trips Santos was allowed to make to the city. Even then, she was forced to stay behind to ensure Juan's return. "You are right," she quietly conceded at last.

"Watch the path in case someone comes this way," he told her gently, switching the radio on and jamming the earphones onto his head.

The US Coast Guard petty officer examined the yawl's papers and the crewmen's passports with his flashlight.

Grapper tried not to fidget and hoped Hawkins wouldn't do anything dumb. He glanced at the Coast Guard cutter. The machine guns and the sailors manning them were silhouetted against the sky, the weapons trained on Grapper.

"That's odd," the petty officer remarked. "It says here that you left the Bahamas the day before you arrived."

Hawkins gulped air audibly.

"Yeah," Grapper answered calmly. "They screwed up on that. I didn't notice it until we left port."

"By then we were so far away we figured it wasn't worth our while to return," Hawkins added hastily.

The petty officer said nothing as he closed the two passport books and handed the documents back. "Actually, we see a lot of mistakes like that," he said finally. "Be sure to get your navigational lights fixed as soon as you reach port," he warned Grapper and Hawkins. "It'd be easy for someone to run into you. If our radar hadn't picked up your mast, we'd never even have known you were here."

"Yes, sir, we'll do that," Grapper readily agreed. "You can never be too cautious when you're traveling on the high seas."

"Yeah," Hawkins grunted.

"I'll let you get on your way, then," the petty officer said. "You should be able to make port before the tropical storm reaches us late tomorrow," he added.

"Storm?" Grapper inquired.

"Yeah, it's going to be a beaut," the officer elaborated. "We received word a few minutes ago that the National Weather Bureau is on the verge of up-

grading it to a hurricane. It's coming from the southeast, so you don't want to hang around."

"We won't," Grapper vowed as the officer expertly swung over the railing of the yawl, landing
in the motor launch moored on the port side of the
boat. The sailor in the launch freed it of the yawl and
started its engine.

As the officer waved congenially and the boat
putted back toward the cutter, Grapper swore under
his breath. "Come on," he growled at Hawkins,
turning away from the rail. "Help me unfurl the gaff
so we can get to full speed and take advantage of this
breeze."

"You think it'll be a hurricane by the time it
gets here?" Hawkins asked anxiously, awkwardly
tugging at the rigging of the rail.

"How would I know!" Grapper snapped, loos-
ing the sail and raising it on its gaff. "Let's get out
of here so we don't have to find out the hard way!"

As the sail billowed in the breeze and the ship
picked up speed, Grapper studied the clouds that
blotted out the stars in the east. Sitting down behind
the helm, he switched on the small light next to the
compass. The front viewing compass swung in its
gimbals as the ship pitched on the waves, enabling
it to remain level regardless of the yawl's motion.

"All right," he said after consulting the map and
using the course protractor to plot their exact route,
"I need some rest. Do you think you could steer for
a while like I showed you?" he asked Hawkins.

"Sure," the other man answered.

"I'm getting us onto the proper heading,"
Grapper instructed, turning the wheel. "Just watch

the lubber mark on the compass and keep us twenty degrees off east. Each notch on this compass is ten degrees, so keep us two notches left of east mark."

"Piece of cake," Hawkins answered, taking the wheel and glancing at the compass.

"I'm going below," Grapper said. "I want to be wide awake when that storm reaches us. Call me if you have any troubles or if the wind shifts," he added, then crossed the swaying deck and descended into the trunk cabin of the yawl.

Hawkins yawned, and then adjusted the wheel so the lubber mark was exactly two notches to the left of the "E" on the compass. For two hours he managed to keep the ship on course as the waves became higher.

Then his eyelids drooped and he fell asleep.

CHAPTER

11

Oz banked the MH-60K and centered it directly over the prone figure floating in the water.

The man appeared to be either completely exhausted or unconscious, bobbing on the surface of the sea and making no effort to signal the helicopter as it circled.

The pilot pulled the control column into its central position to bring the chopper to a near standstill, fighting the gust of wind that strained to push it to one side.

"O.T., are you ready?" Oz called.

"Almost," the warrant officer answered. Since he had more experience at extraction than the other gunner, O.T. had been chosen to rescue the apparently unconscious flier.

The twenty-year veteran stood near the crew compartment door where the SH-60B-style rescue hoist was mounted over its frame. He removed his night-vision goggles and turned on the red emergency lights in the cabin. Then he jerked the cord on his life vest, the gas canister inside inflating the flotation device.

O.T. unfastened his helmet and handed it to Luger. "Is the water warm around here?" he yelled over the noise of the chopper's blades.

Luger shrugged, signaling his uncertainty.

"I hate dropping into cold water," O.T. mumbled, leaning out the side door. He tested the cable and the STABO harness fastener one last time and then stepped out into the darkness, supported only by the thin steel cord.

"O.T.'s outside on the cable," Luger informed Oz.

"Has he got a spare STABO?" Oz asked.

"He's got one," Luger responded.

"Okay then, I'm activating the hoist."

Luger positioned himself next to the winch, the thin steel cable spooling out as the warrant officer was lowered toward the heaving surface of the water.

As O.T. sank into the darkness, he reflected momentarily upon sharks; although he'd heard they weren't as dangerous as most people assumed, he didn't relish putting the theory to the test. He forced the concern out of his mind as his boots touched the water.

"Tepid," he smiled to himself, settling in.

The ocean swelled upward, buoying him on his life vest. The Army airman spit out the foul-tasting brine that splashed into his mouth and then half swam, half floated toward the inert form bobbing eight feet away.

The crewman appeared deathly pale in the intense cone of light from the chopper's landing lights. As O.T. reached toward the unconscious man, he suddenly felt himself being pulled skyward by the cable to which his harness was attached. It seemed to lift him upward as he topped the crest of a wave and the ocean plummeted out from under him.

O.T. cursed as he hung there suspended in mid-air. Looking up, he waved toward the spotlight that hid the helicopter's contours.

"He needs more slack," Luger yelled to Oz.

The pilot responded, irritated at himself for not giving O.T. ample line with which to work. As he activated the winch again, Oz ordered himself to be extra vigilant; he'd been awake too long and was starting to commit errors he couldn't afford to make.

As the line slackened, the sea rose to meet O.T. and within seconds he had splashed his way to the inert Coast Guard crewman.

The man was unconscious but, as far as the warrant officer could tell, didn't appear to be seriously injured. O.T. examined him for signs of broken bones or other injuries that might be exacerbated by the STABO harness. Finding none, he initiated the difficult task of encircling the crewman with the harness.

When the arduous chore had been accomplished, the soldier carefully clipped the ring of the steel cable onto the harness and double-checked it. Satisfied it was secure, the warrant officer splashed away from the unconscious Coast Guard crewman and glanced up at the helicopter hovering above, its bright landing light causing him to squint.

The spray created by the wake of the chopper's blades stung his eyes. Trying to blink them clear, he gave the ready-for-pickup signal by holding his right hand in the air, palm forward.

"They're ready to come up," Luger called to Oz.

"Okay, I'm activating the winch," Oz responded, double-checking to be certain he had the controls set to lift. He tensed his hand on the collective pitch lever to provide for the greater weight the helicopter would acquire when the two men escaped the buoyancy of the sea.

The steel cable reeled the pair in like human fish; within seconds they were alongside the chopper's open door.

Luger reached out and grabbed O.T.'s hand, hauling the warrant officer to the edge of the doorway.

When O.T. had gained his footing, both airmen pulled the unconscious Coast Guard crewman into the chopper.

"They're inside," Luger alerted Oz. "I don't see any wounds, but the airman looks bad."

The Delta medic knelt alongside the unconscious man and started checking him for injuries.

"How's O.T.?" Oz asked.

"Wet and wild," O.T. answered over the intercom, fastening the chin strap of his helmet. "I'm okay." He turned toward the unconscious Coast Guard airman, taking care not to lose his footing in the puddle of water collecting around him, and watched the medic.

The Army corpsman had ripped open the man's life vest and coveralls, pressing a stethoscope onto the pale chest. Listening for only a moment, he relocated the instrument. Still hearing nothing, he pulled one of the man's eyelids open and flashed a penlight into his eye.

The dilated pupil failed to respond to the light. Trying the other eye, the medic discovered there was still no response.

The corpsman sighed, turned toward Luger, and shook his head.

"Damn," O.T. muttered.

"The crewman's dead," Luger informed Oz gloomily over the intercom.

Oz lifted the MH-60K higher into the night sky.

"The Coast Guard choppers should be here in fifteen minutes," he told his crew. "In the meantime, assume your positions at the gunners windows. I'm going to circle and see if we can locate any survivors."

12

Captain Croll polished off another biscuit with relish, licking a bead of orange marmalade from his fingertip. The private dining room in which he sat had been created from one of the officers' cabins left vacant following the mutiny. The shortage of personnel was not without its positive features, he smiled to himself, spearing a piece of sausage with his fork.

Three sailors sat at the table with him. Croll made it a point to give every crewman a chance to eat in the private dining room with his commanding officer during the sailor's off-duty hours. He felt it was essential to avoid the aloofness traditionally adopted by British officers; only if his men trusted him completely and obeyed his orders out of loyalty could his operation continue to succeed. Croll believed there could be honor among thieves and strove to cultivate it on his ship.

Also gracing the captain's table were the three prostitutes and Venessa, the latter stunningly attired in a high-necked black dress scooped low in the back. The captain studied her as she toyed with her food, never once looking up.

"You're awfully quiet today, Fleener," Croll
said, finally addressing the sailor sitting at the end
of the table.

"Yes, Captain. I guess I don't have much to
say."

"You've acquired a nice tan since we got to the
Caribbean," Croll remarked pleasantly.

"Thank you, sir. I guess I'm lucky I don't sunburn too easily."

"Not like Irvane," Crystal guffawed, leering at
the sailor next to her and running her hand over his
thigh.

The sunburned blond sailor smirked. "Too
much Viking blood, Captain," he muttered around
a mouthful of sausage. "If I might suggest, sir, we
could use some sun blocker next time we send a crew
ashore for supplies."

"Your suggestion is duly noted, Mr. Irvane,"
the captain said. "In fact, the ship's doctor has made
the same recommendation." Croll paused to butter
a roll and wondered how much more inane the conversation could become when suddenly his thoughts
were interrupted by a knock at the door.

"Enter," the captain called, replacing his knife
on the edge of the plate.

"Sorry to intrude," apologized Brian Eyestone,
the ship's radio technician, "but we just received
this, sir. It looked important." He handed the captain a sheet of paper and stood stiffly at attention beside the officer.

After skimming the message briefly, Croll rose
from the table and addressed his guests. "Ladies and
gentlemen, if you'll excuse me, I need to make a

course change and prepare a boarding party. Please finish your meal and enjoy your diversions."

Crystal winked at Irvane and elbowed him in the ribs. The three sailors stood at attention as the captain left the table.

"You men will continue to have the day off," he announced on his way out.

"Thank you, sir," the sailors chorused.

As soon as the door closed, the table exploded with hysterical laughter and ribald merrymaking. While everyone else was occupied, Venessa carefully slipped a sharp steak knife into the cloth purse that balanced on her lap.

In the hallway outside, Captain Croll strode down the passageway leading to the main deck and climbed to the bridge. "Beautiful morning," he remarked to Eyestone, pausing to observe the rising sun breaking over a thick shroud of clouds. The sky was painted in streaks of orange and crimson that stretched from the horizon until they were almost overhead.

"Red sky in the morning, sailors take warning," Eyestone recited, half in jest.

"There's usually something to that old saying," Croll asserted. "Look at that bank of dark gray clouds brooding along the southwest horizon," he said, pointing. "Have you heard the latest weather reports?"

"Yes, sir. A tropical depression is developing there in the southeast, just beyond Tobago. There's an advisory from the Coast Guard, but I'm not convinced the storm will materialize into anything serious."

"Keep on top of it," Cross ordered, turning to unlatch the port hatch leading to the bridge.

"Aye, sir," Eyestone responded.

"Good morning, Captain," greeted the petty officer in charge of the bridge.

Croll stood for a few seconds in the center of the compartment, inspecting the crewmen. "Good morning, Mr. Vinson," he acknowledged. "Looks like we received a message from our spy today."

"Yes, sir. Big haul from the sound of it."

"Alter our course to these coordinates and then get the assault team ready," Croll ordered, handing Vinson the radio message. "Which team's on today?"

The petty officer checked a clipboard hanging on the wall. "Mills's group, sir."

"Alert them. Better have a Lynx's crew stand by, too, just to be on the safe side."

"Aye, aye, Captain."

Croll paced back and forth on the deck, checking the equipment on the bridge and nervously surveying the storm clouds that hung ominously on the horizon.

13

Although Oz and his crew had searched for survivors until the Coast Guard's rescue choppers arrived, they'd had no luck. In danger of exhausting their fuel, the MH-60K turned and retraced its route to the USS *Montana,* landing beside the other three Night Stalkers aircraft on the deck. The crew climbed out and leaped stiffly onto the swaying surface.

In the tiny cabin reserved for him, Oz crashed onto his bunk, not even bothering to remove his boots. He slept fitfully for almost five hours before jerking awake as the helicopter he'd been piloting in his dream plunged into the sea. For a moment he couldn't remember where he was; then he lay back in the bunk, shivering in his sweat-soaked clothing.

The pilot blinked in the cabin's dim light and checked his watch—zero eight thirty. Although he felt bushed, he knew he wouldn't be able to sleep anymore.

Meeting Sudden after so many years had dredged up old memories that haunted him, reminding him of the eighteen- and nineteen-year-olds with the eyes of old men that he'd ferried around in his Huey in Vietnam. In the spring of 1971 he'd been stationed near Plateau du Darlac when he'd received orders to airlift a team of Green Berets into the village of Dien Hoa, a tiny hamlet no one had ever heard of before or would ever expect to see again.

Army Intelligence believed the Cong were operating from Dien Hoa, and the Green Berets were supposed to scout the area and terminate any enemy activity they encountered.

The olive-drab Huey's whooping blades generated a down draft that gave the occupants a little respite from the relentless heat of Nam, the blades cutting through the thick, humid air and pushing a breeze downward over the open doors and windows.

As Oz circled the LZ, it seemed "cold" from their vantage point, but there was only one way to verify that perception: If no one zapped them as they went in, it was cold; if they were shot at, then it wasn't. That was the insane logic that seemed to govern the war.

He never even saw the rocket that hit them.

It exploded in the passenger compartment, igniting a claymore mine one of the soldiers carried in his pack. The multiple explosions transformed the servicemen into what looked like lightly charred hamburger plastered over skeletons encased in camo uniforms. Only the "chicken plate" steel armor in the cockpit's bucket seats, plus the venting of most of the claymore's blast out the side doors, protected Oz and his copilot from the shrapnel snapping and ricocheting through the cabin.

The Huey's T-53-L-13 engine and main rotor were severely damaged and the aircraft fell like a rock.

Their plunging descent was broken by the trees surrounding the clearing in which Oz had been attempting to land. The chopper hung up in the branches a moment before plummeting into the elephant grass below, accompanied by a cacophony of rending wood and groaning metal.

Oz fought his way free of the smoldering wreckage of the chopper, stumbling through the thorny brush to the rear of the machine. He reeled with nausea as he first caught sight of the mutilated corpses lying in a tangled knot inside the compartment. His mind spinning, refusing to comprehend what had happened, the youthful pilot sank to his knees and retched.

Somewhere in the distance, with time seemingly suspended indefinitely, he thought he heard someone moan. Staggering clumsily through the thick vegetation that snatched at his clothing and tore at his flesh, he discovered his copilot, nicknamed Snake Hips for some obscure reason, pinned inside under the door, which curled over the man like a huge metal hand. Oz strained at the door.

"You got to get me free," Snake Hips bellowed hysterically.

"I'm not leaving until we get you out," Oz reassured the frightened soldier. "Now push while I pull. Maybe the two of us can get this bent back."

The two airmen strained heroically at the bent metal as chunks of its Plexiglas window cracked and dropped out. At long last the door gave way and Oz pulled it free.

Snake Hips tore at the clip fastening his shoulder harness and scrambled out. "Thanks," he said emotionally.

"Get your carbine," Oz ordered. "I think a welcoming committee's headed our way."

The two grabbed their XM177 carbines and staggered into the thick foliage as a fusillade of AK bullets cut into the heavy growth surrounding them. They ran northward, escaping the gunfire briefly, but the enemy patrol continued after them in hot pursuit, yammering and cursing in their singsong language.

The Americans paused at an open field.

"We ought to go around," Snake Hips whispered.

Oz shook his head. "By the time we got around, they'd be on top of us," he explained quietly. "Come on." He sprinted into the opening, steeling himself for a bullet strike that never came. Snake Hips followed, running as fast as he could.

The two Americans succeeded in crossing the field without drawing fire and darted into the shade of the thick verdure, pausing momentarily to gasp for breath. The foliage gave them some relief from the noonday heat and filled their lungs with the thick humid air that smelled of wet loam and rotting vegetation.

"Watch out!" Snake Hips hissed.

Oz crouched instinctively, bringing his XM177 carbine up and snapping the safety to its firing position with his thumb.

Snake Hips abruptly dived into the brush just as Oz saw the muzzle flash; a fraction of a second later the bullet narrowly passed over his scalp with a sonic crack.

As five Vietcong raced through the undergrowth, their AK-47s blazing on full automatic, Oz returned the fire, knocking one rebel into the brush.

The salvo from the remaining four kicked up plumes of earth on the trail next to the pilot and shattered the compass stitched to his flight vest. Then the revolutionaries hastily took cover in the greenery.

Oz used the opportunity to scramble into hiding himself. At first, he could hear men thrashing in the undergrowth behind him. And then everything grew quiet. He searched the brush for some sign of his enemies' whereabouts.

Suddenly, there was a flurry of shooting in the scrub to Oz's right, the low-pitched AK-47s and the louder XM177 barking out cartridges. Ignoring the stray bullets cracking through the air, Oz rose to a crouch, his carbine at the ready.

As he watched, three Cong bolted out of the brush, crossing a tiny clearing into the vegetation on the opposite side before he could shoot.

Two more of the enemy followed, the first limping badly. The second rebel staggered, blood spurting from a wound on his neck. As the two attempted to cross the clearing, Oz fired. The first VC tumbled like a limp rag doll; the other went sprawling, his twitching feet sticking out of the brush where he had fallen.

The flurry of shooting again stopped abruptly.

In the ensuing hush, even the birds and insects were silent.

Oz glanced at the right side of his carbine and realized the bolt was locked open. Unsnapping the pocket on his flight vest and retrieving another of the short twenty-round magazines, he replaced the expended one in the rifle and slapped the bolt release on the left side of the receiver. The bolt clattered forward, making enough noise to be heard for some distance.

The pilot remained motionless. Still there was no other sound. He dropped the empty magazine and crushed it into the dirt with his boot, rendering it useless.

An AK-47 suddenly initiated another salvo of gunfire.

Bullets cracked next to the pilot's head.

Scrambling to place a palm tree between himself and the VC, he realized that he was hearing muzzle blasts from the knoll above him as well.

He spun and discharged his weapon toward the noise, catching a glimpse of a black-clad figure as he fired. The rebel jerked and fell, half his face blown away by the .223 bullet.

Crouching, the pilot kept the palm to his spine to screen himself from the Cong on the other side. Rising slightly, he studied the area in front of him and then dived back into the foliage when he heard the clack of an AK selector being switched on.

A hail of bullets cracked above his head while another salvo dug into the damp soil and growth around him. Crawling on his belly, hidden by the verdure, he withdrew from the spot on his hands and knees.

And then the shooting stopped.

The American paused and listened.

Someone was thrashing toward him through the brush.

Oz froze with his finger on the trigger of his rifle, squeezing it slightly as the sound grew closer. Then he relaxed perceptibly as he discerned the olive green of a US Army uniform.

It was Snake Hips.

The soldier crawled to Oz.

Despite the fear in the copilot's eyes, he smiled grimly at his equally frightened buddy. A trickle of blood dripped from a wound on the man's upper left arm, while his lower earlobe oozed from where he'd been nicked by a bullet. Both airmen lay motionless on the damp earth.

Oz turned and peered through the thick brush that screened the clearing ahead of him, barely discerning the black forms of two Vietcong not ten yards in front of them.

The pilot signaled Snake Hips, who nodded, and the two Americans rose from the brush, their weapons blazing.

The Cong whirled, answering the Americans with their AK-47s. But the .223 bullets reached their destination and the pajama-clad Vietnamese were dead within seconds.

"Good work," Oz said quietly, glancing toward Snake Hips.

The copilot lay motionless on his back, a tiny

hole on his chest the only indication of the wound that killed him.

Oz inspected the area for several minutes to verify that they'd mopped up the last of the rebels, then knelt and took a deep breath. He grasped Snake His's dog tags, tore them off, and jammed them into his pants pocket. He removed the spare ammunition and pistol from the copilot's flight vest.

Knowing the soldier's XM177 carbine shouldn't be left behind for the enemy, Oz broke it open as if he were going to field strip it and extracted the bolt carrier and charging handle from the gun. He hurled the two parts into the thick brush and then stuck the barrel of the carbine between the fork of a tree and pulled until the barrel bent and the handguards and stock cracked. Then he threw the useless weapon into the foliage.

The pilot knelt in the brush and listened for several minutes. Nothing. He turned back toward his copilot once more, sorry he couldn't take the body with him or at least bury it. But he knew that if the roles had been reversed, he would've expected Snake Hips to think only of his own skin. He glanced at the sun to get his bearings and melted into the jungle.

For three hours Oz dodged the Vietcong patrols searching for him before managing to double around and lose his pursuers. Several days later he was finally rescued by Sudden's patrol.

Oz forced the memories from his mind and threw his legs over the edge of the bunk, landing on the steel deck as quietly as he could in order not to wake Death Song or Luger, who were still asleep in their bunks.

A shower and a change of clothing left the pilot feeling like he'd rejoined the human race. After asking directions from a sailor, he made his way through the swaying corridor toward the mess.

Grabbing one of the metal trays and sliding it along the counter, Oz helped himself to a bowl of steaming hot oatmeal and two slices of buttered toast.

"Ham and eggs?" the cook asked.

"No thanks," Oz said. "But I could use a cup of coffee."

"Help yourself from the dispenser right ahead of you, sir."

Oz picked up a mug from the railed storage compartment and filled it. Turning, he spied O.T. sitting at a table with a sailor.

"Morning," O.T. mumbled through a mouthful of eggs.

"You're up early," Oz remarked, setting the tray on the table and easing himself into the metal folding chair.

"Never sleep well after midnight swims," O.T. replied. "Besides, sleep is for wimps. What's the schedule for today?"

"Since everybody's still dead tired, I think we'll wait until noon to start the first patrol," Oz answered. "I don't want anybody messing up while they're out. Then each chopper will leave on a rotating basis so we'll be able to maintain a twenty-four-hour patrol."

"They say there's a storm moving in," the sailor

informed Oz. "Might even develop into a hurricane."

"Excuse me, sir," O.T. said to Oz. "I didn't introduce you two. This is Master Sergeant Dexter. Dexter, this is Captain Carson, possibly the best copter pilot in the US Army."

"Can you tell he's bucking for a raise?" Oz grinned, shaking the man's hand.

"He's not the only one singing your praises," Dexter declared.

"So how serious is a hurricane in a ship like this?" Oz asked, changing the subject.

"It's not too bad," the sailor asserted. "The *Montana* has weathered more than a few hurricanes in her time. But you might want to check into the dispensary for some Dramamine if you tend to get seasick. We really rock and roll in a major storm."

"Better warn Luger," O.T. snickered. "Judging from how he does in transports, he'll probably be needing it."

"You've got a crewman who gets airsick?" Dexter asked, astonished.

"Yeah," O.T. answered, shoveling the last of his eggs in. "He's fine on choppers, but when he gets into a transport where he can't see outside, his stomach goes nuts."

"That's how most people are with seasickness," Dexter nodded. "Everybody thinks it's the air on deck that makes them feel better when it's really escaping the enclosed room and being able to see what's going on that does it."

"How quickly do the storms come in?" Oz asked.

"You'll need to be careful on patrol," Dexter replied. "Things can deteriorate pretty fast when a storm's approaching. Right now, it's sitting there in the east, building strength feeding off the warm ocean."

"It's headed our way?" Oz inquired.

The sailor nodded. "Most hurricanes travel westward in the Caribbean, and this one is no exception. So, I'm betting we'll be in for it soon."

"Swell," Oz grimaced.

"What's a search party without a hurricane!" O.T. said with a straight face.

The seaman rose. "Well, on that cheery note, I'll leave you gentlemen. I'm on call in fifteen minutes."

"Be seeing you," O.T. called after him as the sailor made his way across the room.

C H A P T E R

14

The wind blew at thirty-five miles per hour, creating mammoth waves that crashed against the HMS *Fox*'s forecastle, the foam sweeping across the deck and erupting into geysers as it reached the capstan.

Captain Croll checked the compass to verify that they were still on the correct bearing.

"We're going to have to get pretty close," Petty Officer Vinson told Croll. "Otherwise we'll probably miss them."

The commanding officer didn't reply but instead checked his watch and turned to the radar technician who was studying the glowing screen in front of him. "Keep careful lookout," Croll instructed. "If they're on schedule, they should be around here somewhere."

"Aye, aye, Captain."

Rain spattered on the glass viewing ports as the frigate pitched about in the angry sea. "Where's that US Navy ship?" Croll inquired.

"She's still forty miles south of us," Vinson replied, momentarily scrutinizing his superior officer out of the corner of his eye.

"I know it's a little risky intercepting the drug shipment," Croll explained to Vinson, "but it's a big haul and I think we can stay hidden under cover of the storm."

Vinson agreed. "The high waves should keep the Americans from detecting us with their radar," he said.

"*If* we can cut off our quarry's radio," Croll added, staring at the gyrating sea.

"Captain," the radar technician said. "Looks like a small ship ahead of us."

Croll strode across the swaying deck and stood over the blue-gray console of the Type 968 surveillance radar. He studied the screen as it swept the target several times, detecting an electronic echo from the approaching ship each time it rode over the crest of a wave.

"I'd say that's it," Croll asserted. "Mr. Vinson, get the Lynx crew in place."

"Aye, Captain."

Within seconds the hangar doors were open and the crew was wheeling the Lynx onto the helideck.

"Instruct Mills's team to get into position," the captain ordered. Then he turned toward his electronic warfare officer. "Engage our EW circuits and jam any radio communications they attempt to send."

"EW circuits engaged," the officer answered from his console.

"Don't let them get a distress call out as we approach," Croll ordered.

"Aye, aye, sir," the officer replied.

The frigate lurched as another wave slammed against its bow.

Below deck in the ship's armory, Mills's team of twelve men loaded and prepared their L85A1 Enfield bullpup rifles and an L86A1 machine gun. The sailors wore foul-weather gear and life vests, carrying magazines of ammunition in canvas pouches attached to belts.

The HMS *Fox* was singularly unsuited for the work Mills and his team were called upon to do. Most of the ship's guns and missiles were designed to destroy or severely damage enemy battleships, submarines, or aircraft. The weapons had too much power for simply crippling a civilian vessel so it could be boarded and seized.

The only weapons systems that had proven worthwhile in pirating a ship were the remote-controlled 40mm/60 Mark 9 antiaircraft guns on either side of the middle deck. But even these were ineffectual at close range because they couldn't be declined to hit their targets; they also required that an enemy be engaged from the side of the ship. Consequently, Mills and his team were essential for Croll's pirating operation.

"Bridge to the armory," the intercom called from the bulkhead.

Mills toggled the speaker, "Mills here."

"Time to head for your positions. Better fasten your wigs on tight—there's a hell of a wind blowing up here."

"We're headed up," Mills answered. "Let's get a move on!" he ordered to his team.

Within three minutes Mills and his men had positioned themselves on the forward deck of the *Fox,* hidden behind the thick metal bulwark of the stern where they would be protected from incoming gunfire.

"We're in place," Mills announced on his portable radio as a wave crashed into the bow, splashing water and spray over the seamen.

"We're closing fast," Croll called. "They're straight ahead, about three miles."

Mills squinted into the storm, unable to distinguish anything other than the gray waves. "We don't have visual, Captain."

"Don't worry, we've got it on radar," Croll shouted. "Just keep your eyes open."

In the bridge overlooking the assault team, Croll turned to his helmsman. "Reduce speed to one-third."

"Speed to one-third," the helmsman echoed, adjusting the lever that conveyed the order to the engine room. In the engine compartment near the keel of the vessel, engineers at the horseshoe-shaped CODLAG control center keyed in the speed change.

The computerized system automatically activated the diesel-powered electric motors as the twin Rolls-Royce Spey gas turbines were placed on standby in the event that a surge of power was called for from the bridge. The changeover was accomplished smoothly by the microprocessor-based system, while the technicians oversaw the procedure on the flow-chart-style monitors. The series of indicators for the ship's twin screws changed from green to yellow as the frigate slowed.

On the bridge far above the engineers, Croll addressed his radar technician, "What's your reading?"

"We're still closing, dead on course, Captain. Half a mile."

"The Lynx crew is standing by, Captain," Petty Officer Vinson reported. "And the fire-control radar and electro-op director is now ready with the Mark 9s."

"Tell the Lynx crew we'll be sending the boarding party with them," Croll stated. "I don't want to put the launch out in these waves. Be sure to remind the pilot to keep low so that US Navy ship can't spot us."

"Aye, sir."

"Captain!" Mills's voice called from the radio. "We have a visual."

"Hail them on your bullhorn as soon as we get within range."

"Aye, aye, sir."

"They're trying to send a message, Captain," the EW officer said. "I'm jamming it now."

"Keep them from getting on the air to attract attention," Croll ordered, aware that even a simple radio inquiry could alert anyone intercepting it to the fact that the British ship was stopping civilians on the open seas. If such a signal were received, it wouldn't take the Coast Guard long to put two and two together.

On the deck below the bridge, Mills lifted the electronic bullhorn to his mouth and hailed the twenty-meter *yate* that was bobbing over a wave toward them. "Prepare to be boarded," Mills's voice boomed over the water.

The drug smugglers below, knowing they couldn't afford to be stopped by a military ship, knelt on the swaying deck and pulled Star submachine guns out from under the canvas where they'd been concealed. As Mills stood above them with his bullhorn, presenting the only human target the men could discern, the five opened fire.

Brass chimed as it dropped onto the yacht's soaked decks; fire and bullets shot upward toward the steel bulwarks of the *Fox* where Mills ducked for cover, the projectiles clanging on the steel plate in front of him.

The British team leader waited a moment for the shooting to subside as the smugglers exhausted their magazines; then he and his men rose, clicked off the safeties of their firearms, and aimed.

As the thirteen British sailors leaned over the bulwark, ignoring the last sporadic firing that came from the *yate,* the small ship's engines roared to a higher pitch as its captain brought it around in an attempt to outrun the larger vessel bearing down upon it.

Mills yelled his order. "Fire!"

The English rifles and machine guns exploded in a barrage that riddled the deck of the yacht as it presented its port side toward them. The salvo pocked three of the drug gunmen who dropped where they knelt. Two of the gunmen remained standing, despite serious wounds washed pink by the heavy rain. They fought to finish reloading their weapons and managed to get off sporadic return fire before being hit by the second salvo from the English sailors.

One of the smugglers tumbled down the stair-well leading to the main cabin while the other fell overboard, disappearing from sight in the choppy sea.

The captain of the *yate*, his shoulder shattered from one of the machine-gun bullets, stood in the flying bridge and continued to swing his ship around, increasing its speed as the stern turned to-ward the *Fox*.

The British sailors on the frigate trained their rifles and machine guns on the man, their barrage of high-velocity slugs riddling the flying bridge. The skipper flopped forward, a spray of blood covering the wheel in front of him.

The engines abruptly ceased as the dead cap-tain's hands clutched the throttle as he fell; the boat coasted to a stop to lay dead in the water, bobbing on the waves.

"Cease fire," Mills ordered. He thumbed on his radio, "Captain, we've neutralized the resistance on the yacht."

"Select five men and go aft to the Lynx," Croll ordered. "You're going to have to rappel down and secure her. Then pilot her to the quarterdeck and we'll unload the cargo and scuttle her."

"Scuttle her, sir?"

"I'm not going to risk any of our crew trying to get the yacht to port in this storm."

"Aye, aye, Captain."

15

The furious wave that slammed against the yawl threw Grapper out of his bunk. Staggering to his feet, he climbed out of the cabin onto the slippery deck of the yacht. "What's going on?" he demanded.

Hawkins blinked groggily in the dim lantern light. "It's getting bad," he said. "I was afraid to leave the wheel to wake you."

"What in the world!" Grapper exploded, staring at the compass. "We're headed west!"

"I only fell asleep for a couple of minutes an hour ago," Hawkins said.

"You're aligned on the wrong heading!" Grapper yelled. "The storm's blowing us *away* from Dominica. Secure the wheel and help me douse the spinnaker."

The two men fought the rigging, struggling to lower the ballooning spinnaker sail that dragged the ship away from its intended destination. The gale-driven nylon canvas bucked like a horse as they fought to secure it, rain splattering against them, instantly soaking their clothes and hair.

"We'll have to close-haul and tack," Grapper

yelled, holding a rub rail to steady himself. "It's our only chance to make Dominica."

As Oz checked their course, the wind battered the MH-60K and whipped the lurching sea beneath them. The black mantle above hinted at the furious hurricane, now designated "Darcy," that had nearly reached the area they now patrolled. The wipers of the chopper swish-sloshed back and forth, furiously attempting to sweep the windscreen clear of droplets.

It was nearing the end of their patrol and the pilot debated whether he should send the next team out or scrub the mission until after the hurricane had passed. It was still possible to observe with the FLIR, which was capable of viewing through the rain using the infrared spectrum in which it operated. Oz finally decided it would be safe to send the next team out, provided they kept their flight short.

He studied the rolling waves on the ocean's surface, which the wind kicked higher and higher as hurricane Darcy approached. He toggled on the radio. "BB-68, this is Sea Wolf One," he called.

"Go ahead, Sea Wolf One."

"We're coming in for a landing."

"Roger, Sea Wolf One, we have you on radar. We'll have our deck crew ready."

Five minutes later the pilot set the chopper down on the swaying surface of the *Montana* and fought his way against the wind to the vessel's superstructure. Just inside the narrow hatchway that overlooked the helideck, he met Sergeant Frank Snyder—the pilot of the next MH-60K slated to go out—and the other three Sea Wolf Four crew members.

"I wouldn't send a dog out in weather like this," Oz told the airmen.

"But you'd send us!" Snyder laughed, anticipating the punch line.

"It's all right," one of the airmen quipped, "our skins are watertight."

"I'm only going to have you stay out an hour," Oz told the soldiers. "The weatherman says you'll have plenty of time to make it back. I wouldn't send you at all but we haven't covered the quadrant to the north yet and I'd like to be sure nothing's going on out there."

"That makes sense," Snyder agreed.

"You'd better get going," Oz said. "Looks like your chopper's in position."

"Yes, sir. See you in an hour."

Oz watched the men as they climbed into the MH-60K, hoping he was doing the right thing in sending them out.

Inside the chopper, Sergeant Snyder spoke through the intercom to his crew as they lifted off. "OK, we're not going to be out in this for long. But while we're out, let's keep our eyes open and try to find something." The pilot eased the control column forward and the MH-60K accelerated, pushing his passengers into their seats.

For thirty minutes they hurtled above the water, seeing nothing but heaving oceans below, their visibility limited to only a few kilometers.

"I'm getting odd signals from the northeast," reported Specialist John Jacobs, Snyder's copilot.

Snyder checked their course on the HSD screen. "All right," he said, "let's circle and we'll take a look at that stretch of water."

Behind the pilot, one of the gunners spoke over the intercom. "We've got zero visibility back here," he said. "The rain's sheeting the ports so badly we can't see anything."

"Just sit tight and don't worry about it," Snyder replied. "We'll be returning to the *Montana* before long."

They flew through the tempest for another five minutes before Jacobs spoke again. "I'm getting a weak radar reading," he said. "Looks like surveillance radar."

"From the *Montana?*" the pilot asked.

"No, wrong pattern," Jacobs replied. "The Navy doesn't have any other ships around here, does it?"

"No, but that doesn't mean much," Snyder answered. "There're all kinds of ships going through here. It could have come from their equipment. Let's check on it so we can at least report we found something out here."

The pilot glanced at the HSD screen for the new heading and then pointed the chopper to home in on the weak signal.

Within minutes, Jacobs sighted the shadowy form of a ship ahead of them. "There!" he exclaimed. "At twelve o'clock."

"I see it," Snyder said. "Looks like a frigate." He fought the controls, forcing the helicopter to head into the wind and stay on course. "What's that behind it. Another ship?"

"Yeah," Jacobs agreed. "Looks like a yacht." He peered through the windscreen, squinting to sharpen his vision. "Are those bodies lying on the deck?"

Snyder studied the yacht closely, discerning the lifeless forms sprawled on the surface of the craft. Lying in pools of blood, too, he realized grimly.

"Sergeant, they're sweeping us with their radar," Jacobs exclaimed suddenly. "Targeting radar from the looks of it."

"Hang on," Snyder warned the crew, stomping on the right pedal and cramping the control column to the starboard. The MH-60K lurched to the right, a gust of wind shoving it with a gut-wrenching thrust. "We don't want to hang around if that's what I think it is," the pilot asserted.

"You think those are the pirates?" Jacobs asked incredulously. "But that's a military ship. Maybe they're just helping the injured people on deck."

"Maybe," the sergeant replied doubtfully, dropping his chopper in an effort to avoid being detected. "We're not going to wait around to find out." He switched on the radio. "BB-68, this is Sea Wolf Four. Come in please. Over."

"Four this is BB-68. Go ahead."

"We think we've located the pirates," Snyder radioed the battleship. "They're using a military ship to cover themselves. I can't see its colors but it looks like a British vessel. It appears that they've attacked a small yacht. Over."

He released the radio trigger on the control column only to be greeted by an electronic humming and chatter. "What the hell?" Snyder exclaimed.

"They're jamming our frequency," Jacobs said.

"How much of my call got through?" Snyder asked.

"There's no way to tell but—Hang on," Jacobs interrupted himself. "They've got their targeting radar on."

"They've launched a missile at us!" shouted one of the gunners who'd opened his window.

Snyder swore under his breath as he shoved on the control column and lowered the collective pitch lever. The MH-60K responded, skittering forward and dropping as it accelerated.

The chopper vacillated in the gale of spray coming from the ocean, snatching at them as they skimmed its surface.

The pilot crossed a trough of water and flew so close to a wave that the landing gear sloshed through it. The water tore at the aircraft, tilting it in the air slightly, inducing a terrific thumping on the underside. Snyder pulled on the collective pitch lever to his side as another breaker towered up in his path; the chopper rose abruptly, narrowly missing the wave.

As the pilot glided around a second surging mountain of water, the noise of the chopper's rotors boomed from the water and echoed across the mountains of churning brine.

"I'm sure it's locked onto us," Jacobs warned.

The distinctive sound of the continuous wave radar from the ship illuminated them to the semiactive guidance system on the GWS 25 missile. The copilot frantically released chaff from the countermeasures pod, hoping it would confuse the oncoming rocket; a metal cloud materialized behind the aircraft but was immediately swept into the ocean by the wind.

"I can't stay this low without colliding with the waves," Snyder declared, lifting the MH-60K to avoid another crest of water hurtling toward them.

The aerial inside the nose radome of the missile continued to sense them. The rocket's computer altered the hydraulics in the projectile's delta wings to home onto its target, following the pinging from the radar echoing from the chopper.

"It's still got us!" Jacobs warned.

For a split second, the missile turned away from the Americans, chasing after a false reflection from a nearby wave. Then it abruptly reacquired its target and curved toward them. The copilot was reaching to activate the 532 countermeasures pod again when the GWS 25 surface-to-air missile overtook them.

No one in the aircrew had time to speak, feel pain, or even be aware they'd been hit. The thunderclap of the warhead swept through the cabin of the helicopter, ripping the aircraft and crew apart with its blast. A split second later the secondary explosion of the MH-60K's fuel tanks created a fireball that was then torn apart by the howling wind as the wreckage of the chopper rained onto the sea.

Captain Croll observed the attack and its aftermath through binoculars, watching as the debris of the helicopter plunged into the ocean. Lowering the binoculars from his eyes, his face was a mask. "Good job, fire control," he said stonily into the intercom.

He turned toward the electronic warfare engineer. "Did you squelch their radio before they got any messages out?" he asked.

"I'm not sure, sir," the man answered. "There was so little warning before they were right beside us. But I think we blanked them soon enough."

Croll swore under his breath and activated his radio. "Mills?"

"Yes, Captain," Mills's voice answered.

"Scuttle the yacht."

"But, sir, we've only got half the load transported to the *Fox*," Mills objected.

"I don't care," Croll replied. "Scuttle her now. We don't have the luxury of waiting to see if that chopper has friends nosing around."

16

"And that's all they said?" Oz asked the *Montana*'s radio technician.

"Yes, sir," the sailor answered, self-consciously pulling at his eyebrow. "They identified themselves, we gave them the go-ahead, and they just said, 'We think we've located the pirates.' And then their signal was lost in electrical interference."

"What kind of interference?"

"It sounded like they were jammed," the second technician said.

"I don't know," his partner shook his head. "That'd take pretty sophisticated equipment to chop up a signal like that. Maybe the storm . . . or a malfunction with their radio."

"No, it was jammed," the other technician said with conviction. "Some of these drug runners have state-of-the-art equipment. I bet—"

"Listen, thanks a lot for your help," Oz interrupted, turning to the ship's commander. "Captain Palmer, if I send out another chopper, how long could it be in the air safely?"

"You're not thinking about going after them,

are you?" Palmer protested. "We had them on radar when we lost contact. They must be fifteen or twenty minutes from us by now."

"How long before Darcy actually reaches us?" Oz persisted.

Palmer crossed to the monitor in the bridge. "We received this from the US Weather Bureau a few minutes ago. It's from their weather satellite," he said, punching the play button on the VCR that was connected to the monitor. A pattern of rotating clouds superimposed over a map of the Caribbean and southern Florida appeared on the screen. "Here's where we are," he said, pointing. "Technically, we're already in the hurricane, but the worst of it hasn't hit yet. We'll be feeling the full effects in under an hour I'd guess."

"How strong will the winds be?"

"They're clocking Darcy at 232 kilometers an hour here where the storm's building," he tapped the screen. "No way a copter's going to fly in that."

"Have your deck crew ready my chopper," Oz said. "We can home in on the area where Sea Wolf Four's last signal was recorded and reach them in twenty minutes. Then we can search and return within the hour since the wind will be at our backs on the return flight. Maybe forty-five minutes round trip."

"That's cutting it way too close," Palmer objected, shaking his head. "I know you're calling the shots on your patrols, but I'm strongly recommending that you reconsider this."

"Thanks, Captain, but we're going. Now, if you'll please have your crew ready the chopper."

"Will do," the captain said. "I won't delay you any longer. You can call your aircrew on that phone there. Franklin," the captain turned toward the sailor manning the console.

"Captain?"

"Have the crew move Sea Wolf One on deck and get her ready for takeoff," Palmer ordered.

The sky was nearly black as Oz and his crew sprinted across the lurching deck of the *Montana*, holding on to the line that had been strung for them between the superstructure and the chopper. The four Army crewmen climbed aboard the MH-60K, slamming the doors shut behind them.

"I'm soaked to the bone," O.T. exclaimed, jacking the cord from his helmet into the intercom. "In fact, even my bones feel soggy."

In four minutes they were airborne. Rainwater poured across the windscreen faster than the wipers could deal with it, compelling Oz to fly by instruments.

The vertical situation display screen in front of him provided information about flight path, horizon, and radar altitude, while the horizontal situation display gave flight projections, navigation reference points, and other pertinent information. Occasionally he checked the FLIR to observe the ocean's surface, while Death Song monitored the radar.

The gale hammered furiously at the MH-60K, the wind tearing at the machine and limiting their forward momentum, although Oz had the control column shoved forward for maximum speed. When the wind dropped, the chopper surged forward.

"We're almost there," Death Song warned. "I've got radar activity at bearing zero five one."

"Let's see what it is," Oz said, kicking the rudder pedal to turn them onto the new course.

The radio crackled, "Helicopter approaching HMS frigate F92, please identify yourself."

"This is Sea Wolf One," Oz radioed on the same frequency. "We're searching for a chopper that was last contacted in this area. Have you had any sightings or communication with them? Over."

"I'm not sure," Captain Croll replied. "We just arrived here, ourselves. But we did encounter a chopper fifteen minutes ago. They seemed to be in pursuit of a small yacht."

"Did you notice if your radio frequencies were being jammed?" Oz asked.

"Funny you should ask that," Croll answered. "Our EW engineer swears someone jammed our radio for a few minutes. A pretty dangerous practice—especially in this storm. Over."

"Can you give us the helicopter's course heading?"

"Not precisely, Sea Wolf One. But they were headed almost due east. Over."

"Thanks, F92. We'll take the new heading and get out of your hair. But please keep a lookout for the helicopter or signs of a wreck. It looks like they may be down. Their fuel would be exhausted by now and they haven't returned to our home ship."

"We'll keep watch," Croll replied. "Good luck with your search. Over and out."

Croll hung up his mike as the American chopper altered its course for the erroneous heading.

"Do you think they bought your story, sir?" the helmsman asked the captain.

"I don't know," Croll said. "They came straight here to search. I'm not sure anybody's going to think it was a coincidence that we happened to be in the neighborhood where they lost their chopper."

"At least no one's connected us with that Coast Guard helicopter," the helmsman said.

"Yeah," Croll nodded. "If they knew that two of their aircraft had vanished when we were nearby, it would cook our goose for sure."

The captain crossed to the barograph. "Looks like we've got quite a storm coming in," he remarked. "Have the crew check to be sure everything is battened down. Then let's head into the wind so we don't get swamped by these waves."

Grapper was chilled by the lashing rain, his hands shaking as he clutched the helm. "Ready about!" he ordered.

Hawkins shivered and wiped the water from his eyes. "Ready," he responded weakly.

"Hard-a-lee!" Grapper yelled, whirling the wheel so the rudder of the ship sprang to the side. The yawl turned sharply upwind, the air spilling from its sails as Hawkins released the jib.

For a few minutes the vessel headed directly into the wind as the air coursed across the deck from the other side of the turning ship. The sails had begun to billow when suddenly the air grew calm and then immediately whipped about in the opposite direction.

With the change in the direction of the wind,

the sail filled abruptly and the boom rushed across the deck, catching Hawkins off guard as he stood on the slick surface. The spar caught the sailor at the knees, knocking him off his feet. He slid along the deck as the wind reversed and blew the boom again, cracking it against the back of his skull. The unconscious sailor fell overboard into the boiling ocean.

Grapper turned the wheel so the ship abandoned its close-haul position and circled. "Hawkins!" he yelled, searching frantically for the injured sailor. "Hawkins!" he screamed again.

He brought the yawl hard about, the wind slamming into the sail, pushing it nearly parallel with the surface of the ocean.

For six long seconds, the boat hung suspended as the ballasted keel balanced the ship. But another blast of wind heeled the yawl even more and abruptly water poured through the lee rail and into the ship's cabin.

Before Grapper could act, the ship lost its balance and plunged onto its side, throwing him overboard into the heaving waves.

The salt water blinded him and burned his throat with its foul taste. Kicking vigorously, he tried to reach the surface, only to discover that his leg was trapped in a line from the yawl. Lungs bursting, he reached down and frantically tried to free his ankle from the line that held him under.

17

Captain Palmer watched silently from the bridge of the USS *Montana* while his crew finished securing the ship against the hurricane that was bearing down upon the vessel.

"Captain, this is the helideck," the intercom called.

"Go ahead, helideck."

"We have the winch ready for Sea Wolf One, Captain."

"Good. They should be here in a few minutes so keep your men alert. I'll notify you as soon as they're on final approach."

"Aye, sir."

The captain surveyed the monocone antenna perched on the forecastle, half invisible in the deluge. He wondered idly if the aerial would be able to weather the storm; the device looked like a huge toy gyroscope made of pipe and wire, and although it was designed to survive winds to three hundred kilometers per hour, Palmer had never trusted its strength.

"BB-68," the transmitter crackled, interrupting

Palmer's reverie, "this is Sea Wolf One. We're—"
The rest of the message was cut by static.

"Sea Wolf One," the ship's radio technician answered, "please say again. Over."

"We're—" Static once more cut the message.

"Say again, Sea Wolf One," the technician directed.

"We're five minutes from you," Oz's voice repeated. "Request permission to land. Over."

The captain nodded at the radioman.

"Permission granted, Sea Wolf One," the technician replied. "Come on in, we've got the ship turned into the storm so the helideck will be a little less windy. Over."

"Thanks, BB-68. See you in a few minutes. Sea Wolf One over and out."

"I hope they make it," Palmer said to no one in particular as he crossed to the radar engineer and studied the luminescent scope in front of him. "Have you got them?"

"Yes, sir. Here," the engineer pointed to a blip. "They're traveling awfully fast for a helicopter."

"They've got one whale of a tail wind," the captain explained. "Pay careful attention to their position in case they go down and we have to fish them out of the water."

The MH-60K was nearly out of control, swept forward by the punishing gale. Powerful gusts of wind accelerated the machine beyond its maximum speed with gut-gripping suddenness.

Oz was aware that the helicopter had been over-designed, with a margin of safety built in so its operational limitations could be pushed somewhat. But it was impossible to know when the maximum speed of the helicopter might be disastrously exceeded.

He gritted his teeth as another blast ripped past, throwing the chopper sideways and forward.

"We're four kilometers from the *Montana* and closing fast," Death Song alerted the pilot.

"O.T.," Oz called, "are you ready with the cable?"

"Ready," the warrant officer answered, steadying himself on the aluminum frame of one of the seats and grasping the heavy cable, its loop ready to be coupled to the cargo hook.

Oz glanced at the HSD and felt the helicopter drop abruptly. Instinctively, he jerked up on the collective pitch lever to counter the down draft that propelled them toward the sea.

He watched intently through the rain-splattered windscreen as a blurred mountain of water loomed in the darkness ahead of them, threatening to engulf the aircraft.

As unexpectedly as it had come, the down draft vanished and the chopper lifted, allowing the ocean to hiss below, its spray blotting the windscreen as they passed. Oz let the helicopter continue to climb until they were at a safe distance above the sea.

The pilot let out his breath as he spied the *Montana*'s navigation lights through the gloom. He clicked on his transmitter. "BB-68, this is Sea Wolf One. I have a visual and am proceeding to your helideck. Over."

Static answered his message and then the radio became intelligible. "We repeat," the radioman on the *Montana* said. "Proceed to helideck. Our crew's standing by. Over."

"We're advancing to the helideck," Oz said.

With the tail wind shoving the chopper forward, the MH-60K refused to come to a stop when the pilot pulled on the control column, tearing ahead instead like a runaway sled on a steep hill.

Oz kicked his rudder pedal to avoid the Tacan antenna and air surveillance radar atop the superstructure. Then he activated the opposite pedal and lowered the collective pitch lever, plummeting them into the shelter offered by the vessel.

The helicopter finally overcame the gust and ranged backward as they dropped into the windbreak of the superstructure. He shoved forward on the collective pitch lever to counter their rearward motion and rotated the chopper around so its nose was facing amidships, centering them above the barely visible landing circle painted in white on the deck.

"Lower the cable, O.T." Oz ordered, holding the chopper above the deck and using the *Montana*'s strobing lights for reference positions. He switched on the radio. "BB-68, we're lowering our cable."

"I'll alert the deck crew," answered the *Montana*'s radioman.

O.T. opened the lower hatch and was greeted by a powerful gust of wind and rain that instantly soaked him. The warrant officer carefully looped the cable around the external sling hook and tugged at it to be sure it was secure. Then Luger and he painstakingly snaked the cable through the MH-60K's lower hatch, watching to ensure that the steel line didn't kink as it unwound.

Two deck hands with ropes tied around their waists staggered under the helicopter as it bobbed in the gale, its thundering blades drowning out the noise of the storm. The ship reeled with the slap of a wave and one of the deck hands fell. As he scrambled to his feet, the other sailor grabbed the end of the line and threaded it into the block mounted on the deck.

Both seaman then lugged the cable to the large winch the crew had prepared to help convey the helicopter to the deck of the swaying vessel. The seamen labored swiftly and silently, since the noise of both the hurricane and the helicopter made conversation impossible.

Within seconds the line was secure. The sailors grabbed the nylon ropes tied to their waists and pulled themselves toward the hatch they'd come through; fellow crewmen on the opposite end of the ropes helped to draw them along, hauling the reeling mariners in like huge fish.

"The winch is ready, Sea Wolf One," the *Montana* alerted Oz seconds later. "We'll activate on your command. Over."

"How's everything look, O.T.?" Oz asked on the intercom.

O.T. knelt next to the hatch and gave the assembly a final inspection as Luger held the warrant officer's vest to be sure he didn't lose his balance and tumble through the opening. "Looks good, Captain."

Oz toggled on his transmitter. "We're ready to land, BB-68. Activate the winch."

The heavy cable lost its slack, tugging the helicopter toward the deck. As Oz carefully lowered the chopper to the rolling surface of the *Montana,* the line was drawn downward, maintaining just enough lift on the chopper to keep the cable taut. The pilot was extremely cautious, knowing that too much lift would break or damage the helicopter or winch, while insufficient pressure could cause the chopper to tumble onto the deck—both with equally disastrous results.

"How're we doing, O.T.?" Oz asked, warily lowering the collective pitch lever.

"Good," the warrant officer answered. "No slack but the cable's not pinging, either."

As the helicopter slowly neared the deck, the chopper's left forward wheel bounced off the surface of the ship, and then all three wheels were down.

"Cut the winch," Oz directed as the chopper was pulled snug against its hydraulic landing gear.

"Power to the winch is cut," the radio replied.

Deck hands rushed through the downpour to get blocks on either side of the chopper's wheels to help keep it in place.

Oz heaved a sigh of relief as he and Death Song quickly went through the post-flight checklist. When they had finished, he spoke into the intercom. "Be sure the doors and windows are locked tight," he cautioned.

"We're secured here," O.T. yelled.

"All right, then let's try to make it to the mess without getting swept off the deck," he declared only half in jest as another team of sailors came through the stinging rain to escort them to safety.

Because there was no hangar on the USS *Montana,* the Night Stalkers' two MH-60Ks and single Apache would sit on the deck through the storm, cables holding them in place while the wind, rain, and waves pounded them.

Fighting his way to the open hatch beyond the X turret of the USS *Montana,* Oz wondered if the three Night Stalkers' helicopters would survive the hurricane out in the open.

As the crew was escorted into the warm interior of the swaying vessel, a team of sailors led by Master Sergeant Dexter struggled on the wet helideck to finish securing the Army helicopter.

"A guy with a pug nose would drown out here," Dexter yelled to the sailor next to him as they unwound the cable from the chopper's hook. The sailor flashed him a wet smile.

"Be sure everything's secured," Dexter shouted, his voice barely audible over the gale.

Three of the sailors in his crew unwound the heavy cables that would prevent the helicopter from rolling or being blown over and then carefully bolted the ends of the lines into place. The other two crewmen helped Dexter fasten the four main rotors to the end of the lines.

As they completed their tasks, the master sergeant inspected the work, blinking the stinging salt spray from his eyes in an effort to see better.

"We're secure, Sergeant," one of the sailors announced.

"Head in," he ordered. "I'm going to check

everything once more." As the deck crew fought their way to the rear hatch, he turned, glancing at the cables holding the MH-60Ks and Apache to the deck. He bent against the wind and tugged at the lines to be certain they were firmly attached to the choppers. As he started to check the final cable, one of the sailors came stumbling across the deck.

"Sarge," the man yelled. "Kane just slipped— looks like he broke his ankle."

Dexter swore under his breath. The new crewman couldn't get out of bed without hurting himself! "Let's get him to sick bay," Dexter barked.

As the two men started across the deck, the steel cable that Dexter had failed to inspect whipped behind them, flapping from the Apache's rotor and twisting against the anchoring bolt that was slowly working loose.

The wind diminished as the HMS *Fox* voyaged into the hurricane's eye, but the waves remained high and lashed at the stern of the British frigate.

"I've got to have full power!" Captain Croll warned over the intercom.

"But, Captain," Master Chief Engineer Ewing replied from the engine room, "our board's lit now. We've got to cut the gas turbines and switch to electric power or we'll burn them out for sure."

The captain took a deep breath and tried to control his frustration. He knew they couldn't risk ruining the turbine engines, and there was no real hurry to put distance between the *Fox* and the American battleship—no one could do anything in this storm.

Plus if he damaged the engines, it would be impossible to get them repaired since they were unable to return to fleet headquarters. Then he *would* have a real problem on his hands.

He took another deep breath and tried to relax. "You're right, Ewing," he conceded. "We can't risk damaging the turbines. Locate the leak and get the engines on line as soon as possible. I want full power available before we exit the hurricane's eye."

"We should be able to find the leak within a half hour," Ewing replied. "My men can have the water out of the vents by then, too. I think it's coming directly through the trunking."

"Put extra men on it if it will help," Croll directed. "Just get it done."

"Aye, Captain." The master chief engineer hung up the intercom phone, his face pale as he turned to the sailor at the horseshoe-shaped CODLAG control center. "Power our electrics, Mr. Hadway," he said.

The seaman carefully tapped the buttons on the board that activated the low-powered but efficient electric motors that ran from the diesel generators, the flow-chart diagram for the engines lighting up on the control center panel. "Our electric motors are powered and the diesel generators nominal," Hadway reported to Ewing.

The master chief engineer double-checked the flow chart and then gave his order. "Cut the Speys," he instructed.

The crewman carefully hit the correct buttons to deactivate the gas turbines. The twin Rolls-Royce engines wound down, their high-pitched whines fading until they were silent inside the acoustic enclosures of their modules.

Ewing watched the board as the engine lights changed color to show their complete shutdown. Satisfied that everything was functioning properly, he turned to the repair crew who waited nervously for the shutdown to be completed. "Truesdale."

"Aye, Chief?"

"Your team will check the chilled water plant for leaks."

Hadway turned around from the console. "The sensors don't show any leakage, Chief."

"I know everything *looks* like it's all right on the board," Ewing countered. "But I'd hate to discover the sensors were wrong or some clown didn't reconnect the circuits correctly during routine maintenance."

Hadway grinned sheepishly.

"So I'll check it for leaks," Truesdale said.

"Right," Ewing agreed. "Carter, you run diagnostics through the computer and see if it can give us anything. The rest of you will inspect every inch of the trunk between here and the cowling. If you find anything—and I do mean *anything*—that looks suspicious, call me immediately so I can have a look. Everybody clear about what we're doing?"

No one spoke.

"Let's shake a leg then," Ewing said. "We've got to be done within the hour or the captain will have our asses tacked to the bulkheads."

18

Captain Palmer stood talking at the front of the gray and white wardroom, a large map displayed on a wide, computerized screen behind him. Oz and most of the ship's officers sat at the tables in front of the skipper, several drinking coffee but most simply listening as Palmer continued his briefing.

The commander expertly compensated for the swaying motion of the deck—the mug of coffee he held didn't spill a drop as he lectured.

"So we're altering our course to make for Pearl Island," he was saying. "We passed through the eye of the hurricane three hours ago and should be clear of it by nightfall. We'll anchor offshore and let the MH-60Ks take the Delta Force troops and our Marine contingent ashore to search the island. If the pirates—assuming there are any—have a home base, intelligence suggests it would be this island or one of the tiny islets around it since they're approximately in the center of where most of the ships have been reported missing."

"Is the island inhabited?" asked the Navy lieutenant next to Oz.

"Our satellites haven't seen anything," Palmer responded, hitting the remote control he held and enlarging the map of the island. "But there's so much foliage in this area"—he pointed to a place on the screen—"that it's possible someone who knows what they're doing could stay hidden from our satellites."

The ensign next to Oz chuckled and shook his head. "No bars or shore leave?" he quipped.

"No wine, women, or song," Palmer said with a straight face. "Strictly business this time, gentlemen." He checked his watch. "We should reach Pearl Island at zero eight hundred, so have your teams ready to board the choppers at that time. With all due respect to our Marine contingent, we'll put the Army ashore first since the Delta Force has had more training in dealing with unconventional warfare. If there are no other questions, gentlemen, I'll see you tomorrow morning."

"Chief, the chilled water plant is free of leaks and the computer hasn't uncovered anything," Truesdale announced to Ewing.

The master chief engineer, balanced atop the swaying cowling on the air intake leading to the gas turbine three decks below, glanced toward the crewman, apparently oblivious to the danger of falling. "Good," he said, half to himself. If there'd been a leak in the chilled water plant, they'd have been in serious trouble. "Truesdale, get over there and help check the trunk. The leak must be somewhere along the air intake."

Truesdale scrambled along the edge of the stack, crouching to maintain his balance.

Ewing paced along the narrow space atop the funnel and watched the crewmen as they worked in the rain, carefully inspecting the cowling for points where water might be leaking in. "Don't miss anything," he warned. "If we don't find the problem here, we'll have to recheck everything until we do find it."

No one cared to think about starting over. Already the wind was picking up and soon they'd be heading into the worst of the storm—without their main gas turbines to help stabilize the frigate if they didn't find the leak soon.

"Chief, I don't think this is it," Hadway yelled, "but maybe you should take a look."

Ewing turned, wiped the moisture from his face with the back of his hand, and stepped across the sloped surface of the stack to examine the area where the crewman pointed.

There seemed to be a hairline crack along the cowling.

The master chief engineer sank to one knee for a closer look.

A barely discernible fissure lay at the anterior surface surrounding the left intake trunk.

"That's not big enough to be our problem, is it?" Hadway asked.

"It probably is," Ewing replied, getting to his feet. "This wind would pile the water over the crack and force it into the intake. It's tiny enough not to give us any trouble except in the high winds we've been in. Truesdale!" he hollered.

"Aye, Chief?"

"Go mix some fiberglass epoxy sealant—a quart should do it. Hadway, you get a heat gun. The rest of you," he said to the four crewmen perched on the stack, "keep looking in case there're more cracks along the cowling."

The sailors promptly went about their tasks, knowing they had only minutes to make the repairs and find other breaks. A torrent was splattering across the cowling when Truesdale returned with a bucket of the epoxy.

"Set it there," Ewing said, chipping away the last of the old tar with his utility knife. "You men get off here so we can have elbow room to work," he ordered the four crewmen.

"Give me the applicator and then help Hadway hold the tarp," Ewing directed Truesdale. "We'll have to keep the heat gun dry if we're not going to electrocute ourselves when we turn it on."

Ewing slopped the straw-colored epoxy into place and then tapped the liquid into the crack with the end of the spatulalike applicator. Once the material was in the fissure, he coated the surrounding metal and tar liberally with the honeylike glue.

When the crack was shrouded, he inspected his work and then laid the bucket aside. Grasping the heat gun, he shook the water from it and glanced at the electrical cable running from the gun down the side of the funnel. "Keep the rain off me the best you can," he charged the two sailors standing next to him. "And don't touch me if I get zapped. If I do get shocked, your job is to get me clear of the gun, not get electrocuted with me. Understand?"

"Yes, Chief," the two sailors answered soberly, exchanging glances.

Their faces were not overly confident, Ewing reflected as he flipped the switch on the heat gun's grip.

The motor in the heat gun purred to life, sending a powerful stream of air across the electric coils and heating the air by the time it was expelled from the machine's nozzle. Drops of moisture were sucked into the machine as well, making hisses of steam when they hit the hot tungsten inside.

Ewing ignored the ripples of electricity that coursed through his wet hands and directed the heated air onto the epoxy, hoping the current going through him wouldn't reach a dangerous level.

As he worked, the waves alongside the *Fox* became perceptibly higher and the gusts of wind more violent. There was little doubt that they were leaving the eye of Darcy and heading into the other half of the hurricane.

As the downpour escalated, the master chief engineer heated the epoxy to cure and harden it. Water splattered him incessantly, increasing the level of electricity leaking from the handle until Ewing's fingers shook spasmodically and his legs twitched.

Finally, the epoxy was hard. Ewing tapped it once to be sure it was cured, then forced his muscles to raise him to his feet. A terrific jolt of electricity coursed through the man's hand, causing him to curse loudly and toss the heat gun over the side of the funnel so abruptly that he startled Truesdale and Hadway.

"You all right, Chief?"

"Yeah, just a little scorched," he laughed, shaking his hand. "Come on, let's climb down before we get blown off."

19

"It's pretty obvious the Navy screwed up!" Sergeant Newport hissed, staring at the blade that now hung at an odd angle on the Apache's rotor.

"Cool it, mister," Oz ordered the pilot of the Apache. "We'll have to make the best of it. The last thing we need to do is stick it to the Navy. Their job's been hard enough."

"It probably is our fault," Sergeant Dexter admitted, standing in the sunlight alongside the two Army pilots on the swaying helideck of the *Montana*. "I don't know how it happened. I thought the lines were secure but—"

"Don't worry about it," Oz reassured the seaman. "I'm amazed the choppers weathered the storm as well as they did. Besides, it looks like just a few bolts are sheared off. That should be relatively easy to repair."

"Yes, sir, it certainly looks that way. And my crew will get on it immediately."

Oz turned to the Apache pilot. "Newport."

"Yes, sir?"

"Get to your quarters and let the Navy crew do

its job. You can catch up with us when your chopper's ready."

"Yes, sir."

Oz glanced at his watch as the airman stomped across the deck. Despite the problem with the Apache, they were still on schedule.

The nearly clear sky was bright with morning sunlight and the sea swelled with waves generated by hurricane Darcy, making the ship rock underfoot as the Army personnel staggered around the deck like drunks.

"The first two squads are ready, Captain," Sudden informed Oz.

"Good job, Lieutenant," Oz replied. "Guess we'd better get saddled up, too."

The two soldiers crossed to the waiting MH-60K and climbed in.

Five minutes later Oz had gone through the short preflight checklist and obtained clearance for takeoff. As he lifted the chopper into the blue Caribbean sky, the aircraft's sister MH-60K rose to follow closely behind. The two helicopters flew at an altitude of only sixty feet in an attempt to keep from being spotted by anyone on the shore of Pearl Island, nearly five miles away.

"We're a little off course," Death Song warned Oz.

The pilot glanced at a CRT screen and adjusted his course slightly, flying from the coordinates displayed from the data cartridge that contained electronic maps for the Caribbean region encompassed by Operation Sea Wolf.

They were definitely off course. He realized

that he'd been watching the ocean rather than his instruments for reference, and the waves, traveling at an angle to their course, had created an optical illusion that slowly diverted him from his path. He toggled on the radio to call the chopper following him.

"Sea Wolf Three, we need to make a course correction."

"We'll be sticking tight, One."

Oz realigned the chopper on course and glanced through his chin window at the turbulent ocean hurtling below. The dark shadows of the two aircraft danced on the sparkling waves while the sun appeared to follow them, its golden light seeming almost unnatural to the pilot after the previous gloomy days of black clouds and rain.

In the passenger compartment, the squad of Delta Force troops fidgeted, anxious to get to land after their grueling time at sea. While sequestered on the *Montana,* the soldiers had spent their time reading old magazines, watching video cassettes, or simply staring at the gray walls of their cabins with only the cleaning of weapons, exercise, and seasickness to break the monotony. The soldiers were now attired in standard camouflaged BDU pants and—in deference to the sultry weather—olive-green T-shirts or bare skin under their armored flak jackets.

The troops were armed with Colt M16 rifles, M203 grenade launchers, and Minimi machine guns, as well as a wide variety of knives and pistols of the men's own choosing. They sat stiffly in their canvas and pipe chairs, shoulder harnesses and battle nerves making it impossible to relax, even though the noise of the MH-60K's twin engines seemed to be trying to hammer their minds into senselessness.

Death Song checked the satellite geographical positioning system for their exact location. "SGPS shows us on course."

"Good," Oz responded. "Sudden?"

"Yes, sir," the lieutenant's voice answered from his headset, which was connected into the helicopter's intercom.

"We're only two or three minutes away from the LZ."

"Lock and load!" Sudden hollered to his team, his voice distorting over the intercom that he'd forgotten about. "Sorry to break your eardrums," he apologized to the aircrew a second later. "Forgot about the mike. I'll get off the line." There was a pop as he pulled his headset jack from its plug in the ceiling.

Oz surveyed the tossing waves that became even higher as they piled into the shallows near the shore of the green island that loomed ahead.

"Sea Wolf Three, let's descend to thirty meters," Oz called to the chopper pilot behind him. He gently pushed the collective pitch lever in his left hand and the MH-60K gracefully dived closer to the rolling turquoise and blue waves.

Oz switched the AN/ASC-15B triservice module to the USS *Montana*'s frequency. "BB-68, this is Sea Wolf One. Come in please."

"This is BB-68. We're reading you loud and clear, One. Over."

"We're almost to our LZ and everything looks

good. We'll let you know if we run into any problems. Over and out."

Death Song studied the HSD screen, then tapped a key on the chopper's computer console. "There's our LZ," he said, pointing. "Next to that tall palm. We're right on the money."

"O.T., signal the Delta Force we're headed in, and then you and Luger arm the Miniguns," Oz directed over the intercom. "Remember that we're *not* to fire unless fired on."

"That's a roger," O.T. replied.

The island's lush emerald foliage of ferns and palm trees was surrounded by a wide sandy beach strewn with driftwood and flotsam from the storm. Oz pulled the control column slowly backward, as did the pilot of the MH-60K tailing him; the two aircraft decelerated as they dropped, skimming above the ocean that lifted and rolled beneath them.

The two MH-60Ks followed the waves that broke on the beach, kicking white foam across the sand as the shadows passed above. A flock of sea gulls scattered ahead of the thumping blades of the helicopters.

"Your guys see anything?" Oz asked over the radio as he swooped toward the beach beyond the reach of the waves.

"That's a negative, One," the pilot behind Oz answered.

"Okay. Stick tight," Oz warned over the transmitter as he lowered his helicopter. With an abrupt end to their descent, the chopper hit the beach, bouncing on its hydraulic landing gear as they smashed into the sand.

Oz and Death Song kept their eyes on the foliage ahead of them, watching for any sign of danger as Sea Wolf Three settled behind them.

The Delta Force troops in the two MH-60Ks leaped into the hot sand, their weapons ready, and scrambled toward the palm trees for greater cover. Within seconds, the soldiers had skillfully blended into the undergrowth and vanished from view.

"Passengers are clear and everything is secured back here," O.T. reported to Oz.

"I'm taking her up," Oz said, lifting the chopper and preparing to circle the area to provide air support if it was needed.

"Sea Wolf One, this is Ground One," Sudden's voice crackled on the radio. "It's clear here. Over."

"Roger, Ground One," Oz replied. "I'll satellite you while you head inland while Three heads for BB-68 for our final squad. Give us a holler if you run into anything and we'll be there to help from the air. Over."

"We won't be shy about asking for help if we need it!" Sudden pledged.

"Sea Wolf Three," Oz called on the radio, "return for the next load of dogs."

"Will do, One," the pilot of the second chopper replied, lifting off the beach to retrieve the third squad of Delta Force troops.

The whooping blades of the MH-60K passed overhead, reminding Sudden of Oz's sharp surveillance. The Delta Force squads trudged through the thick jungle, its air so humid the soldiers found it somewhat difficult to breathe. The island was agonizingly hot and utterly devoid of even a breath of breeze to stir the torrid atmosphere.

"Don't bunch up," Sergeant Young warned his squad in his thick southern accent. Like Sudden, Young was a veteran of Vietnam and was aware of how dangerous a jungle could become if a few determined men decided to turn it into a trap.

The marines had been dropped on the western side of Pearl Island, exactly opposite the eastern LZ where the Delta Force was deployed. This enabled the marines to act as the anvil to the soldiers' hammer as they passed across the island; anyone avoiding detection by running ahead of the Delta Force would likely be driven into the marines' position.

At the same time, if the Delta Force should run into trouble and get pinned down, the marines could approach an enemy from behind and flank them while the two helicopters offered fire support.

The Delta Force platoon proceeded forward, the three squads spread along a wide front to span more ground during the search. Because it would be impossible to locate anyone on the island determined to hide in the thick brush, the soldiers searched for signs of human life: food wrappers, refuse, or footprints.

With each successive step, the troopers became more aware of the weight of their combat gear and weapons. The sultry weather made it difficult to concentrate on their jobs and remain alert. Vines and thorns tugged and cut while insects swarmed from the brush to sting and bite them despite liberal coatings of insect repellent on clothing and skin.

Sudden signaled a halt with his hand and then

motioned to Sergeant Young to approach as the soldiers sank into the foliage and vanished from sight.

"Yes, sir?" Young said, advancing toward the lieutenant. The burly, middle-aged sergeant, his face a mass of wrinkles, sunburn, and peeling skin, squinted up at Sudden.

"How close are we to the lagoon?"

"Let me check," Young answered. He stopped and propped his carbine between his knees, freeing his hands to retrieve a map of the island from his flak jacket. He carefully unfolded the map that, despite the fact that it had been printed by the USS *Montana*'s computer, was surprisingly detailed and accurate.

Young scanned the diagram, glanced at the sun, then placed his compass on the chart to double-check their heading. "Yeah, must be a couple hundred yards ahead. Over this hill we're climbing."

Sudden wiped the sweat from his brow with a dirty hand. "Okay, let's hump to the top of the ridge and then we'll take a ten-minute break. The men look like they need it."

"Yes, sir, they do," Young agreed, folding the map. "I'm becoming concerned about possible heat stroke with three of them."

The sergeant turned and signaled to his squad to continue their advance. The troops materialized from the underbrush as abruptly as they had disappeared into it and silently climbed the hill.

The squad plodded up the incline through the thick verdure. As they neared the top of the ridge, a breeze swept over them, providing some welcome respite from the heat. Nearing the summit, the wind blew even harder, caressing their sweat-soaked skin and clothing.

Everything was far from perfect, however, Sudden reflected as he pushed through the foliage to the top of the ridge. While the draft of air had swept away the humid smell of wet loam and vegetation, it had replaced it with that of rotting fish and an odor Sudden was hard-pressed for a moment to recognize. He unconsciously gripped his carbine as he sniffed the air again to identify the reeking smell.

The stench of rotting flesh, he told himself. And the lieutenant had a feeling deep in his gut that the corpse upwind from them would be that of a human being.

20

"I'm not so sure," Tiffany whispered, brushing a lock of chestnut hair out of her face. "It sounds dangerous to me. We have everything going for us here so why would we want to jump ship?"

The other three women in the dimly lit cabin were silent, vaguely aware of the monotonous rocking rhythm of the vessel and the sound of the ship's engines, barely audible through the steel deck.

"And don't forget about what will happen to us if we get caught," Mandy cautioned, sitting on her wide bed propped up on pillows and feeling very tired after what she referred to as "a busy night."

"Yeah," Tiffany agreed. "You've seen how ruthless the captain can be when somebody crosses him. Besides, we'll be back on the streets in no time with nothing to show for it. Why kill the goose that lays the golden eggs?"

"Maybe that's the point," Crystal put in. "The goose that's laying the golden eggs is going to get cooked sooner or later. There's no way Croll can keep attacking ships without somebody catching on.

Then every ship and plane around here will be blasting him—and us—out of the water."

"That's exactly what I mean," Venessa nodded. "If we stay with this bunch of murderers—and that's just what they are—then we'll be going down with them when they get caught."

"But we have all this money and jewelry they've given us," Mandy protested, liberating a chocolate from the box lying beside her in the bed.

"Having all the cash and jewelry in the world won't do us any good if we're dead or in jail!" Crystal countered.

"You can take what you've earned with you," Venessa explained. "It could help you make a fresh start."

"Do you have a plan or what?" Tiffiny asked, turning toward Venessa. "Maybe if we knew just how dangerous your idea is . . ."

"Whether we agree with you or not," Mandy added, "it won't go beyond these walls. We've got to stick together."

"Yeah," Tiffany agreed. "No matter how crazy your plan is, we'll keep it a secret—as long as you don't do anything that endangers the rest of us."

Sitting cross-legged on her own unmade bed, Venessa studied the faces of the three women around her and wished she knew whether they were trustworthy. But they had been good enough to her so far—and she had to trust someone. "All right," she finally said. "Here's what I have in mind."

It took only a minute and a half to outline her simple plan to the others. They listened in silence until she was finished.

"It's simple and straightforward," Crystal admitted.

"But can we can pull it off?" Tiffany questioned. "I still think we shouldn't rock the boat—so to speak."

"It's real dangerous if we get caught," Mandy said around a mouthful of chocolate.

"It's real dangerous already," Crystal said. "I've heard about how they duked it out with that Cuban ship before Croll took us aboard. Sounds like they could get into a major sea battle again—only this time we'd be in the middle of it."

"If we work together," Venessa said, "we can pull it off. We practically have free run of the ship now. No one would try to question us until we'd escaped."

"*If* we do this, can you guarantee that we'll be able to take the money and jewelry with us?" Mandy demanded. "Otherwise, we'll be flat broke."

"With cash and jewels," Crystal intervened before Venessa could speak, "you can cram a lot of wealth into a suitcase."

"Yeah, I guess we wouldn't need to take much else," Tiffany nodded. "We can buy what we need afterward. But what about food?"

"We won't be at sea that long," Venessa answered.

"Don't the life rafts have emergency rations?" Crystal said.

"We'll worry about the details later," Venessa answered. "Right now, we need to decide whether or not to go through with it."

"We don't even have to decide now," Tiffany

said. "Let's just *consider* it and work out the details. If it looks like it'll work, then we'll do it."

"And if it doesn't look like it will work," Mandy added, "then the idea doesn't go outside this room and we'll sit tight and enjoy ourselves like we have been. I mean, it isn't so bad here, is it?"

"Okay," Venessa agreed, the others nodding. "I'll check on the emergency rations. Mandy, can you find out how soon we'll be getting into port?"

"Yeah, I've got the helmsman wrapped around my little finger."

"Or at least parts of him wrapped around your little finger," Tiffany cracked.

"We need to be getting our cash converted into larger bills and get some kind of luggage," Crystal suggested. "Or maybe some boxes or something."

"But you need to be careful not to give us away doing it," Mandy said. "We don't want to get anyone suspicious."

Venessa smiled to herself. She could already tell the others would assist her with her scheme.

Sudden carefully descended the steep, crumbling bank that led to the lagoon while his troops covered him from the hilltop above. Nearing the bottom of the incline, his foot caught in a thick exposed root and he slid the last few yards, kicking up a sandy avalanche while barely maintaining his balance by clawing at the vegetation.

Reaching the base of the incline, he regained his footing, thankful he hadn't spilled headlong on his face in front of his men. Although the stench of death was heavy in his nostrils, he surveyed the water in the lagoon and saw nothing other than the lifeless fish along the edge of the water where they flopped up and down in the gentle waves.

Somewhere, he told himself, something besides fish is very, very dead.

He walked toward the black water of the lagoon to get a better view of its jagged curve. Realizing it would be necessary to bring the Delta Force troops down to help him search, he turned and signaled his men.

Instantly, twenty-two soldiers materialized from the brush and slithered down the slope, moving almost silently as they came. The third squad of the platoon remained hidden atop the hill to provide cover fire if their buddies below ran into trouble.

"Damn, it stinks!" Sergeant Young exclaimed around his wad of chewing tobacco.

"But do you recognize that smell?" Sudden queried.

"I sure do. And it ain't just dead fish."

"Let's spread out and see what we've got," Sudden instructed. "I'll radio the choppers and let them and the marines know we've stopped to give the area a more thorough search."

The squads went opposite directions along the winding beach. Within minutes, one of the Delta troopers had come sprinting back to Sergeant Young with news of an abandoned boat.

"Let's take a look," Young said. The two soldiers jogged toward a cove half hidden by vines and tall mangrove trees. The sergeant pushed his way through the foliage and discovered a glade that surrounded a large body of water. At the exact center of the still pool was a yawl, lying with its starboard side pointed into the air while its keel and broken masts lay perpendicular to the black surface of the water.

"Well, I'll be damned," Young swore, surveying the giant branches that stretched like a leafy dome above the cove, blotting out most of the sunlight. "Hell, son, that's not a boat, that's a yacht!" Young exclaimed. "The storm must have driven it in here. Go get the lieutenant and tell him we've found something."

The soldier dutifully pushed his way back through the brush.

Young strolled along the sand, swatting at a mosquito that buzzed in his right ear. Puzzled, he studied a light spot he thought he could discern in the shadows around the swamped vessel.

Impatiently he paced along the shore until he could observe the deck of the ship. Were those bullet holes? he wondered. It looked like the evenly spaced pocking of bullets from an automatic weapon.

He continued pacing around the pool for a better look, picking up a dead branch to test the depth of the giant pond; the six-foot tree limb failed to reach the bottom beyond the first few feet out from the shore.

Definitely not a wading pool, Young thought as he threw the branch into the water, sending ripples across its nearly still surface. As he continued to make his way around the pool, he noticed that the shore was composed of tiny bits of broken shells that had been pulverized during countless storms. When at last he arrived at a better vantage point halfway around the cove's circumference, the soldier again turned his attention to the wrecked boat.

No doubt about it, he told himself. There was the bloated body of a man moored to the yawl by a line around his foot, his pale face hidden under the surface of the water.

21

Sudden radioed Oz to report what they'd found and within minutes Sea Wolf One was circling the wrecked boat, unsuccessfully trying to drop a line to the vessel to tow it to shore.

"The foliage is too thick," Oz explained as he hovered above them, half hidden from view by the canopy of trees.

"We can handle it," Sudden replied. "Stand by, we'll get it in a minute." He put his radio into its pouch and turned to the soldiers milling about. "Simpson, wade out and pull the body to shore," he directed.

"It's too deep to wade in," Young said.

"I can't swim very well either, sir," Simpson admitted.

"We could attach a line to the boat and reel it in," Young suggested.

"Okay," Sudden agreed. "I'd like to get a closer look at the boat. Do those look like bullet holes to you?"

"I think so," Young nodded. "Tell you what,

Lieutenant. Being the Olympic swimmer in the group, how about if I volunteer for the job."

"You were an Olympic swimmer, Sarge?" one of the new men asked incredulously. Young, who was tossing his carbine, helmet, and combat vest into a pile on the shell-covered sand, answered the soldier with a cold glare.

The sergeant sat at the water's edge, pulling off his boots and helmet before turning to one of the troopers. "Give me one end of the rappeling line, Mannen," he instructed.

Private Mannen handed the sergeant one end of the line and tossed the coiled nylon rope onto the beach. Then he knelt down to loosen the heavy cord, enabling it to spool out whenever the sergeant needed it.

Without a word, Young clamped the line between his teeth, made sure he had enough slack on the rope, and dived into the water with a splash. He immediately bobbed to the surface, whipping his head back to clear his eyes of water, and then swam effortlessly toward the yawl.

The water was colder than Young had expected—as if it carried the chill of death. For a moment he imagined that other bodies floated just beneath the ebony surface.

He forced the thought out of his mind as he neared the yawl, giving the corpse a wide berth.

As he came alongside the ship, he paused for a moment, treading water and searching for a handhold. Then he spied the railing and reached up and gained a handhold on the brass rod that ran along the aft end of the ship. He lifted himself half out of the water and braced his feet against the submerged rail, freeing his hands to knot the line to one of the cleats on the deck.

He gave the rope a tug to be sure it was tight. Satisfied it would hold, he dropped into the water and swiftly swam toward the shore, again carefully avoiding the body and feeling half sick from the foulness of the air near the vessel.

Reaching the shallows, Young rose to his feet and splashed the last few yards to shore while the members of his squad started tugging at the rope, slowly reeling it in. "Take it easy," Young cautioned. "We don't want to break the rope."

The yawl slid slowly through the water, dragging the bloated body along. Within minutes the boat scraped against the shallow edge of the lagoon ten feet from the shore.

"Stop," Young ordered. "That's as far as it's going. Mannen, secure the end of the line to that tree."

"Okay, Sarge."

"I'll bring the body to shore," Young told Sudden. "I'm already soaked."

The lieutenant turned to Simpson as Young dived into the water. "Get a body bag ready," he ordered.

Young stopped a few feet away from the body, vaguely aware of the odd tattoo on the man's arm, its green and red lines a sharp contrast to the pale pebbly surface of his skin. The sergeant again scrambled onto the brass railing of the ship to free his hands and then removed his Tigarshark from its sheath.

He slashed the rope wrapped around the dead man's ankle, cutting the line in two with a single stroke from the stainless blade. Then he secured the SOG knife in its sheath and let go of the railing, dropping into the water. Taking the free end of the rope in his teeth, he swam the short distance to shore.

As they neared the beach, one of the soldiers waiting to assist swore loudly at the stench emanating from the body.

"Cool it, Private," Sudden told the trooper. "We've got a job to do." The lieutenant waded into the water and helped Young pull the body the last few yards up onto the beach.

As they lifted the stiff body onto the sand, Sudden ignored the man's open eyes, which were turned up in their sockets, and the wounds where some sea animal had feasted. The lieutenant rose to his feet and stepped back. "All right," he said, "get him bagged."

Three of the Delta Force soldiers lifted the corpse, lowered it into the open plastic body bag, and zipped it shut.

"Sergeant," Sudden said. "I want you to go back to the yacht one more time and see if you can find a name or some other ID that might be of help."

"Should I check the inside of the boat?" Young asked, stepping into the water.

"No," Sudden decided. "Let's leave that for some Navy frogmen if we need more information. Locate any name or numbers on the outside, and then we'd better get moving if we're going to meet up with the marines on schedule."

"Yes, sir," Young said, turning and diving into the dark water once more.

"You two move the body to the clearing so the chopper can get to it," Sudden directed as he removed his radio from its belt pouch and thumbed it on. "Sea Wolf One, this is Ground One."

"We read you, Ground One," Oz's voice answered on the radio.

"We've got a package for you. We're moving it into the open. Over."

"Roger, Ground One. I see your men now. That's not one of our guys, is it?"

"No," Sudden answered, realizing for the first time Oz hadn't been told about the body. "We found someone from the boat."

"We'll pick up the package and ferry it to BB-68," Oz said. "In the meantime, Sea Wolf Three will be standing by if you need assistance. Over."

"We'll be talking to you later, then. Over and out." Sudden switched off the radio and watched as Young climbed aboard the deserted ship for a third time. "Keep an eye on him in case he runs into problems," he ordered a soldier who stood on the beach watching.

Sudden turned and pushed his way through the brush until he reached the open. Within moments, Oz brought Sea Wolf One thundering down toward the body bag that lay on the shore.

The pilot pulled the control column to its central position, bringing the chopper to a near standstill above the edge of the lagoon. The Delta Force soldiers below gave the helicopter plenty of room to land as it hovered above them, creating a miniature sandstorm and whipping up a mist that swept above the lagoon.

Observing that the beach was clear, the pilot lowered the MH-60K to the sand. "O.T. and Luger, get the body into the chopper," he directed.

"Yes, sir," O.T.'s voice answered as he and Luger pulled their mike cords out from the intercom jacks, making popping sounds in the other crewmen's earphones.

The two gunners then crossed toward the tail of the chopper into the passenger compartment as the helicopter settled onto the shore. They jumped from the side door and knelt in the white sand, lifting the plastic body bag by its corners.

The airmen gingerly raised the stiff cadaver and lumbered to the chopper, sliding the body through the open side door. Within seconds they had vaulted back up onto the helicopter and Oz had lifted the aircraft into the sky.

The MH-60K rapidly ascended above the emerald crown of Pearl Island and adopted a new heading, its blades thumping loudly above the quiet island as the aircraft sped toward the USS *Montana*.

The cavernous room featured marble statues that resembled prison camp victims, while grotesque modern paintings hung on the walls. The furniture was modern, uncomfortable, and expensive, composed as it was of metal, leather, and glass—cold like the man who owned it. Guards armed with Star Z-70 submachine guns stood woodenly in the shadows beyond the hallway, hidden by the glare from the high-intensity lights that spotlighted the sunken living room like a surgical theater.

Carlos Rodriguez crushed out a cigarette in the chrome ashtray in front of him.

"I understand how we are losing our shipments," he finally said in a throaty whisper.

"You know?" Zammero asked, wondering where his boss's statement was going to lead, since the drug lord's face never seemed to display any emotion.

"Yes, I know," Rodriguez said, sitting motionless and staring at Zammero.

The henchman licked his lips. "Do you want me to take someone out for you?" he finally asked, just to break the silence.

Rodriguez didn't reply. Instead he stroked the amber hair of the woolly monkey that sat in his lap, looking like a tiny, wizened old man. The drug lord continued to study Zammero unblinkingly as did the needle-toothed primate.

Shit, Zammero thought, I hope he hasn't got it into his head that I have anything to do with the missing shipments. The henchman felt trickles of sweat sliding down the small of his back and under both armpits. He wondered if the guards out of sight in the hallway were preparing to shoot him.

Finally, Rodriguez glanced away and spoke. "Think a minute," he rasped. "The Americans aren't intercepting our vessels—there's none of the publicity they always trot out with each little interdiction," he theorized. "And I don't think the Cubans or Nicaraguans are stopping the vessels; they're still interested in transporting consignments for us—though they're not totally above suspicion."

"Then a new player's hijacking our ships?" Zammero queried.

There was no answer for what seemed like an eternity. Finally Rodriguez replied, "Exactly."

Before the aide could relax, the drug lord's icy eyes bore into him again. "I haven't identified who it is yet that's stopping my ships, but I'm putting a end to it," he vowed. "I've loaded my biggest yacht with four Browning machine guns and some of the new RPG-16 rockets we bought from the PLO. That should give us the firepower we need, especially since whoever's been stopping the shipments won't be expecting that kind of resistance."

"But how do they know our routes?"

"Ah, that's a good question, and equally simple to answer when you consider it," Rodriguez said, dropping the monkey to the floor and rising to his feet. "It can be only one person. Just one person knows the exact schedules and routes I set up so the ships won't run into trouble with the government."

"Juan Santos!" Zammero exclaimed. "But how can he get word out to anyone? He's out there in the middle of nowhere and almost never leaves the jungle."

"That's all that kept me from suspecting him earlier," Rodriguez nodded. "But a radio, perhaps. Or a courier. The way he does it isn't important. What's important is that we let him deliver his message once more—then we can surprise whoever has been hijacking my ships."

"And then we take care of Santos?"

"That's why I called you," Rodriguez said, his face still an expressionless mask.

Palmer sat in front of the wide-screen, computerized display at the front of the wardroom while Oz and most of the ship's officers slid into chairs at the long tables bolted to the deck.

As the last officer came through the hatch and settled in, Palmer began. "Captain Carson and I have decided that it would be a good idea to get some input from all of you regarding what we've discovered so far to see if we can make any sense of it," he said. "I'm going to let Captain Carson take over now."

"As most of you know," Oz began, remaining seated, "our search of Pearl Island turned up a wrecked yawl—the *Wild Wind*—and a body, both of which would appear to be linked to the disappearances of ships in this area. And the bullet holes on the deck of the yawl certainly suggest foul play."

Oz glanced at his notes and continued, "The US Coast Guard has already run the *Wild Wind* through their computers and discovered that the ship is registered to Dr. Richard Adams. The Coast Guard then contacted his ex-wife, who claims the doctor left port in Key West with a young woman whose name we haven't yet been able to establish. Captain, can you show us the photos?"

Palmer tapped three buttons on the keyboard beside him and a picture appeared on the wide screen on the wall.

"This photo of the doctor just came in on the receiver a couple of minutes ago," Palmer informed the men, tapping another key. "And this is a picture of the man the Delta Force found lashed to the boat."

"As you can see," Oz resumed, "the body we found isn't that of Dr. Adams."

"Maybe he picked up a new companion," one of the officers suggested.

"It's possible," Oz admitted. "But the Coast Guard stopped the *Wild Wind* several hours before the hurricane hit because she was traveling without lights. The officer in charge of the check says there were two men on board and neither looked anything like the photo of Dr. Admas."

"Furthermore," Palmer added, "one of the two claimed to be Adams, and the documents they produced for the Coast Guard appear to have been forgeries since they don't agree with the registration records in the US."

"The doctor might have been in the cabin," the officer suggested. "That could explain why the Coast Guard didn't see him."

"It's possible," Palmer admitted. "And we shouldn't rule that out since the ship wasn't searched, but it doesn't explain why another guy had his passport."

"So it looks very much like somebody else had his yawl," Oz told the officers.

"Finding the identities of the two men could be the key to discovering what's happening to the ships around here," Sudden suggested.

"Exactly," Oz agreed.

"Did you notice the tattoo on the body?" Sudden asked.

"Yeah," Palmer said. "Our chief medic just finished his examination of the corpse and the apparent cause of death was drowning. He found the tattoo and relayed a photo scan of it and the man's fingerprints to the Coast Guard and Naval Intelligence.

"Here's what the medic found," Palmer said, tapping a key.

The photo of the tattoo and fingerprints appeared on the computer screen.

"It's a stylized anchor with 'RN' in large letters," the captain explained. "It's possible the letters are the man's initials. The anchor suggests he's either been in the navy or associated with shipping, probably for some time—our medic thinks the tattoo is fairly old. The authorities are checking on the fingerprints first; if nothing turns up with the FBI or military records, then the tattoo may give us a lead—but that's a long shot."

"In the meantime," Oz said, "we'll continue our air searches and hope we spot something else."

"Something *is* dangerously wrong," Captain Palmer added. "Keep your men alert and remind them that we're looking for someone who isn't afraid to use automatic weapons and is apparently capable of drowning helicopters. We now appear to have lost both the Coast Guard chopper and Sea Wolf Four. We'll let you know if we get a positive ID on the fingerprints, but until then, let's get on with our jobs."

"We've just received another message from our informant, Captain," Brian Eyestone reported, handing the message to Croll as he stepped through the hatchway onto the bridge.

"Looks like another big shipment," Croll said with a smile as he stepped toward the forward ports.

"Yes, sir."

"How far away is this location?"

"I just checked it, sir," the navigator said. "We can intercept them here," he pointed, indicating the map he'd spread across the table.

Croll studied the chart and nodded.

"Looks like our informant has paid off for us again, Captain," the crewman remarked.

"Have you got a course plotted yet?" Croll inquired.

"Yes, Captain."

"Let's make the change then."

"Aye, aye, sir."

22

Carlos Rodriguez paced the bridge of his thirty-meter yacht, the *Ramera,* as it bumped over the waves in the starry night, its running lights shining brightly to lure whoever was commandeering his drug-laden ships.

An immense .50-caliber Browning machine gun squatted on its tripod inside the armored bridge, its barrel sticking through the firing slit at the front of the bulwark. A metal box of heavy shells lay beside the weapon, with several other unopened cans nearby. The linked cartridges formed a belt that fed from the mouth of the can into the BMG, where cammed claws would pull them through the BMG's mechanism.

"The men are ready," Harlan Logan informed Rodriguez in American-accented Spanish.

"Excelente," Rodriguez answered. He didn't much like the red-haired American—he didn't like *any* Yankee—and the man's Spanish was deplorable. But the human scarecrow was a talented sailor and the captain spoke well of him—so Rodriguez endured his irritating presence.

He glanced over the guardrail at the men and the BMGs hidden fore and aft inside the armor plating designed specifically for the *Ramera*. Though the armor weighed the vessel down and cut its top speed, it would protect the crew and enable them to deal with almost any attack the Colombian could imagine outside of warfare with a military vessel.

In addition to the BMGs, the sailors were outfitted with either pistols or submachine guns should they get close enough to engage an enemy with small arms. And there were the rockets he'd stacked along the front of the bridge; he glanced at the Russian-made RPG-16s. Each launcher fired a seventy-centimeter rocket with a three-kilogram warhead of high explosives. The weapons could penetrate thirty-five centimeters of armor plating and had a useful range of four hundred meters.

That should take care of anything the Brownings can't handle, Rodriguez thought to himself. No one was going to be able to outgun them.

He turned to the ship's captain. "I'm going below to contact my people," he said. "Notify me immediately if you see anything."

"*Sí*, señor, we will," the captain promised, looking like a robot behind the night-vision goggles he wore.

Rodriguez walked the short distance aft to the brass ladder at the rear of the bridge and descended to the deck. Then he turned and climbed down the short flight of steps into the main cabin.

"Get my home on the radio," he ordered the crewman who sat in front of the transmitter. "I want

to see if Zammero has plugged the leak in my operation yet."

"*Sì*, señor," the radioman replied, crushing out
his cigarette and clicking on the switch of the instrument in front of him. He listened intently to his earphones, a frown on his face. "That's odd," he finally
said.

"What's taking you so long?"

"I don't seem to be getting through," he replied. "Let me try another frequency." The crewman spun the dial, but continued to receive only
high-pitched squeals. "Every channel I try goes crazy
a second after I land on it!" he said with chagrin.

"Can you fix the radio?" Rodriguez asked impatiently.

"I don't think it's the radio, señor. Something
else is wrong—some kind of interference."

"*Excusa,*" Logan said, sticking his bony head
into the cabin and addressing Rodriguez. "The *capitán* believes a ship is approaching at high speed with
its running lights off."

"Alert the crew to put on their NVGs and get
ready," Rodriguez ordered. "I'll be there in a minute." Turning to the radioman, he started to speak
and then thought better of it. Whoever was attacking
must have some way to jam their radio, he finally realized. With a sinking sensation, Rodriguez began
to wonder if he had seriously underestimated the capabilities of his enemy.

"Their radio's jammed, Captain," the electronic
warfare officer informed Croll. "It was touch and go
there for a moment, sir—they were trying a bunch

of different frequencies. I finally just blotted out the whole spectrum—except for Mills's radio."

"I'm not sure how wise it is to take out so many channels."

"There's no one in range, sir."

Croll finally nodded in agreement and then turned to the crewmen who manned the other consoles at the back of the bridge. "Any changes on sonar or radar?"

"Negative, Captain," the radar officer answered.

"No change, sir," the sonar technician replied. "Screw count is constant; they're maintaining their speed."

Croll addressed the helmsman. "Full ahead."

"Full ahead, Captain."

The vibration of the twin screws of the engines echoed through the steel keel and ribs of the frigate as the craft throttled to its full power.

"I don't think they'll give us much of a fight," Croll said. "But let's go to battle stations anyway in case Mills runs into trouble."

"Battle stations," an ensign called, activating the proper alarm on the control console in front of him. The ship's lighting went from white to red.

Amid the clanging of bells the crewmen throughout the ship sprinted to their posts with practiced efficiency. Briskly, the various section heads reported on the intercom as their men took their places.

Finally the ensign reported: "All stations manned and ready, Captain."

"Arm all weapons systems and activate fire control," Croll ordered.

"Weapons armed and fire-control radar on line, sir."

"We'll try to get in close and take them with our small arms," Croll said. "No need to waste any of our Exocets—not when it's impossible to replace them. Is Mills's team ready?"

"Yes, Captain," the ensign replied. "They're in position on the forecastle."

Rodriguez studied the ghostly shadow of the approaching ship through night-vision goggles. "Keep our heading and speed constant," he warned the captain. "We don't want them to know we've sighted them. How far away are they?"

The captain checked his navigational radar. "They're still at least two kilometers away," he reported.

"Two kilometers?" Rodriguez repeated in disbelief. "But we can see them from here! The ship must be huge."

"Sí, señor," the captain concurred. "It looks like some kind of military vessel to me."

"Military!" he exclaimed.

"Sí, señor."

Rodriguez considered what the captain was saying. Could the Americans be behind the interdiction of his drug-running boats after all?

Surely it couldn't be.

And yet there was the military vessel, bearing down on them. "Can we outrun it?" Rodriguez inquired.

The captain checked his radar and performed some quick mental calculations. "No, señor. They must be going almost thirty knots—and they may not even be traveling at maximum speed. We can't outrun them."

"Then we'll have to fight them," Rodriguez resolved. "Logan, tell the men to wait until the last possible second before they fire." He turned back to the captain. "Proceed directly at the ship so all our weapons can engage it. Don't veer off until the very last minute."

"*Sì*, señor."

"Logan," he yelled across the deck to the first mate who was instructing the crew below.

"*Sì?*" Logan answered, looking up at the bridge.

"Have the men bring the machine gun from the quarterdeck to the foredeck so they can bring all our firepower to bear on the approaching ship. And hurry."

"Yes, sir," Logan replied, speaking in English in his haste to comply. He crossed the quarterdeck, surveying the life preserver on the bulkhead as he passed, and promised himself that he'd stay nearby. When the shooting started he could grab it and jump overboard in a hurry if it looked like the Colombians were losing the battle.

On the bridge, Rodriguez turned to the two crewmen he had trained to fire the RPG-16s. "Get your rockets ready. I want you to hit the ship as soon as the shooting starts. If we can strike hard with everything we've got, we may be able to escape."

C H A P T E R

23

Mills's team of twelve held their L85A1 Enfield bullpup rifles and an L86A1 machine gun. They wore night-vision goggles, life vests, and canvas pouches on their belts crammed with spare magazines of ammunition. As they normally did when approaching their quarry, the team positioned itself at the forward deck of the *Fox*, hidden behind the thick bulwark of the stern.

"Get ready," Croll's voice warned over Mills's radio. "We're closing fast."

Mills glanced up ahead and detected the yacht, its navigational lights blazing in his night-vision goggles. "I've got a visual, Captain," he reported.

"Good," Croll replied. "Wait for my signal before hailing them."

The *Fox*'s engines shuddered as the ship decelerated to keep from overrunning the yacht. Mills watched as the frigate drew near, towering over the smaller ship. For a moment the British sailor was puzzled that the ship came on without taking any evasive action. Perhaps they thought a Coast Guard ship was getting ready to inspect them, he decided.

"Is that a machine gun on their forecastle?" one of Mills's men asked.

"Shh," Mills told him, "I can't hear the radio. Say again, Captain," he said into the portable transmitter.

"Repeat: Hail them on your bullhorn," Croll's voice ordered.

Mills thumbed the send button. "Aye, aye, Captain." He lifted the electronic bullhorn to his mouth to hail the smaller vessel as it proceeded toward them. "Throw your weapons overboard and prepare to be boarded," his voice boomed down to them, bouncing across the water and echoing from the yacht's bow.

Before he could lower the bullhorn, the *Ramera*'s four .50-caliber BMGs burst to life, cutting into the forecastle of the *Fox*.

Mills stood frozen in surprise while the machine guns bathed his men with fiery tracers that thumped through the steel bulwark and whizzed on to chop into the sailors on either side of him.

The bullhorn Mills held shattered as a slug smashed into it. Dropping the device, he raised his weapon to his shoulder, but before he could fire, one of the projectiles that slashed through the metal hull crashed into his face.

His nearly headless corpse stood at the bulwark for a moment and then fell back onto what was left of his team, which lay sprawled on the deck in a bloody pile.

Seconds after the first deadly salvo from the *Ramera*'s BMGs, the two crewmen on the bridge of the Colombian vessel clicked the safeties off the RPG-16s, quickly aimed through the sights using the range stadia, and pulled the triggers. The rockets lit the bridge with jets of flame that escaped from the open rear ends of the tubes.

The missiles shot from the front of the RPG-16 launchers, dropped slightly as they cleared the railing of the bridge, and then blossomed into flame as their booster engines erupted to life. The projectiles traveled on flat, flaming arcs to the bridge of the *Fox.*

Reaching their targets, both projectiles exploded in a blaze of light that cut into the armor of the bridge and seared the men inside with molten metal and steel shrapnel. The bridge was choked with smoke and the cries of wounded sailors.

The .50-caliber BMGs on the *Ramera* continued to fire, the Colombian gunners too frightened by the behemoth they attacked to quit shooting.

"Steer past them but keep close to their hull so they can't launch any missiles or torpedoes at us," Rodriguez directed the captain. The drug lord approached the two crewmen who were lifting another pair of RPG-16s, readying for a second salvo. "Aim for the rockets on their deck," he yelled above the racket of the machine gun at the front of the bridge. "See those containers ahead of the bridge?" he pointed.

"*Sì.*"

"Hit those."

They might not succeed in getting away, Rodriguez reflected in the abrupt silence that followed as all four BMG crews strung new belts of cartridges into their weapons, but at least they would go down fighting like real men.

Croll blinked in the darkness of the bridge for a moment, dazed by the blast of the two rockets that had cut through the armor plate. The emergency lights finally sputtered on and he tried to rise. His right leg, however, refused to work because of tendons severed by a chunk of shrapnel.

He felt no pain as he clawed his way to a chair, pushing the dead sailor sitting in it out of the way. He pulled himself into a standing position and leaned against the back of the chair.

"Status?" he demanded.

"Most of the men are dead on the bridge, sir," the bloodied ensign at the electronic warfare console answered as he knelt by the helmsman.

"Yes, I can see that," Croll said, looking around. "Get back to your post." He pushed the chair so he could stand by the intercom, then reached over and toggled it on. "Fire control."

"Yes, Captain."

Two more RPG-16 rockets from the *Ramera* arched toward the *Fox* as Croll prepared to speak. The warhead reached the GWS 25 surface-to-air missile cells ahead of the bridge and ignited; a terrific secondary blast shook the bow of the ship as two of the large missiles in the cells exploded. Shards of metal rattled across the forward decks and clanged off the bridge as the nighttime sky lit up briefly and then died away, leaving angry red sparks still glowing on the deck.

"Captain," the voice on the intercom asked, "are you all right?"

"Don't worry about me!" Croll bellowed. "Hit those bastards."

"What did you want us to launch at them, sir?"

"Use one of the STWS-1 torpedoes."

"Aye, Captain. But you'll have to bring us around, sir. Their ship is at one hundred eight-five degrees behind us. They've traveled along our port and are trying to escape aft."

Croll glanced around and found the helm still unmanned, although replacements were starting to stream through the hatchway, their eyes wide with disbelief at the damage inside the smoke-filled bridge.

The captain shoved the chair forward to reach the helm, waving away the medic who was trying to examine his wounded leg. "Leave my leg alone," he ordered. "Tend to the others."

Croll reached the helm and flipped on the intercom to the engine room. "Ahead one-third," he ordered.

"Ahead one-third," the voice on the other end echoed.

The ship's engines rumbled as Croll flung the wheel around to turn the frigate onto its new course heading. He was determined to destroy the men who had damaged his ship and killed almost twenty of his men.

"Hurry!" Rodriguez screamed at the two sailors who readied their rockets for the final strike at the frigate that was now turning to pursue them. "Aim for the radar masts."

He stood clear as the two men shouldered the launch tubes. They snapped off the safeties, aimed, and fired at nearly the same instant; the rockets sped toward the British ship, leaving glowing arcs like giant meteors cutting across the nighttime sky.

One of the warheads smashed against the radar mast, erupting in an explosion that hurled bits of metal over the ship but did little real damage. The second rocket crashed into the stack aft of the mast, leaving a jagged hole in the side of the funnel. The twin thunderclaps of the explosions reached Rodriguez's ears seconds after he observed them.

Rodriguez watched with horror as the *Fox* continued to rotate toward them like an angry giant aroused from slumber. "Get the machine guns moved to the rear of the ship!" he bawled, leaning over the railing of the bridge. He hastened toward the Browning at the front of the bridge and helped the gun crew carry it aft to fire at the ship following them.

"What are they likely to do next?" Rodriguez quizzed the captain who was standing at the wheel of the helm.

The old man replied without thinking, "Torpedoes."

"Can we escape them?" the drug lord asked.

"Might outmaneuver them, if we have enough warning. You might even be able to damage them with the BMGs. But it isn't likely we can do either. We are dead men."

Rodriguez strode to the rear of the bridge and

screamed to the men on the deck below. "Watch for torpedoes. Those manning the two machine guns on the rear of the deck will aim for the torpedoes if you see them. Logan, come up here and instruct the captain which way to turn when you see a torpedo headed for us."

The American swore loudly in English, obviously adding something about Rodriguez to the oath as he headed for the bridge.

Rodriguez ignored the outburst and said nothing. There would be time enough for reprisals later, if they escaped.

The drug lord glanced back at the British ship that was straightening onto course and accelerating to catch them. As he watched, a torpedo leaped from one of the tubes amidships and splashed into the ocean. His eyes riveted onto the water where the bubble-filled wake of the approaching projectile coursed under the surface.

"Torpedo!" one of the crewmen shrieked.

Logan turned to the captain. "It's coming straight at us from one hundred eighty degrees."

The captain hurled the wheel to the left, throwing the yacht onto a new course.

The BMGs erupted from behind the bridge as the Colombian sailors tried to hit the oncoming danger, the .50-caliber bullets raising gushers of water around the torpedo that continued its silent journey toward the yacht.

Rodriguez watched the torpedo alter its course, compensating for the yacht's new heading, as the weapon's sensitive sonar homed in on the pings from the vessel. The projectile seemed to accelerate as it neared the rear of the *Ramera,* whose machine guns continued their heavy fusillade.

A giant plume of water exploded from the ocean twenty-five meters behind the ship, brine showering the men on deck who were too surprised to do anything but stand dumbfounded.

"Cease fire!" Rodriguez yelled at one of the gunners who continued shooting into the ocean. "Save your ammunition for the next one."

"Here comes another!" Logan hollered within moments as the *Fox*'s tubes coughed out a second torpedo, its white wake streaking away from the oncoming British frigate.

This time, all the BMGs on the *Ramera* exploded into action as the sailors manning the weapons strove to destroy the projectile that chased them.

Rodriguez clutched the brass rail, watching speechlessly as the torpedo gained on them. The bullets from the machine guns aligned onto the approaching projectile, but failed to damage it, the slugs from the defensive weapons diverted from their path by the water.

The torpedo continued to close on them and then struck.

The explosion ripped the whole aft deck apart, throwing Colombians and their weapons into the air, riding on a geyser of foaming water. Fragments of metal, wood, and flesh rained down as the yacht started sinking into the ocean, its lower deck flooded by a torrent of water that thundered into the void left by the explosion.

Rodriguez lay unconscious on the bridge as the *Ramera* vanished into the sea.

24

Zammero crept through the jungle, his Star Z-70 submachine gun suspended by a strap from his shoulder and his flashlight stabbing the darkness, enabling him to avoid snakes along the path.

The beam of light did little to dispel the gloom that surrounded the narrow dirt trail where shapes slithered and scampered through the thick vegetation and bats after insects darted through the lower branches.

As the henchman rounded a curve in the trail, the silhouette of the dilapidated shack belonging to Juan Santos loomed ahead, squatting in the tiny clearing. The crickets quieted as Zammero passed, almost as if they suspected the man's violent intentions.

He switched off the flashlight and jammed it into his pocket. Sliding the Z-70 around on its strap, the assassin jerked the charging handle on the left side of the barrel shroud and then released it, leaving the weapon cocked. Then he unfolded the firearm's stock and flipped the selector to automatic.

Climbing onto the rough logs that formed the

porch, he crossed the squeaky boards and tapped at the door with the shrouded barrel of the Z-70.

There was no answer, nor was there any sound within the hut to indicate it was inhabited.

He rapped again, this time more loudly, suspecting that Santos was hiding inside.

"Un momento," a man's voice called.

Footsteps shuffled to the entryway, flaxen slivers of candlelight appearing through the cracks in the door and out from under it.

"Who's there?" Santos queried in Spanish.

"Zammero. I've got a message for you from Rodriguez," the assassin answered, his finger tensing on the trigger as he prepared to shoot through the door. Then he thought better of it. Santos or his wife might escape if he missed his aim and then the door would remain locked.

"My wife is here. Just a minute while I get dressed," Santos said from inside. "I'll come out to talk to you in just a minute."

"The message is for her, too," Zammero replied, gripping his weapon tightly in the darkness. "Actually, it's more of a present," he added. "Rodriguez is giving a bonus to all of us."

"Let me unbar the door," Santos said.

The heavy crossbar slid aside and dropped noisily to the floor. The door creaked open, revealing Santos standing fully clothed, holding a candle in his hand. "What's going on?" he inquired nervously, eyeing the submachine gun Zammero held, its barrel pointed at his chest.

"Stand back," the gunman ordered, stepping into the room and surveying the bed where a still form lay under the blankets. Then he noticed the twine-tied boxes stacked neatly on the floor. "You weren't leaving without saying good-bye, were you?"

"What's this about," Santos demanded.

"Rodriguez knows you've been betraying us," Zammero spat out. "You've been giving away our routes."

"He knows?"

"So you don't deny it! Tell me how you did it. Rodriguez wants to know how you delivered the messages. You can buy a few more precious minutes of your lousy life if you tell me."

Santos studied the gunman, who was careful to keep the muzzle of his firearm aimed at his victim's chest.

"You've got nothing to lose," Zammero added.

"A radio," Santos admitted to buy time. "I keep it here, hidden in the floorboards," he said, pointing to the corner of the room. "Look, I will show you." He cautiously crossed the shack and placed the candle holder on the crude table next to the bed. He paused as if debating whether to remove the transmitter from its hiding place.

"What's wrong with your wife?" Zammero queried, pointing the gun barrel at the still form under the blankets and approaching warily. "Does she want to die in bed?"

"Maria's asleep," Santos explained.

"If she'd *entertain* me for a while, maybe I would spare her life," Zammero snickered, poking the form with the barrel of the Z-70. There was no response. "What's wrong with her?" he demanded.

"Nothing's wrong with her," Santos insisted, turning to face the gunman. He glanced beyond Zammero toward the darkest corner of the shack, which was now behind the assassin.

Zammero finally realized he'd been tricked and whirled around to intercept the woman. With the gun no longer covering him, Santos snatched the barrel of the weapon, locking it in his fists to prevent it from being pointed at him or Maria.

Before Zammero could either jerk the Z-70 free or fire it, he heard the whirring sound of a steel blade rapidly slicing through the air. The sound ended in a whacking thump like that of a watermelon being struck by an ax.

The machete slashed through the crown of the gunman's skull and came to a standstill only when it reached his jaw. His eyes stared straight ahead as Santos's wife tugged at the blade, firmly wedged in the base of Zammero's skull, trying to free it.

Santos released the gun barrel and quietly approached his wife. "It's over," he whispered, taking her by the arms and pulling her away from the machete that she struggled to free, a hysterical cry escaping her lips. He turned her away from the corpse. "It's over. You did fine," he soothed, holding her in his arms as she wept.

"Soon we will be free," he whispered. "Soon."

Palmer sat at his desk in the paneled stateroom studying the screen of the work station, which was tied into the *Montana*'s central computer. The cabin accommodated the captain's bed, a sink, and a private head; on the wall was an intercom and several gauges that displayed the ship's speed and course readings, as well as the status of various stations around the ship.

There was a knock at the door.

Palmer removed the pipe from his mouth. "Come in," he called, glancing up as the Army airman stepped through the hatchway. "Oz. Thanks for coming. I've got some things to go over with you." He motioned to the upholstered chair in front of his desk. "Please sit down."

Oz slid into the seat and waited for the captain to speak.

Palmer swiveled the monitor on his computer around, following Oz to view it. "First off," the captain said, "I'm afraid we're not going to be able to repair the Apache for at least a couple of days. I've got my best machinist busy making the new part— a blade root attachment, I believe—is that what it's called?"

"Yes, sir."

"Well, my best machinist is making one now, so I hope to have the Apache in the air soon, but in the meantime, you'll have to operate with just the two MH-60Ks."

"That shouldn't be too much of a problem," Oz replied. "The Delta Force is doing most of the legwork tomorrow anyway when we search the Lucia chain of islands."

"Yes, well there may be a change of plans there," the captain said, tapping the burnt tobacco from his pipe. "That's the reason I asked you here." He unsnapped a cleaning spike from his pocket knife and went on talking as he cleaned the pipe. "We've just received new data from Naval Intelligence; plus they'll be sending a burst message with additional data sometime soon. Here's what we've got so far."

He tapped a key on the computer and two photos appeared on the screen. "As you can see, the tattoo insignia matches the one shown on this medal perfectly. Do you know who that insignia belongs to?"

"No, sir, I don't," Oz admitted, perplexed that he'd never come across it before.

"Don't feel bad," he said, banging his pipe on the ashtray. "I've seen it before and didn't recognize it myself. It's the Royal Navy insignia—British Royal Navy. Our government has contacted the British and the Royal Navy is now checking the fingerprints we took from the corpse against their records. If he really was in the Royal Navy, we should be able to identify him."

"But will that lead anywhere?" Oz asked.

"Maybe," Palmer answered, retrieving a pouch of tobacco from his desk. "For sure the Royal Navy isn't in the pirate business. But we might be able to get a few clues as to who might be involved if the guy has a criminal record."

Palmer paused to light his pipe and—as if on cue—the work station beeped. He puffed and created a sweet-smelling cloud of cherry smoke as he shook out the match. "This should be our message," he said, swiveling the screen slightly so both men could view it. They watched as the amber letters scrolled onto the black surface.

The message in its raw form was a confusion of letters and other characters, many blinking off and on. "In a moment the computer will decode it," Palmer revealed as the two watched intently. Within seconds, the jumble of symbols was replaced by a coherent memorandum.

SECRET
FR: NAVINTEL
TO: USS MONTANA AND NIGHT STALKER CONTINGENT

1. FINGERPRINTS SUBMITTED HAVE BEEN IDENTIFIED BY BRITISH WAR OFFICE AS PETTY OFFICER STUART GRAPPER; LAST TOUR OF DUTY: THE ROYAL NAVY FRIGATE HMS FOX.
2. APPARENT MIXUP OF RECORDS: STUART GRAPPER WAS LOST AT SEA AND PRESUMED DEAD TEN (10) MONTHS AGO WHEN HIS SHIP, THE HMSFOX, SANK IN NORTH ATLANTIC WITH ALL HANDS ON BOARD. THE ENTIRE CREW WAS LOST AT SEA AND PRESUMED DEAD.
3. SUGGEST YOU RESUBMIT FINGERPRINTS IN TWO WEEKS AFTER ROYAL NAVY RUNS CHECK OF THEIR FILES FOR POSSIBLE ERRORS. IN THE MEANTIME, ROYAL NAVY INVESTIGATIONS ARE BEING INITIATED.

END OF TRANSMISSION

"That's pretty spooky," Captain Palmer remarked, sending another cloud of smoke into the cabin. "Either you found a remarkably preserved body that washed clear from the North Atlantic or there's been one hell of a screwup in the British computers. I'm betting on the latter."

"Definitely a dead end," Oz replied.

"No pun intended?" Palmer smiled grimly. "I can't imagine how somebody could go down in a Navy ship and miss being rescued by the search that must have been mounted. Now to reappear in the Caribbean ten months later—it has to be a bureaucratic screwup."

"Something bothers me about this," Oz said, "but I can't quite put my finger on it. You don't suppose the British frigate we saw when we were searching for Sea Wolf Four could be tied into this?"

The captain mulled the idea over for a few seconds, puffing at his pipe. "That's one kicker of an idea," he finally said, shaking his head doubtfully. "But I can't imagine a ship that size being involved in such a crime. Getting three hundred sailors to agree on anything—especially a decision never to return home and to become pirates—is just beyond belief."

"Yeah, I guess it is pretty ridiculous," Oz agreed, grinning sheepishly.

"Getting to the bottom of this will require meticulous effort," Palmer asserted. "In the interest of leaving no stone unturned—and to get rid of any nagging doubts you may have—let's run the ship's ID number through Naval Intelligence and see where they're supposed to be patrolling."

"Good idea," Oz agreed, rising to his feet. "I've got one more patrol to run before I turn in for the night," he said, "so I'll be seeing you tomorrow, Captain."

"I'll keep you apprised if anything else turns up with our tattooed mystery man," Palmer called to the pilot as he headed for the door.

25

"Are you sure this will work?" Mandy whispered, lugging the heavy box of cash and jewelry toward the stern railing of the fantail. The shadowy deck was lit only by the soft glow from the ship's running lights.

"It's going to work," Tiffany answered in a low voice that was nearly lost in the pounding of the brine churned by the *Fox*'s twin screws.

"Is your life jacket fastened?" Crystal quizzed Mandy.

"I think so." She tugged at the front of it.

"Don't worry about the fit," Crystal advised. "It wasn't designed for someone with a chest like yours. Just so it's tied on."

"If you fall in," Tiffany added, "you won't drown with that vest on. So no screaming if you get wet, or the whole ship will be out here ready to nab us. Tie this line to the box so you won't lose your valuables," she instructed.

"Now how can I fasten that rope to this box?" Mandy demanded peevishly.

"Put the box into the plastic bag we gave you,"

212 • Duncan Long

Crystal replied in vexation. "Then you can tie the line to the mouth of the bag. I swear, God must have given you big boobs to make up for shortchanging you on brains."

"Look, you," Mandy threatened, brandishing a fist.

"Come on, she didn't mean nothing," Tiffany said. "Get the box in the bag and tie this cord to it. Then fasten the rope to your waist."

"You sure these vests will keep us above water with the boxes tied to us?" Mandy asked.

"These vests will float a two-hundred-fifty-pound sailor," Crystal said. "You can damn well be sure it will hold you, even with the weight you've put on."

Mandy gestured with her fist again, "I swear I'm going to pound you!"

"Shhh," Tiffany warned. "Someone's coming!"

The three women ducked behind the rubber lifeboat on the shadowy deck as the footsteps continued coming toward them. Tiffany closed her eyes tight.

The sounds came closer, heading straight for the dingy.

"It's me," Venessa whispered.

"You about gave us a heart attack!" Tiffany scolded.

Venessa squinted in the darkness. "Getting into the boat is the tricky part," she warned. "Fortunately the *Fox* isn't traveling too fast and most of the crew is either in bed or trying to repair the forward half of the ship. The trick's to keep the raft moored to the rail and then very carefully step in."

Venessa skillfully tied the line at the front of the dingy to the rail, remembering how Richard Adams had taken the time to show her how to tie a knot that wouldn't slip loose. She secretly wiped a tear from her eye before she turned to her companions. "Okay, help me lift it over the side."

The four women lifted the boat and simultaneously heaved it above the railing of the fantail.

Venessa was relieved to see that it landed upright and aligned itself on the rope it was tied to, bobbing in the wake of the ship.

"Now," Venessa ordered, "you need to get into the dingy—one at a time."

"My legs aren't *that* long," Mandy protested.

"You can do it," Venessa encouraged. "Keep a hold of the rope so you can climb into the boat. Tiffany, hold on to the line on her box while she gets into the dingy."

"I can't do it," Mandy whined.

"Sure you can," Tiffany told her. "Here, I'll go first."

"I've got something I need to take care of," Venessa disclosed to them. "I should be back in five minutes. If I'm not—or somebody else comes—release the rope and paddle toward the east. You should reach Dominica in just a day or two."

"Be careful," Crystal whispered to Venessa as she walked away.

Without a backward glance, Venessa carefully ascended to the main deck and walked toward the captain's cabin, climbing through an amidships hatch to enter the long passageway that led to his quarters.

When she reached her destination, the guard

stationed in the dimly lit corridor blocked the way. "Sorry, miss," he said in a thick Irish accent. "The doc left orders that the captain was not to be bothered for the next twenty-four hours."

"Captain Croll asked me to visit him," Venessa whispered, winking meaningfully at the sailor.

The Irishman didn't understand.

"Miss, no one said anything about you coming to see the skipper."

"You don't think he'd want the whole crew to know, do you?" she cooed.

The seaman brooded on the thought a moment before he answered. "All right, then, but don't you go exhausting him," he admonished.

Venessa smiled sweetly at the sailor as she entered the cabin and he closed the hatch behind her. She immediately clicked open her purse and removed the narrow-bladed steak knife.

For a few seconds she waited in the near darkness of the cabin, listening to the labored breathing of the sleeping commander. At one point she almost turned to leave, until she recalled the broken body of Richard Adams lying on the deck of his yawl, bleeding to death from his wounds. And she remembered that Croll had ordered the cold-blooded killing.

This is for Richard Adams, Venessa thought, her face locked in a grimace as she raised the knife, gripping it in both hands to plunge it with all her might into Croll's chest.

The guard in the poorly lit passageway didn't notice the blood on her hands and dress as she left the cabin.

Five minutes later Venessa climbed into the dingy, her face hidden by the darkness at the rear of the *Fox*. She hastily released the line and the dingy slowly drifted to a stop while the frigate's engines propelled the ship forward.

"I can't believe it," Mandy remarked as the ship pulled ahead of them. "We did it."

When the women were about fifty yards aft of the frigate, an alarm began to clang and sailors poured out onto the decks of the *Fox*. The ship's work lights flashed on, brightly lighting the enormous vessel.

"Get down!" Tiffany warned. "They're looking for us."

Mandy moaned weakly as a spotlight swept across the water, passing to the right and then to the left of the dingy. Only seconds passed before the beam fastened itself on the dingy, illuminating the women in its blazing brilliance.

"They'll circle around and catch us," Mandy cried.

"I wouldn't be so sure," Crystal dissented. "I have this terrible feeling . . ."

The clatter of two machine guns erupted, their bullets raising plumes of water around the dingy as the gunners acquired their target.

"Jump!" Venessa shouted, plunging into the water to be lost in the darkness.

"No, wait," Mandy screamed hysterically, clutching at the other two women in the dingy as they tried to rise. "I can't swim."

A thumping smack followed by a second discharge from the firearms struck the little craft, and

Tiffany dropped into the dingy without another word, her left lung torn to bits.

"Let go!" Crystal screamed, trying to shake loose from Mandy's iron grip.

"I can't swim," Mandy shrieked, clutching at the other woman's clothes and rocking the dingy.

A third volley clipped through the boat and the two women fell into a tangle on top of Tiffany. The sailors on the *Fox* continued to fire until the rubber craft was completely riddled and was sinking into the ocean, air hissing out of the bullet holes.

"Should we retrieve them?" one of the gunners on the *Fox* asked.

"No need, the sharks will take care of them," suggested a sailor at the fantail.

The officer reeling in the shadows, pressing a bandage tightly to his blood-soaked chest, considered his options for a moment. Finally he hobbled on deck and spoke weakly. "We can't chance having the Americans stumble onto the bodies," he whispered hoarsely. "They're still running patrols in this area. Get a Lynx into the air and let's be sure those murderous bitches are dead and the wreckage cleared."

"Aye, aye, Captain Croll."

26

The sea rolled gently beneath the chopper, the light of the rising moon peeking over the horizon in the west, its reflections scattering on the Caribbean. Oz studied the lunar radiance for a few seconds and then lowered his NVGs to concentrate on the search. The MH-60K flew low, taking advantage of the nearly flat surface of the ocean.

"I've got something to the east," Death Song declared, staring through the starboard door next to him. "They're lit like a Christmas tree."

"Let's take a look," Oz said, pulling the control column to the right and kicking the pedal on the starboard side, angling the MH-60K into a tight turn.

As the aircraft neared the ship, Oz recognized the British frigate they'd encountered previously. A helicopter was just taking off from the vessel's helideck, its landing light illuminating the sea aft of the ship.

"Looks like they're searching for someone," Death Song said. "I wonder if somebody fell overboard."

Oz surveyed the center console and turned to

the military frequency the British ship would be utilizing. "This is NS-1 calling, do you need help searching for someone? Over."

"Negative, NS-1. We're engaged in a training exercise and would appreciate your staying clear. Over."

"Roger. We'll stay clear. Over and out."

Oz tugged the control column and turned to leave the area, traveling in a wide circle that took them away from the *Fox.*

"Captain!" O.T. shouted over the intercom. "The Lynx is firing at people in the water!"

"It's just a training exercise," Oz reassured him.

"No, sir," O.T. insisted. "I'm using my binoculars and there are definitely people and bodies in the water."

"Are you sure they're firing at them?"

"Yes, sir!"

"Hang on. We'll take a closer look," Oz said.

"The frigate's got its navigational radar on," Death Song informed the pilot after checking the scope.

"As calm as the sea is, I doubt if we can avoid their radar even this low," Oz said. "I guess we'll just have to risk the wrath of the British Navy. O.T., are you sure they're shooting at people in the water?"

"Positive."

Oz switched his radio to the *Montana*'s frequency and toggle on the transmitter just as Death Song spoke.

"They're jamming our radio, Captain."

The pilot released the switch, recognizing it was futile to try to send a message.

Ahead of them, the Lynx hovered over a dingy barely afloat on the ocean, three bodies drifting around it facedown in the brine. As the Americans approached the small craft, a head bobbed up out of the water; immediately, a machine gunner in the passenger compartment of the Lynx leaned out of the helicopter and fired at the swimmer.

"Captain!" Death Song exclaimed.

"Arm our weapons," Oz ordered.

Death Song rapidly flipped the switches, arming the missiles and guns on the weapons pods that hung at either side of the MH-60K. O.T. and Luger activated the six-barrel Miniguns pointing from the chopper's side doors.

Oz switched his radio to the British frequency and toggled it on. "This is NS-1. Desist firing or we will take action to terminate it. Over."

"Bugger off, NS-1! This is *our* business," answered the Lynx pilot, circling his chopper around to face the American interloper.

Noting the rockets on the Lynx's pylons, Oz raised the MH-60K above the level of the British aircraft, giving the Americans the advantage of shooting downward if it should become necessary.

Oz watched as the swimmer reappeared, gasping for breath.

A sailor grasping a bullpup rifle leaned from the open side door of the Lynx and took careful aim at the woman.

Before he could shoot, Oz triggered the fire button on the chopper's control column, activating the twin barrels in the MH-60K's machine-gun pod to deter the shooter. The weapons spit 7.62mm slugs that arched on tracers past the Lynx, prompting the gunman to take cover in the helicopter.

The pilot of the Lynx recognized the danger and lifted his chopper, firing his machine guns directly at the Americans as he rose.

The bullets poked into the windscreen of the MH-60K and rattled against its armored skin, failing to do any real damage. Without delay, the Lynx jockeyed for a higher position from which it could launch an air-to-air rocket.

Realizing he had no choice, Oz tapped the fire button on the control column with his little finger three times and three of the unguided folding-fin, 2.75-inch projectiles leaped from their pod, riding forward on jets of flame that lit the side of the HM-60K.

The Lynx pilot hurriedly jerked his helicopter to the side, avoiding two of the rockets. But the third struck the right weapons pod, creating an explosion that hurled unarmed missiles from the aircraft, peppering its side with shrapnel and injuring the copilot. As the aircraft's balance shifted abruptly, sending it into a steep bank, the pilot struggled to regain control.

Taking advantage of the Lynx's situation, Oz pushed on the control column and dropped toward the ocean as the Lynx wheeled away overhead. "O.T., let's try to snatch the girl out of the water," the pilot called on the intercom.

"Yes, sir!"

O.T. and Luger trotted up to the empty passenger compartment and crossed to the side door, steadying themselves on the seats as the aircraft dropped toward the sea. The warrant officer unlatched the starboard hatch, sliding it open to attain access to the winch above the door frame. "Give me a hand here," he hollered to Luger.

The youthful gunner held O.T.'s vest and jacked his helmet phone plug into one of the intercom outlets. "Give us some slack on the winch, Captain," Luger called.

The motor on the winch hummed as its steel line began to unspool. The warrant officer grasped the cable and turned toward Luger, who helped him into a STABO harness. Then the older soldier snapped the hook on the harness as Luger finished fastening it on him.

"Here goes," O.T. said, handing the gunner his NVGs and stepping through the side door, hanging on to the cable.

"He's on the cable," Luger informed Oz. "Lower away, sir."

The winch hummed efficiently as the warrant officer, swinging like a human pendulum, dropped to the ocean below. The frightened girl waved at him frantically from the surface of the water, the rotor wash steaming in a cloud around her.

As O.T. reached the rolling surface of the sea, the young woman swam toward him.

"We don't have time to get you into a harness," O.T. yelled over the noise of the rotors. "Hang on." He grabbed her under the arms and lifted her to him until she could wrap her legs around his waist and lock her arms behind his neck. Then he held her tightly in a wet embrace made frantic by the woman's fear. They left the water as the chopper climbed skyward.

"It's okay," O.T. reassured her as they swung wildly beneath the maneuvering helicopter. He glanced up into the darkness, aware that Oz would never travel so fast with them still hanging below unless someone was chasing them.

As the winch started to reel them toward the side door, O.T. recognized the crack of high-velocity bullets zinging by. "Hang on, we're nearly there," he called to the girl, as much to reassure himself as his terrified companion.

After what seemed like years, the winch finally hauled them alongside the open side door. Luger reached out and pushed against the two to swing them away from the opening, then dragged them into the chopper after they had swung back. O.T. hooked a leg and an arm around the door frame as Luger pulled, and at last the wet man and woman were safely aboard the helicopter.

"Get her fastened into a seat," O.T. directed as the chopper lurched to the side, tracers streaking past. O.T. unlatched his harness, slammed the side door shut, and flipped on the red emergency light in the compartment. Then he turned to the wide-eyed woman staring stupefied at him as Luger snapped her seat belt in place.

"You're on a US Army helicopter and we're heading home," O.T. yelled to her. "Stay in that chair and don't move because it looks like we're going to have to shake some trouble, first."

She nodded imperceptibly.

O.T. and Luger staggered forward to buckle themselves into their gunners positions. The warrant officer glanced through his window in the direction of the gunfire and observed a dark shape following them. He jammed his phone jack into the intercom plug. "We've got the girl and we're secured, Captain," he called.

"Good work," Oz responded. "The others in the water—they look dead."

"The three women down there are dead," O.T. confirmed.

"I'm heading for the *Montana*," Oz said.

"The Lynx pilot's on our tail," Death Song warned. "At seven o'clock."

Oz swore through his teeth as another stream of tracers narrowly missed the chopper. "I didn't think he'd recover," he muttered, glancing over his shoulder to locate their pursuer.

"Missile launch!" O.T. shouted, spotting the telltale jet of light behind the aircraft.

Oz threw the MH-60K into a steep bank that hurled the helicopter toward the ocean, gaining speed as they plummeted. Death Song quickly activated the countermeasures pod and released both a flare and a cloud of chaff, hoping one or both would confuse the homing device on the missile.

The Lynx's AIM-7 Sparrow gained on the helicopter, ignoring the hundreds of bits of chaff that tumbled seaward like a metallic snowstorm. Turning its attention to the flare, sputtering on its tiny parachute, the heat-seeker head drove the four control fins to lock onto it, chasing it as it drifted downward. When the missile neared the ocean, its proximity fuse detected the water's mass and ignited the warhead, creating a giant gusher that lifted into the nighttime sky while its thunderclap reverberated across the sea.

Another volley of bullets rattled off the armor of the MH-60K as the Lynx pilot realigned on the American helicopter. Oz continued his sharp turn, struggling to gain altitude above the British chopper.

"He's at seven o'clock," Death Song warned as the metal detector lights blinked to life with the impact of the machine-gun bullets.

Then the Minigun in the cabin behind Oz thundered to life.

"I've got him in my sights!" Luger shouted on the intercom. "Turn right and I'll have him!"

Oz jerked the control column toward starboard.

"Hold it there," Luger called, firing another thunderous burst from the whirling barrels of his door gun.

The projectiles flashed through the air, stitching into the Lynx as it attempted to veer away from the Americans and escape the murderous hail.

Death Song glanced over his shoulder. "Hard right and we'll be on his tail," he informed the pilot.

Oz jammed the control column fully to the side and kicked the right pedal, submitting the aircraft to a giddy turn as Luger ceased firing. The MH-60K banked sharply to bring them around below and behind the fleeing Lynx, which was headed now for the *Fox*.

"Is he in range for a Hellfire?" the American pilot asked.

Death Song checked his instruments, unsure of

the range with the newly installed missile system. "Yeah, he is," he said.

"Take him," Oz ordered.

The copilot pulled down the monaclelike aiming screen on his helmet, which provided him with a picture from the forward-looking infrared system mounted in the nose of the MH-60K. His finger snaked toward the launch button as he turned his head to center the fleeing chopper in his view; the cockpit computer linked to the infrared sensors traced the motion of his helmet to center the laser on the fleeing Lynx.

He activated the laser slaved to the FLIR of his helmet sight.

The fire-and-forget Hellfire missile's Cassegrain telescope in the nose of the missile locked its microprocessor logic circuit onto the laser flash that briefly appeared on the Lynx. The rocket left its pylon in a burst of flame, quickly accelerating to Mach 1 in pursuit of the British aircraft.

The Lynx pilot recognized what was happening and banked into a mad dive toward the ocean in an effort to shake the oncoming projectile.

The electronic circuits in the Hellfire automatically adjusted the four canard controls to home onto its target and, slapping against the chopper's tail, the warhead detonated with the impact.

The Lynx disintegrated into flame and fragments within seconds, its blazing fuel lighting the sky. The debris from the concussion tumbled end over end into the Caribbean and vanished.

Oz quickly turned the MH-60K in the direction of the *Montana*, shoving the control column forward for maximum speed. While British frigates normally carried only one helicopter during peacetime, he had no way of knowing how many aircraft this vessel conveyed. And he was certain the British commander of the ship would do everything in his power to prevent them from escaping.

"How's the radio?" he asked Death Song.

"Still jammed on both the main and alternate frequencies we've been using with the *Montana.*"

"Think we could reach anyone on another channel?"

"I doubt it," Death Song answered. "They apparently have a pretty sophisticated system that locks onto new frequencies almost instantly. All we had was a carrier wave when they cut off our transmission."

"No wonder we haven't heard anything about their operations," Oz said.

"Missile launch!" Luger warned. "From the frigate."

"It's homing in on us," Death Song confirmed. "I've got its IFF radar interrogating us. They've locked onto us with their gathering beam!"

Oz held the control column forward to maintain maximum speed and slowly brought the collective pitch lever up for maneuvering room. They climbed rapidly as the missile gained on them.

As the rocket neared the aircraft, Death Song tapped the chaff dispenser button. A cloud of metal confetti scattered in their wake, slowly tumbling to the ocean far below. The radar beam guiding the missile bounced and scattered as it struck the spinning chaff.

"It's still coming," Death Song warned, his eyes glued to the radar scope registering the ship's command guidance beam.

Oz simultaneously threw the control column to the left and kicked the left pedal, causing them to dive into a tight circle.

As they started their descent, Death Song released another cloud of chaff. The oncoming rocket drifted off course as the ship's computer tried to determine the precise location of the helicopter. By the time the command guidance beam of the radar gave a clear picture of the chopper, the missile was too low to regain the American aircraft.

Oz skimmed along the surface of the ocean as the six miniature laser sensors in the nose of the GWS 25 missile triggered its proximity fuze. The warhead detonated, sending a fireball skyward while fragments peppered the water around it, raising hundreds of tiny geysers.

"They're sweeping the area with targeting radar," Death Song stated as the MH-60K hurtled precariously over the sea. "Maybe they've lost us."

"Sea Wolf One, this is BB-68. Come in please. Over."

"This is Sea Wolf One," Oz answered, surprised they were already out of range of the British jamming.

"Please return immediately. Do not, repeat, do not approach any foreign vessels. Acknowledge please and then maintain radio silence. Over."

"We read you loud and clear, BB-68, and we are returning. Over and out." Oz released the radio trigger on the control column and spoke into the intercom. "Looks like they know the British frigate is responsible for the trouble out there. I bet the *Montana* will even a few scores."

No one in the MH-60K said anything else as they hurtled toward the American battleship, the moon brightly marking their route like a giant beacon.

27

Croll stood wearily on the bridge of the HMS *Fox* where his crewmen continued to work at repairing the damage done by the RPG-16s. The captain still wore his bloody uniform, his arm in a sling.

"Sir, you need to get into bed and rest," the ship's doctor warned him. "The pain from your knife and shrapnel wounds must make it nearly impossible for you to think. You're lucky to even be alive. If I hadn't found you when I did . . ."

"I can't afford to rest now," Croll interrupted, motioning the nervous medic away.

"But, sir," the medic protested, "couldn't you at least try not to exert yourself?"

"I'll take it easy later," Croll said. "Leave me alone for now."

"Captain, we've got the new forward GWS 25 cells in place," declared a sweaty crewman entering the bridge.

"Good work," the captain said, smiling weakly as he lowered himself into a chair. Suddenly Croll's spirits seemed to sag and his hands shook. "If we don't make land soon and abandon ship, the Americans will be on us like a pack of hounds," he said, his voice fraught with emotion.

The sailors on the bridge glanced at one another.

Croll seemed to regain his composure immediately and rose with a groan. He turned to the navigator. "What's the nearest land, Officer Vinson?"

"Basse-Terre, Captain," the young petty officer replied, turning to his chart for a quick measurement with a pair of dividers. "About one hundred miles northeast. Dominica is one hundred ten due east."

"Which island would be easier for our crew to get lost on?" Croll asked rhetorically, stroking his chin. After reflecting a few seconds, he spoke. "Plot a course for Dominica, Officer Vinson."

"Aye, Captain."

"The Americans don't have us yet, do they?" Croll asked, limping over to stand beside the helmsman.

"No, Captain," the sailor acknowledged.

"Bring us about zero ninety degrees and then take us full speed ahead," Croll directed. "We'll make our course corrections when Vinson has the new heading. In the meantime, we don't want to waste any time. Ziegler!"

"Yes, Captain?" the petty officer asked.

"Go to the hangar and see if there's any way they can get the other Lynx into the air. What's wrong with it?"

"Tail rotor transmission's damaged, Captain."

"See if they can repair it—even temporarily. We could use the air support."

"Aye, sir," Ziegler answered, hastening to the hatch that led from the bridge.

Oz found the situation on the bridge of the *Montana* chaotic as the crew plotted a course to intercept the rogue British frigate. Upon learning about the ship sailing under the British colors, her majesty's government had immediately requested that the Americans stop the bogus ship since the Royal Navy had no vessels in the area capable of handling the job.

The US Navy diverted a strike force consisting of an aircraft carrier and its seven support ships; but even at their maximum speed, the group was still a day away from the Caribbean. Consequently, the task of confronting the fraudulent ship had fallen to the USS *Montana*.

Palmer paced the bridge issuing volleys of commands. "Franklin!" he called, handing a message back to the crewman.

"Yes, Captain."

"Use the positional info we got from the surveillance satellite. Williams!" he shouted across the bridge.

"Sir?"

"Bring us the data from the K-11 spy sat."

"Aye, sir."

Palmer turned to Franklin. "Use the K-11 positional data to plot a course to intercept the—whatever the hell that British frigate's name really is."

"The *Fox,* sir."

"Whatever!" Palmer said. "You can double-check your coordinates with those of Captain Carson—he just left the frigate and it can't have traveled too far since then."

"Aye, Captain."

He turned to his first officer. "Activate our CIWS and let's go to battle stations. I don't want them to get an Exocet at us while our pants are down."

"CIWS activated and battle stations is being sounded!" the officer called, switching on the alarms.

"Commander Carson," Palmer said, striding over to where Oz stood bent over a chart, watching as the navigator plotted the course toward the *Fox.*

"Yes, sir," the American pilot answered, standing upright.

"Sorry to keep you waiting. You need to place your crews on standby so you can get into the air in a hurry. I'll have our deck crew wheel your disabled Apache as close to the superstructure as possible so our defenses will give it some protection if we get into a fight with the Brits." He glanced at his watch. "If they continue their present course, we should intercept them sometime before dawn—probably in about an hour."

"Do you want our choppers to counter their second helicopter if they're carrying one?" Oz asked.

"Right," Palmer nodded. "If they have a second Lynx, it could make things miserable by coming in from behind us. If they don't have one, then I'll be keeping you in reserve—just stay clear of the frigate and let us handle them by ourselves if possible. If something happens to our fire-control radar, then we might also want you to spot for us."

"Yes, sir, I'll start rounding up my men immediately," Oz said, saluting. He left the bridge and hurried through the nearly deserted passages of the battleship, swiftly reaching the large cabin where the Army personnel were berthed.

"What's up, Captain?" O.T. asked as Oz entered the room. The warrant officer sat on the edge of one of the bunks, a tiny magnetic chess set balanced on his knees.

"We need to have our choppers on standby so we can get into the air in a hurry," Oz said. "The *Montana* is under orders to stop the rogue frigate—and will attack it if they refuse to surrender. If that happens, we'll counter the second Lynx the frigate may be carrying and spot for their gun crews if necessary. Otherwise, we're to stay out of the way and let the battleship take care of the frigate."

"What about the Apache?" asked Sergeant Newport, the pilot of the AH-64, sitting up in his bunk.

"You'll have to stick to the ship," Oz replied. "But right now you can help us reload one of the Hellfires from your chopper onto ours in case we need it."

Oz glanced at Sudden. "The Delta Forces will have to sit this one out, too," he said.

"I was afraid of that," Sudden grimaced. "I'll have my guys ready to go, anyway, just in case you need us somewhere other than inside this metal box."

"Okay," Oz conceded, "although I can't imagine your guy'll be needed from here on out unless the frigate somehow makes land."

"Anything's better for these guys than just sitting around," the lieutenant explained.

"Amen to that," Newport agreed, leaving the cabin behind the other Army airmen to help remove the Hellfire from his Apache.

"I'm sure that's an American fire-control signal," Ensign Bammes told Croll as the two studied the screen over the radar technician's shoulder.

"Damn Yanks," the British captain growled. "They've blocked our escape to Dominica. I suppose it would be asking too much to expect them to leave their fire control disengaged."

"Shall we try to go around them, Captain?" Bammes asked.

Croll shook his head. "Even if we managed to elude them, they'd use their surveillance sats to track us down and block our way. Then they'd call in some real muscle and catch us on the open sea." The officer deliberated for a moment. "Our only chance is to fight the ship ahead of us—it's all that's between us and freedom. How far are we from completing our repairs?"

"They're all but done now, Captain," Bammes replied.

"Captain, we're receiving a message from the Americans," Eyestone reported.

"Let's hear it," Croll said, taking the mike from his radioman.

The transmission came over the speaker. "BB-68 calling British frigate number F92. Come in please. Over."

The captain took a deep breath and replied, "This is Captain Croll of the HMS *Fox.* Over."

"Captain, you are directed to come ahead at reduced speed and surrender immediately," Palmer's voice sounded on the radio. "We've obtained permission from the British Prime Minister and the President of the United States to exercise *any* force necessary to stop you. We would encourage you to surrender peacefully and not further endanger the lives of your men. Over."

The British sea captain was silent for a moment and then thumbed on the transmitter. "BB-68, we will reduce our speed and prepare to surrender. We will await your further instructions. Over."

"Stay on your course heading and reduce speed," Palmer instructed. "We've plotted an intercept already. Over and out."

The crewmen on the bridge of the *Fox* stared at the captain in disbelief as he handed the microphone back to radio technician Eyestone.

Croll was quiet for several moments before issuing his order. "Reduce speed to one-third and continue on our present course. We'll rendezvous with the Americans."

"Aye, aye, sir," the helmsman replied, his face a mask.

Within moments the *Fox*'s twin gas turbine engines had slowed, and the nearly silent electric motors took over to push the ship forward at one-third speed.

The crewmen on the bridge stood or sat at their posts in stunned silence; no one spoke until the captain finally addressed them: "Keep our targeting and CIWS radar off, but everyone to battle stations."

Petty Officer Vinson glanced at Croll and grinned as he flicked on the alarm. "Aye, Captain. Battle stations it is!"

28

"According to our computer," the data technician aboard the *Fox* told Croll, "The BB-68 is the USS *Montana.* She's one of the old World War Two battleships the Yanks renovated to keep their Department of Defense out of the hole during the recession."

"What's her armament?" Croll demanded.

The technician pecked at the keyboard and a second chart appeared on the screen. "Their old armament consists of five- and sixteen-inch guns, while the new stuff includes four Phalanx CIWS as well as eight Tomahawk and eight Harpoon missiles."

"How's their CIWS system arranged?" Croll asked.

The technician hit another button. "Their close-in weapons system consists of four 20mm Vulcan Gatlings mounted at—roughly—the four corners of her superstructure. It'd be pretty hard to get anything through those."

"Yes, it will," Cross agreed, studying the diagram on the screen. "Those positions are the Harpoon and Tomahawk launchers?" he asked, tapping the screen.

"Yes, sir, they're nestled in between the CIWS and the superstructure for maximum protection."

Croll unconsciously pulled at his lower lip, mulling over the arrangement. "We're already in the range of the missiles," he remarked. "What's the range for the guns?"

The technician changed the screen to a fourth chart. "Looks like they reach to twenty-seven miles—about the same as our Exocets."

"Interesting," Croll commented. "That'll be all for now." He crossed the bridge. "Mr. Vinson, what's our present distance from the Americans?"

"Thirty-eight nautical miles, sir."

"I've got a plan, Mr. Vinson, but we'll have to hurry if we're to succeed."

"Captain, we've got an emergency message from the commander of the *Fox,*" the radio technician told Palmer.

"Put it on the speakers," Palmer directed, grasping the mike. "This is the captain of BB-68. Over."

"Captain, we've got an emergency," Croll's voice intoned. "We've had a massive fire on our main deck and both of our medics were killed trying to rescue some of the crew. We've got twenty sailors in very serious need of immediate medical help. Over."

Palmer thought a moment, suspecting a trick, but decided he should offer help to the injured.

"We'll send a chopper to airlift the injured to our ship. Over."

"We would appreciate that, BB-68. In the meantime, we've sent our Lynx to you with six of our most seriously wounded crew members. The fire is reaching our bridge and we must sign off immediately. Over."

"I'm sorry, Captain, but I can't let your chopper approach us," Palmer said over the mike. "You'll have to turn your Lynx back. Over."

The radio technician looked up from his instruments. "They're off the air, Captain."

Palmer swore loudly and handed the mike back to the crewman. "I'm betting it's a trick," he said. "Contact the Night Stalkers and tell them to get their copters into the air to check the *Fox*. Tell them to see if there really is a fire aboard. Radar, do you have any sign of an approaching chopper?"

"Aye, sir, we just located an aircraft coming in low between us and the *Fox*."

The captain found himself in a traditional double bind. He'd be damned if he let the chopper in and it turned out to be armed and attacked the battleship; he'd also be damned if he failed to give aid to the wounded or—worse yet—shot down a helicopter loaded with injured men being brought in for medical help. He tried to decide what should be done.

After the MH-60K had traveled eight miles beyond the USS *Montana,* Oz could barely make out the smoke rising from the *Fox* using his NVGs. "BB-68, there certainly appears to be a sizable fire in the

Fox's vicinity," he radioed. "We can see a large black cloud coming from their location. Over."

"Proceed toward them with extreme caution, Sea Wolf One," Palmer said, "and check to see if there actually are injured sailors waiting for transport. They've agreed to shut down their CIWS and other defensive systems, but it looks like it could be a trick. Over."

"We'll move in cautiously. Over."

"Sea Wolf One, do you see their chopper? Over."

"That's a roger. We haven't got a very good look at it but it's approaching and seems to have stretchers mounted on its weapons pylons. Over."

"Let us know as soon as you've got something on the ship's status. Over and out."

Oz switched the radio to the air battle net frequency and toggled it on. "Sea Wolf Three, we're to approach the ship and get a closer look. If there appears to be a real emergency, we'll pick up their injured and ferry them back. But stay alert! No one's convinced this isn't a trick—especially me. Over."

"I read you loud and clear, One. We'll keep our eyes peeled. Over."

"It certainly looks like they have stretchers mounted on the sides of the chopper," Palmer said, studying the incoming chopper through his powerful binoculars whose optics gathered enough light for him to inspect the aircraft. "Keep the CIWS off, but be ready to activate it immediately," he ordered.

"Aye, sir, we'll stay on standby," the close-in weapons system officer replied.

The captain switched the intercom over and spoke into it again, "Deck crew, prepare for an incoming helicopter. Security and medical teams, stand by."

"We're in place, Captain," Master Sergeant Dexter's voice replied from the speaker.

Palmer studied the incoming Lynx once more through his binoculars.

"I've never seen a helicopter with stretchers strapped to the pylons, sir," the ensign next to Palmer remarked.

"I guess the English must still do it," Palmer answered, watching the chopper. "It reminds me of photos of the wounded being transported on American choppers during the Korean War. I guess it's a quick way to increase the carrying capacity of a copter."

"Yeah, you can't stack the wounded in stretchers the way you pack sardines," the ensign snickered.

"That's true enough," Palmer agreed, lowering his binoculars.

"Captain," the ensign cried out suddenly, "the injured sailors on the pylons are being thrown off!"

Palmer lifted his binoculars and stared through the porthole. As the Lynx hung in the air over the ocean, a British crewman was pulling what had appeared to be bodies loose from the pylons.

"Those are dummies!" the American captain shouted, watching the decoy blankets and rags fall away to expose the missiles mounted to the approaching aircraft. Before Palmer could issue the order to reactivate the CIWS, the Lynx's rockets jetted to life and raced for the *Montana*.

The first volley of missiles struck behind the superstructure, exploding into the Tomahawk and Harpoon launch tubes, igniting one of the large warheads in the process. The secondary explosion ripped the noses of the launchers apart, hurling metal fragments and unarmed rockets into the air. The swirling debris rattled the Tacan antenna and bent the SPS-49 air surveillance radar.

The Lynx shot through the thick cloud of smoke rising from the superstructure, swung around, and launched a second salvo of rockets that struck the remaining Harpoon launchers on the starboard side. Another of the Harpoons exploded, shearing off the top of the rear stack, which tumbled over the two fire-control towers and came to rest in a burning mass atop the X turret and the crippled Apache.

"Activate the CIWS!" Palmer screamed into the intercom as he stood on the bridge watching the helicopter wheel around, preparing to fire at him.

"Both starboard Phalanxes are out of commission, Captain!" shouted the CIWS officer over the intercom.

Before Palmer could issue another command, the officer in charge of the forward starboard five-inch gun turret—who had ordered the twin barrels of the weapon raised to cover the chopper—shouted his order without waiting for the directive from the bridge. "Fire!"

The cannons spit their heavy five-inch shells at the helicopter overhead, hovering at nearly point-blank range above the twin muzzles. The shells reached their target and the chopper erupted into a huge fireball that tumbled into the ocean, a whirling mass of twisting rotors and exploding ordnance.

The British timing was off.

The attack on the *Montana* occurred before the two American helicopters could be lured to the decks of the HMS *Fox,* which was littered with burning and smoldering trash that made it appear that the forward deck of the ship was on fire. Instead, Croll ordered the activation of the frigate's CIWS weapons, prompting two GWS 25 surface-to-air missiles to leap from their boxlike launch tubes on the forecastle of the vessel and race toward the American MH-60Ks.

When the CIWS radar was reactivated, Oz responded instantly, knowing that the radar system could only mean a GWS 25 missile was headed their way. He immediately put the aircraft into a steep dive while Death Song punched the chaff button to release a confusing cloud of metal behind them.

Sea Wolf Three, flying above and behind Oz, didn't fare as well, failing to respond the instant the *Fox*'s CIWS radar was activated.

"Look out," the copilot of Sea Wolf Three screamed as he spied the missile climbing toward them.

The pilot of the MH-60K had almost no time to react. Realizing they were lost, he threw his chopper into a dive at the *Fox,* launching his rockets rather than trying to elude the oncoming missile.

The GWS 25 connected an instant later, ripping the MH-60K apart. The debris tumbled through the air as the 2.75-inch rockets the pilot had launched crashed amidships on the *Fox*'s decks, detonating the pair of STWS torpedoes. The blasts lit the night as they ripped the deck open and hurled rubble into the air.

The gathering beam remained locked on Oz's chopper as he dropped at maximum speed, the GWS 25 missile racing after them. Death Song tapped the chaff dispenser button and another cloud of metallic paper poured out, prompting the rocket to lose them and pass alongside.

Oz banked the aircraft to put distance between them and the missile, which was turning back. But the GWS 25 had traveled too far to regain its target; the auto destruct took over, causing the warhead to detonate. Its fireball climbed skyward as metal fragments rained into the open sea.

"They're still sweeping us with their gathering beam," Death Song warned.

Oz hugged the ocean, trying to put distance between them and the *Fox*. He realized they wouldn't be able to outrun a second missile, and there was no time to gain the altitude he needed for their chaff to properly deflect the targeting radar of the ship.

CHAPTER

29

"Get our forward guns into action and stomp those lying SOBs!" Palmer bellowed into the intercom, his fist pounding the bulkhead. Whirling on his radar technician, he shouted, "Give them the coordinates; our fire-control radar is down."

"Aye, Captain."

"Damage report!" Palmer demanded.

"Captain, except for the forward port Phalanx, our CIWS is down. All Harpoon and Tomahawks are off-line—probably destroyed—and the rear stack with the SSC-3 satcom terminal is gone. The fire in our X turret has been contained but the guns in it are inoperational. It looks like the Mk 13 and Mk 38 fire director radar towers are gone. Also, the heli-deck is reporting that the Apache is destroyed and the landing deck is covered with undetonated ord-nance."

Palmer swore long and loudly and then turned to the radio technician. "Can you reach our helicop-ters?"

"Negative, Captain, our radio's being jammed."

"The A and B gunners report they're on their coordinates, Captain," a crewman announced.

"Commence firing," Palmer ordered. "Radar, try to track the shells and see how far they're off. We'll have to do the best we can without a spotter."

He crossed to the front of the bridge and watched as the A and B turrets fired broadside toward the target that was now twenty-five miles away. The huge muzzles belched fire, throwing shadows across the battleship, while the thick black smoke shrouded the vessel for nearly thirty seconds until it was dissipated by the breeze.

"Their gathering beam isn't aimed on us," Death Song announced incredulously, double-checking the radar screen.

Oz pulled the MH-60K into a wide circle, changing course so they'd be harder to find if the radar tried to locate them again. "Why do you suppose they quit tracking us?" Oz queried.

"There's the reason," Death Song said.

Four GWS 25 missiles lunged from their forward launchers ahead of the bridge, their flaming tails slashing through the black sky, propelling them eastward toward the *Montana.*

A second later massive explosions erupted high above the *Fox,* the GWS 25 missiles having reached their targets, exploding on the incoming giant shells fired from the *Montana.* The blasts created huge fragments that scattered across a wide area, tumbling onto the British ship and into the sea around it like steel hail and leaving round black clouds that concealed the stars in the nighttime sky.

Moments later the remaining two shells from the *Montana*'s salvo dropped around the *Fox,* missing their target by several hundred yards and raising giant geysers that churned the ocean with waves that rippled in all directions.

"The *Montana*'s using her sixteen-inch guns on them," Death Song explained, "and the frigate's using its missiles to defend itself."

"How did Captain Palmer know we'd been attacked?" Luger asked from his position behind Oz.

"He couldn't," Oz replied, guiding the aircraft away from the British vessel for a safer vantage point. "There's no way he could've known. The Lynx helicopter allegedly taking injured crewmen to the ship must have attacked."

"And that's why the *Montana*'s using shells instead of missiles," O.T. conjectured. "She must have been severely damaged."

"The captain would have had to lower the CIWS to let the Lynx in," Oz said, keeping his chopper low as it revolved to face the frigate. "There's no telling what kind of destruction they might have caused."

Oz debated what action they should take next. It would probably be best to hang back and let the *Montana* take care of the British frigate, he decided. So he remained in place, low over the water.

Without warning, five shells dropped into the sea, this time exploding in a ring that encircled the *Fox* in geysers. The sixth shell grazed the ship in the fantail, most of the force of the explosion being vented into the sea, raising another giant plume that splashed across the helideck. Chunks of steel pirouetted from the fantail itself, a large piece smashing into the rear radio mast, severing its top. The long section of the mast tumbled to the deck, striking the rear GWS 25 SAM launcher and causing it to topple onto its side.

Another six shells plunged into the ocean, this time landing nearly a half mile from the *Fox,* whose crew worked frantically to reload the GWS 25 on the foredeck.

"The *Montana* didn't get on target very precisely that time," Luger said.

"Maybe their radar's knocked out," Death Song suggested. "All I'm getting from them is their navigational radar; their fire-control signals are missing."

"Maybe we could spot for them," O.T. suggested.

"That's a negative," Death Song replied. "They're jamming our radio frequencies. Where would the EW jamming be coming from on their ship?" he asked. "If we could knock it out . . ."

"It's got to be on one of the masts," Oz said.

"But they've got a collection of those," Death Song declared. "Hitting the right one would be a matter of luck."

"Hang on," Oz warned his crew. "We've got about one minute while the guns on the *Montana* are being reloaded. Let's see what we can do before more shells drop in."

As the MH-60K charged toward the rear of the frigate, the *Fox* launched one of the Exocet missiles on its forecastle, the rocket blitzing away for the American battleship.

*   *   *

"I can't tell if we're reaching the target, Captain," the radar technician on the *Montana* told Palmer. "We're close, but this equipment wasn't designed for fire control."

"I understand that," Palmer said. "Just do your best."

He stared into the darkness through the port side of the bridge, wishing there were some way they could know if the shells were reaching their targets. He glanced toward the A and B turrets forward the bridge. Inside each of the giant mechanisms, crews of seventy-seven labored to reload the six massive guns, while a crew of thirty toiled in the magazine below, straining to move shells and propellent into the elevators that served the ancient weapons.

On the port deck behind the bridge, the Mark 15 20mm Vulcan/Phalanx's radar automatically locked onto the Exocet that streaked toward them, traveling only a few yards above the ocean to remain half hidden by the waves.

In a blur of motion, the Phalanx rapidly pivoted, aligning itself onto the incoming projectile. Before any human aboard the *Montana* was even aware of the danger, the gun's servo motors precisely aligned it onto target, commencing firing with a thunderous roar.

"Captain, incoming!" the radar operator cried.

A tempest of 20mm bullets stormed from its six spinning barrels to tear into the Exocet, which exploded five hundred yards away, splattering in a wide pattern over the ocean.

*   *   *

"The Exocet exploded, sir," the weapon's control officer reported to Croll over the intercom.

"But it failed to reach its target," the sonar technician reported, looking up from his instruments. "No secondary explosions or imploding noise."

"Then our chopper must not have destroyed their CIWS," Croll said, disappointment registering in his voice. He wondered how much damage the Lynx *had* done since the battleship didn't seem to have fire-control radar nor was it launching missiles. That suggested massive damage to the superstructure.

How their CIWS had survived was a mystery, but perhaps only one or two of the Phalanxes remained. "Let's try to saturate their defenses," Croll said.

"We've lost the chopper on our stern," radar cautioned the captain. "It's possible the GWS 25 got it, but since the missile auto-destructed, it's more likely we missed it. They're probably lying low to avoid our radar."

"We can't worry about a gnat when we're fighting a giant," Croll scolded hoarsely. "Let the CIWS handle them if they're still nosing around. Launch the rest of the Exocets," he ordered huskily.

"Aye, Captain."

The three missiles erupted from their tubes ahead of the bridge, scorching the ship with their flames and leaving a dense cloud over the vessel.

"Engineering to the bridge," the intercom called.

Croll limped to the intercom and slapped its switch. "What have you got?"

"Sir, our lower deck's flooding faster than the pumps can handle it."

"Just give me the power I need," the captain croaked, slumping onto the console in front of him. "If we can take care of the American battleship and reach Dominica, we'll be home free."

"We'll do the best we can, Captain, but I can't make any promises."

Croll turned from the intercom, his face ashen. "What's our status on the torpedo tubes?"

"Damage control reports we lost two but two remain operational."

"Mr. Vinson," Croll said shakily, "full speed ahead. Let's get into torpedo range and finish these American bastards off. Tell the forward crew to hurry and get the GWS 25 launcher refilled. We were lucky that last salvo from the Americans was off by a wide margin."

"Sir, the rear GWS 25 launcher was hit by the debris from the Americans' shell," Vinson alerted the captain. "And our stern fire-control radar's down as well."

Croll started to speak, then slid off the console to his knees. He struggled to rise for a moment and then sprawled onto the deck.

"Get the captain to sick bay," Vinson ordered Ensign Bammes and the master sergeant standing next to him.

"I'm only a little light-headed," Croll growled, struggling unsuccessfully to rise. "I'll be okay in a minute."

"You're relieved of duty for the time being,

Captain," Vinson said. "You're injured and unfit for command."

"This isn't the British Royal Navy," Croll protested as two sailors helped him to his feet. "You don't have the right—"

"Have it the way you want it," Vinson said. "You two, take him down to his quarters and keep him there. I'm going to try to get us to Dominica."

"Aye, sir," the sailors answered. They guided the officer through the starboard hatch, half carrying the broken man toward sick bay.

"I've got a king's ransom in my cabin," Croll muttered to the two sailors as they hustled him down a passageway lit by red combat lights. "If you'll do what I say, two thirds of it will be yours. I can also guarantee we'll get to Dominica."

"We're listening, Captain," Bammes said, his companion nodding in agreement. "Tell us what to do."

The activation of the Phalanx alerted the American sailors to the incoming Exocets.

"Radar, what have you got?" Palmer asked, staring through the porthole toward the *Fox.*

"Two—no three—incoming," the technician yelled.

There was no way their single CIWS would stop three Exocets, Palmer realized as the gun fired a long burst and the first warhead exploded nearly four hundred yards from the ship. A second explosion followed, this time merely a hundred yards away from the port.

The Phalanx swiveled slightly to acquire the

third missile, but the automatic gun was too late. The final Exocet reached the ship, exploding against the hull beneath the A turret.

Despite the battleship's twelve-inch armor, the explosion cut right through the protective shield, sending metal fragments and molten steel streaming into the A magazine. Within a fraction of a second, the propellents in the magazine erupted, ripping open the deck and pushing it upward like a banana peel and knocking the A turret askew.

The concussion smashed the safety glass in the ports, showering the bridge with shards and cutting Palmer's hands, which he'd raised over his face. He dropped to his knees and waited for the inevitable. For a brief moment he nurtured a tiny hope, only to have it dashed as the B magazine exploded, rocking the ship with a bone-shaking blast that ripped the few remaining shards from the bridge's portholes.

Palmer staggered to his feet, blood streaming from a deep cut on his temple. He gazed around the bridge, littered now with bits of shattered safety glass and metal.

Five of his sailors were lying motionless around him, the others struggling to rise, groaning from their wounds. Forward of the bridge, a fire raged in the bilge of the forecastle, while the rumblings in the bowels of the ship could only be water rushing into the lower decks.

"Captain?" asked the radar technician, an ugly cut on his cheek.

"Damage report!" Palmer ordered, helping the technician into his chair.

The ensign turned to his instrument panel, but

gazed toward the captain again as another explosion rumbled below them. The ship's decks started to tilt at an alarming angle. "Shall I give the order to abandon ship?" the ensign asked.

"Hell, no!" the captain bellowed. "Give me the damage report. We're going to get those misbegotten SOBs if it's the last thing we do!"

30

Oz approached the frigate at such a low altitude that the helicopter's landing gear momentarily dragged through a high wave, inducing the MH-60K to lose speed before clearing the water.

"What's the first target?" Death Song inquired as they came into range for the Hellfire missiles.

"That's the question," Oz replied. "Let's forget the radio masts and circle around and hit the bridge. If we can knock that out, we'll have them down for the count. Wait a minute—" The pilot rapidly aimed the helicopter by dipping its nose and firing three rockets with a triple tap of the firing button on the control column.

The three Mk 66 rockets raced toward the Oerlikon 20mm antiaircraft gun swiveling toward them, colliding with the automatic weapon that had already started to fire. Three of the heavy slugs from the gun barely missed the MH-60K, one smashing into the machine guns hanging in the right weapons pod. The explosion rattled the chopper and lit a warning light on the panel in front of Oz. Suddenly the 20mm gun was silent, damaged by one of the 2.75-inch rockets that had exploded beside it.

"Close," Oz sighed, circling the frigate to give Death Song a clear shot at the port side of the bridge. "Fire all four Hellfires," he ordered when they were in position. "This may be the last clear shot we get."

The pilot nudged the MH-60K forward slightly and stopped. They were nearing the area protected by the forward GWS 25 missiles, which he could barely see around the bridge. Death Song rapidly aligned his helmet sight onto the bridge and activated the laser designator. He fired the four Hellfires serially, pausing only a moment between fusillades to allow the laser seeker on the nose of each rocket to lock onto target before the next missile followed.

Within seconds the four Hellfires struck, engulfing the bridge in flames and blowing out its newly replaced ports. There was little doubt in Oz's mind that the British sailors inside the bridge had been killed instantly by ricocheting metal fragments.

The GWS 25 launcher swiveled toward them and then abruptly stopped.

"They've shut down their EW and radar," Death Song announced.

"HMS *Fox* calling US copter, come in please," the radio implored.

Oz toggled on the radio. "This is NS-1 answering your transmission, *Fox*. Over."

"We're surrendering, NS-1. Our engine room is flooded—we're dead in the water. Our officers on the bridge are dead and the captain's missing. We'll be needing to abandon ship within the hour if we can't get the lower decks sealed—and it doesn't look like we can. We'll wait for your instructions. Over."

"HMS *Fox,* take whatever action you need to stay afloat," Oz radioed. "Be advised that reactivation of your EW or radar will be considered a hostile act and will be dealt with accordingly. If you abandon ship, your people must stay together so the BB-68 can retrieve them. We will shoot anyone who tries to escape. Over."

"We understand, NS-1. We're signing off the air for now. Over and out."

Oz released the radio switch and spoke over the intercom. "We can't do much with just four unguided rockets and two Miniguns. Do you think they bought my bluff?"

"They don't have much weaponry themselves," O.T. remarked. "In the land of the disarmed, the one-shot gun is king."

"I hope that's true today," Oz said.

Captain Croll surveyed the MH-60K that circled the ship in the darkness.

"Do you think they bought our surrender?" Bammes asked.

"I don't know," Croll replied. "One thing's for sure, though. That pilot can't have much armament left. If we play our cards right we can escape without him seeing us. Lower the launch and prepare to leave. I only want you two to come with me; no one else in the boat."

"Aye, Captain," Bammes answered.

"But what if the chopper tries to stop us?" the master sergeant asked.

"I have a way to stop *him,*" Croll promised.

"We'll get the motor launch ready then, Captain," Bammes grinned.

"I'm taking us higher to see if we can reach the *Montana,*" Oz said. "Keep an eye on the radar and alert me if they switch it on. I still don't trust that band of cutthroats."

"Will do," Death Song answered.

Oz guided the chopper in a wide rising spiral, distancing the aircraft from the *Fox* while remaining toward the rear of the ship to avoid the CIWS missiles. Within minutes, the MH-60K was several hundred feet above the ocean.

"Sea Wolf One calling BB-68, come in please."

"This is BB-68," Palmer's voice answered. "Good to hear your voice—I thought we'd lost you. What's your status there? Over."

"The *Fox* was hit by one of your shells and appears to be sinking," Oz answered. "They claim to have surrendered and are preparing to abandon ship. Over."

"We're not in much better shape," Palmer admitted, "but we're limping toward you now. We've also contacted Navy command now that our radio's no longer being jammed. With any luck, we should reach your position in twenty minutes if you can hold the fort till then. Over."

"Will do. Over and out."

"Captain," O.T. called, "they've lowered a boat and it's leaving the ship at high speed."

"Damn," Oz exclaimed, lowering the collective pitch lever. He took the aircraft past the end of the

Fox, following the boat that now darted past the bow of the British frigate.

Croll glared at the pursuing helicopter, realizing that within seconds it would overtake his fleeing craft.

"Shall we radio him?" Bammes suggested.

"Don't bother," Croll answered. "Just keep going."

The wounded man stood up in the boat and carefully extended the launch tube of the LAW 80 rocket he'd tucked away. With shaking fingers he released the safety on the mechanism and prepared to fire.

Oz hesitated for a moment when he saw the injured man—the captain, judging from his uniform—stand up, his face and uniform matted with blood and his legs so wobbly he could barely support himself. But the LAW 80 was a threat to the chopper, and the man holding it appeared to have every intention of using it.

The American pilot nosed the MH-60K down and tapped the button on his control column, sending a Mk 66 rocket ahead of the motor launch. The missile exploded, rocking the boat and prompting the helmsman to alter its course when the projectile plowed through the erupting water ahead of him.

Croll struggled to his feet and again raised the rocket launcher to his shoulder.

"I guess you're not going to give me any choice," Oz said, tapping the button again, causing another 2.75-inch missile to leap from the aircraft in pursuit of the motor launch. Within a split second, the rocket exploded in the center of the boat, igniting the gas tank.

The fiery blast tore a hole in the bottom of the craft and hurled the three sailors into the water, engulfed in flames. The conflagration burned fiercely for some time as Oz circled overhead, but within a few minutes only bits and pieces of burning debris remained on the surface of the ocean.

Oz hovered over the wreckage for a while, contemplating the burnt bodies floating in the dark sea below. For a brief moment the American pilot almost felt remorse at the passing of these men. But then he remembered his own men—the savage deaths of his friends and countrymen on Sea Wolf Three and Four. He suspected that the sailors below were responsible for those murders, as well as countless others.

"We're not wasting our time trying to recover the bodies," he finally said.

"We're low on fuel, Captain," Death Song advised as the pilot circled back to the British frigate, which had dropped dangerously low in the water.

"Yeah," Oz answered. "I'm checking the *Fox* again to make sure no other clowns are trying to get away, and then we'll head back to the *Montana*. We've done all we can here."

E P I L O G U E

Oz stood on the swaying deck of the USS *Montana,*
which Palmer and his crew had managed to keep
afloat, watching the morning sunlight glistening on
the Caribbean.

"I can't say I've enjoyed my stay on your ship,"
the pilot grinned as he turned toward Captain
Palmer. "I guess I'm the proverbial landlubber."

"I can't much blame you after the last twenty-
four hours," Palmer chuckled, shaking his head.
"Things usually aren't quite so violent out here. You
Army guys must be Jonahs for sure.

"Anyway," he continued with a tired face,
"good luck on your flight to Dominica. I guess we'll
be limping there ourselves with the captured sailors
from the *Fox*—but I suppose you'll be gone by the
time we get there."

"Yes, sir, we have a transport waiting for us."

"Well, good luck then." Palmer saluted.

Oz returned the salute. Then he strode to his
waiting helicopter, climbed aboard, and within a few
minutes the MH-60K was in the air. The pilot circled
the heavily damaged battleship and aligned onto the

course heading that would take them to the waiting C-5A transport. From there, they would head back to Fort Bragg.

Flying toward their destination, Oz reflected on the fate of the survivors of the HMS *Fox* who in a few days would arrive at Dominica in chains and handcuffs. There they would be handed over to the British authorities, herded aboard chartered planes, and flown to England—probably to stand trial for mutiny, a charge the British Royal Navy hadn't brought against sailors for almost a century.

"How's it look back there, O.T.?" Oz inquired over the intercom.

"Everything's fine," the warrant officer answered. "Hey, when we finally get back Fayetteville, let's go to Jake's," he suggested enthusiastically. "I hear they've got a really good band out there."

Oz shot Death Song a knowing look as a loud groan came over the intercom from Luger. The Night Stalkers had finally wised up to O.T.'s taste in raunchy country and western bars.

But all four of them knew they'd be there to celebrate a successful mission, once they got home.

Duncan Long is internationally recognized as a firearms expert, and has had over twenty books published on that subject, as well as numerous magazine articles. In addition to his nonfiction writing, Long has written a science fiction novel, *Antigrav Unlimited.* He has an MA in music composition, and has worked as a rock musician; he has spent nine years teaching in public schools. Duncan Long lives in eastern Kansas with his wife and two children.

'I can't

'I just kno̶͟   ͟ms
up, Sam s͟   ͟ds
eloquently. 'Something since day one... I'm
sorry. Have I embarrassed you, scared you?'

Gemma tried to clear her throat. 'You didn't
scare me or embarrass me.' She went on
firmly in her normal voice, 'No, not at all,
but...'

'But...what do we do about it?'

Margaret O'Neill started scribbling at four and began nursing at twenty. She contracted T.B. and, when recovered, did her British Tuberculosis Association nursing training before general training at the Royal Portsmouth Hospital. She married, had two children, and with her late husband she owned and managed several nursing homes. Now retired and living in Sussex, she still has many nursing contacts. Her husband would have been delighted to see her books in print.

Recent titles by the same author:

THE PATIENT MAN
THE PRACTICE WIFE
A CAUTIOUS LOVING

A FAMILY
CONCERN

BY
MARGARET O'NEILL

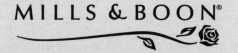

MILLS & BOON®

To my darling granddaughter, gorgeous Georgia Amelia.
Born 16th June 1998

*First published in Great Britain 1999
Harlequin Mills & Boon Limited,
Eton House, 18-24 Paradise Road, Richmond, Surrey TW9 1SR*

© Margaret O'Neill 1999

ISBN 0 263 81946 9

*Set in Times Roman 10½ on 12 pt.
03-0002-53281*

*Printed and bound in Spain
by Litografia Rosés S.A., Barcelona*

CHAPTER ONE

THE waiting room was nearly full and every other person seemed to be coughing and sneezing. There was no one behind the reception desk.

Gemma waited patiently, reminding herself that this was a small village surgery, buried in the heart of rural Dorset. She musn't expect the same fast tempo she had been used to in the busy, high-tech town practice she had left behind her.

'You might have a long wait, love,' one of the coughers and sneezers spluttered out, his voice not only thick with cold but with the local burr. 'Dr Sam's on his own—the old doctor's out on an emergency, Ellie's off sick, and Mrs Mallory can't get here for a bit.'

This mine of information was an elderly man, sitting in one of the front chairs in the waiting area. He smiled cheerfully at Gemma when she turned round.

She smiled back. 'Any idea how long that is likely to be?'

'You can ask the doctor now,' said the elderly man, nodding towards the archway that opened off the waiting room.

A tall, fair-haired man stood in the archway, his head and shoulders bent down towards the diminutive little old lady standing beside him. She was wearing a deaf aid. He said in a loud voice, laying a hand on her tiny shoulder, 'Come back in a day or two, Mrs Bryce, if the tablets don't work. Or if you can't make it to the surgery, give us a buzz and we'll come to you.'

Well, now I know I'm in never, never land, thought Gemma, a doctor who actually *offers* to visit.

The old lady beamed up at him. 'I won't do that unless I have to, Doctor. You know me, like to keep toddling round, stops me old joints from seizing up.' And thumping her stick, she made her shaky way along the short corridor towards the exit.

Gemma nipped in front of her and held open the door. The old lady nodded. 'Thank you, dear.'

The doctor crossed the waiting room and slid behind the reception desk. He pulled a book crammed with names towards him and smiled at Gemma. 'Have you—' The phone rang. He shrugged. 'Sorry.' Then he picked up the receiver. 'Surgery... Right, Pam, keep her warm, give her lots to drink—somebody will be over to see her as soon as possible.'

He added a few squiggles to a memo pad beside the phone, then looked across at Gemma. 'Sorry about that. Now, how can I help you? Have you an appointment?'

He had a nice voice, a rich tenor, tinged with the faintest of Dorset accents. Fringed by thick, silky brown lashes, vivid blue eyes enhanced by the blue of an open-necked shirt—intelligent, enquiring—surveyed her over the desk.

'I've come to register myself and my daughter with your practice—we've just moved into the village—but you're so busy, perhaps...'

He gave her a wide smile. His eyes smiled, too. 'If you *could* come back later, you'd be doing me a favour—we're a bit short-handed this morning.'

'So I gather... Look, could I be of any help?' The suggestion came out in a rush, surprising herself as much as it obviously surprised the doctor, whose eyebrows shot up. 'I'm a registered general nurse with practice experience and have done the odd stint as receptionist.'

Instantly, his manner changed, grew distant. 'Thanks for the kind offer, but I'm afraid I can't take you up on it. You're a stranger, and I can't simply take your word for it that you're fully qualified, Ms...' He sounded faintly apologetic.

'Mrs Fellows,' she said briskly. Her cheeks reddened, her emerald green eyes blazed. 'Of course you can't—it was a silly suggestion. I may be a drug addict or a Nosy Parker wanting a peek at medical files. I'll let you get on, Doctor, and come back later to register.'

You prat, she said to herself as, stiff-backed, she marched down the corridor towards the exit. Fancy making such a fool of yourself and putting the poor man on the spot like that. You and your big mouth.

Sam Mallory stared at her rigid back, her smooth, neat bob of shining reddish brown hair swinging from side to side and at her neatly trousered rounded buttocks. Her back view, he thought, definitely looked cross—more than cross. It radiated fury, with him and with herself he guessed. And her eyes had blazed fury a moment before. *Honest* fury. He whisked round the desk and in a few long strides caught up with her.

He stopped her at the door. 'That was a stupid attitude for me to take,' he said in a low voice. 'It's pretty obvious that you've nothing to hide, but one has to be so careful these days, even in a village like Blaney St Mary.'

Gemma took a deep breath. 'Of course you do,' she said. 'Don't worry about it. Message received and understood. I'll come back this afternoon to sign on.'

'No!' He touched her arm. His touch was light, but she could feel the pressure of his fingertips through her jacket. Her arm tingled. 'Look, can you lay your hands on your registration certificate?'

'Of course I can, and my CV and references—why?'

Her precious documents had been the first things she'd unpacked and filed safely away.

'Will you fetch them? If you're in the village you can't be far.'

Gemma frowned. 'I'm just across the green, but—'

'Please,' he begged, his eyes serious. 'We could do with some help. At present we're without a nurse *or* a receptionist. You're God's gift, manna from heaven, as they say.' He grinned. 'Please, give me a chance to make amends for giving you such a hasty brush-off.'

She swallowed a knot of excitement and surprise that rose in her throat. 'Are you offering me a job, or do you just want help today?'

The phone rang. He took a step backwards and shrugged, then ran a hand through his thick thatch of corn-fair hair. 'Either, whatever… Look, I must answer that. Come back with the necessary and we'll talk—say in about three quarters of an hour. I'll be through with most of my patients by then and my father will be back from his rounds.'

Feeling as if she were walking on air, Gemma floated across the green to Cherry Tree Cottage. The cottage was one of a small terrace facing the wide expanse of grass fringed with trees. She knew she wasn't dreaming, but her conversation with the doctor had a dreamlike quality about it. It looked as if by chance, luck or fate, in one fell swoop she had solved her greatest problem—she was going to land herself a much-needed job. It could, she felt, only have happened in an off-the-map place like Blaney St Mary.

Having to leave London and her job, that had been the only flaw that had presented itself when she had learned that her great-aunt Marjorie, with whom she had corresponded only at Christmas, had bequeathed her the cottage.

But it was a small price to pay for the privilege of owning her own mortgage-free house, rather than a cramped flat. A house to make into a home for herself and Daisy, a real home.

She glanced up the long oval green towards the village school, and prayed that Daisy was settling into her new environment. It was a dramatic change from the large primary school she had been attending. Not that Daisy had had any qualms—she had seemed quite happy when Gemma had left her earlier in the care of the young, breezy headmistress, Joy Scott. But, then, she was a happy little girl. It had been Gemma who'd been nervous.

In reversal of the mother-daughter roles, Daisy had squeezed Gemma's hand with her small, pudgy one, and said firmly, 'I'll be all right, Mummy. I know I'm going to like it here, it's pretty, like a doll's-size school.'

Compared to her old school, a shabby edifice of concrete and glass, it *was* pretty and doll-sized. It was a bungalow-type building, all red tiles and rose bricks, tucked away just off the green amongst trees and flowerbeds and surrounded by a large play area.

Gemma had squeezed her hand in return. 'I'm sure you're going to be fine, love.' She had dropped a kiss on her daughter's soft, round cheek and had smoothed back a tendril of reddish brown hair. 'I'll be here to collect you at three o'clock. Don't go anywhere until I come.'

Miss Scott had said, calmly reassuring, 'Don't worry, Mrs Fellows, there's always someone here to see every child safely off the premises.'

Assured that Daisy was safe till three o'clock, Gemma let herself through the tiny flower-filled front garden into the cottage, ducking beneath the branches of the ancient cherry tree that gave it its name.

Picking her way round the boxes still waiting to be unpacked, she made for the bureau in the sitting room, where she had filed all her important documents. Her registration certificate, CV and references were among them.

Glancing at the glowing reference from Jonathan Willet, head of the busy Nine Elms practice she had worked for until a few weeks ago, she experienced a moment's nostalgia.

It was a fleeting moment gone in a flash, but it triggered off memories and she wallowed a bit as she sat at the kitchen table, nursing a mug of coffee. She had no real regrets about leaving London. She had a few close friends, and they would keep in touch, perhaps visit occasionally. But there was no one she would miss desperately. She and Daisy had always been rather on their own.

A lone parent with a small baby, she'd discovered soon after she and Neil had split up, had little time, money or energy to spare for socialising. Her girl friends and a couple of male friends, doctors and nurses from her training days, were either absorbed in stable relationships or making the most of being completely fancy-free agents. They visited sometimes, and she, with baby Daisy, had visited them—that had been the extent of her social life for the last few years.

Remembering, it brought the sting of tears to the back of her eyes. That was when she could have done with loving parents to support her, she thought sadly. If only Mum and Dad hadn't parted in a messy divorce, weren't living on opposite sides of the world with new partners... *Stop that!* she told herself savagely. Stop getting maudlin. Things are looking up, so don't start feeling sorry for yourself.

Mentally, she totted up her blessings. We're living in a lovely house in a pretty village, and Daisy's school is brilliant—and to top it all, you've *almost* been handed a job on a platter. And it could be a plum of a job in a great set-up with doctors who obviously cared, and all within a stone's throw of home and school.

Two coffees and half an hour later, her heart beating unevenly in anticipation of her interview with Dr Mallory junior—Dr Sam, as the locals called him—Gemma made her way back across the green to the surgery.

The waiting room was empty of patients, but a tall, thin man with a thatch of dark blonde hair, silvered at the temples, was unloading buff record envelopes from a briefcase behind the reception desk. He looked up as Gemma entered. There was no mistaking the blue eyes, the corn-coloured hair. He had to be 'the old doctor'—Dr Mallory senior.

Smiling his son's wide, generous smile in a similarly lean face, he said, 'It's Mrs Fellows, isn't it?'

Gemma, suppressing a surprised intake of breath, returned his smile. 'Yes—but how on earth do you know who I am?'

He raised thick, straight eyebrows. 'You're a stranger—we don't get many of those in the village except in high summer. And the second clue—my son told me to expect you about now, and for good measure gave me a sort of thumbnail description which fits you perfectly.' His eyes twinkled and Gemma wondered just how the younger doctor had portrayed her.

A frisson of pleasure rippled through her at the thought that he had noticed her enough to describe her accurately.

'Oh,' she said lamely. 'I didn't realise that strangers were in quite such short supply. I must stick out like a sore thumb.'

Dr Mallory gave a little snort of laughter, his eyes glinting with admiration. 'Anything but a sore thumb, my dear, I assure you.' He finished unloading the patients' records

from his briefcase and joined Gemma on the other side of
the desk. 'Now, Mrs Fellows, what about you and I going
through to my office and having a chat while we wait for
Sam? Get to know each other a little. He'll join us
shortly—his last patient is with him now.'

His office looked out over a large, walled garden at the
rear of the single-storey surgery block. A mossy, gabled
roof and ancient twisted chimneys were visible between
the tops of trees, above a froth of pink and white blossom.
There was a tall gate in the flint wall opposite the window.

'Oh how lovely,' Gemma exclaimed.

The doctor waved a hand toward the window. 'Our orchard—apples, pears and plums mostly. Blossoming spec-
tacularly early this year, due to an extremely mild winter.
We don't exactly live over the shop, but next door to it.
That's Timbers you can see above the trees. I was born
there and so were all our children. Can't imagine living
anywhere else, though it's too big for us nowadays, even
though Sam has his own self-contained wing. My wife and
I rattle around in it, except when our brood descends upon
us *en masse.*'

His voice had a warm ring to it, making no bones of his
pride in his home and family.

So Dr Sam lived in the family home. Surprising for a
man in what—his mid-thirties? But why not? It made sense
in a house of that size, and was convenient for the surgery.
And his 'wing' is probably several times bigger than
Cherry Tree Cottage—enough to house his own brood of
corn-blonde children?

Gemma pulled her wayward thoughts up sharply.
Whatever had sent them off on such a tangent? The doctor's domestic arrangements were his own affair, and certainly nothing to do with her.

'Have you got a large family, Dr Mallory?' she asked.

'Another son and two daughters, all married, all with offspring.' He grinned. 'But I musn't bore you with family talk—bad as looking at people's holiday snaps. Now, please, do sit down and tell me about yourself. I've only had a brief chat with my son, but I understand you're a qualified nurse. Where did you train, Mrs Fellows?'

She breathed an inward sigh of relief. This was better…this she could handle.

'City Central, but for the last three years I've been working in a London health centre as a practice nurse. I have a current reference from the head of the practice, Dr Willet.' She fished that and her CV out of her bag.

'Jonathan Willet, about my age, a Barts man?'

'Yes.'

The doctor grinned. 'We trained together, met up once or twice on courses since—nice chap.' He held out his hand. 'So, what's my old friend got to say about you, Mrs Fellows?'

Gemma handed him the wallet of papers and blushed. 'He's been very generous about my work.'

'Well deserved, I'm sure.' He put on a pair of rimless half-specs and had just finished reading the reference when there was a tap on the door. 'That'll be Sam. Come in,' he called. He smiled at Gemma. 'This is going to please him. Here, Sam, read this. It's from Jonathan Willet, that's who Mrs Fellows was working for.' He thrust the letter of reference into his son's hands.

The younger doctor gave her a fleeting smile as he took the document from his father. His eyes, she realised, were a more vivid blue than the older man's, and he was a little taller—six feet three or four, she guessed.

He skimmed through the closely worded page and his lean face creased into a wider smile. 'I'm impressed,' he said softly. 'Obviously Dr Willet was sorry to lose you, and presumably you were happy there, so may I ask what made you move to Blaney St Mary, Mrs Fellows?'

'I inherited a house here from my great-aunt, Mrs Rivers.'

'Of course—Cherry Tree Cottage!' said Dr Mallory senior. 'I should have realised. Not that Mrs Rivers spent much time in the cottage, but it's nice to know that it is to be occupied by someone with village connections.'

Sam Mallory laughed. 'Dad, you're coming over all patriarchal again.' He turned to Gemma and pulled a rueful face. 'My father hates change and we've lived in Blaney so long he feels personally responsible for everyone in and around the village.'

Gemma said impulsively. 'I think that's rather nice. Better than being somewhere where no one cares.'

'I'm glad someone appreciates me,' said the old doctor dryly, with a sly look at his son. Then he added formally. 'Welcome to Blaney St Mary, Mrs Fellows. Now to get down to business. I understand you have a daughter—but she can't be very old. Will your husband be able to cope with looking after her, should we offer you the post of practice nurse?'

'Daisy's six, and she started school here this morning. I'm divorced, so there isn't anyone to help care for her. I would only be able to work school hours initially, but perhaps more if I can find a registered reliable child-minder.' With a sinking heart, she looked anxiously from one doctor and to the other. 'Does that put me out of the running for the job?'

They both shook their heads. 'Not at all,' said Sam. 'My mother will always do some part-time nursing to cover out-of-school hours if needed.' He grinned. 'She's brilliant at spreading herself around—a sort of superwoman, my mother.'

Dr Mallory senior grinned in a similar fashion. 'That's for sure,' he said, his voice warm and affectionate. 'School holidays might be a bit of a problem, but we'll cross that bridge when we come to it. By then, both you and Daisy will have made some friends so child-minding may not be a difficulty.' He slanted his son a questioning look. 'So, what do you say, Sam? Shall we take Mrs Fellows on board?'

His voice was teasing. Clearly he'd made up his mind. Her connection with Jonathan Willet had been the clincher, Gemma guessed. What about his son? He had sounded encouraging but... For a second, Gemma found herself holding her breath.

Sam met Gemma's anxious eyes and said softly, reassuringly, 'With a reference like that, how can we refuse?' He held out his hand. Gemma slid hers into it. It felt strong, warm and comforting. 'Welcome to the practice, Gemma.'

Lying in bed that night, Gemma sleepily reviewed the events of the day. It had been a magical day, she thought, a day of small miracles. She had acquired a job and Daisy had loved her first day in her new school, having already acquired a—*best*—friend.

Sharp at three, a noisy crowd of excited children had poured out of school. Daisy had come racing over to where Gemma had stood waiting with several other mums and an occasional dad—hand in hand with another small girl.

Side by side, they had bounced up and down in front of Gemma. 'Mummy, this is Katy,' Daisy had announced breathlessly. 'She's my best friend. Miss Scott said she had to look after me, 'cos she sits next to me at our table.'

'Hello, Katy.' Gemma had smiled down at the skinny, fair-haired little girl with the bobbing plaits. 'Thank you for looking after Daisy. It's nice to have a friend when you start in a new school.'

Katy, suddenly solemn, had said, 'That's what *Miss* said, so I had to show Daisy where everything's kept in cupboards and places so she'll know tomorrow.'

'And now I know,' Daisy had said, with her particular brand of adult pragmatism. 'But we're still going to be best friends.'

'Yes,' Katy had replied, giving an extra big bounce, 'we are.'

A woman who turned out to be Katy's mother had arrived at that moment to claim her daughter. She had introduced herself as Mary Martin. 'I hope Katy hasn't been making a nuisance of herself,' she'd said to Gemma. 'She's an awful chatterbox.'

'Not at all,' Gemma had reassured her. 'She's been looking after Daisy, showing her the ropes, and I don't think anybody could out-chatterbox my daughter.'

'Wanna bet?' Mary Martin had laughed as she had steered Katy away, turning into the lane beside the school.

Gemma and Daisy made their way up the green to Cherry Tree Cottage, Daisy dancing ahead and babbling on about all that had happened at school. It was a typical early April day of scudding white puffs of cloud and high wind. Gemma, half running to keep up with Daisy, decided she would tell her daughter about her new job when they were having tea.

Half-asleep, recalling her daughter's response to the news, she smiled into the near darkness. Moonlight glimmered through the cotton curtains. It had been so typically Daisy. She had slid from her chair, trotted round the table, thrown her arms round Gemma's neck and given her a resounding kiss. 'Now,' she had said, sounding like a wise little old lady, 'there aren't *any* flies in the ointment, are there?' And Gemma had remembered having once referred to the lack of a job as being 'the only fly in the ointment' in regard to the move to Blaney St Mary.

'No flies at all,' she'd confirmed happily.

Gemma snuggled deeper into the duvet, on the edge of sleep, thinking of tomorrow and starting work at the surgery. She was sure she was going to enjoy working with the two Drs Mallory and all the indications were that Mrs Olivia Mallory—Sam's superwoman mother—was going to be fun to work with.

Not that Olivia Mallory had looked anything like the woman Gemma had expected from Sam's description. Like her husband and son she was fair-haired, but unlike them she was short and plump, a bustling little woman with kind hazel eyes.

When Dr Mallory had introduced her as 'Livy, my wife, who keeps us all in order', Gemma had thought he had been affectionately teasing. The idea that he or his son would be ordered about by anyone was a joke for, in spite of their friendliness, they both possessed an air of authority.

Yet within minutes of arriving in the surgery, Mrs Mallory had sent her husband off to his office to catch up with his paperwork and her son off on his house calls. When the men had gone, she said. 'Now, Gemma—you don't mind if I call you Gemma?' Gemma had shaken her head. 'I'll show you round and fill you in on the nursing and reception routine.' She'd opened a door. 'This is…'

Gemma's eyelids closed as sleep overtook her.

On the other side of the green, Sam Mallory was trying to switch off after a hectically busy day. Thank God the regular locum they used was on call for the night.

He sat in his favourite leather armchair in his large, com-

fortable sitting room, nursing a glass of whisky and thinking about Gemma Fellows and the miracle that had brought
her into the surgery that morning. She had been the shining
spot in his otherwise overworked day, a day that had ended
sadly in the death of an old patient.

His mind switched to Tom Bowles. OK, so Tom had
been eighty, chronically bronchitic and had refused to be
hospitalised when pneumonia had set in. Although well
cared for by his devoted daughter, it had been almost inevitable that he should die as a result of this latest attack
of pneumonia. But the fact that Tom had been old didn't
stop Sam from mourning his death.

As a small boy, he had trotted round after old Tom when
he had worked in the garden at Timbers. It had, he recalled
with a smile, been Tom who had taught him the value of
earthworms in the scheme of things. And now he was dead.

Sam heaved a sigh and comforted himself with the
thought that at least he'd got to his bedside before the end,
and had been able to give the old boy an injection to ease
the rattling, painful breathing.

He took a swig of whisky. The rosy firelight, glinting
on the liquid in the glass, reminded him of Gemma's
gleaming red-brown hair streaming out behind her as he
had watched her racing across the green, chasing her
daughter. There was no doubt that the little girl *was* her
daughter—her bronzed red hair gave her away. He had
spotted them as he was leaving a patient's house and had
been captivated by the sight.

How, he wondered—as he emptied his glass, were the
lovely Gemma and her pretty daughter going to fit into
Blaney St Mary? It was a far cry from a noisy, crowded
London suburb. Would they, and particularly Gemma, set-
tle down? He was confident that little Daisy would—chil-

dren were so adaptable—but her mother? Would she hanker after the bright lights, theatres, clubs?

She had explained that she was divorced, but did her exhusband still figure in her life? Or was there perhaps someone else? Someone who might whisk her away—marry her, perhaps? He felt the stirrings of resentment against the man. Pity if that should happen—they needed a nurse of her calibre in the practice.

Who are you kidding? That's not only why you want her to stay. The thought manifested itself from somewhere so deep within him that it scarcely registered. He swore softly under his breath. She was an attractive woman, but surely he couldn't be—

Impatiently he smothered the thought, put the guard in front of the flickering remains of the log fire and took himself off to bed.

CHAPTER TWO

IT FELT good to be in uniform again. Gemma slipped the
navy blue belt round her waist and fastened the elaborate
silver buckle. She was reminded as she fastened it that it
was the last present her parents had combined to give her
when she had qualified ten years ago. They had parted soon
after.

Theirs had been an unhappy marriage, only held together
for her sake until she had been safely embarked on her
career. But as a small child she had been aware of the
cracks. Their parting had been full of recriminations and
bitterness. Even their love for Gemma had been tainted
towards the end because she had tried to act as a go-
between and had only succeeded in upsetting them both.

They had both moved overseas—her mother to New
Zealand to marry a sheep farmer, her engineer father to
South America with his new partner. They kept in touch,
exchanged letters, rare phone calls, Christmas and birthday
cards, but Gemma no longer felt secure in their love. It
was a tenuous, remote thing. There was no one to give her
a hug of reassurance…they had never even clapped eyes
on their granddaughter.

My poor baby, she thought, no caring grandparents and
an immature father who visits erratically, and is either noisily cheerful or painfully morose. In the latter mood he
would make it plain that he was visiting only out of duty.
Would he still make the effort to visit now that they were
living in Dorset, and would Daisy mind if he didn't?

Probably not. Her reaction, when Gemma had explained

that Daisy might not see so much of him, had been astonishingly calm and untroubled. 'P'raps,' she'd said, in her
grown-up, thoughtful fashion, 'Daddy won't be so cross
when he takes me out if he doesn't see me very much.'

Gemma had felt bound to defend him. 'But Daddy isn't
always cross,' she'd said, 'and when he is, I expect it's
because he's got a lot on his mind. He's a very busy man.'

Daisy had given her one of her clear, frank looks, with
eyes as green as her own, and had said matter-of-factly,
'You're busy, too, but you don't get cross like he does.'

Gemma said, 'Oh, Daisy, I do love you.' And with a
hug and a kiss the conversation had ended.

Reliving that conversation, she thought, It's a miracle
that Daisy is such a happy and normal child. Her heart
swelled with pride in her practical, sensible little daughter.

She snapped out of her reverie. She had heard Daisy go
downstairs a while ago, and when she arrived in the
kitchen a few moments later she found her concentrating
on pouring flakes into a bowl, her small hands precariously
juggling with the large packet.

In a rather sketchy fashion she had dressed in the clothes
that Gemma had put out the night before.

She greeted her mother with a beaming smile out of a
shining, clean face. 'Hurry up, Mummy, I don't want to
be late for school and you musn't be late in your new job.'

Gemma dropped a kiss on the top of her head as she
mechanically rebuttoned her cardigan in the right order,
and then began slicing a banana onto her flakes. 'We won't
be late, love. I can't take you to school before half past
eight—there won't be anybody there.'

Daisy squinted at the clock and her lips moved, mouth-
ing, 'Big hand, little hand.' She crowed suddenly, trium-
phantly. 'The small hand's on the eight and the big hand's
a little way past the twelve, so it's just past eight o'clock.'

'Well done, love.' Gemma gave her another kiss and a hug. 'We've bags of time to get to school.'

Olivia Mallory was behind the reception desk when Gemma arrived at the surgery at ten to nine. The waiting area was about a quarter full.

'The calm before the storm,' said Mrs Mallory with a smile, waving her hand over the waiting room. 'These are the patients by appointment. The hassle begins at half nine when the emergency non-appointment list starts. Sam's taking that this morning so be prepared for a few extra dressings and blood tests over and above the list I've prepared for you.'

She handed Gemma a sheet of paper with several names on it and a sheaf of forms detailing blood tests required. 'Booked in bloods to do from yesterday, and three cervical smears. Knowing that I would be covering Reception in Ellie's absence, they were all due to be done by James or Sam, but now thank God, you're here so, bingo, they're all yours.'

Gemma glanced down the list—one of the bloods was booked for nine, another for nine-fifteen.

'Are any of them here yet?'

'Ben Ashley—he's the elderly chap with the red scarf sitting in the front row. He's down for nine-fifteen, but he's always early. Shirley Lowe's your nine o'clock, but by the time she gets her lot off to work and school she's likely to be late. If I were you I'd see Ben first. I'll explain to Shirley if she turns up while he's still with you—she won't mind.'

She gave Gemma a lovely smile, very like her son's, and pushed a stray, greying lock of hair back from her temple. 'It *is* good to have you aboard, Gemma. Do you think you can find your way round the treatment room?'

Gemma nodded. 'Yes, after the comprehensive tour you gave me yesterday I certainly can, and I can't wait to get cracking.'

'Then good luck on your first morning, my dear. Don't hesitate to call if you need me. I can always leave the desk for a few minutes.'

Ben Ashley was chatty and curious about Gemma's reasons for coming to Blaney St Mary, and was intrigued when she explained that she had inherited Cherry Tree Cottage from her great-aunt.

'Nice lady, Miss Rivers,' he said. 'Always ready to pass the time of day when she was here. Can't think why she wanted to go gallivanting abroad so much.'

Gemma, sidestepping the invitation to gossip, slid a needle smoothly into a prominent brachial vein and said, 'You've got wonderful veins, Mr Ashley, like those of a much younger man.'

Ben looked pleased. 'I'm good for another few years, then. That's what I keep telling the doc, but he insists on me having these blood tests every five minutes.'

'That's to keep track of your diabetes,' Gemma explained.

The old man snorted. 'Diabetes! Had it for years. It don't give me any bother so long as I keep taking the tablets.'

Gemma forbore to say that that was because his medication was being kept under close check and the dosage altered if necessary. She withdrew the needle, released the pressure strap and pressed a gauze pad over the small puncture.

'There we are, all done for another four weeks. See you next month, Mr Ashley.'

Gemma followed Mr Ashley out into the waiting room and called for Mrs Lowe.

'She's just arrived,' said Mrs Mallory, 'but she's gone to the loo. I'll send her in directly.'

There was a tap at the treatment room door a few minutes later and a breathless Shirley Lowe entered, apologising profusely. She was a tall, statuesque, handsome woman with a mop of untidy black hair streaked with grey.

'Sorry about that,' she said. 'Have to keep on spending a penny. Dr Sam thinks I may have an infection, though he's tested my urine and found nothing.'

'Sometimes a urine test doesn't reveal an infection, but a blood test does,' explained Gemma. 'And it may point to a specific bug that's causing the problem.'

'And if it doesn't?' asked Mrs Lowe as Gemma inserted the needle and drew up a syringe full of blood.

'Then we have to look for possible mechanical reasons for the frequency.'

'Could a prolapse—you know, of the womb—cause me to want to keep spending a penny? I do sometimes feel as if I'm bearing down.' Her voice trembled, her cheeks reddened.

Surely she couldn't be shy, thought Gemma as she squirted the blood carefully into several glass vials, ready for despatch to the hospital laboratory. She'd had five children, and seemed a sensible, practical person. Obviously she suspected that she might have a prolapse—so why hadn't she mentioned it to Sam when she saw him yesterday? She seemed almost frightened.

Gently she put the question to Shirley. 'If you suspect that you might have a prolapse, Mrs Lowe, why didn't you mention it to Dr Sam? A simple internal examination would have shown whether you have or not.'

Mrs Lowe blew her nose hard and, surprisingly, tears sparkled in her eyes. 'I know it sounds silly,' she said, 'since I've already got five kids, but I'm only in my early forties. Supposing I want more? I don't want to have my womb taken away. I don't want a—what is it, a hysterectomy?' She gave Gemma a watery smile. 'I suppose you think I'm daft, but I just love having a baby around. The traditional earth mother, my husband calls me.'

So that was what was worrying her. 'But you won't necessarily have to have a hysterectomy,' Gemma explained, 'unless it's a major prolapse, and the fact that you're obviously not in acute pain or discomfort virtually rules that out. A repair to your uterus may be all that is needed.'

Shirley Lowe's face lit up. 'And I could still have another baby?'

'I don't see why not,' said Gemma, but added cautiously, 'Though you would have to be guided by the consultant who did the operation.'

'So what do I do next? How do I go about setting things in motion?'

'Let Dr Sam examine you and confirm that you *have* a prolapse, and he'll make arrangements for you to see a consultant at the hospital. Look, I'll go and have a word with him, see if he can fit you in this morning. I can't promise that he'll be able to see you, but if you don't mind waiting, I'll see what I can do.'

'I don't mind if I have to wait all the morning,' said Shirley joyfully. 'My mum's looking after my youngest, so I've got all the time in the world.'

At the far end of the corridor Sam, his head bent over something he was reading, was coming out of his office as Gemma came out of the treatment room. She hurried toward him.

'Doctor, please, have you got a moment?' she called, her voice sharp.

His head jerked up, his blue eyes blazing brilliantly in

the dim corridor lit only by fanlights over the doors. He snapped to attention and gave her a mock salute. 'Yes, ma'am, and good morning to you, too, Nurse.' There was a dry note in his voice, and his lips quirked at the corners in a half smile.

'Sorry,' she apologised as she halted just in front of him, and belatedly wished him a rather breathy, 'Good morning.'

'Not to worry,' he said, and, taking her firmly by the elbow, he steered her in front of him into his office.

'Didn't mean to sound so peremptory,' she said ruefully. 'I just wanted to make sure of getting hold of you before you called in your next patient.'

He was alert immediately. 'Problem?' he asked.

'Rather a request,' said Gemma, and briefly put him in the picture about Shirley Lowe. 'So I wondered,' she added, when she'd finished explaining, 'if it would be possible for you to see her this morning.'

Pushing back the cuff of his shirt, he glanced at his watch. 'Wheel her in,' he said briskly. 'I'll see her before I start emergency surgery.'

'Oh, that's great, she'll be so pleased.'

Sam shrugged. 'Least I can do to set her mind at rest. Besides, if she has got a prolapsed uterus, the sooner I can get her to see someone the better. There's quite a list for gynaecology patients at the General in Shorehampton, and that's where she'll have to go for surgery.'

Gemma pulled a face. 'Tell me about it. It's dreadful in London—every hospital has a list a mile long.' She half turned away. 'Right, I'll fetch her.'

He touched her arm and smiled his stunning smile. 'And by the way, it's Sam—the ''doctor'' bit's only for the patients.'

Gemma dealt with the other booked-in blood, Martin

Carter, after she'd sent a grateful Shirley Lowe on her way
to see Sam.

Martin was a thin, nervous young man of eighteen who
had been seen by Dr Mallory, senior the evening before.
Dr Mallory suspected that he might be anaemic and had
requested a wide range of tests. Martin's veins, unlike the
elderly Mr Ashley's, were flaccid and difficult to find.

'You'll only feel a small prick,' reassured Gemma, when
she found a possible vein on the back of his hand and
began massaging it to bring the blood to the surface.

'I can't stand needles,' the young man exclaimed, going
almost green and looking as if he might faint.

'Would you like a drink of water?' Gemma asked, and
fetched a glass from the basin in the corner of the room.
Well, at least, she thought, if he's scared of needles, he
can't be shooting up hard drugs.

Ten minutes of reassurance and persuasion, and half a
glass of water later, Martin allowed Gemma to take the
necessary blood. He left a little later, making no secret of
the fact that he was greatly relieved that the ordeal was
over.

Poor chap, thought Gemma as she disposed of the syringe and gloves. He hasn't got a clue. If it is anaemia of
any sort, he's going to have to go through this on a regular
basis.

The rest of the morning fled past. The three booked-in
cervical smears were all straightforward, women having
regular check-ups. However, midmorning Sam phoned on
the internal line to say that he was sending in a patient—
twenty-nine-year-old Marian Talbot—whom he had just
examined. She was having problems with acute vaginal
discharge and dysmenorrhoea.

'These painful periods are rather worrying,' he said. 'I
want to eliminate all possible causes. She's nervous and

you will need the same tact and understanding that you exercised with Shirley Lowe. I want a vaginal swab and a cervical smear. I've sent her back to the waiting room till you're ready for her. Any problems, get back to me.'

Marian Talbot *did* need a lot of reassurance, but she was sensible and realised that every possible reason for her condition had to be checked out. During the conversation that Gemma had with her, whilst preparing her for her swab and smear, it emerged that she was a single mother, with a three-year-old son, Tim.

Gemma's heart went out to her. This was a situation that she could relate to. 'Where's Tim this morning?' she asked.

'He's with my next-door neighbour, Betty Bond. She's getting on a bit, but she's marvellous with him—she's a retired nurse. She babysits for me sometimes. I'm lucky to have a good neighbour like Betty.'

'You certainly are,' said Gemma with feeling, knowing only too well the problem of finding a reliable babysitter. It flitted through her mind that if Marian was going to need hospitalisation or a long period of treatment for her condition, she was going to need her good neighbour more than ever.

It was late morning before she had time to stop for coffee. With a sigh of relief, she made her way along the corridor to the small but comfortable staffroom. With Olivia Mallory still in Reception she had thought that she would be on her own, and experienced a little flutter of pleased surprise to find Sam there, pouring boiling water into a mug.

He looked up as she entered. 'I bet you're dying for a cuppa,' he said. 'Dad and I have given you a busy morning. What would you like, tea or coffee?'

'Coffee, please, black.'

He poured water into a second mug. 'With sugar?' he asked.

Gemma hesitated.

'Go on,' he said. 'Be a devil. You don't have to worry about putting on an ounce or two. Anyway, you'll soon burn it off. You'll be helping me with the kids' clinic this afternoon. It's like bedlam—you'll soon work off a few pounds.'

Gemma laughed. 'Your mother did warn me, but I'm looking forward to it,' she said, as he handed her a steaming mug. 'I like working with kids. If I'd stayed in hospital, I think I'd have specialised in paediatrics.'

'Thank God for that,' he said fervently. 'Val Prentiss, who'd been our practice nurse for years but upped and married and moved away, loved it, but her successor didn't. I think that's one of the reasons she left after only a few weeks. She just didn't fit in. She was a restless soul—she barely touched down before she was swanning off.'

His mouth curved into a sudden smile, and there was a humorous yet tender expression in his eyes. 'Let us hope,' he said with quiet intensity, 'that *our* encounter is not to be as brief.' He bent toward her and clicked his steaming mug to hers.

Gemma lifted her mug to her lips and took a sip of her coffee. What did he mean by a brief encounter? Was there a *double entendre* there? Was he talking just about work, or implying something more personal? She wouldn't have put him down as a flirt, but… Better put him straight.

Her pulse quickened a little, but she replied coolly, 'There's no chance of that, Doctor. I'm *not* a free agent, I'm not going to go swanning off anywhere. I'm committed *solely* to my daughter's welfare—our home is here now, and as long as she is happy, here we mean to stay.' Had she laid it on too thick?

The teasing expression in his eyes changed—they were suddenly serious. He put down his mug, ran his fingers through his hair and frowned. 'I assumed as much. I'm sorry if I appeared to be a touch over-enthusiastic, but we've been without a nurse for a month and I was, in fact, making a feeble attempt at a joke. I've now seen you in action, and so far I like what I've seen. I—*we*—would hate to lose you.' He produced a faint lopsided smile, and added, 'Am I forgiven?'

They'd been without a nurse for a month—no wonder they were pleased to have her. Gemma found herself staring into his brilliant blue eyes. They met hers steadily. They were neither teasing nor patronising, just honest, innocent like a clear blue sky on a summer's day.

She nodded and gave him a slight smile. 'You're forgiven,' she said.

'Good.' He picked up his mug and and gulped down a mouthful, then looked at his watch. 'Hell, I'd better be off. I'm late starting my rounds.' And with a brisk nod, he turned and left the room.

Gemma stared at his retreating back as he disappeared through the doorway. She didn't quite know what to make of him. Were his words as innocent as he'd suggested, or had he been making a pass at her? He'd tried to make it plain that he wasn't but, then, he would, wouldn't he, seeing her reaction? He was a charmer, that was for sure, and clearly at ease with women, but with two sisters, that wasn't surprising.

A little frisson of regret rippled through her that she had stated her position perhaps rather too strongly. Poor man. For a moment he'd looked poleaxed by her vehemence,

the expression in his eyes had changed and there had been
a flicker almost of—*hurt*? Or had she imagined that?

Surely a man of his age and experience wouldn't
be…hurt, simply because she hadn't pulled any punches.
Surely he would appreciate her being straightforward and
making it plain that her world circled Daisy's, and that
anything outside of that just didn't interest her.

She pulled her thoughts up short. Of course he wasn't
hurt. She must have misinterpreted his expression. He
might be a country GP, but a man with his looks and from
a distinguished local family would have any number of
social contacts; he probably had a whole retinue of women
whom he could and did date. Why the hell should he be
in the least affected by a brush-off from a thirty-plus
divorcee with a child?

No reason whatsoever, common sense told her. With a
snort of self-derision, she dismissed all thoughts of Sam
Mallory from her mind and set about topping up her
shelves from the stock cupboards and logging her morning's work.

Sam, too, was deep in thought as he drove away from the
surgery. Why had Gemma been so fiercely defensive, almost as if she thought he was going to pounce on her?
Surely he hadn't been that threatening. All he'd meant to
convey was that by the way she had handled the morning's
patients she'd already proved that she was a good nurse,
and the practice wouldn't want to lose her.

It was a genuine compliment to her professional ability,
an acknowledgement that in a few hours she had succeeded
in fitting in. Purely a compliment to her professional ability. *Really?* said the taunting voice of his subconscious.
'Really,' he muttered firmly, under his breath.

Shirley Lowe had been very impressed. 'I like your new

nurse,' she'd said. 'She was so kind and reassuring when I was trying to explain about being afraid of not being able to have any more babies. She must have thought me absolutely bonkers, but she seemed to understand. I think you've got a cracker of a nurse there, Dr Sam.'

Silently Sam agreed. The word 'cracker' just about described Gemma, he thought, both as a nurse and a woman. Warm and vibrant with her glowing reddish-brown hair and emerald green eyes—and fiercely independent beneath that calm exterior. He liked that, liked it very much.

Not sure where his thoughts were heading, he reined them in sharply. Hey, steady man, you hardly know the woman. Give yourself—give *her*—a bit of space. You know you're a sucker for a pretty woman, even a pretty woman with a six-year-old daughter. Just don't get carried away—there's no hurry, she'll be around for the foreseeable future.

Take things nice and easy, he warned himself as he drew up in front of a small bungalow where he was due to see his first patient. Picking up his surgical case was a signal to switch into professional mode as he made his way up the short garden path. He was all geared to deal with old Mrs Smith's chronic emphysema.

Gemma was finding the euphemistically named toddlers' clinic, which included crawlers of ten months, just as hectic as she had been warned it would be, but she was loving every minute of it.

She had wondered after the conversation she'd had with Sam whether working together might be a bit awkward— but it wasn't. Even before the session had started, any awkwardness that there might have been had been broken when he'd handed her a pink plastic Teletubby apron and, rolling up his shirt sleeves, donned one himself.

Gemma burst out laughing at the spectacle of his tall, lean figure covered in the colourful pinny that barely reached the top of his thighs.

'Don't mock, Nurse,' he said with pretended severity. 'Out of long experience I've learned only too well the hazards of dealing with our smaller customers. There's always something coming out of one end or the other. And as a by-product, of course, my pinny does help keep them amused and relaxed.

And he was dead right, she thought when towards the end of the session he was examining a tiny infant of eleven months, his narrow, lean hands moving gently over the small body. The baby was fascinated by the shiny plastic, reaching out to touch the garish images as Sam bent over him.

Sam smiled across at the young mother who was looking anxious.

'Barry's doing fine, Jessie,' he said. 'He's very slightly underweight, but that's partly because he's such an active baby. He's not undernourished, there's nothing to worry about, everything's in good working order and ticking over fine.' As if to emphasise the point, Barry jerked and shot out a jet of urine straight at Sam's plastic-covered front.

The baby gurgled, the young mother giggled nervously and apologised. Gemma grinned and handed Sam a tissue.

'There, Jessie,' he said, with a deep throaty chuckle as he mopped himself off. 'As I said, nothing wrong with any of his working parts.' He picked the baby up and handed him to his mother. 'You can get him dressed now, and we'll see him in four weeks' time, unless you're worried about anything before then.'

Sam grinned at Gemma after Jessie and baby Barry had left the cubicle. 'What did I tell you?' he said. 'To be prepared is to be forearmed. Without my precious pinny, I'd be stinking to high heaven before the session finished.'

Gemma inclined her head. 'I bow to your superior wisdom,' she said with a laugh as she left the cubicle and went out to usher in the next and last patient.

This was a pretty little girl of fourteen months, Patsy Jordan, who'd recently had a repair made to a cleft palate. The repair had been successful, but Sam was keeping an eye on her to assess that the slight deafness associated with the damaged palate was not deteriorating. He examined both her ears whilst she sat on her mother's lap, and gave her several simple sound tests. He referred to a note that he'd made on her last visit, then turned to her mother.

'I think, Maeve, we'd better get Patsy seen by the paediatric specialist she was with in Shorehampton General. Nothing dramatic, but I think there's a slight deterioration which could affect her now that she's just started to talk. I'll write and fix something up. You should hear from the hospital quite soon.'

'Will she have to wear a hearing aid?' Mrs Jordan's voice wavered.

Sam said gently, 'That'll be for Dr Rayburn to decide, but better a hearing aid than that Patsy's growing vocabulary should be curtailed because she doesn't hear properly. Makes sense, doesn't it?' He tickled the little girl under her chin and she gurgled happily, then wriggled down off her mother's lap and made a tottering beeline for the gap in the cubicle curtains.

Gemma dived after her and swung her up above her head. Patsy crowed with delight. Gemma planted a noisy kiss on the soft cheek and Patsy bubbled with laughter.

'She's a lovely little girl,' Gemma said as she handed her back to her mother. 'And if she does need to have a deaf aid, as Dr Sam thinks she might, they're very discreet these days, and Patsy's curls will hide it. No one will ever know that she's wearing one.'

'Thanks for the back-up. That was a neat endorsement of what I told her,' Sam said a few minutes later when Patsy and her mother had left. 'You're very good at this reassuring lark.' He smiled and glanced at his watch, nestling against the fine, golden, silky hairs at his wrist. He looked up and his eyes met Gemma's. 'It's nearly three—time you went off to meet Daisy from school.'

Gemma looked startled. 'Oh, no! I hadn't realised.' She waved a hand round the toy-strewn waiting room. 'Look, Sam, would it be all right if I fetch Daisy and come back to tidy up? She won't be a nuisance, I promise. She won't go wandering about anywhere.'

'I'm sure she wouldn't, and you must bring her over some time to meet us and let her see where you work, but not today. You've had a full first day, so scoot. I'll tidy up.'

Gemma pulled off her apron. 'If you're sure. Next week I'll arrange to pick Daisy up a little later—apparently there's always someone there till at least half past three.'

Sam smiled. 'You do that. Meanwhile, go, woman, go.'

'Bless you.' She turned and made for the door.

As she reached it, he called, 'And, Gemma, thanks for your help. We make a good team.'

CHAPTER THREE

THOSE last words that Sam had spoken—'We make a good team'—came into Gemma's mind many times over the next couple of days. They *were* a good team. They had worked together smoothly and efficiently, dovetailing in with each other in the toddlers' clinic. There had been no hitches, the atmosphere had been great and the toddlers and their mothers had responded.

Over those two busy days she also felt that she had become part of the practice team as a whole, working harmoniously with both Dr Mallory senior and his lovely wife. They made her so welcome that she already felt that she belonged.

She just hoped and prayed that Ellie Peterson, the receptionist, who, according to Sam, had been with them for yonks, and who was due to return on Friday, would accept her as readily as the Mallorys had. If she didn't, she thought, butterflies fluttering round in her stomach, the situation could be turned on its head. Both Sam and his parents obviously thought the world of Ellie and would value her opinion as a loyal and trusted employee.

Ellie, a pretty, petite woman with a creamy complexion, huge, spaniel-like brown eyes and shining black hair swept neatly back into a chignon, welcomed her with a rather reserved but genuine smile when she arrived for duty just before nine on Friday morning.

'You're Gemma, of course,' she said, leaning across the reception desk to shake hands. 'I'm Ellie. Mrs M.'s been telling me what a tower of strength you've been over the last few days whilst I've been laid low. I'm so glad. The Mallorys are such a lovely family and work like Trojans to keep the practice functioning to their high standards.'

'Yes, I can see that,' said Gemma as she shook Ellie's hand. 'They've been so kind to me, made me feel very welcome.'

Ellie nodded. 'We're one small happy family here, and you'll be one of the family in no time. If Mrs M. approves of you, you're in.'

Gemma laughed. 'Don't the two doctors have any say in the matter? Suppose they disagree?' She still found the thought of the two tall, lean, clever men being bossed by the cuddly Mrs Mallory laughable, though she had seen it happen on her first day.

Ellie chuckled. 'They wouldn't dare,' she said. 'They trust her instinct, and so do I. I've never known it to be wrong, and she's given you the OK, so welcome to Blaney St Mary, Gemma.'

'Thanks. Now I'd better get stuck in—what have you got for me?'

'Quite a list—it's weight-watchers, or general fitness and exercise day, as Sam prefers to call it. He's always at pains to explain that having too much cholesterol and being over-weight are not the same thing—you can be fat outside and thin on the inside. It's being generally fit that matters, and that applies to both the over- and the underweights. Here are their record cards and diet sheets.'

Ellie handed Gemma a pile of cards. 'With a few exceptions, most of the people you will see this morning are the oldies, or mums at home with young children. There's an evening session for people who are at work, but Mrs M. or one of the doctors will deal with them.'

Gemma raised her eyebrows. 'Wow, there are quite a

few. Surely there can't be that many people in the village with weight problems?'

'It's bus day. They come in from the surrounding hamlets and smaller villages,' Ellie explained, and added, her eyes twinkling, 'and even here in the wilds of Dorset, we're familiar with the current thinking on health and diet—preventing heart disease and so on. Blame it on television. Now, if…'

Her voice trailed off as the door flew open and a man staggered in, carrying a boy who looked to be about six. Blood was pouring down the boy's face from a gash on his forehead. 'Quick, help me,' the man gasped. 'It's my boy, Brian, he's been cut, he ran into the greenhouse door.'

The boy lay in his arms, limp and apparently unconscious.

'Bring him through here,' said Gemma briskly, leading the way to the treatment room. She called over her shoulder, 'Ellie, get one of the doctors.' Ellie was picking up the phone even as she spoke.

'Put Brian on the couch,' Gemma directed the distraught man.

She grabbed a handful of tissues from the dressings trolley and mopped up some of the blood, which was obliterating one side of the child's face, praying that his eye had not been injured. With glass you never knew. It appeared undamaged. She heaved a silent sigh of relief and with a fresh handful of tissues continued to wipe away more of the blood.

Sam arrived as the boy moaned and began to come to. The bleeding was easing off, no longer pouring, though still oozing freely.

Brian suddenly opened his eyes wide and stared at Sam. He looked puzzled, but both his pupils were normal and equal, Gemma and Sam noted with relief. They were both aware that a skull fracture was always a possibility with a head wound, especially if a patient was unconscious.

'Looks like he fainted with shock,' Sam murmured, as he pulled on plastic gloves. He bent over the boy. 'Brian, it's Dr Sam—can you hear me?'

They heard a whispery, 'Yes.'

'You've hurt yourself,' Sam said gently. 'Daddy's brought you to the surgery. I'm just going to look at this cut you've got on your head.'

Brian whimpered. 'Daddy.'

His father took his hand. 'It's all right, son, I'm here.' He looked at Sam and pleaded in a low, shaky voice, 'He's going to be all right, isn't he? He's bleeding so badly.'

Sam gave him a quick glancing smile. 'Head wounds do bleed profusely, Hugh, even quite small ones. I'll be able to tell you more when I've cleaned him up.' He turned to Gemma. 'Let's have some gauze swabs and forceps, please, Nurse.'

Gemma, anticipating his request, had a receiver, several forceps and a bowl full of swabs and antiseptic at the ready.

With infinite care, in case there were slivers of glass embedded in the damaged tissue, Sam swabbed the wound. Brian whimpered occasionally as he worked, but for the most part seemed reassured by Sam's soft voice and gentle fingers.

'Looks clean,' he muttered after a few moments, dropping the blood-soaked swabs into a receiver that Gemma placed beside him. She handed him another pair of forceps loaded with a dry swab, and he applied a little pressure to the open wound to stem the bleeding. With his other thumb and forefinger, he experimentally eased the two edges of the cut together.

'I think we can get away without stitching this,' he said

with a grunt of satisfaction. 'It isn't as deep as we thought at first. So what I'm going to do, Hugh,' he explained to the anxiously hovering father, 'is hold the wound together with fine strips of special adhesive tape.'

He smiled down at Brian, squeezed his small shoulder and said softly, 'Brian, you heard what I was telling Daddy. We're going to mend this cut by pulling the edges of it together. Before I do that I'll put something on your head to make it numb and cold so you won't feel anything very much. Do you understand old chap?'

'Yes.' Then, predictably, he went on in a quavery voice, 'But it won't hurt, will it?'

Sam said evenly, 'It shouldn't do, but it might feel a bit sore so we'll give you a tablet to swallow to help that. But it won't take too long to do—it'll soon be over. Now, are you ready, Brian? Shall we make a start?'

Brian whispered, 'Yes.' He closed his eyes.

While Sam had been talking, Gemma had laid up the dressings trolley with antiseptic and an anaesthetising agent, scissors, gauze swabs, forceps and narrow-strip adhesive dressing tape and a medicine measure containing a junior aspirin.

Brian was given the aspirin, and the local anaesthetic was applied to his forehead and given a few minutes to take effect. Then Sam got to work. Quickly and evenly, keeping the two edges of the wound in alignment, he applied, in criss-cross fashion, the narrow strips of tape that Gemma handed to him.

It was as neat a bit of 'stitching' as she had seen, she thought. 'Nice work,' she murmured, as she covered the injured area with a window dressing so that they could keep an eye on the wound whilst it was healing.

'Thanks.' Sam smiled down at Brian. 'All done, old chap, you were very brave.' He gave the boy a conspiratorial wink. 'I think you deserve something from the sweetie jar—let's see what Nurse can conjure up for you.'

For an instant, his blue eyes, full of warmth and humour, caught Gemma's in a twinkling sideways glance, and she was acutely aware of the sheer masculine charm of the man behind the caring doctor. The glance caught and held briefly and she felt a little dart of pleasure shafting through her and momentarily found herself smiling into his laughing eyes.

The moment passed—it might never have happened. Smoothly transferring her smile to Brian, Gemma reached for the sweetie jar.

While Brian was choosing a brightly coloured lolly, Sam gave Hugh instructions about keeping the boy quiet and warm for the rest of the day. 'And call me at once,' he added, 'if he is sick or there is any change in him that worries you. And give him plenty of fruit juice to drink. Bring him back the day after tomorrow so that I can see how his wound's progressing.'

The rest of the morning flew past, as Gemma weighed and in some cases measured height, advised and reassured. Most of the patients were fighting to lose a few—or many—pounds, but one or two were underweight. Ralph Wyman, forty-eight, was one such patient.

Gemma checked his notes, before calling him in to the treatment room. He was making a long, slow recovery from stomach cancer. The affected part of his stomach had been successfully surgically removed, and he had just completed a course of chemotherapy. He was a writer, a widower and lived alone in an isolated cottage a couple of miles outside the village. Recently he had suffered several small fits, had been diagnosed as mildly epileptic and had

had his driving licence withdrawn, hopefully only temporarily till his epilepsy was under control.

'This patient is *seriously* underweight,' Sam had written
rather despairingly. 'Please encourage him to eat *anything*
that he fancies, particularly food high in carbohydrates and
proteins. And advise to eat little and often...this is one
patient who can afford to snack between meals. I can't
seem to get through to him.'

That, thought Gemma, was surprising. It was difficult to
imagine Sam at a loss with a patient, but for some reason
he apparently didn't gel with Ralph Wyman. Well, even a
doctor as good as Sam Mallory can't win them all, she
thought.

She went to the door of the waiting room and called for
Mr Wyman, and watched as a tall, thin beanstalk of a man
uncoiled himself from his chair and loped tiredly across
the room.

He was thin to the point of gauntness, his cheeks sunken,
his skin unhealthily pale and dry, his grey hair thinning at
the temples. He walked with a stoop, but he produced a
rather sweet, weary smile when Gemma invited him to sit
down. 'I suppose,' he said wryly, 'that you're going to add
your voice to the others and lecture me about eating.'

Gemma grinned. 'That comes within my remit,' she acknowledged gently, 'but I don't think I really need to, do
I? *You* know that you're bordering on the edge of malnu-
trition and making a mockery of the successful operation
to remove the growth. You're not apparently suffering
from nausea, or having pain when eating—so why don't
you eat, Mr Wyman?'

'Never been much interested in food and I forget when
I'm writing.'

'And by the time you remember, you're past it—right?'

'Spot on, Nurse. My wife used to keep me tanked up,

but…' A shadow passed over his face, and it looked suddenly very bleak.

Gemma's heart gave a jerk of sympathy but, keeping her voice even, she asked, 'How long since your wife died?'

'Three years—seems like yesterday. Thought by moving here away from our circle of well-meaning friends I'd somehow come to terms with it, but I haven't so far.'

'But you didn't bargain on getting ill yourself, did you?'

He pulled a face. 'No, that's for sure.'

'Do you manage for yourself, or have somebody in to clean for you?'

'A Mrs Fairbody descends on me three times a week.' One side of his mouth quirked into a lopsided grin. 'And she is,' he said.

'Is what?' frowned Gemma. 'You've lost me.'

'A fair body…what my mother used to call, a fine figure of a woman.' His weary grey eyes brightened for a moment.

Gemma smiled her appreciation. Thank God he'd managed to hang onto a sense of humour. 'Nice one,' she said. 'Now does she do, or would she do any cooking for you?'

'Been desperate to get her hands on my pots and pans since day one.'

'Then let her loose in your kitchen. Let her spoil you. Tell her you're to have *small*, nourishing dishes at frequent intervals to build you up. Cauliflower cheese, egg custard, stewed fruit, chicken soup, pasta dishes—she'll know what to do, she'll fill up your freezer in no time. You're much more likely to eat if there's something ready to hand.'

Ralph Wyman stared at her in silence for a moment, then drew in a deep breath. 'Is that it?' he said. 'Aren't you going to read me the riot act about making myself eat, and so on?'

She shook her head. Some instinct told her that the time for pussyfooting around with this sad, intelligent man was past. Somehow she had to get through to his self-respect, his sense of self-worth. He may not care if he lived or died—but she did. The time for begging for his co-operation was over.

'What's the point, Mr Wyman? You don't need me to tell you what you should do. If you want to survive, you've got to make yourself eat, or you'll be back in hospital on drip feeds, and that would be a waste of everyone's time and money and set you back months. There isn't any other answer—your cure lies in your own hands.'

His exhausted grey eyes searched her face. 'You pretend to be hard, Nurse, but you really care, don't you?' He stood up, wafer-thin, and leaned across the narrow desk where Gemma did her paperwork. 'At a guess,' he said softly, 'I'd say you weren't a stranger to a share of life's traumas.' He straightened up, squaring his shoulders. 'Right. I take note of what you've said. Thanks for being honest with me.'

He went quietly out of the door, closing it softly behind him.

Gemma gazed at it, deep in thought. Had she been right to take a tough line with the frail, unhappy man who had just passed through it? Should she have tried to coax him a little more, rather than pass the buck to him? Had she stepped out of line, exceeded her brief? Would Sam approve of what she had done?

The door opened slowly and Sam's handsome, corn-bright head appeared round it. 'I did knock,' he said apologetically, his eyes twinkling.

Gemma felt a little ripple of pleasure trickle through her. It *was* good to see him after the grey, sick, sad Ralph Wyman. He glowed with health and positively lit up the

room. 'Sorry, didn't hear you. Please, come in. I was thinking about poor Mr Wyman.'

'Poor Mr Wyman is why I'm here,' said Sam. 'I saw
him leave, wondered what you made of him. He's on my
conscience. I feel that we should be doing more for him.
What do you think, Gemma?' He perched himself on a
corner of the desk and his eyes, grave now, searched her
face intently, trying to read what was there.

She met his gaze frankly. 'I think that he hasn't made
up his mind whether he wants to live or die, and until he
does there's precious little you or anyone can do for him.'

'You mean, he doesn't care because he is still grieving
for his late wife?'

'Yes.'

'Early on I tried to get him to talk about it, but he's an
intensely private person. Did you manage to get anything
out of him?'

'Just the fact that he misses her dreadfully.'

'Did he actually admit to that?'

'Yes.'

'Well, that's something. He just clammed up on me,
virtually told me to mind my own business. Any luck on
the eating front?'

'I'm afraid I got rather tough with him—told him it was
up to him to play ball with us, otherwise his op and sub-
sequent treatment had been a waste of time. Whether he
will or not, remains to be seen. He seemed to be grateful,
for what he called, my honesty, but whether it'll have the
desired effect I don't know.' She felt her cheeks colour
faintly. 'I'm so sorry if I've pushed him too far. I should
have consulted with you first—I may have done him more
harm than good.'

Sam shook his head. 'No,' he said decisively. 'You
looked at him with new eyes and made a clinical judge-

ment. It may have been just what he needed, to be forced to look at himself. Nothing else was working, there is nothing to lose.' He slid off the desk and smiled down at her. 'I trust your judgement implicitly. I place great store by professional instinct backed up by sound knowledge and, quite properly, you acted on yours.'

He crossed the room, but paused at the door. He dropped his voice a notch, and asked rather throatily, 'So, how do you feel at the end of your first week, Gemma—any regrets about joining us?' He raised one eyebrow in a humorous question. A faint smile hovered round his wide, generous mouth.

'None whatsoever,' she replied without hesitation. 'I feel as if I've worked here for years, not barely a week. I feel that I...'

'Belong?' he suggested softly, his eyes holding hers across the width of the room.

She stared into their brilliant blue depths. 'Yes,' she breathed.

Sam gave her a dazzling smile. 'God bless your great aunt Marjorie for bringing you to Blaney St Mary,' he said.

Some timbre in his voice sent a pulse beating madly in her throat. She fought to ignore it, got her breathing under control and smiled back. 'Amen to that,' she said firmly. 'It's the best thing that ever happened to Daisy and me.' Daisy! The beating pulse in her throat, slowed, returned to normal. 'We *both*,' she added, with emphasis, 'feel as if we belong.'

Amusement flared in his eyes—the emphasis on both, hadn't been lost on him. 'Ah, yes,' he murmured, 'Daisy! We've yet to meet Daisy. Why don't you bring her over to say hello after school—I've a gap between surgeries this afternoon. And Mum comes over on a Friday to help Ellie with the week's paperwork, and even Dad may be back from his house calls so she can give us all the once-over.'

'Thank you, she'd like that very much. She's an awfully curious child and full of questions about everything and everyone. I have to give her a blow-by-blow account of all that's happened every day.' She frowned. 'Oh, Lord, does that make her sound as if she's a precocious little monster?'

He laughed. 'Not at all. It sounds as if she's an intelligent, loving little girl who likes to keep tabs on her mum.' He looked at his watch. 'Time I was off—see you later.'

With a half salute, half wave, he whisked himself out of the door and she listened as his long, loping footsteps receded down the corridor.

The rest of the morning passed without incident. Two of her overweight ladies were jubilant at having lost a few pounds, and a bluff, middle-aged gentleman waiting for a hip replacement reached his goal weight and was over the moon.

'At last, to be free of this pain will be a miracle,' he said.

At lunchtime, when the surgery closed for forty-five minutes, Gemma dashed over to the cottage for a snack and to do a bit of tidying up, but returned in time to have a coffee with Ellie before they opened up again. Ellie lived in a small village some miles away and didn't go home to lunch but had a sandwich in the staffroom.

'I have a standing invitation to the Mallorys for lunch but I only occasionally take advantage of it,' she explained with a diffident smile. 'Feel they don't always want me hanging around.'

'Very sensible of you,' agreed Gemma. She took a sip of coffee. 'I suppose your husband doesn't get home for lunch very often—he's something to do with farming, isn't he?'

To Gemma's surprise, the expression on Ellie's gentle face hardened. 'He's out all hours. He deals with farm machinery selling and repairing.' She sounded bitter and resentful and a faint wash of colour stained her pale cheeks. 'I think he thinks more about his beastly tractors than he does about me,' she added with a bleak little laugh.

Not knowing what to say, Gemma remained silent and stared down into her mug. She was totally unprepared for this outburst.

Ellie took a slurp of coffee. 'Sorry, not fair to you, shooting off like that,' she said. 'Didn't mean to embarrass you…unforgivable of me. It's just that sometimes it gets on top of me. He seems so wrapped up in his bloody machinery we just never seem to have time to talk any more. I have the feeling that he's avoiding me.'

Tell me about it, Gemma felt like saying, remembering the last year or so of her marriage to Neil and the fabrications he had made for getting home late.

Instead, she said gently, 'Men and their machines, they're like little boys, aren't they? And most of them are not good at talking, discussing their emotions. Perhaps he would like to talk but doesn't know how to begin.'

'Perhaps.' Ellie clearly didn't believe it for one minute. She pinned a smile on her face and made an obvious effort to pull herself together. 'Now, spill the beans about yourself,' she said. 'Mrs M. tells me that you have a little girl— lucky you.'

'Yes, Daisy, she's six, and I think she's God's gift to the world, but, then, I'm prejudiced. You'll meet her this afternoon. Sam kindly suggested that I bring her in and give her a guided tour so that she's familiar with where I work. He thinks it will be reassuring for her.'

To Gemma's surprise, Ellie blushed furiously and her eyes brightened. 'How like Sam to think of something like that,' she said. 'He's marvellous with children, he's got a way with them.'

'Yes, he certainly has. It was obvious when we did the toddlers' clinic that he has an affinity with children.'

'I think perhaps it's because he is the oldest in the family. According to Mrs M., he was always good with his younger brother and sisters but, then, he's a rather special sort of man, don't you think?' Ellie's voice was full of admiration—and something more besides?

Good Lord, I believe she fancies him, Gemma thought. I wonder if he realises it? I wonder if that's why she and her husband...

Ellie repeated, 'Well, don't you think he's rather special? All women do.' She sounded slightly aggressive.

Tread warily, thought Gemma, and said carefully. 'I don't really know him well enough to comment—after all, I've been here barely a week—but from what I've seen, I think all three Mallorys are rather special.'

Ellie said brightly. 'Yes of course, they are.' But Gemma felt that she had expected a more fulsome answer in praise of Sam, or was the mild-mannered receptionist suspicious of her?

She looked at her watch and with an inward sigh of relief realised that there was no further chance to pursue the subject as it was a quarter to two and time to open for afternoon surgery.

The Friday afternoon surgery was mainly taken up with the small diabetic clinic. During the course of the afternoon Sam sent several patients through to Gemma in the treatment room to be weighed and have urine tests, and in two cases to have dressings renewed to typical slow-healing ulcers—in one case on the toes, in the other on the shin.

She also had to book in some patients to come back on Monday for blood tests. These couldn't be done in the afternoon because they had to be despatched to Shillingbury Cottage Hospital, ten miles away, for laboratory examination before twelve each day.

Sam rang through just after half past two to say that he was sending in the last patient. She was a newly married, newly diagnosed, young diabetic who had recently moved into the area. He wanted her weighed and measured and booked in for a blood test on Monday.

'Here's another chance for you to do your Florence Nightingale bit, Gemma,' he said. 'The poor girl needs bags of reassurance and TLC. Her name's Cathy Burns, and she's worried that having diabetes will stop her having a baby. Do confirm what what I've told her, that there's no reason why she shouldn't have a healthy baby as long as she sticks to her diet and medication and has regular check-ups.'

'Will do,' said Gemma, impressed yet again by the deeply personal interest he took in his patients.

But when Cathy left twenty minutes later, she was still only partially convinced. Gemma had given her some leaflets about diabetes in pregnancy for her and her husband to read, and had promised that when Cathy came back on Monday for her blood test they would go into the subject in greater depth.

Somehow she must convince Cathy that generally it was safe for a diabetic to have a baby, provided she obeyed all the rules, but quite how she was going to do this she wasn't yet sure. Perhaps there was another young diabetic mother in the practice catchment area with whom she could put Cathy in touch. She would ask Sam and Dr Mallory senior if either of them had a patient who fitted that category.

A few minutes later, pondering on this possibility, she

sped up the green to collect Daisy from school and put her in the picture about visiting the surgery.

The visit, though short, had been a great success, Gemma reflected, lying in bed that night waiting for sleep to come. Daisy had been her usual happy, outgoing self, neither pushy nor shy, shaking hands composedly with Mrs M. and Ellie in Reception and later with both the doctors. All of them, experienced professionals that they were, had welcomed her without talking down to her.

Except for the children's corner in the waiting area with its brightly coloured toys and books, there wasn't much to interest a six-year-old girl. But Daisy had jumped at Sam's suggestion that she might like to see the treatment room where her mother worked most of the time. She had been impressed by the gleaming glass and chrome cupboards and dressings trolley, and, curious as ever, had wanted to know what various receptacles and instruments were called, repeating the names after Gemma.

The highlight of the afternoon, however, was when Sam offered her the sweetie jar. He explained that the sweets were kept to offer children who had been brave when they'd had to have something not very pleasant done to them to make them better.

About to dip her chubby hand into the jar, she hesitated and, ever practical, said slowly, 'But I haven't been brave, so is it all right for me to have one?'

Smiling, Sam said, 'It certainly is, Daisy. Let us say that it is because it is the first time you have come to visit— it's a welcome to Blaney St Mary.'

Daisy beamed. 'OK,' she said, and, her green eyes sparkling, pulled out a bright red lolly.

All in all, thought Gemma drowsily, it had been an interesting day to end her first week—meeting Ellie, little Brian with the cut on his forehead, sad, thin Ralph Wyman, Cathy Burns, diabetic, afraid to have a baby…must try and help her…

CHAPTER FOUR

GEMMA surfaced on Saturday morning when Daisy bounced into bed beside her. She opened sleep-bleared eyes and groaned as her daughter burrowed into her and gave her a smacking kiss on the cheek. She gave her a fumbling kiss in return and stroked back the tangle of curls from round the happy little face.

'Hello, darling,' she mumbled, squinting over Daisy's head at the clock—nearly eight. She'd had a wonderful night.

'Hello, Mummy. My room's full of sunshine—why isn't yours?'

First question of the day, thought Gemma. 'Because your room faces east and the sun rises in the east and the earth turns to meet it, and mine faces the opposite direction, west, so I get the evening sunshine,' she explained. 'But if you pull back the curtains, love, we can look at the blue sky, watch the clouds sail by and have a cuddle while we plan what we're going to do for the day.'

'Scrumptious,' crowed Daisy, hopping off the bed and over to the window which overlooked the green. She pulled back the chintzy curtains and bright daylight filled the room. Birdsong filtered up from the front garden through the open casement.

Daisy bounded back onto the bed and curved herself against Gemma. She exhaled a huge sigh of contentment. 'Isn't it funny, Mummy?' she said. 'I like school very much, but I like it when I'm home with you, too, just you and me.'

53

Gemma felt a warm glow in the pit of her stomach, not just caused by her daughter's neat round bottom which was pushed into it. 'Poppet,' she said, kissing the top of Daisy's head, 'you have the knack of saying the right thing at the right time.'

'What's a knack?' asked Daisy.

To the best of her ability, Gemma explained what a knack was.

Daisy pondered this a moment. 'So it's a nice thing,' she said at last dismissively. She gave a wriggle of excitement. 'So what are we going to do today, Mummy?'

'I thought we'd go into Shillingbourne and explore and do some shopping. With summer on the way, you can do with some new shorts and sandals—you've outgrown last year's.'

Daisy shot up in bed and turned round to look down on Gemma, her face shining. 'Can I choose, Mummy, please, please? I know exactly what sandals I want—they must be red.'

'We'll have to see what we can get, love. There aren't as many shops as there are in London. Shillingbourne's a country market town.'

They had a wonderful day in Shillingbourne, which turned out to be much larger than Gemma had expected and full of graceful old Regency buildings. There were loads of shops, ranging from the high class and elegant to the cheap and cheerful. They found Daisy's red, fashionably chunky sandals in the children's department of Browns, a sort of local equivalent of Harrods. The sandals were pricey, but Gemma didn't mind. They were beautifully made and fitted well, with sensible room for growth.

The shorts, together with a couple of jazzy T-shirts, were purchased from a stall in the market. They were so cheap that Gemma, egged on by Daisy who thought they were 'scrumptious'—apparently the present *in* word in the village school—went wild and bought herself amber drop earrings from the next-door stall. She felt terribly extravagant, but comforted herself with the thought that it was in celebration of their first week in Blaney St Mary.

Just like Daisy's lollipop, she thought, recalling Sam smilingly offering Daisy the sweetie jar in the surgery and explaining that it was by way of being a welcome-to-the-village present. It was a nonsensical, silly thought, and gone in a flash.

They lunched in the sunny garden of an ancient pub tucked away off the high street. After lunch they located the library, joined immediately and chose several books each from the packed shelves. Then they went in search of the leisure centre and registered as members of the adults' and children's swimming clubs.

The leisure centre was surprisingly well equipped. Daisy, who had been swimming since she was three, was to be allowed access to the junior pool.

Their last port of call, before leaving Shillingbourne, was to the superstore on the outskirts of the town. Gemma, who had so far only shopped at the village post office stores, stocked up on the basics to fill her larder and fridge-freezer.

In the magazine section they found a Walt Disney video on special offer which Daisy had been coveting for weeks. Still feeling in a celebratory mood, Gemma agreed to buy the cartoon on condition that Daisy contributed a minuscule amount of her pocket money toward the purchase.

Knowing that it was one of her mother's few house rules that she use her pocket money for just such luxuries, Daisy joyfully consented.

Both happy and content, they drove home through the

winding lanes and steep hills of Dorset in high good humour. They sang enthusiastically—'Twinkle, twinkle little star' and a whole host of nursery rhymes and children's hymns, which were great favourites and still apparently being sung in the village school.

They had just finished singing 'All things bright and beautiful' when they drew up outside Cherry Tree Cottage. To their surprise, Miss Heinman, their next-door neighbour, was limping—badly limping—down the garden path, stick in one hand and clinging onto the cobbled wall between the cottages with the other. She had obviously come from their front door.

She was as white as a sheet and her face was contorted with pain. She looked as if she was about to collapse at any moment.

Gemma was out of the car in a flash and racing over the narrow strip of pavement and up the garden path, reaching the elderly woman just as she began slipping to the ground. She lowered her gently the last few inches and propped her against the wall.

Miss Heinman fluttered open her eyes. 'Thank goodness you've come,' she murmured. 'I've hurt my leg… knee…ankle…I thought…you being a nurse, but I don't want to be a nuisance.'

'You're not a nuisance. I'm sorry I wasn't in. Don't worry, we'll soon get you sorted out.' Gemma turned to Daisy, who had followed her out of the car, and handed her the the bunch of keys that she'd snatched from the ignition. 'Open the front door, love, and then go next door and ask Mr Roberts if he'll bring round Mrs Roberts's wheelchair and help me get Miss Heinman into the house.'

Round-eyed but composed, Daisy took the keys and did as she had been bade. Mr Roberts arrived quickly with the wheelchair, but it took some time for them to get Miss

Heinman into the cottage, with Mr Roberts pushing the chair and Gemma supporting the injured leg to ensure that it didn't suffer further damage.

Once inside the sitting room they transferred Rose—as Mr Roberts addressed Miss Heinman—to Gemma's sofa, with her swollen, twisted leg, on cushions. Seeing that she was reasonably comfortable, Mr Roberts left to attend to his invalid wife, who, he explained, got agitated if left on her own. He took the chair with him but promised to bring it back again if it was needed.

'That Dorothy Roberts makes a fool out of Jim,' said Miss Heinman in a quivery but disgusted voice when he had gone. 'She's a whiner—he waits on her hand and foot.' She winced as Gemma carefully removed the elderly lady's torn stocking and gently examined her leg. 'Not that I can talk, putting you to all this trouble. So what's the damage, Nurse? Will I be able to walk on it soon?'

'Not for a day or so at least, and that's if it turns out to be simply a twisted knee and a sprained ankle. If it's anything worse—'

Miss Heinman interrupted, 'Oh, my dear, do you think it might be worse? How infuriating.' Her colour was improving now that she was off her leg, and she seemed more annoyed than frightened at the prospect of more serious injury.

Gemma said gently, 'I honestly don't know. You may need to have an X-ray to establish the extent of the damage. I'm going to phone the surgery and ask one of the doctors to come and have a look at it. Meanwhile...' She turned to Daisy who was standing quietly by, watching what was going on with keen interest. 'If you would fetch some towels from the linen cupboard, love, and then fetch the freezer bag from the car, we'll give Miss Heinman the ice treatment.'

'What's that when it's at home?' asked Miss Heinman as Daisy went bustling importantly off on her errand, clearly thrilled to be helping.

Gemma explained that it meant packing bags of frozen vegetables or ice cubes round the knee and ankle joints to reduce the swelling.

In no time at all Daisy was back with the towels, and while Gemma spread them on the cushions beneath the injured leg she bustled out to the car and fetched the freezer bag.

The next ten minutes were busy ones. Gemma phoned the surgery and left a message on the answerphone to be switched through to whichever doctor was on duty. She then packed frozen peas and beans round the distorted knee, and ice scrapings from the freezer, collected by Daisy in plastic bags, round the inflamed, swollen ankle.

'I'd like to offer you tea,' she explained to Miss Heinman, 'but it's safer not to, just in case there's something broken and you have to have an anaesthetic. I don't think that's the case, but we'll have to wait for the doctor to give his verdict. But I can give you an ice cube to suck if your mouth is very dry.'

'Thank you, but I'll live,' said Miss Heinman in a rather caustic tone. 'Now, tell me—'

The door bell rang. Gemma said, 'I guess that's the doctor. Daisy, love, you go and let him in.' But before Daisy, who was usually like greased lightning, could move, Sam Mallory was filling the sitting-room doorway, tall and lean and smiling his wide, warm smile.

'Front door was on the latch,' he said, 'so I let myself in.'

Gemma felt her heart do a curious little flip and found herself returning his smile with a wide one of her own. *Déjà vu*, she thought. It was a repeat of what had happened yesterday when he had come into the treatment room, hard on the heels of poor, sick Ralph Wyman. Now, as then, his thick thatch of corn-coloured hair gleamed and his blue eyes dazzled, and he exuded confidence and reassurance.

'Oh, please, do come right in,' she said. 'It's Miss Heinman you've come to see. She's had a fall and hurt her leg.' She had been kneeling beside the sofa, repositioning the bags of frozen peas and beans, but now stood up.

Sam nodded and crossed the room in a few long strides. 'So you said in your message.' He crouched down beside the sofa and took the elderly woman's hand in his. 'Hello, Miss Heinman. In the wars again? Last time it was a broken arm, and this time your leg. You know, at ninety you lead a very adventurous life. I don't know what my father's going to say about this latest episode.'

The old lady snorted. 'Your father doesn't expect me to keep myself wrapped in cotton wool, any more than he will when he reaches my age. And Mrs Fellows here doesn't think my leg's broken, only sprained or something, and she seems to know what she's about. I hope you appreciate her over in the surgery. As you can see, she and little Daisy have been making me comfortable between them.'

'Indeed they have,' said Sam, flicking a 'well done' smile at Daisy and a slanting, twinkling look up at Gemma. She was flushing slightly. Her elderly neighbour's warm praise surprised her. 'And, yes, I assure you, we do appreciate her in the surgery. Now, tell me how you hurt your leg whilst I have a look at it.'

He bent over the grossly swollen limb and began examining it with firm, experienced fingers, concentrating hard as he exerted a little extra pressure round the swollen knee joint—almost, thought Gemma, as if he could 'see' with his fingers.

While he worked, Miss Heinman explained how she had stumbled at the foot of her garden path, twisted her ankle and banged her knee against the gatepost. 'Which is why,' she said in her rather terse manner, 'I decided to seek Mrs Fellows's help. I didn't think I'd be able to reach up and open my front door, and one garden path is as long as the other. I did not, of course, know that she was out.'

Sam finished his examination and sat back on his heels. 'Well, it's a good job she returned when she did,' he said cheerfully. 'The ice treatment has prevented the swelling getting any worse. As far as I can see, you've sprained your ankle and strained your knee, but there's nothing broken.'

'So no hospital?'

'No hospital, at least at present, but you're either going to have to go to your niece over at Bourne End or have someone in the house with you. I'm going to strap you up with a support bandage from foot to thigh, and I forbid you to put any weight on it for several weeks. You'll have to use two sticks and hop.' He spoke with not altogether pretended sternness. 'Now, what's it going to be—Bourne End or Mrs Carter to live in for a bit?'

Gemma marvelled, as she had several times over the last few days, at the in-depth knowledge that the Mallorys and Ellie had about the patients and their families. There was no such thing as distancing themselves from their patients in Blaney St Mary. It gave her a definite glow to think that in time she, too, would be in that privileged position.

Miss Heinman opted for her niece at Bourne End because Mrs Carter was going to stay with her sister for a few days.

'Good,' said Sam, with obvious satisfaction. 'Molly will look after you, and that big, strong son of hers will make light work of lifting you when it's necessary.'

It was an hour and a half later before Gemma and Daisy had the cottage to themselves.

Sam had departed long since to make other visits, after efficiently strapping up Miss Heinman's leg, administering a painkiller and phoning her niece, Molly, to put her in the picture.

'I'll be over to see you at Bourne End on Monday,' he had promised Miss Heinman, before leaving.

On his way out, without the least facetiousness or patronage, he had thanked Daisy for helping to look after his patient.

Daisy had looked at him with serious emerald green eyes. 'I just did what Mummy told me,' she'd said.

'That's the best sort of help a professional can have,' he'd replied.

Gemma accompanied him to the front door.

Dusk was settling over the green. Sam paused on the doorstep. 'Thanks for all you've done for the old lady,' he said. 'Things might have been infinitely worse if you hadn't taken her in hand. I'm sorry you got involved on your day off, but it's the sort of thing that happens in this village.'

'It's one way of getting to know your neighbours,' Gemma replied dryly. 'To date I haven't done more than pass the time of day with Miss Heinman and the Robertses.'

'The villagers, especially the oldies, do tend to keep in-comers at a distance till they get to know them. This little episode will build up your Brownie points no end, a sort of baptism of fire. Anyway, thanks for all you've done. Hope you can relax tomorrow and enjoy the rest of the weekend off.'

Sunday started off well. The day was blustery and chilly and punctuated by frequent bursts of heavy rain. But

Gemma and Daisy happily dodged the showers to attend the eleven o'clock special children's service, held in the ancient little church tucked away just off the green. They were there at headmistress Joy Scott's instigation.

'Do come,' she'd pleaded when Gemma had dropped Daisy off at school on Friday morning. 'It's only held once a month, and most of the school will be there. It's all very informal, more or less conducted by the children themselves, with a little guidance from the vicar and myself. The children read or recite pieces or poems they have chosen.' Her eyes had twinkled. 'Many with only a fleeting connection with Jesus or the bible story, but what the heck? If anyone can understand, *He* can.' With a laugh, she had pointed upwards.

Gemma had been intrigued. 'We'll be there,' she'd promised.

They thoroughly enjoyed the quirky service, which lasted only forty-five minutes, but by the time they had said their goodbyes to Daisy's school chums and their mums, who were there in force, it was nearly half past twelve when they wended their way homewards across the green.

There was a red, low-slung, lethal-looking sports car with a black hood standing outside the cottage.

Daisy said, 'Wow, what a scrumptious car—red, like my sandals.'

Gemma shrugged. 'I can't think of anyone we know with a car like that. Must be somebody visiting the Robertses.'

But as they crossed the road dividing the green from the terrace, the car door opened and a familiar figure climbed out and leaned on the low roof, watching them approach.

Both Gemma and Daisy came to an abrupt halt. This is

where the weekend comes apart, thought Gemma, her heart dropping with a metaphorical thump into her stomach.

Daisy said in a small voice, 'It's Daddy.' She slipped her hand into Gemma's.

Gemma breathed in deeply. 'So it is,' she murmured through tight lips.

Neil was the last person she expected or wanted to see. What was he doing in the wilds of Dorset? When she had told him that they were moving to Dorset, he'd intimated that they wouldn't be seeing much of him when they were 'out in the sticks'. Relief had flooded through her. Alleluia, fewer erratic visits.

It would have been different if Daisy enjoyed her outings with him, but she had recently made it abundantly clear that she didn't. He was too volatile, moody, quickly got 'cross', as she put it.

Gemma squeezed Daisy's hand and, trying to put warmth and reassurance into her voice, said, 'Come on, love, let's go and say hello to Daddy.'

Neil was in one of his expansive, showing-off moods. He swung Daisy up in his arms and kissed her noisily. 'Hello, poppet, what do you think of Daddy's new car? We'll go for a spin in her presently.'

'Not in that lethal object in these narrow lanes you won't, especially the way you drive,' said Gemma firmly. She added, hoping that Daisy wouldn't be seduced by the gleaming red vehicle, 'Besides, we've made plans for the day. It was silly to come all this way without making sure that we would be here.'

Neil lowered Daisy to the ground. She moved a step or two towards Gemma, but for a moment hovered uncertainly between them.

Gemma fished the key out of her bag and beamed Daisy

a reassuring smile. 'You go and open the door, love, and we'll show Daddy round.'

'OK.' Daisy almost snatched the key from her and hurried up the garden path.

Neil shrugged and a pleased expression replaced the pout that he'd assumed at Gemma's criticism of his driving. For a fleeting moment she experienced a little spasm of pain—regret—in the region of her heart. He looked, she thought, almost as young and handsome as he had on their wedding day, the eternal Peter Pan. If only...

If only he had learned to grow up, accept the responsibility of a wife and baby, instead of running away. But he just hadn't been able to hack it. If he had, they might have still been together providing Daisy with the ideal two-parent background.

Ideal! That was a hoot. Her parents' marriage hadn't exactly been made in heaven.

Neil was saying in a smug voice, 'Didn't think about you not being in. I'm house-partying with some people in Hampshire—business acquaintances, very dull, but useful. Realised that it was practically next door to you so excused myself to buzz over. Have to get back for drawing-room tea—they're an old-fashioned lot—but I'm all yours till then.'

'Lucky us,' muttered Gemma drily but softly so that Daisy wouldn't hear the irony in her voice. 'You'd better stay for lunch.' She turned and marched up the path, leaving him to follow.

'Happy to accept your gracious offer,' he said, close on her heels.

For Daisy's sake, Gemma worked hard at making Neil's visit a success.

It poured with rain and they were unable to make their planned walk to the top of Round Hill, much, she thought, to Neil's relief. He was a city man, from his sleek designer haircut to the soles of his expensive shoes. As walking was out, they sat round the kitchen table and played board games.

Neil was at his charming best, fulfilling his role of the caring father so successfully that Daisy, who had been rather subdued over lunch, visibly began to relax and enjoy herself. It was lovely to see her giggling and behaving as a six-year-old should, instead of being guarded and watchful as she often was in his presence. If only he was always like this when he visited. If only...

He left just before four, full of promises about visiting again soon. The rain had stopped and a washed-out sun peeped out between a gap in the clouds.

Empty promises? wondered Gemma as she and Daisy accompanied him to the gate. 'Do phone before you decide to come,' she reminded him, and at the risk of spoiling the rapport of the afternoon added, 'and, please, remember what I said about not taking Daisy out in that death trap.' She glanced at the sleek red car standing at the kerb. 'I mean it, Neil.'

He shrugged. 'Don't worry, we'll think of something, won't we, poppet?' As he had when he'd arrived, he swung Daisy up into his arms and gave her a resounding kiss, before setting her down on the ground. Then, to Gemma's utter astonishment, and before she could take evasive action, he put his arms round her, drew her close and aimed a kiss at her mouth, which she averted by turning her head to one side so that it landed just below her ear.

He let her go so suddenly that she rocked on her feet as she staggered back.

Daisy squeaked in a trembly, accusing little voice, 'You *kissed* my mummy. You *never* kiss Mummy.'

'Well, so I did,' he said, sounding pleased with himself,

ignoring Daisy's shocked surprise. And with a smirk he turned on his heel, crossed the pavement, lowered himself into the death trap, noisily gunned the engine into life and drove off at a cracking pace.

Gemma seethed but kept a rein on her temper—Daisy was already confused enough. She laid a comforting and protective hand on her small daughter's back and propelled her up the path toward the cottage. There was going to be a hell of a lot of explaining to do. Blast you, Neil, blast and damn you for spoiling things yet again.

Sam, returning from an emergency call-out to a baby with a middle-ear infection and cruising slowly up the other side of the green, witnessed the entire episode.

He tried to interpret what he'd seen. Who was the idiot who'd taken off at nought to sixty in the ten-mile-an-hour restricted zone round the green? The idiot who'd made a fuss of Daisy and had attempted to kiss Gemma? Even from a distance he could have sworn that she hadn't wanted to be kissed, the way she had staggered back from the man.

What sort of a *friend*, if that's what he was, would try to force a kiss on a woman in broad daylight?

He stopped the car and stared across at Cherry Tree Cottage. Were they all right, Gemma and Daisy? They had somehow looked vulnerable as they had walked up the path. Or had he imagined that? Should he find some excuse to call on them? After all, Gemma worked for the practice. OK, she'd only worked for them for a week, but just the same...

'God help me,' he muttered. 'I'm getting as bad as Dad, doing the paternal caring bit. Keep your distance, Mallory, she wouldn't appreciate you butting in one bit.'

He sighed heavily, and with uncharacteristic clumsiness and a clash of gears cruised back to the surgery.

CHAPTER FIVE

The week following Neil's disturbing visit had been a busy one for Gemma.

She and Daisy paid a flying visit to Shillingbourne after school on Monday afternoon to buy curtain material, paint and wallpaper to redecorate Daisy's room. It needed doing, but it was more a gesture on Gemma's part to reassure Daisy that all was well. She had been considerably rattled by Neil's silly behaviour on Sunday.

Daisy didn't refer to the kiss, but had been thoughtful and quiet when he'd left and had followed Gemma about like a shadow whilst she was preparing supper, occasionally giving her a hug. Gemma had given her hug for hug, read an extra bedtime story and suggested the trip into Shillingbourne the following day.

The shopping trip worked wonders, and Daisy, who had still been rather subdued when Gemma had left her at school on Monday morning, was by that evening her usual bubbly self.

It had been a busy week at the surgery, too, as they got to grips with a mystery bug which was making the rounds. Friday was no exception.

Gemma was in the middle of a long list of bloods when Sam appeared in the treatment room between patients. On account of the bug, his house calls had doubled and she had seen little of him over the last few days. The semi-retired Dr Thorn, who lived in a neighbouring village, had been covering much of his surgery work, but wasn't on duty that morning.

Sam greeted her with a tired smile without its usual dazzle, and lines round his mouth were etched deep. Amazingly, though, his blue eyes remained as brilliant as ever.

Her heart went out to him. Astonishingly, a curious desire to hug him, as she hugged Daisy, swept over her. She squashed the outrageous desire and said softly, 'You look exhausted. Can't you get someone else in to help?'

'Bob Carstairs is covering tonight, as well as Saturday and Sunday. He's a locum in a million, and dear old Richard Thorn is covering tomorrow's calls so I'll be off the hook for much of the weekend.'

'Good, you'll be able to go to bed and zonk out.'

'Tempting,' he said, his smile widening, 'but what a waste of time. There are better things to do than sleep.'

Like wining and dining some gorgeous female and dancing the night away, thought Gemma savagely. The savageness of the thought shook her. What the hell was she thinking about? What was it to her whom he wined and dined? She looked pointedly down at her watch.

'Sorry,' Sam said at once. 'Enough chat, you're busy. Can you fit in another blood, please, and a urine test and do a throat swab?'

He handed her some lab forms. 'It's a young woman, Alison Graves. She's new to the area and not very communicative. I haven't got any notes for her. I'll have to ask for them to be faxed through from her last GP. She's presenting with a range of symptoms that could be anything from glandular fever to something more obscure. I want wide-spectrum blood tests, and her urine tested for the obvious—glucose, blood, pus, and so on. I've given her a specimen pot and she should be in the loo, producing a specimen, right now.'

He frowned. 'I rather think we might be looking for one of the autoimmune diseases in its infancy. She complains of feeling the cold, especially in her hands and feet, indicating a circulation problem, Raynaud's probably, which we can do something about. And I thought I could detect a few blemishes across her cheek-bones, which might indicate... But they were very faint. See what you think, Gemma. I'd be grateful for any feedback you can give me. The sooner we can get her sorted, the better.'

'Well, I'll just about manage her before twelve, if...' She raised her eyebrows and inclined her head toward the door.

Sam laughed. 'I'm gone already.' he said.

At the end of her list, Gemma called Mrs Alison Graves in from the waiting room. Alison was tall and skinny, with lank, long, badly tinted fair hair. She was heavily made up.

With ill grace she slouched down in the chair that Gemma offered and handed her the pot containing her urine specimen.

'Dunno why the doctor's going to all this trouble,' she grumbled. 'I thought he'd just give me a tonic or something, so I can get on with my life—if there is any life in this God-awful place. I've just moved, for heaven's sake. That's why I'm so bloody tired.'

'I know exactly how you feel,' Gemma replied with a smile, as she dipped a test strip into the urine. 'I've not long moved myself—it's an exhausting business. But as Dr Sam's seeing you for the first time, he needs to find out if there's any other reason for the symptoms you describe, before prescribing anything. He's a very thorough doctor.'

'Yeah, and cool and dishy with it,' said Alison, with a hint of animation.

Yes, cool, dishy and caring, thought Gemma as she examined the multicoloured testing strip. Everything was negative. 'Well, you'll be glad to know that that's clear. Now, if you'll take off your jacket and pull up your sleeve, I'll take some blood and we'll get it off to the lab for examination. That may give us a clue as to why you're not feeling a hundred per cent.'

She had no problem finding a prominent vein under the bright lights of the treatment room, and was easily able to slide in a needle and take as much blood as she needed to fill the numerous specimen bottles she had lined up.

When she had completed the operation, and whilst Alison, her head slightly bent, was busy rolling down the sleeve of her blouse she took the opportunity to surreptitiously inspect her face. Yes, as Sam had thought, illuminated by the bright lights, though almost concealed beneath the heavy make-up, were the faintest of blemishes across her cheek-bones and the bridge of her nose.

Telangiectasia—sometimes called the butterfly rash— typified certain immune diseases. Sam's hunch had been right. Alison Graves was suffering from more than simple tiredness. With a little flutter of pleasure, she realised what a compliment he had paid her by asking for her opinion, just as he had with Ralph Wyman. It gave her a really warm feeling of being wanted and useful, but, then, that was typical of the whole set-up here at Blaney St Mary.

After seeing Alison out and parcelling up the morning's specimens for collection later, she looked at her watch. It was too late to see Sam now and pass on her findings— he would be out on his rounds. She would have to tell him this afternoon during the toddlers' clinic. The knowledge that they would be working together after nearly a week of seeing so little of him gave her a curious little fizz of pleasure.

Although it was after twelve, she decided that she must

have a coffee to sustain her till lunch time. Ellie was in the staffroom, also taking a late break.

'Mrs M.'s holding the fort,' Ellie explained. 'It's been like a madhouse out there this morning, what with the phone going non-stop and people going on holiday wanting to book for various jabs. Not to mention the hay fever sufferers booking in for their anti-allergy jabs. You're going to be busy on those next week.'

'Oh, well, that's par for the course, especially at this time of year,' replied Gemma, spooning coffee into a mug. She poured on boiling water and with a sigh of relief sat down in one of the comfortable old armchairs next to Ellie.

'But I think the bug may be on the wane,' said Ellie. 'Fewer of the calls seem to have been in connection with that this morning, though I haven't done a proper count, so keep your fingers crossed.'

'I certainly will,' promised Gemma, 'Both Dr M. and Sam are looking pretty ragged—they're working flat out.'

Ellie peeped at her over the rim of her mug. 'Yes.' Her cheeks flushed slightly. 'I think Sam in particular looks tired. He's been bearing the brunt of it, he's so protective of his father.'

'Tries to be,' agreed Gemma. She glanced at Ellie's flushed cheeks. Not for the first time she wondered if Ellie had a thing about Sam. A little voice inside her hoped not, but she didn't know why. 'But Dr Mallory's been working his socks off too. The only time I've seen him lose his rag was when Sam offered to do some of his calls as well as his own—the old doctor blew his top.'

'Yes, well, he would, wouldn't he?' said Ellie. 'He's such a dear. Sam's going to be just like him one day, don't you think?' She sounded rather wistful, hopeful that Gemma would agree.

'Well, he could do worse,' said Gemma drily. Then, to

change the subject, she asked, 'Doing anything nice over the weekend?'

Ellie pulled a face. 'Visiting my in-laws in Bournemouth. It'll be ghastly. Dave's not looking forward to it either. They never let up, but it's been ages since we visited. If only…'

Wondering if Ellie wanted to talk, yet not wanting to pry, Gemma said cautiously, 'What do you mean, they never let up?'

'About me not producing a baby. As if it's my fault. My God, if only they knew how much I wanted one, only I can't… We can't…' She blinked back tears from her brown eyes and compressed her lips.

Gemma couldn't keep the surprise out of her voice. 'But surely, that's none of their business?' She reached out and touched Ellie's arm. 'I'm so sorry.'

Ellie stood up abruptly and took her mug over to the sink and began washing it. 'I'm sorry, too, coming apart like that, but you're such a good listener and it is nice to have someone near my own age to talk to.' She blew her nose hard and started toward the door. 'Must go now or Mrs M. will be sending out a search party,' adding, as she stood in the doorway, 'you don't know how lucky you are to have Daisy.'

'Oh, but I do,' Gemma said softly, and then went on, 'Ellie, if you think it would help to talk, I'd be only too glad to lend an ear.'

Ellie produced a watery smile. 'Thanks, I'll hold you to that.' Then she whisked herself out of the room.

Gemma made a point of getting back early from lunch to prepare the room for the toddlers' clinic. It took time to distribute the toys, set up the weighing and measuring equipment and lay up a basic trolley in the examination cubicle. It was her second toddlers' clinic. Her spirits, which had been a little low following Ellie's disclosure, soared.

She was on her way back from Reception with a formidable pile of records when Sam caught up with her, taking her by surprise.

She breathed out a startled, 'Oh.' She quickly recovered herself and added, 'You're early.' Then she asked suspiciously, 'Have you had lunch?'

He chuckled. 'You're as bad as Mum, always worrying about the inner man, but, yes, thank you, I have eaten. Finished my visits quicker than I expected.' He glanced sideways at her, his blue eyes twinkling, laughter lines deepening round his half lowered lids.

'We mothers tend to worry about things like that,' she said primly. She had no idea why, but it was suddenly important to remind him that she was a mother.

'Touché!'

They reached the clinic room, and he pushed open one side of the double doors and flattened himself against it. 'After you,' he said, his voice suddenly husky.

'Thanks.' There was a sudden tenseness between them. She found herself trying to make herself as small as possible as she slid past him, but with her arms full she was unable to avoid brushing against his chest. She shrank some more. He breathed in sharply—or had she only imagined it?

'Here, let me.' His voice was gruff, deeper. He took the records from her, his hands touching her bare inner forearms as he scooped them up. The soft flesh tingled. He dumped the files on her desk, then slowly turned to look at her. For a timeless, breathless moment their eyes met and held in a vibrant silence.

There was about a yard separating them. With a step he closed the gap. 'Gemma!' He lifted his hands as though to cup her face. Cup her face... Kiss her... Her eyes still locked with his, she took half a step backwards.

Slowly he let his hands fall to his sides. Then he, too, stepped back a little. The merest shadow of what might have been a smile touched the corners of his mouth. He closed his eyes for a second, cleared his throat and said very softly, 'I can't explain that, Gemma. I just know there's been something...' Palms up, he spread his long, narrow hands eloquently. 'Something since day one, the day we met, when you appeared in the surgery and offered to help. I'm sorry. Have I embarrassed you, scared you?'

His eyes were as brilliant as ever, but no longer dancing. they were thoughtful, serious, as they were when he was dealing with a distressed patient.

Gemma's heart pounded against her ribs, her mouth went dry, her thoughts raced. Should she make a joke of it, laugh it away? It had only been a look after all. *Only*! Her mind was empty of jokes and she could no more laugh than fly.

She stared at him, as if seeing him for the first time— taking in his leanness, his height, the high forehead and the thatch of bright, fair hair springing from his temples, the darker, thick, straight brows, the patrician nose and the firm yet tender mouth.

He was almost too perfect, she told herself. It was difficult to find a flaw in the man, not just physically but in his temperament. But there must be one.

But she didn't want to find a flaw! Perhaps there was the occasional man who wasn't flawed. Something stirred deep within her—a longing, a hope, a joyful awareness, a strange sensation of elation. It had been so long since...

She tried to clear her throat. 'You didn't scare me or embarrass me.' She went on firmly in her normal voice, 'No, not at all, but...'

'But…what do we do about it?'

He didn't need to elaborate further. It couldn't be pushed away, ignored—it was too significant. She kept her voice level. 'What, indeed?'

'Talk?'

'I think we must, but when… There's Daisy…Daisy!' She looked at him, a thousand questions in her eyes.

His voice was gentle. 'I haven't forgotten Daisy—she's the chief reason we must talk, Gemma. Can I call tonight casually—as a neighbour, a friendly visit?'

There was a hum of voices and the sound of footsteps in the corridor.

There were a dozen reasons why he shouldn't, but many more why he should. It was an unreal situation. Feeling as if she were caught up in some fantasy, Gemma nodded. 'About eight. Daisy stays up till half past on a Friday, but I want her to know that you're there.'

'Not arrive like a thief in the night,' he murmured, as a knock came at the door. 'I'll be there.'

Gemma forced herself to concentrate on her work. She helped mothers undress and dress small bodies; she weighed, measured, reassured and administered injections with her usual calm efficiency. Sometimes she assisted Sam with an examination when a child was being difficult and the mother unable to cope.

They were almost at the end of the clinic, and Sam was examining his last small patient in the cubicle, when a young chap in tattered jeans and a scuffed leather jacket suddenly appeared in the waiting room. He was awkwardly carrying a tiny child who looked to be about a year old. The infant was grizzling, a low, exhausted grizzle that told Gemma it had been going on a long time. Skinny little bare legs were drawn up to its little pot belly, visible between a nappy that stank to high heaven and a too small, grubby jumper.

The young man said, 'They told me out there to bring 'im in 'ere. Can you stop 'im crying? 'E's bin doing it all night.' He thrust the bundle at Gemma. Wordlessly she accepted the pathetic little creature from him and cuddled it to her. 'Oh, an' they said to give you this.' The young man, who looked to be in his teens, handed her a temporary resident's form.

'Name: Gaz Formby', Gemma read. *Gaz?* Date of birth… She stared at it in disbelief. The infant was twenty months old, not twelve as she'd guessed. It was seriously underweight. 'And you are Mr Formby?' She spread a paper sheet on the desk and carefully laid the baby down. In one practised movement she removed the filthy nappy, and with moist wipes began cleaning up the tiny sore bottom.

'Naow, my name's Steve Beck. I'm 'is dad but 'e's got 'is mum's name, only Tracy's not well, like, so she's stayed 'ome.'

'Home being a farm near Bourne End,' said Gemma, glancing at the address on the TPR form. The name rang a bell and she recalled that Bourne End was the village where Miss Heinman had gone to stay with her niece. Gently she wrapped Gaz in a small blanket, then sat down behind the desk and cuddled him on her lap. The grizzle died down to a whimper. 'Is the farm warm and comfortable?' she asked.

'No, it ain't,' said Steve truculently. 'Anyway, we don't live in the farmhouse but in a grotty caravan in the yard. Tracy's uncle owns the farm and caravan, lets us stay in it in return for 'elp about the place. It's a dump, but better than nothing.'

As Steve was talking, Sam was showing the last mother and toddler out of the cubicle.

He crossed over to the desk and looked down at the now almost quiet infant, lying in Gemma's arms. Gently he touched a sallow little cheek, then looked up at Steve. 'Would that be Alf Formby's pig farm?' he asked.

'Yeah,' replied Steve, sounding defensive.

'You're right, that caravan's pretty grotty. It must be difficult to manage, especially with this little chap.' He smiled at Steve and then at Gemma. 'OK, Nurse, let's have…'

'Gaz,' she said, holding back a grin. It was such an odd name for such a tiny scrap of humanity.

Sam clearly agreed with her as his eyes, glinting with humour, met hers. 'Gaz,' he said without a tremor. 'In the cubicle so that I can have a look at him.' He moved across the room and Gemma followed. Steve stayed where he was. Sam paused. 'Aren't you coming, Mr…?'

'Beck, Steve Beck.' Steve shook his head. 'I'll wait 'ere if it's all the same to you—I'm a bit queasy like.'

Sam gave him a reassuring smile. 'Fair enough. I'll give you a run-down when I've finished,' he promised.

Fifteen minutes later he was explaining to Steve that he was going to admit Gaz to the paediatric ward in the cottage hospital at Shillingbourne for assessment and investigation.

'There are several things that could be wrong with your son,' he explained to an obviously bewildered young father. 'It could be simple colic, giving him a pain in his guts, or it could be something more complicated than that. He will have to have scans and tests to determine whether there is anything seriously wrong. He's also very undernourished and needs a special diet to reverse that condition.'

'When will 'e 'ave to go in, then?'

'I want to get him admitted immediately. I'll arrange an ambulance straight away. You can go with him, although you'd have to find your own way back, or follow on in your car—you've got some sort of transport?'

'Van. But what about Trace? She'll be gutted if I don't get back to tell 'er what's 'appened.'

Sam said, 'I'll go over and see her, but it won't be till after my surgery which is due to start shortly—that'll be about six. In the meantime, I'll try to get in touch with Alf Formby and ask him to give her a message.'

Steve said angrily, 'Fat chance. The old bugger don't answer the phone if 'e's out with 'is pigs.'

'There's no need to phone,' interjected Gemma firmly. 'I'll go over to Bourne End and explain the situation to Tracy after I've fetched Daisy from school. Just point me in the right direction.'

'That'd be great. Problem solved.' Sam smiled at her, a wide, special smile that conveyed more than words could possibly have done, and his voice was warm with approval.

A wave of pleasure washed over her at his easy acceptance of her offer. He hadn't sounded surprised or tried to deflect her, but accepted it as he would if his mother had made the offer. She positively glowed, feeling that she was indeed part of the small happy family unit, just as Ellie had predicted.

Half an hour later Gemma and Daisy were on their way to Bourne End. Daisy accepted the change to their usual routine and the reason for it quite happily. In fact, she was thrilled to bits to be visiting a farm, especially a pig farm.

'Will I be able to touch them?' she wanted to know, bouncing up and down with excitement. 'I'd like to, 'specially if there are piglets. I've never seen pigs close up, except on television.'

Bearing in mind Steve's description of the farmer and Sam's rather grim expression when he'd mentioned the name Alf Formby, Gemma tried to cool down Daisy's enthusiasm. He didn't sound the sort of friendly type who would welcome visitors.

'I don't know if the farmer will let us get too close to them,' she cautioned, 'and I don't know how long I'll be with Tracy. I want you to stay in the car while I'm talking to her. We'll see if we can look round afterwards.'

Daisy's pretty little mouth turned down at the corners. 'Oh, Mummy, can't I, *please* just get out of the car. I won't go anywhere, promise.'

Gemma half relented. 'We'll see, love. It might be too muddy.'

Daisy stuck a small red-booted foot in the air and waved it about. 'Oh, Mummy, don't be silly. Don't you remember? I've got my wellies on because it was raining when I went to school this morning.' She was triumphant.

Gemma grinned. 'OK, you win. You can stand outside the car, but you musn't go anywhere until I've finished talking to Tracy.'

They reached the farm at the end of a long rutted lane a few minutes later. It was a low, rambling building which might once have been charming but now looked drab and badly in need of repair. To one side of it across a dirty, untidy yard stood a shabby caravan. It was deep in afternoon shadow and there was something almost sinister about about the whole set-up. There was no sign of life.

No wonder poor little Gaz is so grubby and undernourished, thought Gemma. His parents are little more than children themselves, yet are somehow trying to manage in a place like this.

Daisy was staring, wide-eyed, at the battered caravan. 'Mummy, is *that* where Tracy lives?' she whispered.

'I believe so, love. I'll knock and find out. I'll try not to be too long. You can get out and stretch your legs, but stay near the car.'

'I *think* I'll stay in the car and read my book,' said Daisy with a slight wobble in her voice. 'I can't see any pigs about and I don't think I want to look round *this* farm—it's creepy.'

Gemma gave her a hug. 'I'll be as quick as I can,' she promised.

She got out of the car and crossed the yard to the caravan, wrinkling her nose as she caught a strong whiff of pig.

Fifteen minutes later, she recrossed the yard and let herself back into the car. She smiled at Daisy, though she'd seldom felt less like smiling after her confrontation with Tracy. 'There, I wasn't long, love, was I?' she said, as she did up her safety belt.

'You were *ages*,' accused Daisy, pouting a little. 'Can we go home now, please? I'm hungry.'

Gemma kissed her quickly on the cheek, before putting the car in gear and starting off down the lane. 'Thanks for being so patient, darling. We'll be home in two shakes of a lamb's tail,' she promised, before it occurred to her that four-legged beasties might not be favourites on the agenda at this moment in time. The Formby farm had definitely been a disappointment. 'And why don't you choose what we'll have for supper tonight as it's Friday?'

Predictably, Daisy, any petulance forgotten, chose baked beans on toast with a sunny-side-up egg on top, her all-time favourite.

Over supper, Gemma struggled to put out of her mind the shocking, unpleasant interview she'd had with Tracy Formby. There was time enough to discuss that with Sam when he called later. Her heart quickened with pleasure at the thought of seeing him, but her stomach churned. Should she tell Daisy that he was coming, or wait for him to arrive? Perhaps the right moment would suddenly materialise when she could mention it casually.

Resolutely, she made herself concentrate on fielding Daisy's questions and asking some of her own. Over pudding, ice cream and mashed banana, another favourite, she asked what homework project Daisy had been given to do over the weekend.

Daisy's chubby little face lit up. 'We've got to draw a coloured picture of the front of our house and count the windows in it and 'scribe it in words,' she said. 'I'm glad. I like drawing and writing.' She half slid off her chair. 'Can I go and count the windows now, please?'

'Finish your pudding first, love, and then we'll both go and count them.'

They stood in the garden a few minutes later, looking up at the front of the house. Daisy counted five windows. One each side of the front door, the sitting room and the dining-room windows, and three above tucked under the gabled roof, the main bedroom, landing and bathroom.

Daisy slipped her hand in Gemma's and sighed contentedly. 'I *do* like living here, it's much nicer than London. My teachers are nice and the people are nice at your surgery, aren't they, Mummy?' She turned her smiling face up to Gemma's.

'They certainly are, poppet.' It was a golden opportunity. 'By the way, Dr Sam might call in later. He wants to talk to me about a patient he asked me to see this morning and the girl I went to see this afternoon. Sorry to bring shop talk home, love, but we've been so busy...'

'Oh, goody. I like Dr Sam. What's shop talk?'

CHAPTER SIX

SAM arrived promptly at eight. Gemma, trying to ignore the way her heartbeat quickened when the doorbell rang, marched firmly along the hall and flung wide the front door.

He was silhouetted against the red glow of the setting sun streaming across the green.

'Hi!' They both spoke simultaneously, breathily, then burst into laughter.

Sam, his eyes brimming with amusement, said, 'Shall we begin again?'

Gemma chuckled and the knot in her stomach dissolved. 'Good evening,' she said, bowing her head slightly in the manner of the gracious hostess. 'Please, do come in.'

'Thank you.' Grinning, he stepped into the small hall, towering over her.

Daisy came bounding out of the dining room, a bundle of energy in her jazzy pyjamas and huge fluffy slippers. 'Hello, Dr Sam. I'm ready for bed and I've had my bath, but I stay up till half past eight on Friday and Saturday nights as a treat.' She beamed him a dimpling smile. 'Would you like to see my homework? It's a drawing.'

Sam nodded and smiled down at her. 'I'd *love* to.' He accepted her hand, which she tucked confidently into his, and allowed himself to be led into the dining room.

'It's a picture of our house, but I haven't finished yet,' she explained as Sam bent over the table. She began pointing out the salient features, naming the various rooms behind the windows.

'And that's Mummy's room with the flowery curtains, but my room's not there, it's at the back and faces east and I've got blue curtains with birds and trees on.'

'What sort of birds?'

'Oh, robins and blackbirds and…'

Gemma stood just inside the door and surveyed the two bent heads so close together. Tendrils of Daisy's vibrant, red-bronze tresses seemed to reach out to touch Sam's thick, straight, corn-blond hair. She found herself holding her breath not wanting to disrupt the tableau. A curious sensation surged through her.

They looked so *right*, together—there was no other word to describe it. Like father and daughter, came the extraordinary thought.

She felt herself blushing and squashed the thought. She cleared her throat, but her voice still came out sounding husky.

'Would you like a drink, Sam? Coffee, wine?'

He lifted his head and smiled over his shoulder. 'Wine would be nice,' he said. 'A dry white if you have it.'

Was it her imagination at work again, or did *his* voice, too, sound huskier and deeper than usual? And had his smile a special quality about it?

'Right, coming up,' she murmured, as she drifted, feeling curiously detached, towards the kitchen.

The feeling of detachment and euphoria persisted as at Daisy's request the three of them played noisy games of Snap and Pairs Sam and Daisy each won games, with Gemma trailing a dismal third each time. She was accused by Daisy of not concentrating, and serenely agreed. Just as she found herself agreeing when Daisy's bedtime approached and, backed up by Sam, her happy little daughter begged to be allowed to stay up till nine o'clock.

Daisy, wide-eyed with astonishment, gave her a life-threatening hug, and then, to his pleased surprise, did the same to Sam.

By the time she was eventually settled for the night, and Gemma and Sam, calling a final cheerful goodnight, made their way downstairs, it was half past nine. It had been a strange, unreal experience for Gemma, finding herself sharing Daisy's bedtime ritual with anyone. A new experience for both of them, and Daisy had revelled in it.

Feeling thoroughly bemused, Gemma followed Sam down the stairs. She couldn't believe how easily she had been outwitted by her daughter who, out of the blue, had invited Sam to admire her newly decorated bedroom and had then cajoled him into reading a bedtime story.

'Sorry you got trapped into that,' she apologised stiffly, leading the way into the sitting room. She indicated an armchair. 'Please, sit down.' Suddenly, without Daisy's presence, she felt uptight and breathless. What had she let herself in for when she had agreed to him visiting, talking—what had they got to talk about? A look! Eye contact! A wordless exchange of vibes!

Sam grinned. 'Don't be. I'm a sucker for Thomas the Tank Engine, and it was a joy to read to Daisy—she's a darling.' And you're a darling too, he wanted to say. Beautiful, desirable, and I'd like to kiss your lovely mouth. Instead, he said softly, 'Relax, Gemma, love, I'm not going to pressure you. We're only going to talk.'

Love! What did he mean—*love*? He said that to patients, especially children whom he wanted to reassure. She herself said it to reassure. *She* didn't need reassuring. 'I *am* relaxed,' she insisted, trying to sound firm. She was let down by her voice, which came out a little squeaky.

He ignored the squeak, nodded and sat down. 'Do you think I might beg another glass of wine?'

She had just sat down in the opposite armchair, but

catapulted to her feet. 'Oh, of course, I'll fetch the bottle from the fridge.' She bolted from the room.

In the kitchen, she stood motionless for a moment, taking deep breaths, fingers pressed against her hot cheeks. 'Get a hold of yourself, woman,' she muttered. 'You can handle the situation. It's no big deal.' Liar! OK, so it is a big deal. It's the biggest, maddest thing that's happened to you since Neil took off. This thing between you and Sam. But you're older and wiser, and forewarned is forearmed. All you have to do, Gemma Fellows, is to play it cool.

Play it cool! She snatched the ice-cold wine from the fridge and loaded it onto a tray with two glasses, added bowls of crisps and nuts and, keeping her back ramrod-straight, marched along the hall to the sitting room.

Sam was leaning back in his chair, his eyes closed, hands linked behind his head, long legs stretched out before him, feet crossed at the ankles. He was sound asleep.

Gemma stood, looking down at him. Her heart contracted. He looked totally at ease, younger and unexpectedly vulnerable, the tired lines round his mouth smoothed away.

Taking infinite care not to wake him, she placed the tray on the small round table between the chairs. But for all her care he heard her and his eyes flicked open to reveal brilliant chips of blue, immediately focused and alert.

'Good Lord,' he said, sitting up straight. 'Sorry about that. It's this room. It's charming, all these muted colours, gracious yet cosy. I'm afraid I dropped off.'

'Don't you think that the fact that you've only had a few hours' sleep over the last week, as well as working flat out during the day, might have something to do with it?' Gemma said drily. She felt good all at once, no longer tense and nervous but mature and practical, able to handle anything or anyone, even this charismatic man who threatened the defences she had long ago erected.

He grinned. 'Yep, you could be right. It has been a bit of a marathon, but that's to be expected in general practice, especially a virtually two-man one like ours.'

With a steady hand Gemma poured the wine and handed him a glass.

'Have you ever thought of taking on a third partner, not just relying on occasional help?' she asked.

Sam took a sip of wine. 'Dad and I have thought about it, but dismissed the idea. We're managing with Richard Thorn and Bob Carstairs, pro tem. They're both doctors we can trust to look after our patients the way we do and, believe me, doctors of that calibre are not thick on the ground.'

His eyes met Gemma's. The twinkle died out of them and they were suddenly bleak. 'That must sound incredibly conceited,' he said, his voice harsh, 'and we certainly haven't the monopoly on caring, but caring doctors seem to be few and far between these days. Some think you clock on at nine and off at five.'

'Tell me about it,' Gemma said bitterly. 'There are a lot of nurses who think like that too, especially in hospital. It's a techno-gadget-led career, with good old-fashioned TLC coming second best. And agency nurses being used instead of permanent staff. And untrained people being given jobs to do that they shouldn't be, and all due to cuts and bad management.'

She paused for a moment, then laughed uncertainly, and her eyes, which had glittered angrily, softened.

'Sorry, rather a hobby-horse of mine. I can quite see why you and your father are reluctant to invite in another partner—you've such a unique set-up here. I never dreamed that I would be lucky enough to work in a place like this.' She lifted her glass in a sort of salute.

Sam leaned across and clinked his glass to hers. 'The luck is ours, Gemma. You fit in perfectly, this is where you belong—in Blaney St Mary.' His voice was like a caress, soft, warm, slightly husky, and his eyes suddenly full of tenderness.

Deep, sea blue eyes. I could drown in them, thought Gemma, and felt her lips forming the words to say it out loud. She drew in a sharp, painful breath and looked down into her drink. Oh, that would be just great! Pull yourself together, woman. You've been paid a compliment—think of something gracious to say.

She could find no words, gracious or otherwise. The seconds, perhaps minutes, ticked by. Painfully conscious of the steady tide of give-away red creeping into her cheeks, she said abruptly, 'By the way, Tracy Formby, little Gaz's mother, I went to see her…'

Her voice trailed off. It sounded like what it was, a totally artificial diversion. She could feel Sam's eyes focused on her face, and forced herself to look up and meet them, almost afraid of what she would find there.

The tender expression was still there, but laughter was there too. He'd seen through the diversion, but chose to go along with it.

'And how did the poor girl take the news about Gaz?' he asked, his voice calm and professional, every inch the concerned doctor.

Gemma gathered together her tattered wits. If he could be so professional, so could she. After all, she'd started this particular ball rolling.

She said evenly, 'Remarkably well. In fact, she didn't care a damn, or pretended not to. I'm not sure which. She seemed to hate the poor little chap. Her indifference, her abusiveness, shook me, though it shouldn't have done. I've heard it all before. And there's no reason why she shouldn't have come to the surgery. She isn't ill, at least…'

'At least?' Sam prompted.

'As far as I could make out, she hasn't got a temperature, hasn't vomited or had diarrhoea, which seems to put the current bug out of the picture. I just think she couldn't be bothered. But she's a bag of nerves, thin, chain smokes, looks as dirty and neglected as the baby.'

Sam frowned. 'Any sign she's doing drugs?'

'Not that I could see, but she was wearing a long-sleeved shirt and jeans so I couldn't see her legs or arms. And they're obviously church-mouse poor. I wouldn't have thought they could afford even the cheapest soft drug, never mind the hard stuff.'

'That's never stopped an addict before. And she smokes—that costs. I dare say she spends more on ciga-rettes than food. But you're probably right— She's not into drugs or she'd have been to the surgery for a fix on pre-scription.'

His frown deepened. 'What a pathetic little family they are.'

Gemma looked across at him and felt the sudden sting of tears in her eyes. 'Pathetic's the word for it. I was *so* angry with her at first for neglecting the baby and not seeming to care.' Her voice wobbled. 'But thinking about it, talking about it…that horrible caravan…little Gaz… How *could* they manage? She's not much more than a child herself, and neither is Steve. At best, bringing up a baby is hard work. For them it must be hell. *Hell!* Oh, Sam.'

The held-back tears rolled down her cheeks. Suddenly Sam was there, drawing her up out of the chair, holding her in his arms, folding her against his chest. He nuzzled the top of her head. She could feel his warm breath stirring her hair. He tilted her head and kissed her forehead, her eyelids, her wet cheeks, and then her mouth, gently but firmly.

It was a long, lingering, loving kiss, a kiss to reassure, to let her know that he was there, would be there whenever she had need of him. At last he lifted his head and cupped her face with his long, narrow hands and wiped the last of her tears away with his thumbs.

His eyes smiled into hers. 'You needed that, love,' he said softly. 'We all need to cry sometimes. It's the best therapy, bar laughing.'

Gemma sniffed and he fished a clean handkerchief out of his pocket and held it to her nose. 'Have a good blow,' he said, a smile tilting the corners of his mouth.

She blew noisily into the large square of snowy-white cotton. 'Thanks.' She smiled up at him, a quivering smile, her mouth trembling with the effort. 'Sorry, shouldn't have broken down like that, very unprofessional.'

He pressed a forefinger to her lips. His brilliant eyes held hers.

'Unprofessional be damned. If anyone deserves to give way to a good howl, you do. In just over a couple of weeks you've moved house single-handed, started Daisy off at a new school and yourself off in a new demanding job. This afternoon's episode with little Gaz just acted as a catalyst. Brought back memories of the struggle you had to bring up Daisy on your own. I'm right, Gemma, aren't I?'

She nodded.

He stroked her cheek. 'And you had Miss Heinman to cope with last weekend, *and* for good measure you've decorated Daisy's room. Good Lord, woman, you must be exhausted.'

'Yes, I think I am a bit tired,' she admitted, feeling suddenly intensely weary.

Sam smoothed her hair back from her face and kissed the corners of her drooping mouth.

'Bath and bed,' he said, turning her round to face the door.

'But…' She waved her hand over the table with the empty glasses and bowls of nuts and crisps.

'No problem. I'll tidy up and see myself out.'

With his hands on her shoulders, he steered her to the bottom of the stairs. 'Up you go, love.'

He gave her a gentle shove and she slowly mounted the first few steps. She was halfway up when he said softly, 'What are you doing tomorrow, Gemma?'

She paused and looked down at him over her shoulder. 'We're going to Shillingbourne, shopping and swimming, in the morning.'

'No plans for the afternoon?'

'Depends on the weather. If it's fine we thought we might climb up Round Hill—they say the view from the top is fantastic.'

'We used to call it Kite Hill when we were kids. Has Daisy got a kite?'

'No.'

'If I supply a kite, may I join you, or is this a strictly mother-and-daughter outing?'

Gemma's pulse rate doubled. She shook her head. 'Not at all, the more the merrier.'

'About twoish?'

'Fine.'

By midway through Monday morning, the weekend was for Gemma but a dream, as work took over with a vengeance. But between patients memories of it kept flitting into her mind. She could almost *feel* the wind lifting her hair as she and Sam and Daisy stood on the top of Round Hill on Saturday afternoon.

Ruthlessly squashing the vivid picture of an ecstatic Daisy, guided by a laughing Sam, controlling the soaring, swooping kite sailing high above their heads, she went out to the waiting room to call in her umpteenth patient, a Mrs Gloria Watson.

Mrs Watson was a cheerful, heavily pregnant lady in her late thirties. She was wearing large, sloppy men's trainers with a neat maternity trouser suit.

She beamed at Gemma as she limped over to a chair and sat down. 'Thanks for squeezing me in, Nurse,' she said. 'I don't want to worry either of the doctors if it's not necessary. I hope you'll be able to help me. Ellie says you're brilliant.'

'Competent, rather,' said Gemma with a laugh. 'But I warn you, I'm a bit rusty on my midwifery.'

'Oh, it's nothing to do with this.' Mrs Watson patted her bulging tummy. 'That's fine. It's my big toe. I stubbed it last night, tripped up a step. It bled quite a bit and hurt like mad. The nail was a bit wobbly so I put an Elastoplast on it, but it's stuck and bled a lot when I tried to remove it this morning. That's why I'm wearing my husband's trainers—they're more comfortable than any of my shoes.'

'I did wonder,' said Gemma. She placed a stool under the injured foot. 'Right, let's have a look at your poor old toe.'

The toe was a mess, oozing blood and pus, the nail half hanging off. Gemma cleaned it up with antiseptic, applied an anaesthetiser, and with infinite care removed the shattered nail where it was still attached to the damaged nail bed. The area round the toe was swollen and bruised.

Mrs Watson hissed in a couple of sharp breaths, but otherwise maintained a stoic silence.

'Well done.' Gently Gemma swabbed the exposed raw
flesh with more antiseptic. 'Having a nail removed is a
painful business.' She ran her fingers lightly over the big
toe joint and smaller bones adjoining it. 'And I think you
may have broken a bone or two as well as ripping your
nail off. I'll have to get one of the doctors to check it to
see if it needs to be X-rayed. And you need an antibiotic
to counter the infection. I'm just going to cover it with
gauze until one of them can take a look at it.'

It was a smiling Sam who breezed in a few minutes later
in response to her phone call to Ellie. Gemma returned his
smile and her heart fluttered like a cloud of butterflies in
her chest—she hadn't seen him since Saturday.

He crouched down in front of the patient and whistled
softly between his teeth when he saw the injured toe. He
sat back on his heels. 'I'm afraid you'll have to go into
Shillingbourne Cottage for an X-ray, Gloria, to establish
whether you've broken anything. Meanwhile…' he
quirked a quizzical sideways glance up at Gemma, one
eyebrow raised a fraction higher than the other '…I think
a Kaltostat dressing to clean up that pus and a small padded
splint to keep the toe in alignment, don't you, Nurse?'

His eyes glinted, her heart thudded. She nodded. 'Fine.'
Her voice came out as a throaty murmur, and she repeated
loudly. 'Fine.'

A hank of hair fell across Sam's forehead and she had
to resist the sudden desire to smooth it back in place. What
on earth? Her cheeks burned and she busied herself disposing of the dirty implements and bowls on the trolley,
fervently hoping that he hadn't noticed anything amiss.

He stood up and smiled down at Gloria. 'I'll get in touch
with the hospital right now. See Ellie on your way out—
she'll tell you when to go for your X-ray, which should be

later today. And I'll leave your prescription for an anti-biotic with her.'

He paused at the door. 'And promise me you won't try to drive yourself into Shillingbourne. I know you think you're tough as old boots, but that just wouldn't be on.'

Gloria grinned. 'OK, promise. Mum'll take me if Phil's working. She insisted on bringing me in this morning. She's outside in the waiting room.'

'Sensible woman, your mum,' said Sam, and with a nod and a smile for both of them he took himself off.

'If I weren't happily spoken for,' sighed Gloria, 'I'd go for our Dr Sam in a big way. He wouldn't know what hit him. Of course, I've known him since for ever. He used to be quite a lad, played the field. I heard that he nearly got caught once, but wriggled off the hook.' She sighed again. 'But he's gorgeous, isn't he, Nurse?'

You can say that again, thought Gemma. 'He's very nice,' she mumbled as she bent over the injured foot. What did that mean—wriggled off the hook? With practised fingers, she fixed the dressing and the splint in place with a firm supporting bandage. 'I'm afraid you won't be able to get your trainer on,' she explained, when she'd finished bandaging from toe to ankle, gently easing the thick sock over the bulky dressing.

'Not to worry,' replied Gloria cheerfully, and with Gemma's support hobbled out to the waiting room to join her mother.

There were four more patients for Gemma to see before lunch. Working on autopilot and concentrating fiercely, she dealt with them with her usual calm so that none of them guessed at the turmoil she was in. But it was a relief when the session ended and she could get ready to go home for lunch to think. She had to get herself straightened out.

She had nearly made a fool of herself in front of a patient. Supposing she had pushed back that lock of Sam's hair… It didn't bear thinking about. It was ridiculous at her age—frightening to think that she had so nearly given herself away. What on earth was happening to her?

Ellie called to her as she was letting herself out of the staff door, wanting to know if she would be back early for coffee. Gemma had decided to skip that ritual for once, but couldn't refuse the pleading tone in Ellie's voice, and confirmed that she would.

She tried to make sense of what was happening to her and Sam as she nibbled at a sandwich a few minutes later. What was it between them? Simply chemistry, all body scents and hormones? Lust rather than love? And was it affecting him as strongly as it was her? Did she invade *his* mind as he did hers?

He'd been so gentle and kind on Friday evening when he'd mopped up her tears and comforted her. It had been exactly what she'd needed then, but if…*if* this seemingly mutual attraction was going anywhere, she would want more than avuncular comfort from him, a replacement father for Daisy. She would want companionship, laughter, sex and promises of something more to come…

The thought stopped her in her tracks. What the devil was she doing, even thinking along those lines? Dear God, she hardly knew the man and here she was making some sort of future plans round him—and all on the strength of eye contact and body language and one real kiss. That farewell kiss on Saturday had been something! There had been nothing avuncular about *that*.

Altogether, Saturday had been brilliant: Kite-flying on the hill; a farmhouse tea in a village in the valley the other side; walking back home with a tired Daisy riding high on Sam's shoulders. It had been a happy family outing.

What else could it have been, since it had been largely

devoted to entertaining Daisy? But, then, for years her weekends had been devoted to Daisy and, being the sort of man he was, Sam had sussed that out for himself.

The easy companionship had continued after Daisy had gone to bed. They had watched a film and had held a post-mortem on it as they'd consumed the bottle of wine Sam had brought with him. She had accused him laughingly of trying to get her tipsy.

He had gone along with the cliché. 'What, so that I might have my wicked way with you?' he'd said with a leer, his blue eyes blazing. They had even flirted a little, keeping it light, veering away from anything serious—until he had kissed her goodnight. That had been anything but lightweight.

Standing in the hall just inside the front door, Sam said with sudden deadly seriousness, looking into her eyes with an intensity that was almost frightening, 'Is there any reason why I shouldn't kiss you as I want to kiss you, as you deserve to be kissed, Gemma?'

There was Daisy, and a dozen other reasons—most of them to do with the fact that no man had figured seriously in her life since she'd parted from Neil. The barricade she had erected then had remained intact.

'No,' she whispered.

'Your ex?'

'Is very ex.'

'Positive?'

'Positive!' She *was* positive.

'And there's no one else?'

'No one.'

He bent his head and his mouth closed over hers, at first tenderly then savagely, and she had responded like a flower in the desert thirsting for rain. Their bodies had melded, soft breasts crushed painfully to hard chest; hip to hip, thigh gyrated against thigh, rousing, exciting; tongues explored, teeth nibbled lips.

Sam gave a groan. His hands, which had been cupping her buttocks, crept up her back and slid up into the thick bob of her hair. He tilted back her head and rubbed his nose to hers. 'Oh, Gemma, I don't know what you've done to me,' he murmured thickly, 'but you've made your way deep under my skin.'

The murmured words had come like manna from heaven—under his skin, that's just where she wanted to be. Gemma shivered, her heart hammered as if it would bound from her chest—but suddenly out of the blue warning bells rang in her head. This isn't right, it's too soon, they seemed to clamour. She eased herself away from him, gently but firmly. 'I think you'd better go,' she said, her voice quaking.

His intelligent eyes gazed steadily down into hers. 'You want more time.' It was a statement not a question.

'Yes.'

'You have it, love.' His voice was gentle. 'Just think about it. See you at the surgery on Monday.' And turning on his heel, he let himself out of the front door.

Think about it. She'd done precious little else but think about it since then. The memory of that kiss and its implication had been with her all through Sunday. Somehow she had survived the day without rousing Daisy's suspicions.

It had helped that they went to tea with her best friend, Katy. While the two girls had played together, Gemma and Katy's mother, Mary, had chatted about this and that and laid the foundation for future friendship. But that had been Sunday—today's revelation by Gloria Watson about Sam's youthful past, especially the bit about him sliding off the hook, was a whole new ball game. It had suggested that he had backed off from commitment. Neil had been good at backing off from commitment. Or was there another explanation?

The chiming of the grandfather clock jerked Gemma back to the present, reminding her that it was time she returned to the surgery and her chat with Ellie.

Ellie had barely got started on a résumé of her disastrous weekend with her in-laws when the patients' doorbell pealed several times in quick succession.

They abandoned their coffee and made for the door.

'Somebody sounds frantic,' said Gemma, as Ellie punched in the security sequence to release the outer and inner doors.

An elderly man, grey in the face, stood on the doorstep. He was shaking badly and clutching the left side of his chest. 'Pain,' he said. 'Terrible pain.' He sagged against the doorframe. Gemma and Ellie caught him as he slid towards the ground.

'Know him?' asked Gemma, as between them they half carried him, his feet dragging, into the waiting room.

'No, I'm sure he's not one of ours. There was a car parked at a crazy angle to the kerb—must be his. Is he having a heart attack?' puffed Ellie as they laid the man gently down on the floor.

'Possibly.' Gemma was taking the man's pulse at his wrist. It was weak and uneven. 'Loosen his tie, Ellie, and fetch the mobile oxygen pack and a blanket, then get hold of Sam or his father, or both. We're going to have to carry him to the treatment room.'

Both doctors came within minutes, and the four of them carried the man to the treatment room. Breathing raggedly through the oxygen mask, he came round as they lowered him onto the couch. He stared blearily up at the strange faces and frowned and fumbled at the mask.

Sam bent over him. 'Best keep it on, old chap,' he said, plugging his stethoscope into his ears as Gemma unbuttoned the man's shirt. 'I'm a doctor. You're in the Blaney St Mary surgery.'

The sound of voices filtered through from the waiting room.

'Doesn't look like he's going to arrest,' murmured Dr Mallory, 'but he's going to have to be hospitalised. Sam, you and Gemma carry on here, Ellie will phone for an ambulance and then between us we'll sort out the invading hordes—OK by you?'

'Fine.' Sam nodded and began his examination. A few minutes later he straightened up. 'I think you've had a mild heart attack,' he told the elderly man gently. 'Have you had any heart trouble before, Mr...?'

'Blake.' The colourless lips trembled. 'No, I haven't. Is it serious, Doctor?' He put out a shaky hand.

Sam took it and gave him a reassuring smile. 'All heart attacks are serious and have to be followed up, Mr Blake, but yours is a mild one, a warning to take care. Now, I'm going to give you something for the pain and arrange for you to go into hospital for tests. Is there anyone we can notify?'

He gave the name of his daughter who lived in London, and gave her telephone number. Gemma made a note of it as he reeled it off. He was a widower, holidaying in Shillingbourne. Would they let the hotel manager know? He was worried about his car. He was agitated, worried about everything.

Sam gave him a painkilling injection and a mild sedative to calm him down. He and Gemma both assured him that they would take care of everything. They stayed with him, monitoring his heart, blood pressure, pulse and respirations until the ambulance arrived twenty minutes later. They saw him into the ambulance, then, standing side by side on the gravel strip outside the surgery, waited until it had departed and their patient was safely away.

Their hands were almost touching. Gemma felt the hairs on her bare forearms stir. He had his shirtsleeves rolled up and she could feel the warmth radiating from his skin, was aware of the curling fair hairs on *his* arms, glinting in the sunshine. Her cheeks flushed, she glanced sideways at him. 'I must get on, I'm miles behind with my list.'

His fingers closed over hers. 'Don't go.' His voice was low, urgent. 'Another minute's not going to make any difference.' He squeezed her hand tightly. 'Gemma, about Saturday, can we...?'

His voice was drowned out as a red sports car roared round the green and screeched to a halt at the kerbside in front of them. He stared. The car looked familiar. Of course it was. He'd seen it outside Cherry Tree Cottage the Sunday before last when he'd witnessed that strange little tableau...

'Bloody hell!' He looked at Gemma. He couldn't read the expression on her face. 'Do you know this maniac?' he asked.

She nodded. 'Yes,' she hissed through clenched teeth. 'I do. It's Neil, my ex-husband.'

CHAPTER SEVEN

AN INCREDULOUS expression swept over Sam's face. 'So this the husband who is supposed to be *very ex*,' he ground out. Dropping Gemma's hand as if it were on fire, he turned and disappeared through the surgery door.

Gemma stood like a statue staring after him. What did he mean—'very ex', in that sarcastic tone? And what was Neil doing here? And why, oh *why* had he come when she and Sam—?

'Surprise, surprise, Gem, darling.' She turned back to see him bounding across toward her, a boyish, exuberant smile on his face, doing his Peter Pan act.

He skidded to a halt in front of her, scuffing up the gravel. Just like a small child, she thought crossly.

'Hello, sweetie, long time no see.' He bent his head as if to kiss her. She stepped smartly back.

Sweetie! She hated him calling her sweetie, always had. It grated. She wasn't dead keen on Gem either—it was what he used to call her. She'd loved it then when they were young and in love, but now... She didn't want to think about that.

'Rubbish, Neil, you were here just over a week ago, and I told you then about coming without phoning first. Right now Daisy's at school and I'm working so I suggest you take yourself off somewhere and come to the cottage at four o'clock when we'll both be home.'

Give me time to prepare Daisy, she thought—and with the thought a wave of sadness that she had to be prepared for a visit from her father.

Neil's full lips—too full—turned down at the corners. So different from Sam's finely sculpted lips, sprang another thought. 'Couldn't you hook her out of school early?'

'No, and, anyway, I'm working. See you at four at the cottage.' Turning on her heel, she let herself into the surgery.

Ellie looked surprised to see her. 'Sam said you'd got a visitor and might be a while and suggested I might change some of your appointments,' she said.

'Did he now?' Gemma produced a tight smile. 'No need. As you see, I'm here. But be a love and phone the school, please, and tell them that if I'm late collecting Daisy…' She hesitated. Neil wouldn't, would he, take her out in that lethal car of his? 'They're not to let her go with anyone else.'

Ellie looked at her, her eyes popping with curiosity.

Not surprising, thought Gemma. It must sound a bit cloak and daggerish. 'I know it sounds odd, I'll explain tomorrow, but don't say anything to anyone else, Ellie, please?'

Ellie shook her head. 'Not if you don't want me to.'

'Thanks.' Gemma smiled an apology to a couple of patients waiting behind her and fled to the treatment room.

She crushed thoughts of both Sam and Neil out of her mind and got on with her list. As Ellie had warned, there were a number of people wanting jabs before going on holiday or hay-fever sufferers needing antihistamines, in addition to the normal chores.

She was surprised to find that a number of those wanting holiday jabs were off to some far-flung places. She found herself administering vaccines against a range of diseases from cholera to typhoid. This had been the norm when she was nursing in the London practice, but unexpected in rural Blaney St Mary—at least, she thought with a snort of self-disgust, to a townee like me. Why, because someone lives in the country and speaks with a thick local burr, should they be content with the Costa Brava? How patronising could you get?

The list went without a hitch until Jo Pullen and his wife came in for first-time jabs. They were off to Saudi Arabia. Jo Pullen was a heavily built, middle-aged man who nearly fainted at the sight of the needle. He had to be persuaded by Gemma, and jollied along by an exasperated Mrs Pullen, that he would feel little more than a scratch before he would even roll up his shirtsleeve.

'So you say,' he said grimly, squeezing his eyes shut as Gemma swabbed his arm and bent over him with the syringe. 'But I can't abide needles, that's why I don't like going further afield than Brittany—that suits me fine.'

'All done,' said Gemma seconds later, putting a tiny dressing over the minute puncture mark.

Mr Pullen opened his eyes cautiously. 'You mean, you've finished?' he asked. 'But I didn't feel a thing. You're a wizard, Nurse.'

'If you say so, Mr Pullen,' replied Gemma, smiling at him and his wife. 'So tell me, why are you going to Saudi Arabia this year instead of Brittany?'

Mrs Pullen answered. 'We're going to see our son. He works in Saudi and is treating us to this holiday. I'm looking forward to it. It'll make a nice change, and it'll be lovely to see him and his family.'

'All sand and flies, I dare say,' grumbled Mr Pullen, but he smiled. He tapped his arm and rolled down his sleeve. 'But at least the worst is over, thanks to you, Nurse.'

Gemma saw them out and called for her next and last patient—Mrs Janice Norton—for removal of stitches from a hand wound, she saw from her notes.

Janice had a tiny baby secured to her chest in a front

sling and was struggling with a reluctant, grizzly small boy of about three with her one good hand, the other hand being bandaged.

Gemma went to meet her. 'Let me help,' she offered, and, gently but firmly detaching the boy from his mother, led the way to the treatment room.

Surprised, the boy stopped grizzling and stared up at Gemma. She smiled. 'My name's Gemma,' she said as she sat him down on the spare chair. 'What's your name, love?'

He stuck his thumb in his mouth and continued to stare.

'It's Adam, Nurse.' supplied his mother. 'He's a bit shy with strangers.'

'He'll grow out of it,' Gemma said, handing Adam a picture book which he took with one hand whilst keeping his thumb plugged into his mouth. 'Is he at playschool yet?'

Janice said wryly, 'You've got to be joking. The nearest one's in Shillingbourne, and it's expensive. No way could we afford it. But he's already booked in for the reception class at the school—he can go there when he's four.'

'Oh, well, not to worry, he'll soon have his…brother, or is it sister…?'

'Sister.'

'To play with,' Gemma said cheerfully. She stroked the sleeping baby's soft cheek. 'Now, let's have a look at this hand of yours, Janice, see if the stitches are ready to come out.'

She unwound the bandage and removed the dressing that had been applied over the diagonal wound. 'It's looking good, coming together well. Dr Sam did a neat bit of stitching. I'll remove most of them, but one or two will have to stay in for another couple of days.' She glanced at the young mother. 'I dare say you've been using it more than you should—yes?'

Janice shrugged. 'Can't help it with these two to see to.' She dropped a kiss on her baby's head and smiled across at Adam, still sucking his thumb but absorbed in the book. 'Especially as Adam's a bit mummy-sick at present.'

Deftly, Gemma began removing the stitches—sibling jealousy? she wondered. 'Do you let Adam help you with the baby?' she asked, keeping her voice low. 'Let him hold her sometimes, help when she has a bath?'

'Oh, I wouldn't dare. He's clumsy, he doesn't seem to realise that Tansy needs to be handled with care.'

Poor Adam! There was no doubt that he was loved, but... Gemma finished removing all but three stitches, swabbed the palm with antiseptic and applied a small, waterproof dressing to the healing area.

'Come back and see me in three days and I'll take out those last few stitches,' she said.

She sat back in her chair. Now comes the tricky bit, she thought. This poor woman's anxious and unhappy. I must try and help. Still keeping her voice low, she said, 'Why don't you explain to Adam that because Tansy is small she has to be treated gently, like he was when he was a baby. Sit him down somewhere safe and show him how to hold her, ask him to help you push the pram—anything to make him feel involved. And try to give him a little time on his own and throw in lots of hugs and kisses.'

Janice frowned. 'I haven't been neglecting him, if that's what you think.' She sounded indignant. 'But there's so much to do, and my husband comes in at all hours, wanting a meal. I just get so tired.'

Wanting or demanding? 'Janice, it's crystal clear that you haven't been neglecting Adam, that you love him to bits, but make sure that *he* knows that. The baby inevitably takes up so much of your time that he may be feeling a bit left out. Perhaps your husband could—'

'*No!*' An explosive no. 'He's too busy and…to tell you the truth, Nurse, he isn't too keen on the kids.' Her voice dropped to a whisper. 'He didn't want to have children. I think he's a bit jealous of them.' She crossed over to Adam and removed the book from his hand. 'Come on, love.' she said huskily, helping him down from the chair. 'Let's go home to tea and watch something on the telly.'

My word, thought Gemma, have I said too much or too little?

Janice paused at the door. 'Thanks, Nurse, I'll remember what you've said, it makes sense. I don't know why I hadn't realised what was happening.' She pulled a face. 'I must be thick, but things will be different from now on.'

'You're tired, not thick, Janice. Why don't you make an appointment to see Dr Sam? Your hormones may be all over the place—they often are when you've had a baby. If it is that, he might be able to prescribe something to sort them out.'

The young mother's face lit up. 'It would be brilliant just not to feel so exhausted. I'll make an appointment right now. Thanks again, Nurse, you're a gem.'

A gem! How ironic. Thoughtfully, Gemma tidied the treatment room, disposing of dirty dressings and wiping down surfaces. Had she been too optimistic with Janice, suggesting that Sam might come up with a miracle pill to cure her postnatal exhaustion? No, it had been the right thing to do. Even if he didn't produce a magic pill, he would listen, offer guidance and show that he cared. To someone like Janice, who seemed to be starved of caring— certainly by her husband—that could work like magic.

Sam! Just saying his name in her head, it did strange things to her heart, making it leap about inside her chest like a wild thing. She sat down hard on a chair. This was ridiculous. She shouldn't feel like this, especially after the way he'd walked away from her with that caustic remark when Neil arrived.

Oh, God. Neil. She looked at her watch. A quarter past three. She'd have to scoot if she was to have time to explain his arrival to Daisy.

Daisy was subdued when Neil arrived, returning his noisy kiss with a cautious one of her own. But she smiled, if a little hesitantly, when, with a flourish, he produced a large, oblong, beautifully wrapped package and handed it to her.

'There you are, poppet, to remind you of how much Daddy loves you.'

'Thank you, Daddy.' Her voice was trembly with excitement, her round face rosy as she laid the parcel on the table and knelt up on a chair to open it. Her nimble fingers made short work of removing the outer wrappings.

Gemma tried not to mind her eagerness, her ready acceptance of the present from the father whom she half distrusted. She's only six, Gemma reminded herself, it's only natural. But, oh, please, my darling, she prayed silently, don't be fooled by him. He's still the same irresponsible man who walked out on us, couldn't handle being a father. Expensive presents can't alter that.

It *was* an expensive present—an angelic-faced, elegantly dressed doll in pink satin, a walking, talking, laughing, crying, singing doll.

For a moment, speechless, Daisy stared at it, stroked its rose-tinted cheek with a chubby forefinger, then lifted it reverently from its silk-lined box and cuddled it close.

Her green eyes sparkled. 'Oh, Mummy, isn't she beautiful?' she breathed.

'Beautiful,' Gemma agreed, pumping enthusiasm into

her voice. She touched the gold-tinted curls. It was a little girl's dream doll. God knew how much it had cost. For once she envied Neil, or rather envied the fact that he could afford to buy a present for their daughter that brought such a glow to her dear little face.

Not, she reminded herself, that Daisy glowed like that only for expensive presents. She would do the same for much simpler things, like a book or paints or crayons. She was an unspoilt, easy-to-please child, but there was no doubt that the doll had hit a high spot. And why not? For once Neil had got it right. Be generous to him.

She ruffled Daisy's hair. 'You're a lucky girl,' she said. 'Don't you think that Daddy deserves a thank-you kiss?'

Daisy leaned across the corner of the table and kissed his cheek. 'Thank you, Daddy, for my beautiful, beautiful doll.'

'What about this one, then?' said Neil, offering his other cheek.

Daisy kissed it quickly, then scrambled back onto her chair.

'I could do with a hug too,' he said. 'Come here, poppet.'

A small frown creased Daisy's forehead, but she slid off the chair and, cuddling the doll, walked round the table.

Oh, Neil, don't push it, Gemma prayed. Don't make a big deal out of it. Just give her a quick hug and let her go.

He didn't hear her prayer or, if he did, ignored it, pulling Daisy roughly onto his lap and demanding another kiss as well as a hug. So what was new? He never had been sensitive to her thoughts or the vibes she had sent out to him in those early days of their marriage when she had still loved him. But be fair, she told herself. Not many men are intuitive or perceptive. You've got to spell everything out for them.

Sam is, murmured an inner voice. Is he? So why did he march away from me this afternoon? Why didn't he *see* that I was upset by Neil's arrival instead of—?

'Daddy, please, let me go. You're hugging me too tight and you're hurting my dolly.' Daisy's voice shattered her thoughts.

'Neil!' Gemma said sharply. 'Let Daisy get down— *now.'*

'Jealous.' He leered at her, grinning.

'No, but she's thanked you. Don't spoil it. Let her go, you're frightening her.' She put steel in her voice. 'I mean it Neil.'

Neil loosed his hold a little and looked down at Daisy. 'I don't frighten you, do I, poppet?'

Wide-eyed, Daisy stared up at him. She shook her head slightly. 'But I want to get down, please, and so does…Rose. She wants to get down, too.'

His mouth went sulky. 'Oh, well, if that's what you want.' He almost pushed her off his lap.

Clutching her doll, Daisy stood for a moment looking uncertainly from her father to her mother. A tug-of-war kid, thought Gemma, her heart going out to her small daughter.

She said softly, 'Listen, love, why don't you go and phone your friend Katy and tell her all about…Rose. Use the phone in my room.' She looked hard at Neil, willing him not to say or do anything to upset Daisy further. 'Katy,' she explained, 'is Daisy's best friend at school.'

Daisy's eyes were shining as she sidled towards the door to the hall. 'Oh, Mummy, can I? That's brilliant.' She whisked out through the door, banging it closed behind her.

Silence descended like a blanket as Gemma and Neil stared at each other across the table.

Ignore what's happened, Gemma told herself. Be pleasant, sociable. 'Would you like something to drink?' she asked. 'Coffee, tea?'

Still looking sulky, he grunted. 'Got anything stronger?'

'I thought as you were driving…' She hadn't thought anything of the sort—she'd known he'd want something stronger.

'Wine—red, white?' Deliberately she didn't mention the half-bottles of gin and whisky, survivors from her farewell party when she'd left London.

'Well, if that's all you've got… Red…please.' Suddenly the boyish smile was back. 'Nice to know you still care, Gem, about me drinking and driving. Don't want me to have an accident.'

'I don't want *anyone* to have an accident, especially one that can be avoided,' she said repressively. 'I saw what drinking and driving could do when I worked in Casualty.' She made for the door. 'I won't be a moment, the wine's in the kitchen.'

He was standing at the window, staring out across the green, when she came back. She crossed the room and stood beside him, handing him a glass.

'Cheers.' He clinked his glass to hers.

'Cheers.' She couldn't think of anything else to say, just longed for him to be gone. The thought brought a lump to her throat. She had loved him once…so much. If only, if only…

He knocked back the wine in one long swallow, then looked at his watch. 'Damn, have to be off, though I wish I could stay…' He gave Gemma a long considering look, and before she could move he planted a wet kiss on her mouth. 'You know, Gem, we should get back together again, you and I.'

Speechless, Gemma gaped at him for a moment, then found her voice. 'And Daisy?' she asked drily.

He shrugged. 'Of course, Daisy. Goes without saying.'

The tenderness of her thoughts a moment ago seeped away. 'That's big of you.'

He ignored, or didn't notice, her sarcasm. 'So, what about it Gem? Shall we give it a go?'

Gemma drew in a deep, deep breath that came from way beneath her diaphragm. 'I think if anything had better go Neil, it had better be you, right now.'

He looked at her, no, leered at her, and said, sounding almost triumphant, 'Afraid of falling for me again, Gem, or haven't you got over the first time?'

Gemma stared at him in disbelief. Of course she'd got over him. Did he really imagine that she could still love him after the way he'd deserted her, leaving her with a baby, knowing that her parents were living abroad? That she'd been on her own? His conceit was breathtaking, but, then, that was all part of the little boy act.

Extraordinary that he was such a whiz kid in the business world. Probably much of that was due to his charm, and he had oodles of that—and knew how to use it. Thank God, she was now immune to his charm.

She removed the empty glass from his hand and said blandly, 'The first time was the last time, Neil. Now it's time you were off. You've got a dinner date.'

'Yes, but I'll be back…soon.'

Please, not soon. 'Next time, please, phone.'

They moved out into the hall. He looked up the stairs.

'I'll say goodbye to Daisy for you,' Gemma said, making her voice casual, hoping he wouldn't insist on saying goodbye himself. Daisy, she thought, had had just about enough of her father for one day, and *she'd* certainly had enough of her ex-husband.

A few minutes later, with a sigh of relief, she watched as he noisily revved up the engine and drove away.

* * *

Gemma lay awake much of the night going over the events of the day, and rose feeling ragged.

Neil's suggestion that they get back together made her furious, and a touch scared, though she wasn't quite sure why. He wouldn't deliberately physically harm her or Daisy, but he was given to little boy tantrums when he couldn't get his own way, which was disconcerting to say the least.

As for Sam's curtness, that still hurt and made her heart ache. *Why* had he acted so out of character, so rudely? What had he read into Neil's arrival? What had made him suddenly turn to ice when only minutes before they had been working side by side on the elderly Mr Pullen? She would tackle him about it at the first opportunity.

She worried, too, about Daisy, and her reaction to her father's visit. Silly, really, she told herself, as Daisy had gone happily to bed with Rose lying in state beside her, seemingly having forgotten being over-hugged by Neil. As if to confirm this, Daisy bounced into her room minutes later, her usual happy, chatty self, carrying Rose with exaggerated care. The episode was clearly forgotten.

The church clock struck a quarter to nine as Gemma made her way across the green to the surgery. Perhaps, she thought, like Daisy, Sam and I can forget yesterday's incident. She smiled wryly. Who are you kidding? she mused as she let herself in through the staff door. He'll probably avoid me like the plague and won't give me a chance to ask why he'd reacted as he had.

As it happened, fate decided that even if he'd wanted to, he couldn't ignore her. His corn-bright head bent in his usual solicitous manner, he was giving an arm to an elderly lady leaving his office. He looked up as Gemma closed and locked the staff door.

'Morning.' His voice was clipped.

Gemma's heart turned over several times. 'Morning,' she replied, mustering a smile and a nod that included the patient.

The tightest of smiles touched Sam's lips. She was near enough to see that it didn't reach his eyes. They were unreadable, the laughter lines radiating from them just lines. Maybe he was simply tired, he'd been on call last night.

In a toneless voice he asked. 'May I have a word, Nurse, please, if you can spare a moment, in my office in, say, five minutes?'

Gemma beamed, though her heart thudded into her shoes. He sounded so stiff, formal, unfriendly. 'Fine. I'll be there, Doctor.'

She let herself into the staffroom. She shrugged herself out of her jacket, ran a comb through her long bob of hair and stared in the mirror. Jade green eyes stared back at her, thoughtful, puzzled—sad! Why sad? Because Sam…because Sam's bitterly angry with you, she told her reflection, and that hurts. Angry! With little reason, she reminded herself sharply. For heaven's sake, where's your spunk, woman? You're the one who has a right to be angry. He's the one who walked away.

OK, supposing he was angry because Neil had arrived, driving dangerously like a bat out of hell. Surely that wasn't enough to ignore him the way he had or to humiliate her. It was almost as if he had a personal motive for refusing to stay to be introduced. But that wasn't possible. He not only didn't know Neil, he didn't know anything about him. She'd hardly mentioned him, except to acknowledge him as her ex-husband.

Ex-husband, that's what seemed to be bugging him. No, not ex, but *very ex*. He'd said it when he'd turned on his heel, almost as if he didn't believe it. Did he think that because she and Neil were divorced he shouldn't come anywhere near her? Surely he appreciated that ex-husband didn't mean ex-father, and that for Daisy's sake he was entitled to visit.

Or did he think…could he possibly think that Neil still held a place in her affections? Was that what the sarcasm had been about?

Did he resent it, loathe it, because he felt he had a *right* to? She almost stopped breathing for a moment as the thought sunk in, swirled around in her head… OK, they were mutually attracted—no, more than that, his kiss had said more than that the other night.

Five minutes, he'd said—five minutes had passed. Her chest full of butterflies, she made her way slowly to Sam's office. She tried to marshal her muddled thoughts, but they refused to be marshalled, and she found herself just as muddled when she knocked on his door and entered in response to his invitation.

His back to the door, he was silhouetted against the window looking over the walled orchard and twisted chimneys of the manor house. Gemma stood just inside the door, tense and expectant, waiting for him to speak.

After what seemed an eternity he turned round. Against the light she couldn't see his face clearly, or the expression in his eyes.

He said abruptly, 'I must apologise for the way I behaved yesterday. I shouldn't have walked away from you as I did. I should have waited to be introduced to…' he hesitated '…your husband.'

His voice was colourless. Gemma felt as if her heart were being squeezed by an ice-cold hand.

'Ex-husband.'

Sam took a step forward. She could see his face now.

He was frowning, his mouth a firm line, his eyes were so dark they were almost navy blue.

'Are you sure he's really ex?' His voice had hardened. Where was the kind, caring doctor, the kind, caring man, the man of perception?

Gemma felt a mixture of disbelief, anger and intense sadness surging through her. She had thought that this man knew her—and she knew him—but...

'I said ex the other night, and I meant it. Why don't you believe me?' Her voice came out in a vaporous whisper. Her lips felt white, it was painful to speak. She felt her eyes glistening with held back tears. She clenched her teeth—*no way* would she cry. For heaven's sake, there was nothing to cry about—he was simply a man like any other man.

Sam took another step forward, his eyes searching her face. He punched one fist into the other. 'Shi—' He bit off the word. He reached out a tentative hand and touched her shoulder. 'Gemma, I don't know how to cope with this...this jealousy.'

Jealousy! All the thoughts in her mind tumbled together. '*Jealousy*,' she repeated incredulously. Incongruously she remembered that Neil had accused her of jealousy when he'd cuddled Daisy.

'That's right, good old-fashioned jealousy...' The internal telephone on his desk sprang into life. He muttered under his breath as he turned and snatched up the receiver. 'Yes?' he barked, then said more quietly, 'Sorry, Ellie, what can I do for you?'

Gemma stared at the back of Sam's bright head, her tumultuous thoughts spiralling. *Jealousy!* There was an old song about jealousy... The murmur of Ellie's voice penetrated her thoughts. She caught the words 'came off his bike' and 'grazed legs'. An accident... Making a conscious effort, she snapped into professional mode.

Sam was saying, 'Can he walk? Good. Gemma's here. We'll come through and take him to the treatment room. Anyone with him? No? Then you'd better let his mum know, Ellie.'

He put down the phone and turned back to face Gemma. His lips were curled in a lopsided, sardonic smile. 'Sorry about that, might have known it would happen. Another half-finished conversation bites the dust. I'm afraid duty calls. Young Jason Lowe has come off his bike—cuts and abrasions. Sounds like a longish clean-up operation so let's get cracking.'

Gemma followed him out into the corridor.

Lowe! Shirley Lowe, query prolapsed uterus, had been one of the patients she'd seen on her first morning.

'Is he one of Shirley Lowe's brood?'

'That's right. She'll bawl him out for cycling too fast, then kiss him to death. Good mother, Shirley.'

Thirteen-year-old Jason was big and bouncy like his mum. He managed to keep some sort of smile on his face during most of the time it took for Sam and Gemma to work on his extensive grazes, though at times it was rather a grim smile. He had skidded on his left side, causing abrasions and what amounted to first-degree burns from his cheek to his ankle.

Slowly, painstakingly, working side by side—Gemma on the leg, Sam on the boy's face and arm—they used forceps to pick out minute pieces of gravel and dirt from the sore areas, and then gently swabbed them clean with an antiseptic. As always, they worked together in perfect, professional harmony.

Sam had to stitch a small, deep cut on Jason's cheekbone, just below his eye. 'You were lucky there, old son,' he said, as he put in the last stitch. 'Just missed injuring your eye. I'm going to take a look a look in it to make sure that it hasn't been damaged.'

Taking his time, he examined Jason's eye carefully through the ophthalmoscope and pronounced it clear.

He slanted a glance at Gemma. 'All finished at my end. How are you doing, Nurse?'

His words were formal, but his voice was husky, warm…intimate, Gemma thought, her heart hammering out an extra beat.

She straightened up. 'Just finished, Doctor,' she said, matching his formality, 'but I'm not happy about leaving the leg uncovered. Jason's wearing shorts now, but he'll be wearing trousers to school and they're going to rub those sore places.'

Sam nodded. 'Yes, I agree.'

'The best thing,' he explained to Jason, 'would be to leave the wounds exposed—they tend to heal better that way. But, as Nurse pointed out, you'll be wearing trousers to school so we'll have to cover the sore areas with some specially treated dressings to keep them clean and promote healing.'

'If I didn't go to school,' said Jason, grinning cheekily at Sam and Gemma, and at his mother who had just arrived, 'I wouldn't have to wear trousers, would I?'

Shirley lightly cuffed the good side of his face. 'That's enough cheek,' she said severely, though her face was wreathed in a smile of relief. 'It's school for you tomorrow, if Dr Sam thinks that's OK.'

'That's fine by me,' said Sam, 'but don't go kicking a ball around for a day or two, Jason, and make an appointment to come back to see Nurse in five days' time to have your stitches out and the dressings checked.' He stripped off his plastic gloves and tossed them into the bin. 'Now

I'm off to see some of my other patients. Nurse will fix you up with dressings.' And with a nod to Shirley and Gemma, he was gone.

Gemma spent the rest of the morning making up for lost time and didn't even snatch a coffee-break. Remembering her promise to Ellie to fill her in on Neil's visit yesterday, she was relieved for the reprieve. Not that it would last. Ellie would expect the full story over their usual lunchtime coffee.

As it happened, she had a further reprieve. When she went into the waiting room to summon her last patient, Mrs Mallory was manning the desk.

'Poor Ellie has a raging toothache and has gone to the dentist,' she explained. 'I've told her to take the afternoon off, so I'm holding the fort for the rest of the day.'

The phone was ringing as Gemma let herself into the cottage at lunchtime. She stared at it till the answerphone clicked on. Before he spoke, she knew that it was Sam. His clear tenor voice filled the small hall.

'Gemma, this is Sam. I won't see you this afternoon. Doing a stint at Shillingbourne Cottage in Theatre. But we must talk. Will call about ninish after Daisy's tucked up. If I don't hear from you, will assume this is OK.'

In between patients, as she worked her way through her list that afternoon, she debated with herself whether to leave a message saying no, or not to ring, which was the same as saying yes. By the time she collected Daisy from school she'd decided not to ring... Sam was right, they *had* to talk.

CHAPTER EIGHT

GEMMA had a tray loaded with bubbling coffee and a plateful of savoury and chocolate biscuits at the ready when Sam arrived at ten. One look at him and the words 'You're an hour overdue—this is a funny sort of nine o'clock' died on her lips.

She led him through to the sitting room, and said firmly, 'You'd better sit down before you fall down. You look exhausted.'

She had been psyching herself up for this meeting all afternoon, but from the moment she had opened the door and seen him, her nervousness had vanished. He'd looked tired this morning, but now... She recognised the drained look. 'Did something happen in Theatre?' she asked, her voice soft, gentle.

Sam sank down into the squashy armchair. 'Last patient on the list, young woman, girl really, only seventeen, appendicectomy, should have been quite straightforward. Well, it was, until she arrested—twice—just as we were finishing off.'

Gemma poured fragrant black coffee, handed him a cup and offered the biscuits. 'Take a handful—you need a sugar boost. Did she...?' Her eyes asked what her lips could not.

Sam shook his head. 'No. We resusced her both times, but it was touch and go, still is. She's in pretty poor shape in Intensive Care. The billion dollar question is—why? Why the sudden collapse? Why did her heart suddenly succumb to the strain of a simple operation? Heart, lungs—

everything—appeared normal when Roger Hayes, the anaesthetist, examined her on admission… It only left one real possibility…'

'Cerebral embolism or aneurism?' Gemma whispered.

'Yep. We took some X-rays and it turned out to be an embolism. It showed up clearly, but no way could poor old Roger have known about it. The girl hadn't a history of headaches or dizziness or anything associated with a blocked artery to the brain. Having surgery apparently just triggered it off, and the strain of the extra pressure was too much for her heart even though it had previously been ticking over fine.'

He stared down at his coffee, his hair gleaming in the lamplight. A hank of it fell over his high forehead and Gemma longed to stroke it back.

He lifted his head and stared at her, his eyes full of sadness. 'So frightening to see this fit, sporty girl lying there in the ICU, just hanging on. Poor kid. I saw her this afternoon when I was doing a round on the ward, and she told me how much she was looking forward to running a marathon in aid of leukaemia sufferers in six weeks' time. Wanted to know if she would be fit enough to run by then. Fat chance of that now even if…'

'She survives?'

'Yes.' He looked grim. 'For God's sake, she's had a stroke, Gemma, a girl of seventeen. From the position of the block, it looks as if she'll have left-side paralysis. She's an athlete. What is she going to do with her life when she's half-paralysed?'

'Sam, I know it's a cliché, where there's life and so on— but it's true.' She laid a hand on his arm—a comforting hand, a small enough gesture when she would have liked to have held him close, kissed his stiff, cold lips and warmed them. 'We've both seen things like that happen before, for no rhyme nor reason, and patients come through. And there's so much being done for stroke victims now, especially young ones. There's no reason why she shouldn't make a complete recovery. It is possible.'

He stared down at her hand resting on his arm, and then up into her face. His eyes brightened a little. 'You're dead right, of course. Not only might she pull through, but she might make a full recovery. I needed to hear that. I can think of some women who would have bawled me out for being late, but you didn't. You've even let me talk about it.' His lips curved into the semblance of a smile. 'I'm grateful.'

Gemma smiled back. 'No need to be. I'm a nurse.'

Some women would have bawled him out! Women he knew intimately? Stop second-guessing! There was no reason to suppose there were a host of other women in his life now, even if, according to Gloria Watson, there'd been plenty in the past, and one of them had been special. No, Gloria hadn't said that, she'd said… Oh, what did it matter what she'd said? It was only gossip.

There's no smoke without fire, whispered a nasty little voice at the back of her head.

Of course he was attractive to, and attracted by, women, and treated them with a special courtesy. But, then, so did his father—it was part of the Mallory charm. Not that it was anything like Neil's hollow charm—was it?

As for his social life outside the surgery, that was a mystery. Perhaps in his rare off-duty periods he pursued a wild life in Shorehampton or Bournemouth, but if he did she knew nothing of it. In fact, she knew very little about any part of his life when he wasn't working, except what he'd told her on that glorious kite-flying Saturday afternoon, and that had all been about family—his parents and his brother and two sisters…

'Do you think I might have another coffee, please?' Sam was holding out his empty cup and wearing a quizzical, lopsided smile. He was looking a little less tense.

Gemma snapped out of her reverie. Her cheeks reddened. 'Oh, yes, of course,' she said breathily, taking his cup and crossing to the side table to fill it.

Had he noticed that for a moment she'd been lost in thought? Her hand shook slightly as she poured. What had she been thinking about, letting her mind wander when Sam was eaten up with concern for his patient? *Some nurse—some confidante!* How could she?

She handed him his brimming cup. Behave as if nothing happened, get back to basics. 'Any chance of finding out what caused the embolism, or is it going to remain a mystery?'

Sam took a huge swallow of coffee. 'Might do. They'll run a huge battery of tests and might come up with some answers. But as you reminded me, in our line of work the unforseen, the unexpected can happen, and sometimes there isn't an obvious answer. It's the sort of nightmare situation we have to live with, leaving one always wondering if one could have done just that little bit more. Poor Roger's worried witless, wondering if he missed something when he examined her.'

'Could he have?'

Sam shook his head. 'Not very likely, he's very experienced, thorough, an excellent anaesthetist. But it's always possible, though there was nothing in the girl's history to indicate that anything might go wrong. She was admitted yesterday, had the usual four-hourly obs taken—all were normal. No abnormalities in the blood tests that were taken. She's an athlete in the peak of fitness. The embolism was a freak accident. All that we can do now is hope she pulls through.'

He looked at his watch and frowned. 'Wonder how she's doing?' He looked across at Gemma as though she might have the answer.

'Why don't you ring and find out?' she suggested practically.

The frown disappeared, to be replaced by a brief smile. 'Brilliant idea,' he said, as if she'd suggested phoning the moon. 'Why didn't I think of that?'

Because you're pretty shattered, she thought, and clever men like you often miss the obvious.

He pulled his mobile out of his pocket and punched in a number.

Gemma busied herself gathering up the dirty cups and empty biscuit plate—he'd eaten the lot. She heard him ask if Dr Hayes was still there—apparently he was. Sam asked to speak to him.

'Would you like a sandwich?' she mouthed, while he was waiting to be connected.

'Please.' He touched the back of her hand with his fingertips. It was a fleeting, feather-light touch, but her skin was still tingling when she reached the kitchen.

She made a pile of chicken sandwiches, armed herself with two glasses and the half bottle of whisky she had denied Neil, and returned to the sitting room.

Sam was perched on the edge of his chair, his mobile still in his hand. His face was unreadable. Good news or bad? Let it be good! He's had enough for one day.

'Well?' Her voice came out a breathy whisper.

He stood up and pocketed his mobile and stared at her as if surprised to see her. 'She's holding her own, seems to have stabilised. Not out of the woods yet, but if she maintains the status quo for another hour they reckon she'll be fit enough to be helicoptered down to Bournemouth for specialised assessment and treatment.' His mouth tilted in a tentative smile. 'It's better than we could have hoped for a few hours ago.'

'Oh, Sam, I'm so glad. The sooner she can have treatment the better. It'll give her a fighting chance of overcoming the paralysis, won't it?'

'That's the latest thinking—to get cracking on massage, physiotherapy and speech therapy within hours of a cerebral accident taking place. And as you reminded me just now, some patients make a remarkable recovery. Please, God, it's true of this youngster.'

His blue gaze, soft and melting, melded with hers. 'Oh, Gemma.' He reached out and took both her hands in his. He raised them to his lips and brushed a kiss across her knuckles. Then he drew her into his arms and cradled her head against his chest.

It felt familiar, she felt at home. His heart beat firmly but a little fast beneath her ear. He nuzzled the top of her head with his nose and his lips and his chin. It felt incredibly sweet, safe, being there in his arms. They stood together for seemingly endless minutes, swaying gently, clinging together, supporting each other.

This is how it should be, she thought, each of us supporting the other. How can you possibly know that? You hardly know each other, and supposing there was something in what the Watson woman said? protested a small, sober little voice. Supposing there was something in his past and he wasn't the perfect man, the perfect doctor. Her heart told her that it didn't matter.

'Doesn't this feel *right*?' murmured Sam, echoing her thoughts, his breath stirring her hair.

'Mmm…just what I was thinking.' She burrowed deeper against his chest and the long, strong column of his throat.

'We're on the same wavelength, Gemma, have been since that first morning when we met.' His voice was muffled, buried in her hair. He lifted his head and put a finger beneath her chin and tilted it upwards. 'A few weeks ago…a lifetime ago…but time doesn't matter, we belong together, my love.'

The pretty little carriage clock inherited from her great-aunt Marjorie gave out eleven silvery chimes—and then there was silence, a velvet-deep silence.

For a moment, as if they were one, almost drowning in each other's eyes, they both held their breath.

A dozen thoughts raced and tumbled around in Gemma's head just as her heart seemed to tumble round in her chest, refusing to be still. She struggled to get her thoughts together. What did he mean, belong together? Was he talking marriage or something else? And what about Daisy, her baby—where did she fit in? Had he forgotten Daisy? The small voice fired out one question after another.

It was all very romantic, talking about time not mattering. Perhaps it didn't to the two of them, but it did to Daisy. With Neil as a role model for a father, she would need *time*, and plenty of it, to accept a man into her life…or anyone perhaps on a permanent basis.

Her world revolves around you! reminded her voice loud and clear.

If he's suggesting marriage or a partnership. Her thoughts faltered as she was drawn deeper and deeper into the blue pools of his eyes. Perhaps he didn't mean that, perhaps he means just sex…

She swam up to the surface and exhaled her long held breath, breaking the silence. 'What do you mean?' she whispered. 'Belong together? I don't understand.'

Amusement flared in Sam's eyes. 'My word,' he murmured, 'the wheels have been churning. I could almost read your thoughts…'

Could he? Her cheeks went pink…

'There's no mystery, my love. Belonging together means what it says—I belong to you, you belong to me. You and me and Daisy, together.'

'Oh,' The word was breathy and drawn out. 'You didn't forget Daisy!'

'Bloody hell, do you think I would?' His voice was suddenly cold. He eased away from her and put his hands on her shoulders. '*Did* you, Gemma?'

A shutter slammed down over his eyes, leaving them cold to match his cold voice. Gemma shivered and felt the blood drain from her cheeks. He was so angry.

'I—I—' she stuttered. 'I didn't know… You see, Neil—'

'What's Neil got to do with it? You're supposed to be divorced, but he's always hanging around.' Sam's voice was icy. 'Have you still got a *thing* for him, Gemma? Tell me honestly.'

His eyes bored into hers, his fingers bit into her shoulders.

The biting fingers rallied her. She said quietly, 'You're hurting me, Sam.'

He swore beneath his breath and released his hold on her shoulders. 'Oh, Gemma, my dear love, I'm so sorry—the last thing I want to do is to hurt you, but that man makes my hackles rise.'

'But you don't know him.'

'Don't need to,' he ground out. 'A maniac who drives like he does and has obviously damaged you in the past—that's enough for me. Dear God, the thought of him and you…'

Her heart gave a leap. She wanted to wipe the pain off his face, the pain that said as clearly as if he had spoken…I love you, it proclaimed loud and clear.

She said very gently, 'Sam, there is no him and me. He

has access rights to see Daisy, that's all, and he only exercises them when the mood takes him. He isn't a very good father, never was, couldn't face up to his responsibilities, opted out soon after Daisy was born. Comes back to play daddy occasionally, but sometimes it's months between visits.'

He cupped her face in his hands. 'Is that why you found it hard to believe that I included Daisy in my future plans for us, because he has no sense of responsibility?'

'Yes. Oh, Sam, I'm so afraid for Daisy, she's had so many ups and downs in her short life. He's made promises that he hasn't kept, sometimes spoils her, sometimes ignores her, sometimes even frightens her…'

Incredulity, horror, anger flared in his eyes. 'Do you mean he threatens her physically?'

'Do you think I'd let him? No, in spite of his temper he's never done that. Rather the reverse. He's sometimes too affectionate and retreats into a stony silence if Daisy doesn't respond as he thinks she should. And that frightens her and makes her feel guilty for upsetting him. He's like a chameleon. She doesn't know what it's like to have a man around who is solid, dependable.'

Sam kissed her nose. 'I'd be solid and dependable, Gemma. Just give me a chance to prove it.' His voice was husky, his lovely blue eyes, warm and tender, devoured her. With his thumbs he traced the contours of her cheekbones. He kissed her eyelids. 'You're a beautiful woman, my darling, and you've been on your own too long. All I want to do is to take care of you and Daisy, and the sooner I can start the better.'

My darling! And said so tenderly, it sounded good. Too good to be true?

'Fine words butter no parsnips.' Gemma recalled the words of a dear old lady whom she had nursed. 'What does it mean?' she had asked. 'It's easy to make promises, quite another matter to put them into practice,' old Mrs Thompson had explained tartly.

A little shiver of apprehension ran up and down Gemma's spine. Was Sam making rash promises that he wouldn't be able to put into practice? He was a fancy-free bachelor. Did he really want to give up that freedom to care for her and Daisy? And *if* he had let one woman down… She should ask him if it was true. She would, but not now. He'd had enough for one evening. And so had she. She couldn't bear it if…

All that mattered was Daisy's happiness. Everything was happening too fast. The bottom line was—

'Gemma, come back to me, please.' Sam's voice, soft but firm, lasered through her thoughts. He dropped his hands from her face and moved back a step as if sensing that she needed space. 'Tell me what's wrong.'

He sounded so kind, so understanding—everything Neil was not. 'How do you know that anything's wrong?' she countered, trying a tentative smile.

'Your beautiful eyes and face are a dead give-away, they're very expressive, so, please, tell me what I can do to make things right.'

'Give us time, much more time. It's all so unreal. We know so little about each other. Daisy especially needs time. I won't be rushed, I must be sure that she likes you and trusts you enough to—' The words came tumbling out in a rush.

'Let me in?'

'Yes. There's just been the two of us for so long. I'd be a rotten mother if I rushed things just because…' She flushed a little. 'Because you and I, on the strength of hormones and vibes—'

'Have fallen in love and want to be together?'

Gemma moistened her lips with the tip of her tongue. 'Yes,' she whispered.

Sam's mouth crooked into a lopsided smile. 'Then we won't rush things. We will be old-fashioned and conventional and take time to get to know each other. I will court you, and after a decent interval propose, with Daisy's love and approval. For I intend to win her love, Gemma, and I intend being the best father in the world to her, make no mistake about that. She will be loved and cherished as every child should be.'

He cupped her chin in his hands again and looked down into her upturned face. 'You do believe me, Gemma, don't you? *I* keep the promises I make.'

His sweetness made her want to cry. But should she...? No, she had no doubts. 'Yes, Sam, I believe you. Thank you for understanding.'

'What's to understand? It's what mature love is all about, keeping promises. I'm no youngster mistaking lust for love, or a man who has never grown up to appreciate what commitment is. I won't let you or Daisy down, dear heart.' He kissed her gently on the mouth as the carriage clock chimed the half-hour. 'And now I'm away while we're still on the respectable side of midnight, or tongues will start wagging too hard. They'll start soon enough anyway—someone's bound to have seen me arrive.'

Gemma laughed a little uncertainly. 'Why will they wag?'

Sam gave a deep-throated chuckle. 'Because we're news. We're not in the big city now. We'll be the talk of the village, the young doctor, whom many of them have known since he was a baby, and the beautiful new nurse. Lovely, juicy gossiping point, even in this day and age.'

Gemma said drily, 'I suppose they'll rate me as a sort

of seductress, you know, the gay divorcee out to get her man. As long as Daisy—'

'Daisy won't suffer, love. You've already established yourself as a good mother and a kind and caring nurse. The gossip will be curious but kind so, please, don't worry about it. Now, I'm really off. Goodnight, my love, sleep well. Thanks for the coffee and sympathy and, most of all, thank you for loving me.'

He gave her another quick kiss, whisked himself out of the room and moments later she heard the front door close behind him.

She went to bed prepared, almost hoping, to lie awake for hours, mulling over the evening's events. She wanted to examine it minutely, from the moment Sam had arrived to when he had said goodnight. But she got no further than when Sam had wrapped her in his arms and held her against his broad chest. Remembering his heart beating a little fast but strongly beneath her ear, she was lulled to sleep, and slept till Daisy bounced into her room at seven o'clock next morning.

Daisy was full of chat about the day ahead. 'Don't forget that Katy's coming to tea, Mummy.'

Gemma smiled down into the bright, beaming face. 'I haven't forgotten, love. What do you think she would like to eat?'

'Fish fingers and baked beans—they're her favourites.'

'Right, so shall it be. And what about pudding?'

'Strawberry ice cream with a banana cut into circles. Oh, and gingerbread men.'

Thank God for simple tastes, thought Gemma, giving Daisy a hug and a kiss. 'I think we can manage that, kiddo.'

* * *

Having deposited Daisy safely at school, Gemma made her way, her head bent deep in thought, towards the surgery.

After last night how were she and Sam to greet each other, work together? Would it be embarrassing? And his parents—how would they react to the situation? They'd made her so welcome as a member of the staff, but how would they feel about her as a potential daughter-in-law?

She tried to picture it from their angle. A single mum with a small daughter, whom they hardly knew. Surely they would feel that their beloved eldest son was making a mistake. And what about Ellie, who had confided in her and had a crush on Sam—would she feel that Gemma had betrayed her?

Sam had made it all sound so easy. He would court her—nice old-fashioned word, 'court'. Daisy would get to know him, learn to love him, everything would be wonderful. All part of the miracle that had brought her to Blaney St Mary.

'Hi, isn't it a perfectly *beautiful* morning?'

Gemma jerked up her head. Sam's voice was husky, a tone lower than usual, rich with double meaning. He was walking towards her, with Rufus and Rex, the family Labradors, loping along on either side of him. He stopped just in front of her. The dogs sniffed at her with their soft muzzles and waved feathery tails.

Gemma stroked their silky heads, and her heart, already churning as her turbulent thoughts whizzed round in her head, churned some more as her eyes feasted on the man before her. He stood tall, lean, muscular, his bright fair hair glowing in the early morning sunlight and enhanced by a turtle-necked creamy sweater.

Memory stirred as Gemma stared. Substitute silver armour for the creamy sweater and he was a double for the picture of Sir Galahad, the gallant knight in her favourite book of legends which she'd drooled over as a child.

She made her lips move. 'Yes,' she breathed. 'It *is* a beautiful morning, but—'

'But?'

'Why are you out walking the dogs at this hour?' Her voice remained a breathy whisper.

'It's my late start morning—first patient's booked for nine-thirty.'

Gemma cleared her throat. 'I know, but you usually catch up on paperwork and phone calls on late start mornings.'

Sam's eyes, incredibly blue, incredibly warm, twinkled like mad. 'This morning I decided to break with tradition and go to meet my love, and be seen to be courting.' He leaned forward and tucked a strand of hair, lifted by the light breeze, carefully behind her ear. A casual gesture, but he made it seem like a caress.

'Oh.' The breathiness was back. Gemma glanced quickly round to see if they were being observed. There were a few people walking their dogs and a few children dawdling to school.

Sam chuckled. 'Nervous of attracting attention, love? Well, I dare say there are a few lace curtains twitching, and that innocent gesture will start tongues wagging. But does it matter? The sooner everyone gets used to seeing us around together, the better.' His eyes swept over her face. 'You don't mind, do you, Gemma?' He touched her cheek lightly with his fingertips. 'As I said last night, any gossip will be friendly gossip.'

Gemma touched the spot on her cheek that he had touched. Her eyes smiled into his. 'No, Sam,' she said softly, lingering over his name. 'I don't mind, just as long as Daisy isn't harmed by rumours before I can explain to her about you and me.' She forced her eyes away from his and fumbled for her fob watch beneath her jacket.

'Lord, I shall be late. We'll have to talk some other time.' She began walking quickly towards the surgery.

Sam and the two dogs fell in beside her. 'This evening?' he asked. His face curved into a smile. 'And I promise you, rather earlier and less harrowing than last night—before Daisy goes to bed. Just a casual visit, like the other night when I dropped in. That was quite a success. Perhaps we could fix something for the weekend, as we did then, not kite-flying this time but something else. There's a steam rally over at Lower Boxley, with a train for the kids to ride on. Daisy would love that. How about it, Gemma?'

They reached the surgery and walked round the side of the building to the staff door. His hand brushed against hers and she shivered with the sheer pleasure of his flesh touching hers.

'Cold?' he asked, his eyes flaring with amusement.

Gemma shook her head. He knows that I'm not, she thought.

He dropped the dogs' leads. 'Stay,' he commanded. They lay down, their heads resting on their paws. 'Good boys.'

He turned to Gemma and held wide his arms. 'Come here,' he said softly, but still with a note of command in his voice.

'We shouldn't, not here...' Gemma murmured and stepped forward into his arms.

For a few moments he held her as he had the previous night, cradling her head against his heart. He kissed the top of her head then tilted her face and kissed her mouth, his tongue teasing her lips apart to explore the soft, moist interior. Their tongues entwined, their warm breath mingled.

Gemma's legs felt as if they might give way. She could hardly breathe. With an effort she pulled her face away from his. 'Must go,' she muttered. 'Please, Sam, let me go.'

He rubbed his nose to hers and let his arms fall to his sides. 'I love you,' he said, and, picking up the dogs' leads, turned and walked away.

CHAPTER NINE

GEMMA tidied herself up in the cloakroom, running a comb through her hair and touching up her 'kiss-proof'—not against *that* sort of kiss—lipstick over her smudged, bruised lips. She stared into the mirror over the basin, trying to assess if anyone would notice that she had been so thoroughly kissed. The dreamy look in her smoky green eyes was a dead give-away, she thought, smiling at her reflection. But what the dickens? She was feeling on top of the world.

She went through to Reception to collect her list, and came down from cloud nine with a jolt. Olivia Mallory was manning the desk. Normally, working with Mrs M. was a joy, but this morning was nowhere near normal, and the last person she wanted to see was Sam's mother, and be inspected by those kind but shrewd hazel eyes. What on earth would she have thought had she seen her practice nurse wrapped in her son's arms, being kissed senseless, only minutes before?

Gemma's heart beat a tattoo against her ribs, and her puffy lips felt dry as she approached the desk and arranged a smile on her face. 'Hello, Mrs M. This is a surprise. I thought Ellie would be back this morning.' Her voice, meant to sound bright and breezy and, oh, so casual, came out sounding as if she had a bad dose of tonsillitis. She cleared her throat.

Olivia Mallory glanced up from the pile of records she was dealing with and gave her a quick wide smile, just like Sam's, then pulled a face. 'Poor Ellie. She expected to be back, but she had a rough time when she saw her dentist yesterday. He found an abscess beneath the tooth that was giving her pain. She's on penicillin but is feeling pretty ropey so I've told her to take a couple of days off.'

'Poor old Ellie. And poor you. Weren't you going to meet a friend in Bournemouth tomorrow to go shopping?'

'With luck, I still will. Helen Brodie's back from holiday and has agreed to hold the fort tomorrow. You haven't met her yet—she's our occasional relief receptionist.'

Gemma nodded. 'Yes, I know. Ellie's mentioned the name. I look forward to meeting her.' She glanced at her watch. 'Goodness, I'd better get cracking or my patients will think I've deserted them.' She picked up her list and fled to the treatment room away from those shrewd eyes.

By concentrating like mad, she managed to keep her tumultuous thoughts at bay as she worked her way through her list of patients.

It was a mixed bag, starting with a couple of cervical smears, women who hadn't been able to get to the regular session the previous week. Both were perfectly straightforward and easily dealt with.

They were followed by Jamie Hooper, a small boy with stitches to be removed from his knee. It was a tearful episode, but mercifully brief, with Jamie brightening up as soon as it was over and Gemma offered him the sweetie jar. He chose a green lolly, and cheekily admitted to his mother, who had been even more nervous than he, that it hadn't hurt much. She hugged him and told him that he was a brave boy, and with effusive thanks to Gemma led him away with promises of more goodies to come.

Tidying up in readiness for the next patient, Gemma thought how apt the saying was that children made cowards of us all. For a split second she thought of Daisy. When would she have the courage to break the news to her daughter that they would be seeing a lot more of Sam in the future and that he might become a more permanent fixture in their lives? How would Daisy take it? Would she hate the idea? And if she did, what then?

Sam! Just thinking about him, it made her pulses race and her cheeks flush. Furiously squashing the thought and willing the blush to subside, she went out to the waiting room to call in her next patient.

Elderly Mrs Green was anaemic and had come in for her monthly injection of iron. She'd had several previous injections, but remained nervous about them.

'That nurse who was here for a short while a few months ago hurt me something awful,' she said. 'Gave me a dreadful bruise. Mind you, to be fair, I do bruise easy.'

'Then I'll be extra careful,' Gemma promised as she swabbed the upper and outer quadrant of the elderly buttock with antiseptic. Then, holding the muscle firm, she popped in the wide-bore needle and slowly released the Imferon that she had drawn up into the syringe.

A few minutes later, exclaiming that she'd hardly felt a thing, a relieved Mrs Green left the treatment room.

The rest of the morning was busy, and Gemma didn't even stop for coffee. It was nearly one o'clock and she was clearing up after her last patient when Sam appeared in the doorway.

Her heart gyrated as his eyes feasted hungrily upon her.

'I was hoping,' he murmured, his rich tenor voice warm and husky, 'that we might have lunched together, but I have an emergency call-out and I'll have to go straight on to take surgery at Little Wickford after I've sorted it out, so I won't see you till tonight, my love.'

My love! He made it sound so proprietorial, as if only he had the right to say it. She wanted to leap across the room and throw herself into his arms, feel them wrapped hard around her as they had been this morning. She wouldn't see him till tonight… Tonight seemed a lifetime away.

'Oh, well, not to worry,' she heard herself say in an airy, doesn't-matter sort of voice. 'I've oodles to do in my lunch hour.'

Sam's vivid blue eyes twinkled with laughter. She might have known he'd see right through her. Bravado, that's all it was and he knew it. She felt her own eyes twinkling back at him—it was wonderful being on the same wavelength, the right vibes winging their way between them… Please, let Daisy—

Sam said softly, 'I've got to go, dear heart, but I promise you all is going to be well.' Lifting his hand in a farewell salute, he turned and walked away down the corridor.

Dear heart! My love! He made them sound so precious, made her feel so special. It was like being in love for the first time. Her cheeks flamed, her heart stood still—she *was* in love for the first time.

What about Neil—hadn't he been her first love? *No!* It was crystal clear. What she had felt for Neil hadn't been love. Not true love. He had needed mothering, or something like that. It was hard to remember. Sex had come into it, but not this overwhelming, consuming passion that she felt for Sam.

Yet this was a passion that was about more than sex— a passion to share everything, to be as one. To care for each other and care for Daisy.

She did a little pirouette of sheer joy, finished clearing up, called goodbye to Mrs M., who was on the phone, and let herself out through the staff door.

It was true that she had oodles do in her lunch hour. She'd promised Daisy that she would make gingerbread men for their tea that night. She prepared the ginger biscuit

mix whilst eating a sandwich and gulping down a cup of
coffee. In the middle of rolling out the mixture it suddenly
dawned on her that, with Katy coming to tea, Sam
wouldn't be able to visit.

Her heart plummeted.

'Oh, no,' she groaned. 'Why didn't I think about about
it before?'

She knew why. Because she longed to have Sam there
in her own house, wanted to see him sitting at her table
playing silly games with Daisy, as he had before, looking
as if he belonged. And because he had bewitched her when
he had uttered the words 'my love' and 'dear heart' with
that particular throb in his voice, leaving her breathless and
tongue-tied.

Well, she would have to untie her tongue and ring him
and tell him not to come. She groaned again. It was the
last thing she wanted to do so she'd better get on with it
while she had the strength of mind to do so.

She picked up the receiver and rang his mobile. He answered on the second buzz.

She blurted out quickly, 'Sam, I won't keep you a moment, but don't come tonight. Daisy's got a schoolfriend
coming for tea.'

'So…why should that stop me?' He sounded amused,
his voice drawling.

'Well… Because…' she faltered. 'I don't know really,
it's just that…' Her voice petered out.

'One small girl will go home and tell her mummy that
Dr Sam visited Daisy's house. Is that what it is, Gemma?'

He was laughing at her, teasing her. She hadn't expected
that. What had happened to the vibes, the being as one? A
wave of anger and bewilderment washed over her. She
could picture his face, his twinkling eyes, his wide curving

smile. Why was he laughing at her? Didn't he realise that she was worried because of Daisy? Daisy would be—

'Are you all right, love?' his voice was no longer teasing, but soft and gentle.

She wanted to shout, No, I'm *not* all right. I'm mixed up and anxious and feel guilty because I let myself fall in love with you. And for all I know you might be as bad as Neil and go off and leave us, like he did, like you left that girl. But the words wouldn't come, they stuck in her throat.

'Gemma?' He sounded puzzled. 'Look, if it bothers you that much, I won't come tonight but, please, tell me what's wrong. Is it Daisy?'

His tender tone melted her insides, turned them to mush.

'Yes, it's Daisy... I'm so afraid that she will be hurt by the gossip.' Her voice was a wobbly whisper. 'I know you said she wouldn't be, but...' Her voice almost dried up, then she blurted out, 'Is it true—did you desert a girl when you were younger?'

She almost dropped the receiver. She was appalled. She shouldn't have asked him over the phone—perhaps she shouldn't have asked him at all. Yes, she should. For Daisy's sake—her own sake—she had to know. She stared at the the silent phone. 'Sam...'Her voice shook. 'I must know.'

'Of course you must.' His voice was flat. 'But it was so long ago...'

'You thought that I'd never hear about it?' Her mouth felt dry, sour.

'No, Gemma, because it was an unpleasant incident that happened a long time ago and isn't relevant to us. I certainly wasn't deliberately hiding anything. I would have told you about it some time when we were exchanging mutual histories.' He spoke coolly, rationally.

'Some time!' The bitter taste in her mouth came through

in her voice. This was the man who had seemed to be flawless. 'Would you, I wonder?' She made an effort to pull herself together. 'But I musn't keep you, you're working.'

'I'm in the surgery and haven't opened up yet, though I can hear patients arriving.' He paused for a moment. 'Gemma, I must come tonight. I don't know what gossip you've heard, but you should hear the full unabridged version before condemning me out of hand. I'll come after Daisy's friend has gone, if you prefer.'

She made up her mind suddenly. Never let it be said that she hadn't given him a fair hearing. 'No—come as you planned, sixish.' She gave a funny, cracked little laugh. 'I'll save you a gingerbread man.'

'I *love* gingerbread men.'

The afternoon seemed endless. There was an empty, cold space in Gemma's chest where her heart should have been, but the world went on. Patients still needed attention.

She had just finished treating her last patient on the afternoon list when Dr Mallory rang through and asked her to clean and dress a foot wound.

'And give him a shot of anti-tetanus, and codeine for the pain. But don't be late collecting Daisy from school,' he said in his usual courteous, thoughtful manner. 'Old Harry will be happy to wait for me to see to him after I've finished here if you can't manage it.'

Gemma assured him that it was no problem. She had plenty of time—one of her patients hadn't shown up. 'So who is old Harry?' she asked.

'Trotter.'

'Should I know him?'

Dr Mallory chuckled. 'Probably not. He's on our list, but not what you would call a regular. Last saw him offi-

cially about five years ago when his wife died, though I
drop in on him from time to time. He lives about three
miles from the village. He's ninety-five and hiked in this
afternoon to have his foot looked at.'

'*Hiked!* With an injured foot?'

'That's Harry, a tough old bird. Wouldn't have come
but thought he was bleeding a bit too much, and it was
giving him gyp—his word to express what must be excru-
ciating pain. Just as well it bled—washed some of the
muck out of it. I've dowsed it with antiseptic and put on
a temporary pad and the bleeding's eased, but it needs a
Kaltostat dressing and a protective pad.'

'How did he injure his foot?'

'Sliced into it with the edge of a sharp spade just below
and between his big toe and the next toe, in the soft tissue
between the metatarsus. Went right through his wellie,
might well have had a couple of toes off. He nicked a
blood vessel but miraculously seems to have missed the
tendons and bones, though I don't know how.'

'Oh, well, an X-ray will show if they're damaged...'

'An X-ray.' There was a chuckle at the other end of the
phone. 'I suggested it, of course, but Harry flatly refused.
Short of manhandling him to the hospital, there's nothing
I can do about it. But the old boy's probably right about
there being no long-term damage. He knows the score.
He's had many minor, and not so minor, injuries over the
years and has survived them virtually unaided. But I've
put him on an antibiotic and threatened him on pain of
death to complete the course.'

He paused, then added, 'Take good care of him, Gemma.
He's rather a special old guy, he's known me since I was
a baby—that's sixty-odd years ago. He was already a married man with a family when I was born. Knew me as the

young Dr James, just as Sam is now known as the young doctor.'

There was another pause, then he said softly, 'He was at our wedding, you know, together with most of the village. And who knows? If Sam gets his act together and doesn't leave it too long, he'll be at *his* wedding, too. And that would please the old boy nearly as much as it would please us.' He cleared his throat and became suddenly brisk. 'But that's enough of this maudlin nonsense. I'll leave Harry in your capable hands, my dear.'

Or not so capable, Gemma thought, replacing the receiver with hands that trembled slightly. She was shaken by Dr Mallory's potted family history, especially his reference to Sam and marriage. Marriage to Sam. This morning when he had kissed her it had been practically a dead cert. Now, because of listening to Gloria's gossip, she was hovering on the brink of—

The thought pulled her up short. What was she thinking about? Whatever Sam's explanation for something that had happened in the distant past, and whether or not she accepted it; their relationship had hardly got off the ground, and as yet Daisy knew nothing about it. Daisy was the important factor. Other people hardly mattered, not even the kind, benevolent Mallorys, whose approval she would like to have. It was for Daisy's sake she had to know the truth.

She took a deep breath. Enough thinking—better get cracking and get on with work. Nice, straightforward work—she knew where she was with that.

Thank God for antibiotics and anti-tetanus, she thought a few minutes later as she bent over Mr Trotter's foot. She removed the pressure pad that Dr Mallory had left *in situ*, revealing a mucky wound which looked as if it could do with all the protective cover on offer.

The bleeding had stopped, leaving a gungy mess of dirt and dried blood in the long cut carved by the corner of the sharp spade. She sprayed analgesic round the wound, then, using a needleless syringe to squirt in normal saline, she swabbed away the dirty effluent as it oozed out.

Old Harry watched with interest, seemingly indifferent to the pain that the procedure must be causing in spite of the analgesic spray.

Gemma sniffed. She recognised that smell from her schooldays. Riding lessons—stables—horses—manure! She wrinkled her nose and glanced up at the old man.

'Would I be right in thinking you were digging in horse manure when you sliced into your foot, Mr Trotter?'

'That's right, m'dear, I was dunging me roses, nothing like dung for roses.'

Or for bugs, thought Gemma.

'All done,' she announced ten minutes later as she strapped the thick protective pad in position over the Kaltostat dressing. 'But you must come back in five days' time so that I can renew the dressing. Meanwhile, don't get it wet and please don't remove it. This wound's going to take some time to heal.' Carefully she eased his boot on over the bulky dressing.

'It's only a bit of an 'ole,' Mr Trotter replied grumpily. 'It'll mend in no time.'

'It won't if you interfere with it, I can assure you.' Gemma made her voice very firm, but injected into it a note of humour. 'And you'll get me the sack if anything goes wrong with it. Dr Mallory will think that I haven't done my job properly.'

The old man stared at her and ran calloused fingers

round his bristly chin. 'You blackmailing me, missus?' he asked, his faded eyes twinkling.

Gemma gave him her nicest smile. 'Could be,' she said cheerfully, 'but the doctor will be mad at me if it doesn't heal, that's for sure.'

'Oh, well, suppose we can't have the old doctor blowing his top—I've a lot of use for the old doctor, and the young 'n too.' He stood up and hobbled toward the door. 'I'll be in next week, m'dear.'

'You do that and make my day,' said Gemma, with a laugh as he left the room.

He was, as Dr Mallory said, a special old guy.

She tried to still her thoughts as she crossed the green to meet Daisy and Katy from school, but they continued to nag persistently. It had been a day of significant happenings, from Sam's kiss in the morning to the treating of old Harry at the end of the day, which had been triggered off by the conversation with Dr Mallory.

How proud he was of his family's long involvement with the village, underlining the close rapport that he and Sam and Mrs M. had with their patients. And how sure he seemed that it would continue into yet another generation. It implied that their association with Blaney St Mary was set in stone. How did she feel about that? Just supposing, how would Daisy feel if...?

She gave an anguished sigh and a mental shake and shut down on her teeming thoughts as she reached the school gates. The rest of the afternoon would be devoted to the children.

They had just finished tea and were debating which video to watch, *Mary Poppins* or *Snow White*, when the doorbell rang.

Gemma looked at the clock. Just after six—it had to be Sam. She felt queasy. This was going to be quite an ordeal.

She stood up. 'I'll go,' she said, but Daisy beat her to it, slithering down from her chair and racing out into the hall, with Katy hot on her heels. Gemma, her heart thumping painfully in anticipation, brought up the rear. Daisy flung open the door.

Sam, accompanied by Rex and Rufus, was standing in the porch.

The children uttering delighted oohs and ahs, and draped themselves round the necks of the handsome, tail-waving Labradors.

'I was walking the hounds,' Sam explained to Gemma over the girls' heads, 'and I thought that Daisy and her friend might like to meet them.' A smile of sorts touched his lips, but didn't reach his eyes.

Daisy looked up, her face very bright and alert. 'How did you know that Katy would be here, Dr Sam?'

Trust Daisy to see through that little fib. How would Sam explain it away?

Quite simply. 'Because your mummy told me that she had to hurry home at lunchtime to make gingerbread men because your friend was coming to tea.' He grinned down at both girls. 'I love gingerbread men and, to be honest, I came in the hope that there might be one going spare.'

Smooth!

'Oh, there is,' said Daisy enthusiastically. 'There's more than one, isn't there, Mummy?'

Gemma said brightly in the manner of a good hostess, 'There certainly is and Dr Sam is welcome to one, but not out here on the doorstep. Do come in, Sam.'

'And the hounds?'

'Of course, they're most welcome.'

She stood back as he and the dogs, led by Daisy and Katy, filed into the sitting room. His brilliant blue eyes inscrutable, he stared down into her face as he passed.

Gemma lowered her head, afraid of what he would read in her eyes. Love, hate, mistrust!

The girls took over the hostessing, stationing Rex and Rufus on the hearthrug and steering Sam to a seat at the table.

Daisy placed a plate of gingerbread men in front of him and pleaded for a game of something. 'Like we had before when you came—cards or junior Trivial Pursuit,' she said.

Gemma said with a high, tinkling laugh, 'Give Dr Sam a moment to catch his breath, love. And perhaps Katy would rather watch a video, as you planned.'

Katy shook her head. 'No, thank you, I'd like to play cards. I can see the video any old time.'

Implying, thought Gemma, that playing cards with the doctor was a treat not to be missed. She felt that the situation was getting away from her, and wondered why she'd insisted that Sam should come as arranged before...before she'd accused him, on the strength of gossip, of deserting some girl in his past. They wouldn't get a chance to talk so what was the point?

'Oh, well, in that case, if the doctor doesn't mind.' She made herself look at Sam and produce a smile. 'Would you like a drink—wine or something stronger?' He didn't look in the least bit rattled, but maybe he was feeling as edgy as she.

He looked down at the tall glasses in front of the girls. He picked a glass up and sniffed it. 'Ginger beer would suit me fine,' he said, to the girls' delight.

Sam knew an endless variety of children's card games. The girls wanted to know how he knew so many games.

'Legacy of my misspent youth, wet afternoons and a large number of younger relatives to be entertained,' he said with a laugh, slickly dealing out cards for Chase the

Wicked Lady. He explained the simple rules and they had a noisy, hilarious session.

Occasionally his eyes, still unreadable, met and held Gemma's. Was he angry with her for listening to gossip, and would he be able to explain it away? Please, let him, she prayed inwardly. Don't let him have run away from commitment.

The Wicked Lady was followed by Catch a Thief and Three in a Row. The girls clamoured for more, but an hour later Sam stood up and announced that he must go.

'A doctor's life doesn't end when he sees his last patient for the day,' he said with a laugh, dismissing their entreaties to stay. 'I have phone calls to make, you might call it my homework.'

The girls giggled. 'Homework's for learning things,' said Daisy. 'I thought doctors knew everything.'

'I wish,' Sam replied, pulling a doleful face. 'In my job you go on learning for ever. So I'll be off, ladies. Thanks for the games. You were both brilliant, we'll make card-sharps of you yet.'

'What's a card-sharp?' they asked in unison.

Sam grinned. 'Someone who's sharp at cards,' he said. He called the dogs who were dozing in front of the elegant steel fireplace, filled with a blaze of flowers on this warm spring evening and commanded them to say goodbye. To the girls' delight, Rex and Rufus each offered a regal paw.

Gemma was confused. How were they going to talk if he whisked himself away now? 'I thought you might stay for supper,' she said in a faltering voice.

'As I say, I've phone calls to make.' His voice was brisk, decisive. He moved toward the door. 'Goodbye, girls…Gemma.'

What did he mean, goodbye? It sounded so final, a brush-off. Gemma sucked in a frightened breath and got to her feet. 'I'll see you out.' The girls began standing up. 'No,' she said sharply. 'You stay here. I want a word with Dr Sam.'

She followed him out to the hall. He strode quickly to the front door, opened it and stepped out into the porch.

Gemma fought for breath and words. 'Sam…' She reached out and touched his arm.

'I'll be back at nine,' he said, 'after Daisy's in bed. We'll talk then. It's up to you whether you tell her that I'm coming.' His voice and eyes were expressionless. He turned and strode down the path.

Stunned, Gemma watched him go. She had never felt so forlorn or bereft in her life.

He arrived dead on nine o'clock. He nodded an acknowledgement of her stumbling greeting, and preceded her down the hall into the sitting room.

Her hands, already cold and clammy with nerves, seemed to get colder. She waved at the drinks tray on a side table. 'Would you—'

'No, thanks, I want a clear head for this.' His eyes bored into hers. Legs wide in a very masculine pose, he stood with his back to the flower-filled fireplace. 'Gemma, do you love me?'

'I…I…'

'Well, do you or don't you? Very straightforward question. I don't want to hear about your reservations, whether connected to Daisy's feelings or the short time we've known each other. I want to know if you love me.'

Gemma sank down onto the sofa. That was the last question she'd expected. Neither had she expected this almost arrogant attitude. Rather she had thought that he might be a bit on the defensive, angry perhaps but eager to explain himself.

She was holding her breath. 'Yes…' The word came out on a gusty sigh.

Sam nodded. 'Good. Now we've got that out of the way, I'll tell you as briefly and concisely as I can why I *deserted*—your word—a young woman nearly ten years ago.' His face looked both grim and sad.

Gemma made a dismissive gesture with her hands. 'Sam, please… I didn't mean…'

'But you did, which means you want answers.' He pushed his hands into his trouser pockets.

Gemma stared up at him. 'You mean you *did* desert someone.' She clenched her fists. She didn't want to hear this.

'I had a sort of semi-serious relationship going with a staff nurse. I ditched her when I learned that she was sleeping around with half the hospital. A day or two later she announced that she was pregnant. I was pretty sure the baby, *if* there was one, wasn't mine. She was on the Pill and I was taking precautions.'

'And did you sleep around, Sam?' Her voice was cold.

'No, not when there was something going between Joy and me.'

'I see,' Gemma said thoughtfully, her voice less chilly. 'So, was there a baby?'

'No…though I didn't know that for some time. Joy took herself off, disappeared, rumours circulated. But the possibility that I might have fathered a baby shook me to the core. Made me grow up, turned me into…' he gave a wry smile. '…the mature, sober adult that you see before you. I'd been a bit wild, but not too wild to know that I might have had to accept responsibility for a new life.'

In two strides he crossed the room, sat down on the sofa beside her, and took her hands in his. 'Which is why, my love, you can trust me to care for you and Daisy, because had there been a baby I would have loved and cherished it, as all children should be loved and cherished.'

Wave after wave of relief washed through her. He wasn't perfect, but he was the man she'd thought him to be, a man to be trusted, depended upon. She drew her hands from his and slid them up round his neck. 'Oh, Sam, I do love you,' she murmured.

'The feeling's mutual,' he said, gathering her into his arms.

He left half an hour later. 'Like I told the girls, I do have phone calls to make,' he said, adding, 'by the way, Mother has asked me to pass on an invitation to you and Daisy to come to tea next Sunday. She thinks it's time you met the family. It's one of our regular get-togethers.'

'But…we don't know them,' she faltered.

Sam grinned. 'Precisely—the idea is that after Sunday you will.' He touched her cheek. 'You must come. Daisy will love it, meeting all my nieces and nephews.'

She experienced a moment of panic. 'Have you told your mother about us? Was tea your idea?'

The lopsided grin that turned her insides to marshmallow tipped the corner of his mouth. 'No, love, I haven't told her, but I have a hunch she knows. Very perceptive, my mother. And tea was her own idea.'

She smiled. 'OK, then, if Daisy's happy about it, we'll come.'

CHAPTER TEN

GEMMA saw little of Sam over the next few days. Her list, already packed, continued to lengthen as the pollen count rose and the need for antihistamine injections grew with it.

As for Sam, his house calls doubled as the tummy bug, in the mysterious way that bugs did, made a return visit to Blaney St Mary and the surrounding villages. This had a ripple effect on the surgery, and Helen Brodie, standing in for Ellie, was kept busy answering the phone and making appointments.

On Thursday evening, Sam sandwiched in a brief visit to the cottage between calls. He arrived as Gemma was coming down the stairs, and she saw his silhouette through the coloured glass of the door panels.

She put her finger to her lips as she opened the door. 'Daisy's only just settling,' she murmured. 'If she hears you come in she'll be down like a shot.'

Sam grinned and nodded. 'Sounds as if she'd be pleased to see me.' He followed her into the sitting room. 'And are you pleased to see me?' he asked, swinging her round into his arms. He didn't wait for an answer, but lowered his head and showered darting kisses on her upturned face. Eyes, nose, cheeks, neck and finally mouth. He teased apart her lips with his tongue and explored the moist softness within.

Gemma strained against him, soft breasts to hard chest, and kissed him back, fiercely, hungrily. Her hands cupped the back of his head, locking his face to hers till they were breathing each other's breath.

The insistent burring of Sam's mobile in his top pocket shattered the blissful moment.

He groaned and lifted his head, forcing it back against the pressure of Gemma's hands. He was breathing heavily, deep, rasping breaths as he fumbled in his pocket for the phone. 'Love you,' he muttered as he switched it on. 'Dr Sam,' he said briskly, and listened with a frown to what was being said at the other end.

The voice was shrill and frightened—a child's voice? Gemma got her own breathing under control and eased herself out of the arm that still encircled her.

The voice trailed off into sobs.

Sam said with quiet authority, 'Heather, listen to me. Don't try to get her up from the floor, but roll her onto her left side, making sure her head is turned, and put a cushion at her back so that she won't roll over. Then hold her hands and talk to her. I'll be with you in a few minutes.'

He switched off and smiled a small rueful smile. 'Sorry, Gemma, love, must scoot. One of my young single mums in trouble, sounds as if she might be fitting. Apparently, she's twitching and unrousable. She's not been very well lately, has a slight heart problem due to rheumatic fever as a child, but there was nothing I could pinpoint. This may give me a lead.'

While he'd been speaking he'd moved towards the door and into the hall. Gemma followed him. 'That was her eight-year-old daughter, Heather, phoning. Nice, sensible kid. I've known her since she was a baby. She was my first home delivery when I joined the practice. Against all the odds, Stella's made a super job of bringing her up on her own.'

They reached the front door and he bent and gave her a quick abstracted kiss on the cheek, but his mind wasn't on it. Gemma guessed that it was already with his patient. 'See you tomorrow at the surgery, love,' he said as he strode down the path.

'Hope all goes well,' Gemma called, as he reached the gate.

'Thanks.' He didn't look back, but waved his hand as he slid into his car. Seconds later, he pulled swiftly away.

Gemma watched as he circled the green and headed north out of the village. Her heart went out to the young mother and the little girl, Heather. One of her recurring nightmares was what would happen to Daisy if she herself was taken ill. How would she cope? Who would she call on for help? In a medical emergency, of course, she could phone the surgery, just as young Heather had done, no problem…

But in the long term and if she died…?

There was only Neil, unpredictable and unreliable, unfit to take custody of Daisy full time. And, of course, her own parents, but which one? Neither knew Daisy, both had partners who might resent the intrusion of a small girl into their lives. On the other hand, they might do battle over who should care for her, using her as another tool to hurt each other. She shuddered at the thought of Daisy going to either of them, or to Neil.

That left Emma, her best friend and Daisy's godmother. But at this moment in time she was nursing in a remote corner of India, and letters took for ever to reach her. In any case, in a year's time she might be in Africa or any other trouble spot in the world where the charity she worked for might send her. No, Emma was a non-starter. The most she could do was offer support from afar.

At least, Gemma thought, staring unseeingly at the television screen, financial security was less of a problem now. The cottage could be sold and the proceeds used to secure Daisy's future in practical terms. She drew in a deep, painful breath. But money didn't buy love, and love was what Daisy would need if anything happened to her. And who would be prepared to give her that?

Sam, of course, shouted a voice in her head. He's already said that he wants to love and care for Daisy. But that's when we're married, cut in a panicky, doubting thought. The voice was scathing. And you think that he would turn his back on her if something happened to you and you weren't married? Get real, woman. He's a man in a million who would cherish Daisy as if she were his own.

And Daisy has already said that she likes him, the voice reminded Gemma—right from his first visit. On the kite outing, other visits, he's always brought a touch of magic with him... There's already a rapport between them. So tell Daisy that he wants to marry you, give her a chance to tell you how she feels. But we've known him for such a short while, hardly time for her to...

What's time got to do with it? A few weeks is a lifetime to a child. Daisy probably feels that she's known him for ever. She's always talking about 'Dr Sam this' and 'Dr Sam that', isn't she?

True! Gemma got up and switched off the television, and turned and stared at herself in the mirror over the fireplace. 'Right,' she told her reflection sternly, 'I shall talk to her tomorrow directly we get home from school, and be totally honest with her about how Sam and I feel about each other, and ask her straight out how she feels about Sam as a stepfather.'

Supposing she's dead against the idea, wondered her treacherous thoughts. Her stomach churned sickeningly at the thought, but her resolve remained firm and, metaphorically squaring her shoulders, she took herself off to bed.

She dreamed about a small girl—not Daisy—drowning, and being plucked from the water by Sam. Tanned, tall, lean and muscular. he bent over her and began resuscitating her on a sandy tropical beach. His face was fierce, intense, as he worked on the fragile little body, a lock of blond hair falling over his forehead.

Abruptly the dream ended and Gemma woke up. Had the little girl been saved…or hadn't she? And did she represent the child, Heather? She couldn't wait to get to work to find out from Sam what had happened to Heather and her mother.

Ellie was behind the reception desk when Gemma went through to collect her list. She looked pale, but otherwise much her usual self, bright-eyed, smiling, calm and collected.

In fact, thought Gemma, there was an aura about her. She was looking quietly radiant, and smiling a Mona Lisa, enigmatic-type smile.

'It's good to see you, Ellie, and, considering what you've been through with that abscess, you look great.'

'I feel it. The antibiotics worked brilliantly, and…' Ellie thrust a list and pile of records toward her. She gave an un-Ellie-like giggle, leaned across the desk, and whispered, 'I'm pregnant. Only a few weeks, but I've tested and I'm positive.' Her pale cheeks flushed. 'Oh, Gemma, I can't believe it after all this time. I'm so happy, and Dave's over the moon. He's actually going to take me out for lunch, and he hasn't done that for yonks.'

Holding back all the cautionary warnings that she felt she should make about it being early days, Gemma said, 'Oh, Ellie, that's wonderful news. I'm so pleased for you. You must tell me more later.' She reached across and gave Ellie a kiss on her cheek. 'But I've got to dash right now. I must see Sam before I start, if he's free.'

'His last patient's just gone. You can catch him before he buzzes for his next one.'

'Thanks.'

Gemma made for his office and knocked on the door. He called to her to come in. He was busy at his monitor, and didn't look round as she slipped into the room.

Her breath caught in her throat. Looking at him, her heart felt as if it were being squeezed tight, her insides melted. He looked so like the man in her dream, bending over the fragile body of the little girl, as then a lock of fair hair falling over his forehead as he peered at the screen.

In a low, husky voice, she said, 'Sam, I don't want to bother you but...'

He swivelled round in his chair and beamed a lopsided smile at her. '*You* could never bother me, Gemma. What about a good-morning kiss?' He opened his arms wide.

She shook her head. 'No fear, I'm staying right here. Someone might come in.'

His eyes gleamed wickedly. 'Not without knocking, and I can always tell them to go away.'

Resisting the temptation to throw herself into his arms, Gemma laughed and kissing the tips of her fingers, blew the air toward him. 'There's your kiss. That's all you're going to get this morning, so make the most of it.'

He heaved a theatrical sigh and let his arms fall to his sides. 'You're a hard woman, Nurse Fellows. So, if you're not here to give me a proper kiss, what brings you to my office?'

'Stella—the emergency you were called out to last night. Her little girl Heather phoned. I haven't been able to get them out of my mind.'

The wicked glint faded, and his eyes suddenly filled with compassion. He said gently. 'I can imagine, a single mum, a small daughter, like you and Daisy. Is that the comparison you were making?'

'Something like that.' No way did she want to tell him in detail the thoughts it had triggered off. 'Please, tell me what happened. Did you have to send her to hospital?'

'No. She was conscious when I arrived, almost back to normal. Don't think it was a true epileptic fit, more a Stokes-Adams syndrome episode. I'm going to arrange for her to have some more cardiac investigations. Could be that she's a suitable candidate for a pacemaker.'

'And Heather. Did you leave her there alone in the house, a little girl trying to look after her mother?' She tried, unsuccessfully, to keep the tone of accusation out of her voice.

'No, love,' Sam said drily, raising a surprised eyebrow. 'You don't really think I'd do that, do you? I arranged for the woman next door, who is a good friend and neighbour, to stay the night with them.'

Gemma's cheeks reddened. 'No,' she whispered, 'I didn't really think you would leave them high and dry to manage for themselves. I don't know why I said that. I'm so sorry. It's just that I couldn't stop thinking about them…'

'And if something like that could happen to you and Daisy?'

She nodded.

He crossed the room and took her in his arms. 'Not,' he said, 'whilst I've breath in my body. If anything happened to you, love, I would take care of Daisy.' He kissed the top of her head. 'OK?'

'OK,' she quavered.

The rest of the day passed in a flash. The usual mixture of patients came and went. She took blood, gave injections, applied dressings, cleaned and stitched wounds and reassured. Always there was a need for reassurance. Just, she thought dreamily, a warm glow spreading inside her, as Sam had reassured *her*.

She wrenched her thoughts away from Sam, and concentrated on the job in hand, the re-dressing of a particularly unpleasant varicose ulcer that was slow to heal.

'Come back in five days, Mrs Snow,' she told the patient. 'If it's not improving, I'll talk to one of the doctors about trying a new treatment.'

She looked at her watch after Mrs Snow had gone—ten to three, time to clear up before fetching Daisy from school.

Fetch Daisy from school and... Her stomach clenched, she felt breathless, nauseated... She was going to ask her small daughter the most important question in her young life. There was no way of softening or embroidering it. When it came down to it, the question was—would she or wouldn't she accept Sam as her stepfather?

It began to rain as Gemma and Daisy started up the green. It had been raining on and off all day, short, sharp showers from dark clouds interspersed with brilliant blue skies.

'April showers,' said Gemma, opening up her yellow umbrella, bright with red poppies, and cuddling Daisy to her side so that they were both protected from the darting rain.

'But it's May,' protested Daisy, at her most pragmatic, 'so it's May showers.'

Gemma laughed down at the dear little upturned face. 'OK, poppet, I concede. It's May showers.'

'What's concede?'

'To give in,' Gemma explained as they reached the cottage.

They left their wet macs in the hall and went straight through to the kitchen, warmed on this rain-chilled spring afternoon by the elderly but functional Aga.

'I've got a treat as it's Friday,' said Gemma, going to the fridge and removing a large bag. She held it aloft. 'Cream chocolate doughnuts and, drinkwise, you can name your poison, love—Coke, limeade, lemonade?'

Daisy clapped her hands. 'Cream doughnuts, yummy, and I'll have Coke, please, Mummy.' She giggled. 'It rhymes—Mummy, yummy.'

Gemma felt a little catch in her throat. She thought, She's always extra bubbly on Fridays, on account of us spending the weekend together and planning what we're going to do. So what about this Friday? This Friday which will alter our whole lives? This Friday that will mark the beginning, the end, or at least might put a hold on, my relationship with Sam.

She tried to squash the nausea that gripped her stomach as she poured the Coke. Some splashed on the table.

'Mummy, why are your hands all shaky?' Daisy asked.

Gemma sat down at the opposite side of the table with a loud bump and took in a long, deep breath. She produced a smile of sorts. 'Because, Daisy, love, I have something to tell you, and I don't know how to begin, how to explain. I just want you to know that I love you more than anyone in the world, and I want you to be happy—I want us to be happy together, always.' Her voice came out as if she had a cold.

Daisy, her mouth ringed with cream, about to take a second bite of her doughnut, stared at Gemma, and her eyes were suddenly filled with tears, which brimmed over and trickled down her cheeks.

'Mummy, don't die, please, don't die.'

Gemma knocked her chair over in her haste to get round

the table. She knelt beside Daisy and folded her in her arms, hugging her tight and kissing her wet cheeks.

'Darling, I'm not going to die,' she murmured between kisses. 'Oh, baby, whatever made you think that?' She rocked her backwards and forwards.

Daisy heaved in a sobbing, trembling breath. 'You sound so funny, as if you want to tell me something bad, something that will hurt.' She blinked at Gemma through her tears and scrubbed at her eyes with balled-up fists. 'Are you sure you're not going to die, or go away and leave me? Promise you're not going to, Mummy, promise me!'

Gemma hugged her even tighter. 'Darling, I promise. I'm as fit as a fiddle, I'm not going to die. And *I* don't think what I have to tell you is bad, and I hope it won't hurt you. But it will surprise you and I want you to think about what I have to say very carefully. There's no rush and you can ask me anything you want. Will you do that, sweetheart?'

Daisy lifted her head, which had been buried in Gemma's neck, and stared her straight in the face for a moment, her green, tear-filled eyes unwavering.

'It sounds very important,' she said in a whispery voice.

'It is, love, it's something that will change our whole lives.'

'We don't have to go back and live in London, do we?' Daisy's voice rose to a squeak. 'I'd hate that. I want to live here always, in the village with Katy, and I want you to work at the surgery with Dr Sam and everyone, and be happy…' Her voice trailed off.

Gemma's heart jumped at her mention of Sam. It was like an omen, it had to be her cue. All she had to do was pick the right words. Keep it simple, her instincts told her.

She cupped Daisy's tear-stained face in her hands and kissed her on her nose. 'I want all those things too,' she said softly, 'and so does Dr Sam. He doesn't want us to go away, ever. He has asked me to marry him, but I said I would have to ask you first.'

She fought to keep calm, but her heartbeats hammered against her chest wall and thundered in her ears.

All sorts of expressions flitted across Daisy's face, ending with a frown. 'Will Dr Sam be my daddy if you marry him?'

'He'll be your stepfather. Daddy will remain Daddy, he's your natural father.' Please, don't let her ask what natural means, not now. I'll explain it some time.

'Will Daddy still come to visit?'

'Yes.' Don't enlarge upon it, she warned herself. This was going to be a long session. Her knees were numb. She dropped her hands from Daisy's face, dragged a chair round the table next to Daisy's and shifted onto it.

Daisy looked thoughtful. 'Will Dr—? Oh, I won't be able to him call him Dr Sam when you're married, will I? What will I call him?'

Gemma thought she might faint, though she'd never fainted in her life. Did this mean what she thought it meant? She cleared her throat. 'Do you mean that you think I *should* marry Dr Sam?' she asked, trying desperately to sound matter-of-fact.

Daisy pursed her rosy lips and nodded, slowly bouncing her reddish-brown curls. Her pursed lips curved into a smile. 'Yes,' she said at last. 'I think it would be brilliant if you did... I like Dr Sam. In fact, I think I love him. I'm glad he's going to be my stepfather.' She looked at Gemma thoughtfully. 'So, what do you think I should call him, Mummy?'

Gemma, dizzy with happiness, hardly able to take in the fact that Daisy actually wanted her to marry Sam, unable to think straight, smiled at her through eyes misty with tears. 'I don't know, love,' she said tremulously. 'I think we'd better ask him.'

The conversation for the rest of the evening was mostly about the wedding. Daisy wanted answers. When would it be? Could she be a bridesmaid? Gemma, making a terrific effort to concentrate, explained that it wouldn't be for a while yet, that she and Sam had a lot to talk about and there was much to be arranged, but, yes, of course, she would be a bridesmaid. They talked colours and styles of dresses and all the fairy-tale things that small girls associated with weddings.

Gemma, weak with relief and happiness, romanticised with her. She had no idea what sort of a wedding Sam envisaged, but somehow they would fit in all Daisy's ideas of what it should be.

Bubbling over, Daisy wanted to know if she could ring Katy and tell her that Mummy was going to marry Dr Sam. Not for the moment, Gemma explained. Sam hadn't yet told Dr Mallory or Mrs M. that they were going to get married.

'We wanted you to be the first to know,' she added, 'because you are the most important person in our lives. I know it's hard for you to keep a secret from your best friend, but just this once, love, you must.'

'When do you think Dr Sam will tell Dr Mallory and Mrs M.?' Daisy asked.

Gemma smiled and kissed her small nose. 'Just as soon as I let him know that we have your blessing, poppet.'

'Oh, have I given you my blessing?' asked Daisy.

'Yes, love, that's exactly what you've done.'

Daisy gave a huge sigh and yawned. 'I'm glad,' she said. 'It sounds nice, a blessing. Now I think I'd better go to bed. I'm pooped.' She gave a little chuckly laugh. 'That's what Katy's granny says when she's tired—pooped.'

Gemma phoned Sam as soon as soon as Daisy was tucked up in bed and fast asleep. He was on call till midnight when Bob Carstairs would relieve him, but she caught him between patients.

She said breathlessly, as soon as he answered, 'I've told Daisy.'

He whistled in a breath through his teeth. 'And…?' His usual clear tenor sounded gravelly.

'She's over the moon, thrilled to bits, can't wait for us to get married.'

She heard him take in another deep breath. 'Hallelujah. Thank God for that. I was so afraid…'

'So was I, but you said all would be well and that's how it's turned out.'

'I'll be over.'

'But you're on call.'

'So? My mobile works as well in your house as in mine.' He clicked off.

He arrived a few minutes later, and gathered her in his arms as soon as he was in the hall. He gave her a hard, long kiss, not particularly sexy but very satisfying, a married sort of kiss, she thought. Without warning, he swept her up in his arms carried her into the sitting room.

'Happy?' he asked in a low, throaty voice as he lowered her to the floor.

'Unbelievably. I feel as if a huge weight has been lifted from my shoulders. Oh, Sam, I can't tell you how deep-down scared I've been, wondering how to tell Daisy, dreading that she would hate the idea of us getting married, and wondering what we would do if she did.'

She sagged suddenly against him. 'I'm pooped,' she said with a rather hysterical giggle. She looked up into his gently smiling face. 'That's what Katy's granny says when she's tired,' she explained solemnly.

Sam tightened his hold round her and sank down onto the sofa, cuddling her to him. He rocked her to and fro like a baby. 'You're emotionally exhausted, dear heart,' he said softly. 'You must go to bed and have a good night's sleep.'

'I like it when you call me dear heart,' she murmured, snuggling against his chest. 'It makes me feel safe and...'

'Cherished!'

She smiled sleepily. 'Yes, that's the word. I don't think I've ever been cherished before.'

'Then prepare yourself for a lot of cherishing in the future, but right now it's off to bed with you.' As if to endorse his words, his mobile chirped into life. He kissed her forehead and pushed her off his lap. 'Go on—bed,' he said sternly, steering her towards the door. 'I'll let myself out.' He clicked on the switch.

'Dr Sam,' she heard him say as she made her way up the stairs, pausing halfway up to blow him a tired hit-or-miss kiss.

He grinned, a lopsided, loving grin. 'Goodnight,' he mouthed. 'Sleep tight.'

She did. She fell into bed and remembered nothing else till the morning.

Saturday passed as most Saturdays did, in a welter of small routine activities. Though she missed him dreadfully, Gemma was rather glad that she wasn't seeing anything of Sam that day. He had surgery in the morning and a GP meeting in Bournemouth, spanning the afternoon and evening.

It was a good opportunity, she thought, to keep everything as normal as possible, as if nothing momentous had happened to alter their lives. So she and Daisy went swimming and shopping in Shillingbourne as usual, but plans for the future kept popping into the conversation and they were both on a high.

Daisy kept up an endless stream of chatter. The matter of what she should call Sam when he became her stepfather was still top of her agenda. 'I shall ask him tomorrow,' she decided, 'at the tea-party.'

'Perhaps,' Gemma suggested, 'it would be better for the three of us to sit down together and talk this over in private. There will be a lot of people there and they might not all know that Sam and I are getting married. He might only have told Dr Mallory and Mrs M.'

She couldn't have been more wrong. The whole family had been put in the picture by the time she and Daisy arrived at the manor house.

Sam greeted them with the news as he threw open the massive iron-studded front door and welcomed them into the timbered hall.

His eyes met Gemma's over Daisy's head. 'Sorry, I've rather jumped the gun. I just couldn't wait to tell everyone about us,' he said, pulling a rueful face. 'Don't be mad at me.'

Before she could answer, Daisy said in her practical little voice, 'Mummy won't be mad at you, 'cause she loves you.'

Sam crouched down so that his twinkling eyes were on a level with hers. 'Are you sure about that, Daisy?'

Daisy nodded. 'Oh, yes, pos'tive.'

Sam smiled. 'May I give you a kiss?' he asked softly.

'Because you're going to be my stepfather?'

'That, and to thank you for being prepared to share Mummy with me.'

Daisy dimpled. 'And because I gave you my blessing?'

Sam grinned. 'Got it in one,' he said.

Daisy offered a rosy cheek. 'Just here,' she said, pointing to a spot in the middle.

Sam gave her a loud, smacking kiss.

'And this one.' She offered the other cheek and he repeated the kiss.

'Now, let's go and meet everyone,' he said, taking each of them by the hand and leading them across the gleaming oak floor towards one of the heavy wooden doors opening off the hall. They could hear laughter and the sound of voices as they approached.

Gemma stopped as they reached the door, and took a deep breath. 'I'm scared,' she murmured. 'You've got such a big family, we've got no one.'

Sam kissed her cheek noisily as he had Daisy's. 'My family is your family,' he said softly, 'and they're all dying to meet you both.'

Sam was right. It was obvious that his brother, Luke, and his sisters, Mattie and Ann, and their respective partners, Jane, Mark and Simon, were eager to welcome them. They weren't in the least bit fazed by the fact that Sam was proposing to marry someone whom he'd only known for a few weeks. Everyone seemed to think it was a brilliant idea.

'It was the same with Mark and me,' Mattie confided to Gemma. 'A case of love at first sight. We got hitched six weeks after we met. The parents were thrilled to bits. But, then, that's how it was for them, too. They clapped eyes on each other for the first time over an anaesthetised patient in Theatre, and, bingo, that was it. They wanted to be together and got married in no time flat. They have a thing about togetherness.'

That was true if the rest of the afternoon was anything to go by. Everyone went out of their way to make Gemma feel wanted, close.

And Daisy was having a wonderful time with the other children. After tea, Nicola, Paul, Fliss and Tom, with two-year-old Lucy clutching Daisy's hand, all trooped out to the orchard to play. Mrs M. and Dr Mallory, humping his year-old grandson Frank on his broad shoulders, went along to supervise them.

Gemma guessed that it was a diplomatic move to give the younger members of the family a chance to talk amongst themselves, four pairs of people with much in common. She heaved a sigh of pure pleasure as for the first time in many years, she basked in the delight of being one of a pair and part of a family.

The party broke up at seven. Tired children were reunited with their parents and deposited in various cars parked on the drive. Goodbye and thank-you kisses were exchanged, promises made to phone, and repeat congratulations called to Sam and Gemma.

Gemma turned to Mrs M. and Dr Mallory as the last of the cars disappeared down the drive. 'We must go now,' she said, holding out her hand. 'Thank you for a lovely party and making us feel so welcome. You have an absolutely super family.'

'And you're part of it now,' replied Mrs M., ignoring Gemma's hand and giving her a hug and a kiss. She bent down and kissed the top of Daisy's head. 'And you've brought us another grandchild.'

Dr Mallory kissed them both too. His blue eyes twinkled as Sam's did. 'Nice to have you in the family firm as well as the medical one,' he said to Gemma, his voice rather gruff. 'Could have predicted this the day you joined us.'

Gemma looked startled. 'How?'

He tapped his finger to his nose. 'Intuition, my dear. Women don't have the monopoly, you know, and if I thought you were a cracker, I knew damn fine that Sam would, too.'

CHAPTER ELEVEN

THE days following the party flew by, happy, busy days for all of them. The news of the engagement spread like wildfire, and all the village showered Sam and Gemma with good wishes.

Gemma told Ellie early on Monday morning, wanting her to be the first to know outside the family. And Daisy was given permission to tell Katy of the engagement.

Secure in the knowledge that she was pregnant, Ellie was beside herself with delight. 'You and Sam are so right for each other,' she said, giving Gemma a hug. 'And how perfect for Daisy to have a man like him for a father. He's a very special sort of person and will love her as if she were his own.'

'I know,' replied Gemma, hugging her back. 'He thinks the world of her, and she adores him. Oh, Ellie, I can't believe this is happening to us. Everything I could ever have hoped for has come true since we arrived in Blaney St Mary. It's the magic of the place.'

'You brought the magic with you,' said Ellie, misty eyed. 'I've got pregnant and you've got Sam.'

It was eleven-thirty on the following Thursday morning when the comparative peace of the surgery, with its steady hum of conversation from the waiting patients, was suddenly shattered.

From the car park in front of the building came the unmistakable sound of a vehicle hitting a solid object, metal crumpling against stone.

Dr Mallory and Sam emerged from their consulting rooms at one end of the corridor as Gemma erupted, almost at a run, from the treatment room at the other end. Ellie, at the reception desk, had a head start, but Gemma and Sam overtook her and were first through the main door.

A low-slung red car was straddling the pavement, with its long nose buried in the cobbled wall fronting the car park. Slewed round in the mouth of the car park was a Land Rover. Sam realised, as he and Gemma sidled round it to reach the damaged car, that it belonged to Steve Smith, the patient he had just examined.

Steve was climbing out of the Land Rover, looking pale and shaken. 'Weren't my fault. Bloody fool was turning in too fast—almost ran into me!' he shouted loudly with a quiver in his voice.

Sam called firmly, 'It's OK, Steve. Stay there, sit on the wall and take a few deep breaths.'

The driver of the sports car was slumped over the steering-wheel, his head resting against the cracked but unbroken laminated window.

Sam opened the driver's door. 'The idiot isn't wearing a seat belt,' he ground out under his breath. 'May have a whiplash or worse.'

Dr Mallory and Ellie arrived.

'Anything I can do, Sam?' Dr Mallory asked briskly.

'Take a look at Steve Smith. He's a bit shocked and not too brilliant. Been having some trouble with his angina and this hasn't helped. You go, too, Ellie. Gemma and I can manage here.'

'Will do.' Dr Mallory strode away to where Steve was sitting on the wall. Ellie followed him.

Gemma stared at the car, suddenly realising how familiar it was. She felt the blood leave her cheeks. 'Oh God it's Neil,' she whispered, pushing past Sam and crouching down to peer up into the driver's face. 'Neil, can you hear me?'

Neil groaned and tried to lift his head.

'Don't move suddenly, old chap,' said Sam sharply, placing the palm of his hand lightly on Neil's head. 'You may have hurt your neck. Stay put for a moment.' He touched Gemma's shoulder. 'Gemma, we need a support collar and my emergency bag,' he said gently but urgently. 'Will you fetch them, please?'

Gemma looked up and nodded. She rose a little unsteadily to her feet. Years of training and of dealing with crises came to her aid. 'Of course,' she said in a small but firm voice. 'Anything else?'

'Take Ellie with you and get her to phone for an ambulance. Report possible whiplash and/or head injury, and let them know that there might be other injuries. Then she can phone Mum and ask her to come over. And she can make an announcement to the patients to the effect that we'll all be running a bit late.'

It was reassuring to be given orders in his calm, authoritative voice, and a relief to be doing something constructive. Gemma relayed the messages to Ellie who was helping Dr Mallory support Steve Smith back to the surgery.

Her mind was in overdrive as she collected the bag and a collar and sped back to the car. Her emotions were mixed. She was shocked and anxious about Neil, and prayed that he wasn't badly injured, but she was angry, too. How typical of him to be driving without a seat belt. Would he never grow up? Now that the initial shock was over, she was astonished at how curiously detached she felt, as if the driver of the car was a stranger, not her ex-husband.

Now if it had been Sam... Hissing an expletive through clenched teeth, she clamped down on the thought.

Sam was still bent over at an awkward angle, supporting Neil's head and talking to him in a low voice, when she reached the car.

He glanced Gemma a quick, reassuring smile. 'You get in the passenger seat and fix the collar, love, while I ease his head up.'

Very gently, with one hand on Neil's forehead and the other steadying the crown of his head, Sam tilted him back, enabling Gemma to fit the collar beneath Neil's chin and round his neck, keeping his head in alignment with his spine.

'That more comfortable, Neil?' Sam asked when they'd finished.

'Mmm,' Neil slurred. Had he heard? Was he answering the question? Gemma kept her eyes glued on his face, willing him to full consciousness.

Sam looked across at her. He seemed to have homed in on her thoughts. 'If you can find me the ophthalmoscope, love, I'll examine his eyes. Might give us a clue to what's happening.'

Gemma said. 'Oh, yes, of course,' in an abstracted voice. She fumbled in the emergency bag and found the instrument.

Sam took it from her and bent over Neil. Carefully he parted his eyelids. 'Hmm, pupils are equal and there's normal dilation,' he grunted after a moment. He touched Neil's face. 'Come, on old chap, time to wake up,' he said in a clear, firm voice.

Neil muttered something and his eyelids fluttered a couple of times and then remained open. He frowned. 'Where the devil...? Oh, yes—hit the wall.' A look of panic came into his eyes. 'Can't move,' he mumbled.

'You're not supposed to,' said Gemma softly. 'You've got a neck brace on in case you've sustained a whiplash injury.'

'Right,' breathed Neil through gritted teeth. He was ashen. 'But it's my bloody leg that's giving me hell.'

Gemma heaved a sigh of relief. Thank God he was conscious and fully alert.

'Which leg?' asked Sam.

'The right, my knee feels as if it's busted.' His voice cracked, his face was contorted with pain.

Gemma took his hand and squeezed it. 'Hang in there,' she murmured softly.

'OK, I'll take a look at it as well as I can,' said Sam, 'but I don't want to move you until the ambulance arrives, because of a possible neck injury, so I'll have to examine it on the spot. Pain anywhere else—chest, stomach, arms?'

'Nothing to speak of,' Neil slurred, his teeth still clenched together.

'I'll have to cut your trouser leg off above the knee.' Sam crouched down to bring himself level with the injured limb.

'Christ, what does that matter?' Neil mouthed thickly. 'Just get on with it.'

Gemma handed Sam scissors from the bag. He nodded his thanks and began snipping away the expensive material. The cut-off trousers revealed a hugely swollen, grossly inflamed and distorted knee.

Sam crouched down on his haunches and examined the joint with careful, sensitive fingers.

'Not surprised you're in a lot of pain,' he said. 'Your knee's badly dislocated, and there might be a fracture concealed by the dislocation. It's a hospital job. Needs an orthopaedic surgeon to tackle it and it'll have to be X-rayed to determine whether there is a fracture and the dislocation needs to be reduced under anaesthetic. But I can give you something for the pain—that'll help a bit. Draw me up 50mgs of pethidine, please, Gemma.'

As if on cue, the ambulance was heard approaching as Sam injected the painkilling drug. 'It works quite quickly—should hold you till you get to hospital,' he said kindly.

Neil grunted out a feeble acknowledgement, but his eyes sought out Gemma's. 'Come with me, Gem,' he mumbled.

She managed a smile. 'Just try to stop me,' she said, stroking his forehead and just touching his cheek with her lips. It was a cool, distant kiss of comfort. I ought to be feeling more than this professional compassion, she thought, but I can't.

The transfer to the ambulance by the skilled crew took only a few minutes.

Sam took her hand briefly as his eyes met hers for an instant. 'Take care,' he said softly. 'I'm only at the end of the phone.'

'Thank you.' Her eyes tried to tell him how much she loved him. 'I'll try to get back in time to collect Daisy from school.'

Sam's eyes conveyed their own message of love. 'Don't worry about it,' he said. 'I'll collect her. And tell Neil not to worry about the car. I'll take care of everything.'

And he would, thought Gemma as she climbed into the ambulance, her heart bursting with pride at the thought of his capacity to care. He was, as Ellie had said, a very special sort of man.

The church clock struck six as Gemma got out of the taxi in front of Cherry Tree Cottage. She heaved a huge sigh as it drove off. How good it was to be home. She felt as if she had been away for days instead of hours. Hours spent talking to Neil, every moment of which had emphasised the chasm between his upbeat lifestyle and hers. It seemed incredible that they had once been husband and wife, and that he, Peter Pan character that he was, was her sensible little Daisy's father.

Bone- and mind-weary from the emotional and physical stresses of the day, she heaved another sigh. She wanted a drink and something to eat, but most of all she ached to see Daisy and Sam.

They should be coming any minute if Sam had timed it right from the phone call she had made to say she was leaving the hospital. Shielding her eyes from the summer evening sun, she looked across the green. And there they were, running towards her, hand in hand, Daisy's little legs going like pistons to keep up with Sam's long strides which he was slowing to accommodate hers.

Daisy flung herself into Gemma's arms, her chubby little face screwed up with anxiety. 'How's Daddy?' she panted. 'Is he going to be all right?'

Gemma hugged her tight. 'He'll be fine, love. He had a lot of X-rays which showed that he hasn't broken any bones. But he's hurt his leg and it's bandaged up and he'll have to walk with crutches for a bit, but otherwise he's OK. He sends you his love and a big kiss.'

He hadn't, he was feeling too sorry himself, but Daisy needn't know that. It was a necessary little white lie.

'Will he have to stay in hospital?'

'No, he's going to stay with friends. They came to fetch him while I was still at the hospital. That's one of the reasons I've been rather a long time, waiting for them to come.' She smiled lovingly at Sam over Daisy's head. There was so much she wanted to tell him.

His eyes were brimming over with tenderness. He said softly, 'You look whacked, love. You've had a long, wor-

rying day—you need a stiff G and T.' He steered them up
the garden path, relieved Gemma of her shoulder bag and
found the key.

'I've had a long day, too,' said Daisy, as he ushered
them into the hall. 'I think I need a G and T.'

Drunk with tiredness, Gemma leaned against Sam and
laughed helplessly. It was a typical Daisy remark.

Sam chuckled. 'You can have a C and L,' he said, as
unceremoniously, to Daisy's delight, he swept Gemma up
into his arms, carried her through to the sitting room and
dumped her on the sofa.

'Thanks,' she murmured, and, sinking back against the
cushions, closed her eyes and listened through a haze of
exhaustion to the conversation between Sam and Daisy.

'What's a C and L?' asked Daisy.

'Coke and lemonade with chunks of ice in it—scrumptious. You fetch the bottles and the ice from the kitchen
and I'll mix the drinks.'

Daisy sped off to the kitchen, bustling back a few
minutes later with the bottles and ice precariously balanced
on a tray.

Sam smartly took the tray from her.

'Wow,' she said, her eyes shining. 'I've never had Coke
and lemonade before.'

'Special occasion,' replied Sam.

'Why's it special, because of Daddy not having to stay
in hospital?'

'That, and because tonight Mummy and I are going to
fix the date of our wedding. I think it ought to be soon,
don't you, poppet? Like we said this afternoon, the sooner
the better.'

Gemma's eyes flew open. 'What do you mean, fix the
date of the wedding?' She looked uncertainly at the two
loved faces. 'Sam...I thought we'd decided to wait before

fixing anything. We need time, so much to talk about, like where we're going to live…and Daisy needs time…' Her voice trailed off.

Daisy slid off her chair and crossed the room to perch on the side of the sofa. 'No, I don't, Mummy.' Her voice was very earnest. Her straight eyebrows came together in a frown over her neat little nose. She took Gemma's free hand in her two small pudgy ones in an adult, reassuring sort of way. 'I love Sam and you love him too,' she said, 'and I want us to live with him in his house. There's lots of room, it would be like here only bigger, and when I have brothers and sisters we'll need more room, won't we?'

Gemma's mind boggled. What the devil had they been talking about while she'd been sitting by Neil's bedside?

'Out of the mouths of babes and innocents comes devastating logic,' murmured Sam. His eyes twinkled madly, his mouth quirked into his heart-stopping, lopsided smile.

Daisy turned an enquiring face to his. 'What's logic?' she asked.

Sam's eyebrows shot up in surprise. Then he took in a deep breath. 'It's—'

Gemma gave him a warning glance and shook her head. Now was definitely not the time for a philosophical lecture that would lead to further whys and whats. He would soon learn that the questions were endless.

She said quickly, 'I'll explain later, love. Right now…' she put her glass down with a shaky hand '…I think you deserve a hug.' She opened her arms wide.

Daisy scrambled into them. She tilted her head to one side. 'Why do I deserve a hug?'

'Because you are right, both of you.' She included Sam in her smile. 'There's no reason on earth why we shouldn't be married as soon as possible.'

'*Wow!*' Daisy sighed. 'That's scrummy.'

'I second that,' said Sam, crossing the room to perch himself on the arm of the sofa. 'It's a brilliant, very intelligent decision.' He dropped kisses, first on Daisy's head and then on Gemma's. 'Now, how about if I cook us omelettes for supper—a big one for me, medium one for Mummy and a small one for Daisy?'

'Like the three bears,' said Daisy. 'Daddy bear, Mummy bear and Baby bear.'

'That's us,' said Sam.

By eight o'clock, an excited but finally pooped-out Daisy was safely tucked up in bed and Gemma and Sam were seated side by side on the sofa. They were acutely aware of each other, of the warmth and vibes flowing between them and the intense longing to be in each other's arms, yet by unspoken agreement they kept an inch or two of space between them.

There was the matter of Neil and the accident to be sorted out and put into perspective. Gemma knew that his arrival so dramatically on the scene needed to be explained. Sam would have guessed that she and Neil would have talked while they were waiting at the hospital. He had avoided probing whilst Daisy was still around, but he must be itching to know what she and Neil had discussed.

Well, here goes, she thought. She held up her glass of red wine so that evening sun slanted on it, making it glow like a jewel.

She took a sip. 'Funny,' she mused, 'how easily Daisy was reassured about Neil once I explained that he had only minor injuries. I thought she might be more upset. Not that they've exactly got a strong father-daughter relationship. And you'd already briefed her about the accident so she was prepared for what I had to tell her.'

'Yes. I explained what his injuries might be, but kept it low-key. And I had the impression that as long as he wasn't at death's door, she would take it in her stride, as, in fact, she did. But, then, that tallies with being six years old and talking about somebody who plays a very limited role in her life, doesn't it?' There was a curious note in his voice.

'Yes.' Gemma turned to look at him.

He was leaning forward, his elbows on his knees, cradling his glass in both hands and peering down into the ruby red liquid. 'The thing is,' he continued softly, 'although I didn't know your ex-husband, except for the short while that I treated him today, he's played a major, rather than a limited, role in my life.' His fingers tightened round the stem of his glass till his knuckles whitened.

Gemma frowned, a frown which he didn't see because he was still staring into his wine. 'I don't understand what you mean,' she said, wanting to take the glass from his hands and massage the tense fingers.

He turned his head sharply and focused his eyes, dark with pain, on hers. 'What I mean, Gemma—' his voice was thick, low, husky '—is that from the first time I saw him, driving away from the cottage like a maniac, I've been jealous as hell of him, just knowing that he was around somewhere...

'Of course I didn't know then that he was your ex-husband. I saw him kiss you, thought he was someone special to you, and then when he turned up again at the surgery... God help me, I could have killed him. I came to the conclusion that you were still in love with him and were encouraging him back.'

He took a huge gulp of wine. 'And even today, in spite of everything, just for a moment or two I wondered. You were so tender with him, held his hand, kissed him...and then knowing you were together at the hospital all those hours, talking.' He shrugged and dredged up a wry smile. 'Well, let's say I had a job to keep my mind on my work.'

Gemma looked at him with astonished eyes. 'Oh, Sam, how could you think that? If we hadn't been finished years ago, today's accident would have convinced me that I didn't love him. All I could think of when we were treating him, before we knew that he wasn't critically injured, was thank God it wasn't you lying there.'

She drained her wine in one swallow and put her glass down with a shaky hand. 'And if it weren't for Daisy, I would never see him again. Not that we will be seeing so much of him in the future—he's been promoted and he's off to Australia to open up an office in Melbourne. He won't be able to come back from there every five minutes.'

Sam inhaled deeply. 'That,' he said in a deeply satisfied voice, 'is great news. I presume he hared down to see you to boast of his promotion.'

Gemma was surprised by his uncharacteristic sarcasm. 'No, he came because I had written to let him know that we were getting married.'

He frowned and slammed his glass down on the table. 'Did you *have* to write?' His usual cool seemed to have deserted him.

Gemma rested her hand on his arm. 'Sam, it was a courtesy letter on account of Daisy,' she said gently.

'Sorry.' He pulled a face. 'Of course it was, but where he's concerned... Truth is, love, I'm just so scared of losing you, after waiting all these years for you to come along, that I can't see straight.' He picked up her hand and pressed her palm to his lips. 'So, *please*, marry me and put me out of my misery. I'll get a special licence or whatever and we'll nip in to the nearest registry office and do the deed.'

Gemma took hold of both his strong, lean hands and held them prayer-like in her own. 'No, not a registry office, my darling. I don't mind what sort of wedding we have, but Daisy does, and so do your parents. They want you to be married in the village church as they were, with Uncle Tom Cobley and all, and particularly—'

'Old Harry Trotter,' Sam broke in. He grinned his lop-sided grin that made her heart flip like a mad thing. 'So be it, a fairy-tale wedding it will be, with all the trimmings.' He pulled her into his arms. 'And to be honest, I'd rather have it this way. Though I'd have married anywhere to please you, to make sure of you.'

He bent forward and planted a kiss on her nose, then freed his hands, which were still clasped between hers, and took her into his arms and onto his lap. 'Because I'm like Dad, I like continuity. I love being part of this small community, knowing my young patients and their parents, and often their grandparents. I couldn't live or work anywhere else. And I want you and Daisy to love it too.'

'Oh, Sam, we already do,' she said firmly. Her green eyes blazed. 'This is where we belong—with you in Blaney St Mary. You're stuck with us for good, I'm afraid.'

He nuzzled the top of her head and trailed kisses over her face and neck, beneath her chin and up to her mouth. She closed her eyes and waited for his kiss, but it didn't come immediately.

She opened her eyes. 'What's wrong?' she whispered.

'Nothing's wrong,' he whispered back. 'I was just feasting my eyes on your dear, lovely face, absorbing the fact that if I cherish you I can feast upon it every day for the rest of my life.'

Gemma said breathlessly, 'You're a romantic old thing, aren't you?'

He wrinkled his nose. 'I'll disregard the ''old'' and have

you know that all Mallory men have a strong romantic streak in them—that, and the virtue of keeping their women. When I say ''I do'' at the altar...' he raised a questioning eyebrow '...*when*?'

'Six weeks' time, end of June,' Gemma said promptly.

'I promise you, it'll be for keeps.'

EPILOGUE

TIMOTHY and Tara bawled their heads off throughout the baptismal service.

'Good sign that, they be crying out the devil,' sang out Old Harry Trotter from the midst of the congregation in the nave of the church.

Several people nearby shushed him, but the Mallory family, grouped round the ancient font, smiled at each other. It was a typical Harry remark.

Daisy whispered to Katy, who was standing beside her close to the font, 'They must have a lot of devil in them—they cry an awful lot.'

''Spect they'll grow out of it,' Katy whispered back.

'Yes, when the devil's all cried out,' replied Daisy in her pragmatic fashion.

Gemma and Sam, overhearing the whispered exchange, smiled down on them, and then across at their two noisy offspring in the arms of their respective godparents.

Sam clasped Gemma's hand tightly and gave her his special, just-for-her smile. The awareness vibes were bouncing back and forth between them. They were both remembering!

It was a year to the day that they had stood at the altar and made their vows. A June day just like today, with brilliant sunshine pouring through the magnificent stained-glass windows in a mosaic of colour. Lozenges of red, green and blue splashed on the heads of the congregation, on the wooden pews and stone-flagged floors and on the brass urns full of lupins and delphiniums and branches of white, sweet-scented syringa.

The scent of the mock orange blossom had filled the church then as it filled it now, only then it had mingled with the scent of the mimosa and white roses in her bouquet, a bouquet cleverly imitated in Daisy's tiny posy. Just as Daisy's dress had been a replica, except in colour, of Gemma's—Empire-line in style, with tiny puff sleeves, the muslin falling in graceful folds from the high bodice. Daisy's was a soft rose pink, Gemma's a creamy gold.

Gemma's eyes prickled with happy tears. It had been a lovely wedding day. She reached out and lightly touched Daisy's head—it had been her day too.

Daisy turned and glanced her a dimpling grin and took in a deep breath, wrinkling her nose. 'Nice,' she mouthed.

Gemma nodded. Was she associating the scent with the wedding? she wondered.

Sam's hand tightened on hers and she lifted her head as the vicar marked first Timothy's then Tara's small foreheads with water from the font...

'In the name of the Father, the Son and the Holy Ghost, I baptise thee,' he intoned in his strong, carrying voice. 'And now,' he said, 'on this happy day, by special request from Daisy, the twins' sister, we will sing "All things bright and beautiful".'

The congregation rose to its collective feet, the organ burst forth and several dozen voices were raised to the ancient beams as they sang their hearts out to the old favourite, Daisy's shrill little treble competing with Sam's vibrant tenor.

It was nearly midnight. Gemma and Sam sat side by side in the huge, canopied four-poster that would have put any modern king-size bed to shame, each feeding a baby. Sam was supplementary bottle-feeding Tara, Gemma breast-feeding Timothy.

The room was dim, lit only by the orange glow from the bedside lamps. And it was quiet, except for an occasional glug from one or other of the sucking babies. Gemma was supporting Timothy, whose rosebud mouth was firmly latched onto her nipple, with one arm resting on a pillow, and with her free hand she was entering the day's events in her diary.

Not having a hand free, Sam had an open book propped up against his hunched-up knees, but he wasn't reading. A dreamy smile on his face, he was watching Gemma and his son.

'I wish I could paint,' he said softly. 'You look exquisite when you're feeding the babies. I'd love to capture the look of you on paper.'

Gemma chuckled her sweet husky laugh. 'You've taken zillions of photos and nearly worn the video camera out,' she murmured, leaning over to brush his night-bearded cheek with her lips.

'Not the same,' he said. 'I want to *taste* you.'

'Be my guest.' She laughed, tilting her head so that the lightly tanned column of her throat was exposed.

'Idiot, you know that's not what I mean, although, come to think of it…' He leaned closer and licked her neck with little flicking movements of his tongue… 'Mmm, tastes good.'

Gemma laid down her pencil and closed her diary.

'Finished?' Sam asked. 'That was quick. I thought to-day's entry would have taken half the night.'

She smiled at him. A rich smile, full of love—sexy love, maternal love, tenderness.

'What was there to say?' She bent and kissed her son's cheek and raised her shining emerald green eyes to Sam.

'Except that today was a perfect ending to a perfect year? I wouldn't have changed it by one iota. You've loved and cherished Daisy and me, just as you promised. And to crown it all, you put the cherry...' She dimpled. 'No, two cherries on the cake. I feel the most blessed woman in the world.'

The church clock chimed a measured, sonorous twelve.

With a noisy slurp, Tara finished the last of her milk. Sam pulled hard at the bottle to release the teat from the rosebud mouth. It came away suddenly with a loud sucking plop.

Sam grinned and stared down at his small daughter. 'How do you do that with such a pretty little mouth—apply suction like a vacuum cleaner?' he asked.

Tara stared up at him with wide eyes, not quite blue, not quite green, and gave a satisfied burp and a beatific smile.

'I think that's all the answer you're going to get,' said Gemma with a soft chuckle.

Sam leaned across and kissed her. 'You know, dear heart, Tara's mouth is exactly like yours.'

Gemma looked down at her son. 'And Timothy's got your nose,' she said.

Sam laughed. 'Then honour is satisfied. They're a nice mixture of Fellows and Mallory.'

'I think Old Harry would call them a pigeon pair,' said Gemma.

Sam kissed her again. 'I like it,' he murmured. 'I can live with that.'

MILLS & BOON®

Makes any time special

Enjoy a romantic novel from ***Mills & Boon®***

Presents...™   *Enchanted*™   TEMPTATION.

Historical Romance™   ✚ MEDICAL ROMANCE™

MILLS & BOON®

MEDICAL ROMANCE™

A SON FOR JOHN by Gill Sanderson
Bachelor Doctors

Since qualifying Dr John Cord had concentrated on work, trying to forget that he had loved and lost his Eleanor. But his new Obs and Gynae job brought her back into his life. Even more shocking was the sight of a photo on Ellie's desk of a young boy who was clearly his son!

IDYLLIC INTERLUDE by Helen Shelton

Surgeon Nathan Thomas borrowed his step-brother's Cornish cottage, only to find himself next door to a beautiful girl. Not one to poach, Nathan was horrified by his instant attraction to nurse Libby Deane, assuming she was Alistair's girlfriend.

AN ENTICING PROPOSAL by Meredith Webber

When nurse Paige Warren rescued a young Italian woman, she phoned Italy leaving a message for 'Marco', but Dr Marco Alberici—an Italian prince!—arrives in person, disrupting her surgery and her hormones! Should she really accept his invitation to return to Italy?

0002/03b

FREE!

4 Books
and a surprise gift!

We would like to take this opportunity to thank you for reading this Mills & Boon® book by offering you the chance to take FOUR more specially selected titles from the Medical Romance™ series absolutely FREE! We're also making this offer to introduce you to the benefits of the Reader Service™ —

★ FREE home delivery
★ FREE gifts and competitions
★ FREE monthly Newsletter
★ Books available before they're in the shops
★ Exclusive Reader Service discounts

Accepting these FREE books and gift places you under no obligation to buy; you may cancel at any time, even after receiving your free shipment. Simply complete your details below and return the entire page to the address below. *You don't even need a stamp!*

YES! Please send me 4 free Medical Romance books and a surprise gift. I understand that unless you hear from me, I will receive 6 superb new titles every month for just £2.40 each, postage and packing free. I am under no obligation to purchase any books and may cancel my subscription at any time. The free books and gift will be mine to keep in any case.

MOEB

Ms/Mrs/Miss/Mr ....Initials ....
BLOCK CAPITALS PLEASE

Surname ....

Address ....

....

....Postcode ....

Send this whole page to:
UK: The Reader Service, FREEPOST CN8I, Croydon, CR9 3WZ
EIRE: The Reader Service, PO Box 4546, Kilcock, County Kildare (stamp required)

MILLS & BOON®

Makes Mother's Day special

For Mother's Day this year, why not spoil yourself with a gift from Mills & Boon®.

Enjoy three romance novels by three of your favourite authors and a FREE silver effect picture frame for only £6.99.

Pack includes:

Presents...
One Night With His Wife by Lynne Graham

Enchanted
The Faithful Bride by Rebecca Winters

TEMPTATION.
Everything About Him by Rita Clay Estrada

Available from 18th February